1 0 AUG 2015		8/4 col

Please return this book on or before the date shown above. To renew go to www.essex.gov.uk/libraries, ring 0845 603 7628 or go to any Essex library.

Essex County Council

D1514385

30130503235877

Tremanyon – A Shadow Falls

© Carol Symons

Cover design: © Tracy Saunders
Cover Image: V&A Image/Victoria & Albert Museum, London.

First Edition published 2010

Published by:
Palores Publications,
11a Penryn Street, Redruth, Kernow, TR15 2SP, UK.

Designed & Printed by:
The St Ives Printing & Publishing Company,
High Street, St Ives, Cornwall TR26 1RS, UK.

ISBN 978-1-906845-21-6

DEDICATION

MY GRANDFATHER WAS a wise and wonderful man, firm but fair, and I spent many hours in his company. He would always have the answers to a small child's questions of Why, What, Where, When and How. We would walk and he would talk, and I would learn.

We gathered primroses from the banks and hedgerows along the winding country lanes of my childhood, and here I learned that the new leaves, emerging from their sometimes sticky or hairy buds, were not always green. They were also bronze or purple, almost silver or white, and even yellow as well as bright or dark green.

In the autumn we would wander those same country lanes to pick blackberries. Although he was still a fit and upright man, at this time of the year Grandpa would always carry a walking stick, with a hooked handle in order to reach up and pull over those stems, way up there out of reach, which always carried the largest of those juicy black fruits. Now I learned that dead and dying leaves are not always brown, but gold, orange and red, the flame colours of an autumn bonfire.

In summer and winter too we would walk along the sea's shoreline in search of Amber and Carnelian, walking always into the sun to catch the light shining through those opaque gems. Here Grandpa would explain the mysteries of the sea and how the waves and white horses would form far out to sea – way beyond the horizon that was visible to us. We discovered egg cases and seed pods from distant shores, feathers and fossils, and he taught me to look for the things that were not really hiding, but a little further away, just not right there in full an open view.

He taught me that beauty is something deeper than the outside wrapping, and that I should not be fooled by the glitter and tinsel of the pretty parcel. Something wonderful can come from within a plain brown paper packet he told me. These lessons were learned quite hard sometimes, for a small child, by example and simple means. I remember, even today, a boiled sweet that came in a lovely golden wrapper that I expected to contain a delicious soft centred chocolate, but this was to be a lesson within a lesson, for it demonstrated the fact that something which did not have external beauty could give longer lasting pleasure.

He taught me to look for the beauty within the person. Not to be swayed or impressed by what I saw on the outside, or by wealth or material assets. He taught me to look for kindness and understanding, together with a generosity of spirit, and to understand that honour among men was important, as too was a true and honest love. I learned without realising that I was learning and, although he was a headmaster, there was never a scholastic approach to his teachings.

Grandpa encouraged my love of reading, and from an early age we would read together. The one book which so vividly springs to mind is that of the Children's Water Babies, an adaptation from the book of Charles Kingsley. I still have this book today, and I realise now that this story fitted with my grandfathers great sense of morals and justice, and Mrs Doasyouwouldbedoneby has travelled with me from that time onwards.

He also encouraged me to write poetry and short stories, and that a good story should have a beginning, middle, and an end.

My story does contain all three. It has a beginning, set in the period 1700–1800 at the rebirth of the Manor of Tremayne – Tremanyon. The middle, though cloudy, is surely unfolding day by day, and the end is as clear as the beginning and set in modern times.

So Grandpa, this first book 'the beginning', is for you. I only wish that you were here to read it.

It is also dedicated to the house that was my home. A home so dear to me that it will always be home in my heart . . . The home I think of with such love. I stood on those stairs the day I was married . . . my sons were born there . . . It will forever and always be "My Home".

This book, the first in a series about Tremanyon,
is dedicated to my dearly beloved grandfather,
Percival Horace Pike
and to my wonderful mother in law
Emily Symons
also to Trewince, and my home in Cornwall.

Tremanyon
A shadow falls

CAROL SYMONS

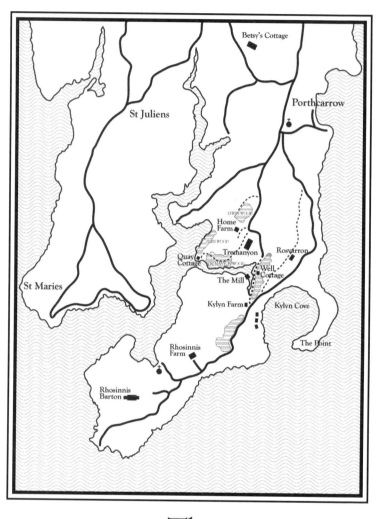

The
Rhosinnis Peninsular

CHAPTER SEVEN

CHAPTER EIGHT

Chapter One
1747 – *Ginifur*

IT WAS A soft and golden evening of late summer, the sun about to dip below the gently rolling hill on the far side of the river where the dark brown cows were ambling leisurely back from the afternoon milking.

Ginifur Retallick sat on the step of the single storey cottage, a bowl in her lap and a filled pot of peeled potatoes by her side. Fifteen years of age, she was maturing into a beautiful young woman. Her long dark hair was pulled loosely back from her face and tied with a scrap of bright green ribbon at the nape of her neck. Her honey coloured complexion was flawless and her eyes a curious shade of green, with the sparkle of youth. The cotton dress she wore had seen better days. It was well worn, and had been cut down to fit from one of her mother's dresses that were stored in the chest in the single roomed cottage. The dress was covered with an overskirt, and both were pulled up above her knees as she enjoyed the last of the evening sun.

Ginifur placed the knife in the bowl on top of the peelings before placing the bowl down by her side and, wriggling her toes, she hugged her knees to her chest. She looked out at the river tinged with the reflection of the evening sun, the water lapping at the foot of the steps on the quay. She never tired of sitting here. In winter or summer, sunshine or rain, the view was the same one she would see every morning as she would awaken in her bed. Ginifur loved the mornings and the evenings with their special sounds and soft colours.

The fish cellar was just below the cottage, next to the quay, and Ginifur could hear the comfortable rumble of barrels as her father prepared for the next days packing of the pilchards.

Ginifur was born in this cottage on a bright sunny May morning, shortly after her father and mother had taken up positions on the Tremanyon Estate. Her mother, Sara, had been a ladies maid before she died during childbirth ten years ago. The child, a boy, did not survive his premature delivery into the world and Simon Retallick, Ginifur's father, relied on Ginifur to take care of both of them and the house, for his days were filled from dawn to dark. This was true especially now for besides dividing his time between the boats and the fish cellar, he added the temporary post as gamekeeper for John Retallick, Simon's father, had retired as gamekeeper and the position had yet to be filled.

Suddenly Ginifur shivered, she wasn't cold but instinctively she felt for the shawl on the step behind her, and pulled it up and over her thin bare shoulders. Warily she arose from the doorway and lightly, on bare feet, she stepped towards the low wall that surrounded the tiny garden. She listened to the silence that surrounded her, an eerie and unnatural silence. Not the silence of other early evenings. She listened for the birds in the blackthorn bushes, but only silence met her, for the birds that were chirping merrily only a moment ago had ceased their joyful evening song. Her clear green eyes cast a glance across the river. The surface of the water was mirror clear. Nothing moved, even the fish had stopped jumping. A sudden rustle of the leaves in the bushes caused her to pull her shawl closer around her shoulders and she turned towards the young beech wood that had been planted along the creek during the year of her birth. Slowly, and unusually fearful, Ginifur moved towards the end of the cottage, her eyes darting here and there. Looking, searching. But searching for what? The rustling of the leaves increased and, as her hand pushed a wayward lock of hair from her eyes, she focused them on a point at the top of the wood.

A wisp of misty grey smoke was caught in the growing breeze, hovered briefly and was quickly dispersed. Ginifur stood very still as another dark cloud formed, larger than the first, which rose lazily above the trees, spreading and taking longer this time to vanish. The rustling increased as the wind grew stronger and, with it, the next wisp became a plume of dark smoke that was quickly gathered up and scattered across the darkening sky. Ginifur took a step back as she realised what was the source of the smoke and, turning quickly, she ran out through the small gate between the fronds of Tamarisk hedge and down the grassy bank towards the quay below.

The gate to the cellar was standing wide open as she ran through. "Da. Da. The Big House. The Big House . . ." She called out.

Simon looked up in amazement as he rolled the wooden barrel out of the net locker, beneath the cottage, in readiness for the women who would come to fill them with the pilchards already stacked into the salted baulk in the centre of the cellar.

"Ginny. Slowly child, what's ado?" Simon was about to laugh at his daughter, his only child, hurtling towards him across the uneven floor of the open cellar. Hewn from the natural grey rock, the cellar floor was crossed with channels to run off the excess oil from the fish into the pit at the far end. From here it would be collected and barrelled separately for pilchard oil, also known as train oil, was used to light many of the lamps in country cottages throughout Cornwall. He paused and righted the barrel, hands on his hips as he straightened his back, and saw her frightened face. "What's amiss Ginny?"

"The Big House Da, the Big House. I think it's afire." She glanced up at the fast moving clouds that had miraculously appeared to mar this once beautiful evening. "And there's a storm brewing Da, a good'n."

Simon waited to hear no more and raced from the cellar with his daughter close on his heals. "There Da, see the smoke!" Ginifur pointed above the trees, now bending with the beginning of the storm that was about to hit the South West with a ferocity not seen for many a year.

Simon's eyes fastened on the spot above the wood for only a brief second and then he set off at a running pace, up the steep hill, towards the path that would lead him through the Big Wood and to the house that was hidden beyond. As she watched her father's receding back, Ginny stood mesmerised by the sight of the smoke now forming into great clouds and darkening the sky above.

Simon stopped only once. Looking back over his shoulder he called. "Ginny, go to the Mill. Get help. Get everyone Ginny, everyone." His voice carried down on the east wind but Ginny was rooted to the spot, watching everything before her as if caught in some terrible childish nightmare. "Ginny! Ginny!" Simon stopped once more, as he reached the path through the wood. "Ginny. Now child. Now."

Ginifur, startled, suddenly comprehending the urgency in his voice, moved quickly on her bare feet. Gathering up her skirts in her hands, she darted out through the gardens and across the field to the lower corner of the wood. Fleet of foot, like a startled young deer, she sprinted along the river path towards the mill at the head of the creek. Ginifur rarely wore shoes, she possessed only one pair that she wore to Church or on high days and holidays, and the soles of her feet were like supple leather. She felt neither twig nor stone as she hastened along the narrow path beside the river but,

11

by the time she had reached the bridge over the stream, the fire had a strangle hold on the Big House. Dusk was falling fast, and now the darkening sky above the brow of the hill was glowing red, gold and amber as long fingers of flame clawed angrily up into the sky.

Ted and Davy, the miller and his son, together with his wife Suzie and the younger children, stared in horror as Ginny shouted and waved to them as she approached the house on the other side of the creek. By the time she had reached the bottom of Fern Meadow, they were already hurrying to meet her. "Do 'em know at Primrose Bank? Has Charlie gone up?" Called Ted.

Breathless now, from her running, Ginifur shook her head. "I don't know." She gasped.

"We'll go up that way then." Ted had reached Ginny ahead of his wife and family and, thrusting the tiny gate open he led the way up the steep narrow path to the cottage in the trees, calling out as it came into view. "Charlie! Lily!"

Charlie was at work in his garden and lent on his fork as they neared him. "What's the shoutin' fer?" Charlie's face creased into a frown, and his wife appeared at the cottage door.

Ted's pace didn't let up as he rushed passed the cottage, calling back over his shoulder. "The Big House Charlie . . . It's on fire."

Charlie's mouth dropped open as he turned around. But the cottage was hidden in the trees. He could see nothing beyond their immediate boundary. Then he realised that there was an ethereal glow about the trees, and wisps of pale grey smoke were beginning to filter through the higher branches. After Ted and Davy had quickly passed by, followed closely by young Ginny Retallick and Ted's wife and children, Charlie noticed an alarming crackling and splintering of wood and timber, resembling that of a giant bonfire. Like the one on Rhossinnis Head, when they were sending a warning to ships. Flinging his fork to one side, Charlie grabbed the bucket of stones that he was clearing from the vegetable patch. He discarded them quickly, scattering them back across the dry earth, and ran from the garden. As he ran past the cottage he called out to his wife. "Bring any buckets ye 'ave in the 'ouse Lily, and be quick 'bout it mind." He shouted as he too headed up the path.

Lily, a short stout woman, trundled back into the cottage rubbing her floury hands on the pinafore tied about her thick waist. She emptied one bucket, spilling the potatoes across the floor, and the second, full of freshly drawn water from the well, she threw on the plants outside. Then, as quickly as her short and ungainly body would allow, she set off in pursuit of her husband.

As Charlie came out of the trees, at the bottom of the 'Master's Drive' that skirted the Lower Lawn, he saw Ted, Davy and Ginifur climbing the 'Ha Ha', the dividing hedge between the upper and lower lawns. He stared in horror at the sight before him. The beautiful Queen Ann Mansion was ablaze. Flames licked angrily out of the roof and every window on the first floor.

By the time they converged on the drive, Simon had organised a relay of water buckets. It appeared that all the house servants had escaped and, although suffering severely from shock, they rallied together with those who had raced up from the village, in an effort to stem the fire.

Ted glanced quickly about him. "Where's the Master?" He shouted above the roar of the flames.

Simon shook his head. "I think he's still in there. Maud took his supper to his room a short while afore the smoke crept into her attic room. She managed to get down the staff staircase to the kitchen, but by the time she had raised the alarm the landing was ablaze. Sam and Adam attempted to use the back stairs to reach the landing but they were beaten back by the flames and the heat. They were lucky enough to get out alive." He called back in answer as he continued to keep the water buckets moving.

Ted ran to the back of the line in an attempt to help, knowing in his heart that their efforts were going to be in vain. The wind sucked the flames higher and higher, and the greedy roar of the fire vied with the howling wind. The flames now engulfed the whole of the first floor. Without warning the drawing room windows exploded outwards, splintering with a resounding crack and sending shards of glass flying onto the fire fighters, cutting a few bare arms and uncovered heads but mercifully missing their faces. A gasp of horror, tinged with fear, rose up from the crowd as angry flames spat out at them from the gaping holes. The heat was now so intense that the band of firefighters was driven away from the front of the house. Any hope of getting near to the house with buckets of water was quickly dismissed and regrouping themselves upon the lawn, as the crackling became an unbelievable din, they could only watch as the stones began to shatter in the extreme heat of the fire. Slowly but surely, the crowd was beaten further and further away, until they formed a tight knot at the bottom of the garden. Women wept silently, or so it seemed, in the roar of the fire, as the men watched in horror and anguish.

Maud sat hunched up upon the bottom step of the granite stairway that divided the upper lawn into two. She buried her head deep in her lap, her hands covering her ears in an endeavour to block out the terrible noise. Ginny, trembling with fear herself, approached her gingerly. Sitting beside Maud, she placed a comforting arm about her shoulders. Maud was the oldest of the servants in the Big House. She was, or had been it would now appear, the Master's servant since she was a girl. After the Mistress died she and the butler, Mr. James, had been his faithful companions until the end. And it must be so, thought Ginifur, for no one could possibly live through a fire such as this.

Suddenly, with an enormous crack that could have been mistaken for an explosion, the front of the house crumbled and the roof fell in. The crowd on the lawn let out a final gasp of horror as they glimpsed the staircase, rising grotesquely through the smoke as the flames began to subside.

The crowd was silent. They stood huddled together, staring at the remains of Tremanyon, and as the shock and horror slowly turned to reality, tears ran silently down their cheeks. Men and women together, all united in their grief, could not turn their heads away from the devastation. Only Maud refused to look back to see the extent of the damage, continueing to bury her head in her skirts. All that remained was the staircase, and the arched window at the back of the house, whilst pockets of flames crackled and spat amongst the rubble and burning timbers.

It was some time before anyone opened their mouth to speak. It wasn't until it dawned on Hannah that she was now homeless, and let out a painful cry before uttering, between sobs, "Where am I goin' to go? What are we all to do?" that the enormity of the situation began to take its hold.

"Don' 'e worry Hannah." Samuel Sawle put a comforting hand on her shoulder. "Ye can move in with we. The little 'uns can squeeze up, and there will be plenty of room."

"I've lost me best dress, and all me wages." Hannah bleated, remembering the dress that her mother had so painstakingly sewed for her before she left Gorran to take her position at Tremanyon. And the little painted tin that her father had found for her to keep anything that was left over from her wages. She had saved one whole pound and five shillings and sixpence. It had taken the thrifty Hannah her entire three years to save it. It was all in silver three pence pieces. A fortune for Hannah, who was saving her pennies to help with setting up home when she married Billy Stevens next spring. With a bump she sat down on the lawn and cried as the other servants, who had also lived in the house, tried to come to terms with the loss of their own precious belongings, and most likely their jobs and their home.

The cook, Mrs Teague, rung her hands as she stared in disbelief at the glowing embers still flickering and flaring in the growing wind. The butler, James Tyler, usually haughty and unapproachable, stood with his shoulders drooped forward and his head hung low as he tried to hide his own grief at the loss of his Master and friend. His normal severe expression softened into understanding and sympathy as he glanced at old Maud, crumpled ungainly on the step a few feet away from him. Where would she go now? he wondered, for she was far too old to find new employment. He shivered as he realised that he too was getting on in years, and that it would be no easy task for him to find a new position let alone one as good as the one that he had enjoyed until now.

As the wind increased in speed, blowing in from the east, Samuel was the first to move. The coachman gathered up his brood and pressed them before him, with Adam pulling the weeping Hannah up towards the top of the lawn.

Simon approached the shaking form of Maud, still being comforted by Ginifur, and the nearby butler. "We have only a humble dwelling, as ye know Mr Tyler, but we would be happy to share it with ye until our futures are settled." He offered.

James Tyler nodded briefly. "That is thoughtful of you Retallick. If I may spend the rest of the night with you, I shall have to leave at first light and make my way to Truro."

Netty Teague picked up the edge of her once white, starched *pinny* and wiped her eyes as she searched the crowd for Tom, her husband. He had been helping to man the pump at the back of the house and she hadn't seen him since they stopped hauling all those buckets. "Where's Tom?" She grabbed at the nearest arm. "Where's Tom?" She asked again and again. And then, as her voice nearly broke with fear, she called out. "Has anyone seen my Tom?"

Simon turned. "Didn't he come down with the others?" He too searched around the lawns for the head gardener.

Samuel hesitated as he steered his family homewards. "Tom stayed at the back of the 'ouse. 'e stayed t' watch the Garden

Cottage in case the flames jumped across. It's a good job the new roof is slate and not the ol' thatched one."

Every eye was drawn to the remains of the Big House, and the arched wall that linked it with the adjoining cottage as Tom appeared on the side lawn, and called out. "Netty? Is my Netty there?" Netty Teague broke away from the crowd and waddled quickly towards him.

Tom spied Samuel and his family making their way towards him. "Your cottage be safe Sam, ye can take the little un's 'ome now. The 'orses 'av calmed down too, none of 'm are 'urt."

Sam reached him ahead of his family. "Thank 'e Tom. I was some worried about they 'orses. The one thing they really hate be fire, but whilst there was a chance of savin' the Master." He glanced at the pile of rubble and smouldering timbers.

"I know." Tom followed his gaze. " 'e didn' stand a chance Sam. We did the best us could, 'n ye 'n young Adam couldn' 'ave done more. Ye was lucky to get away with yer own lives, I be thinkin', just look at yer 'air, 'n Adams too!"

Sam studied his son briefly, taking in the singed locks of hair that hung to his shoulders, before fingering his own and smelling the burnt ends. He hadn't thought about it until this moment. He had simply grabbed Adam by the hand and raced to the side door. No, he hadn't considered any possible outcome from his actions, he had only thought about rescuing the master. At the sudden thought that he might have, quite possibly, pulled Adam to his death and left his family fatherless, his legs trembled and he gripped a hold of Adam's shoulder, lest he should stumble and fall. Adam glanced at his father's face. Even through the smoke stained skin, he could see that his face had blanched and his eyes were wide open, showing the whites of his eyes. Old for his years, Adam understood his father's delayed shock and positioned himself carefully at his side in order to offer him disguised support. Now, as the fire had died down, suddenly there was a brief lull in the wind and the night was uncannily quiet. They could hear Simon calling out the servant's names, in order to ascertain that they had all escaped without injury.

"Did 'em all get out?" Asked Tom.

"I think so, all 'cept the master."

"Get on 'ome Sam. I see 'e 'ave young Hannah too. There's nought more 'e can do 'ere t'night." As Tom spoke he placed an arm about his wife. "Ye be shiverin' lass. Are 'e cold?"

16

Netty grinned in spite of herself. Lass, indeed!! She was nearly forty-five years old. "We've lost everythin' Tom. Our 'ome, our savings and our livin.'"

Tom squeezed her waist gently. "No we 'aven't lass. We've not lost everythin'. We've still got each other." With his free hand he indicated the Garden Cottage, unoccupied since Squire Durance's sister died three years hence. But it was still cleaned weekly, and everything was just as she had left it. "And at least, fer the time bein', we'll 'ave a roof over our 'eads. Now, where's Maud and Mr Tyler, they will need a bed too. It'll mean ye'll 'ave t' share a bed with old Maud, and Mr Tyler 'n me'll bed down in t'other. The twins can sleep on the floor downstairs fer the night and in the mornin' us'll see what us can salvage."

"Simon offered t' take Maud and Mr Tyler t' Quay Cottage." Netty informed him.

"That was good of un, but their cottage only 'as one room. I'm sure the Master would want us t'use the cottage 'ere, and I'm sure that Mr Tyler would agree."

Soon after the villagers had made it safely back to their homes the wind increased in severity, blowing slates from roofs and submerging tiny fishing boats in the unprotected harbour. The little cottage beside the river felt nothing of this storm, protected from the east winds by the hill behind it. The trees beside the ruins of the Manor house took the brunt of the wind, and although it continued to force the embers into short bursts of flame there was nothing left in the ruins to burn. As the sky lightened from the east the wind finally eased, and the storm blew further on, out to sea.

Tom and Mr Tyler had struggled to lift and carry Maud up the narrow and twisting staircase in the Garden Cottage to one of the small rooms under the eaves where Netty, assisted by the kind hearted Ginifur, undressed her, washed the smoke stains from her face and then tucked her up in the double bed that Netty would have to share with her that night. All through the dark of the remaining night, with the wind howling around them, Maud lay on her back staring up at the ceiling. As the moon, dodging in and out from behind the dark scurrying clouds, cast eerie and unfamiliar shapes about the room her eyes never closed, blinked infrequently and when the dawn finally broke and Netty awoke she found her lying exactly as they had left her.

Netty sat up in bed. "Maud!" She laid a hand gently upon her shoulder, but Maud didn't move. There was no sign of recognition in her eyes and her tight lips didn't part. For one awful moment Netty thought that she was dead, until she noticed the slight rise and fall of Maud's ample bosoms beneath the cover. "Maud!!! It's Netty." She tried again, but to no avail. Finally giving up on waking her bed companion Netty put her feet to the floor, she had slept in her under garments and reaching for her dress she pulled it quickly over her head, screwing her nose up at the smell of the smoke that permeated each fibre. With no comb handy Netty pulled and straightened her fine grey hair with her fingers, twisted it into a bun at the nape of her neck securing it with the pins that she had removed the night before and made her way down the stairs.

Tom was already up and about. A bright fire was burning in the hearth and he had brought in a dozen eggs from the hen house, a comb of honey from the hives in the garden and gone over to the Home Farm for some milk from the dairy. He also managed to scrounge a small loaf of bread and a large piece of heavy cake from Mrs Polaughan, the farm bailiff's wife and she had also pressed him to take a large pat of butter that she had rested overnight and a few spoons of dried nettle leaves to make some tea. "How's Maud?" He asked as Netty entered the tiny kitchen.

"I don' like it at all." She told him. "She aven't spoke a word, nor moved an inch all night. I don' even think she 'av slept. She just lies there, starin' at the ceilin'."

"I'll get Mr Tyler to look at 'er. We'll see what 'e thinks us should do."

Tom had also lit the range and the kettle was spluttering away as the twins, Bess and Betty, stirred and rubbed their eyes. "Come on you lazy bones." Netty admonished them "Stir yerselves, 'n 'elp me t' get some breakfast." As she spoke the front door opened and Mr Tyler bent his head to enter the long, low ceilinged room. "Good mornin' Mr Tyler. I've got some breakfast on for ye." She said as he slumped into the only comfortable chair in the room and stared morosely at the fire twinkling in the grate.

They sat in silence eating the eggs that Netty had coddled in water, and the bread and heavy cake spread thinly with butter. Netty had brewed the nettle tea and there was a large jug of fresh butter milk for them to share too. They hardly tasted their food as they ate slowly and without appetite.

The silence was broken by a knock on the door. Someone else had found it difficult to sleep. Samuel's head appeared around the door as he asked for Mr Tyler. His cap in his hand and his head

18

bent low, because of low the beams supporting the floor above, he coughed to clear his throat before speaking. He could still feel the smoke on his lips and in his lungs. "Mr Tyler, Sir!!"

James Tyler looked up and spoke for the first time. "Samuel!"

"I been thinkin' Sir. Didn' we oughta inform someone, 'bout the fire I mean, and o' course, the Master?"

James Tyler passed a hand across his face before answering. His eyes slowly lost their far away expression as he struggled to fix his mind on the matters that needed his attention. His back straightened perceptibly as he took a deep breath. "Of course, you are quite right Samuel." He looked about the room. "I wonder if there is writing paper." James Tyler pushed himself out of the chair as his eyes alighted on the bureau. Crossing the room he gently pulled at the lid. To his surprise it was unlocked, and he lowered the door to reveal paper, ink and sealing wax, together with an assortment of quills. Pulling a small chair towards the desk he sat slowly down and began to write.

They watched and waited in silence. The only sounds to be heard were the scratching of the quill on the paper and the crackling of the fire in the grate.

James Tyler folded the letters carefully. Then, lighting a taper from the fire, he sealed them with wax and addressed them before turning to Samuel. "Get young Adam to saddle the fastest horse in the stables, and then come to see me." He instructed. "I want him to take these letters to Tregony."

Netty suddenly remembered Maud and prodding her husband to get his attention, she mouthed her name silently to him. Tom took the hint. "Mr Tyler. I'd be obliged if ye was t'look at Miss Bottings. Her avn't spoken nor moved since she was put t' bed last night. She appears t'be awake fer 'er eyes be open."

James Tyler nodded before asking. "What do you think Mrs Teague?"

"I don' rightly know Mr Tyler. T' tell the truth I'm affeared for 'er. I am that. I think 'er mind 'ave gone. Like Annie Scott when she watched 'er 'usband and son drown while they was tryin' t' rescue the passengers from the Santa Maria."

James Tyler paused before pushing himself from the chair. "Perhaps you will come up stairs with me Mrs Teague." He suggested. After he had visited Maud it was his opinion that she was in need of medical attention, and thus instructed Adam to call at the doctor's house on the way home.

Adam set off mounted on the light grey, the fastest horse in the stables. He was instructed by Mr Tyler to ride to Tregony and inform the authorities of the fire at Tremanyon. He also carried with him a letters for Mr Franks the Master's solicitor, and the bank. Adam was to ensure that they were safely aboard the mid morning coach for Truro. On his return he was to come by way of Ruan Lanihorne with a request for the doctor to call at the Garden Cottage, to see Maud Bottings.

* * *

In the cold grey light of dawn they gathered once more about the shambles of stone and timber still crackling and spitting as unrelenting pockets of fire refused to relinquish their hold on the once beautiful mansion. Now, as the crowd grew larger and the servants were joined by onlookers from the village, they stared at the burned out shell. All that remained was the charred staircase and the half landing with the arched window shattered by the heat.

Slowly, a steady stream of villagers arrived to offer their help. Word had quickly spread of the plight of those who lived and worked at Tremanyon, and they had brought with them, in Morley Pascoe's old trap, a veritable selection of food. They had brought vegetables from their small gardens, onions, potatoes, carrots and autumn cabbages. Fish from Solly Treffry, mackerel caught fresh this morning, and fresh bread and heavy cakes made by the women. Tied on to the seat, beside old Morley was a large wicker basket filled with an assortment of clothes.

Netty stared at it all in amazement. "We can't take these!" She announced. "None of 'e 'ave clothes enough to spare. Tis too generous. Far too generous."

Morley looked down from his advantageous height. "Ye can take 'em Netty Teague, 'n ye will. Cut 'em down to fit they twins, or yourself or young Hannah. Whatever the folks in the village 'ave, tis far more than ye 'ave right now. There be a pair of trousers fer Tom too. They'm seen better days mind, 'n there be a shirt or two that will need some attention, but the material still be good."

Tears filled Netty's eyes. "How will we ever repay ye all?" She whispered.

"Think nothin' of it Netty. What are us folks for if we can't 'elp they less fortunate." He climbed down with great difficulty, and

20

then lifted the basket to the ground where the twins helped Netty to carry it to the cottage. Pushing the twins before her, they were still in a daze, Netty set off with the very welcome gifts as Tom and Samuel returned from their search of the back of the house

Mr Tyler and the Reverend Siley Pratt were in earnest conversation on the side lawn and Tom hesitated as Mr Tyler beckoned to Sam. "Samuel. Come over here a moment, please."

As Tom turned to walk away he grimaced and muttered quietly. "Whatever 'e wants, if it involves that Right Reverend Gen'leman, I'd watch meself if'n I was ye" Samuel nodded and made his way towards the solemn pair.

"The Reverend has kindly offered a home to Hannah until her future is settled." James Tyler informed him. Sam frowned. "She could help his wife with the housework and the children, in return for a roof over her head." James Tyler continued. "It must be crowded for you in the coach cottage, and the last thing you need is another mouth to feed."

Sam suppressed a scowl and sharp retort. He knew what it was like in the Reverend Siley-Pratt's house. Hadn't Mary Pipe been given into service in that house? And look at her now, poor thing. Cowered and frightened, afraid of any strange noise, hiding from friends and strangers alike and peeping out at the world from behind covered windows in her Gran's house. What would become of poor Mary when Granny Pipe died? She couldn't live forever, even though she had outlived all her children.

"Samuel!" James Tyler reminded him that he had spoken, but realising that they were all under a great strain he allowed for his lapse of attention and waited.

"No, Mr Tyler." Sam blurted out sharply. "Hannah will be just fine with we." James Tyler was obviously taken aback with Sam's terse reply and so he added the simple explanation. "She 'ave taken to the little un's, and is 'elpin' Tess who is tired with the young'n on the way."

Reverend Siley Pratt raised himself to his full height, and looked down his long crooked nose. His gaunt narrow face and strange appearance was not enhanced by the severity of his black clothes. Sam couldn't help but think that he looked more like the devil himself than a man of God. "You must think of Hannah's future." The Reverend retorted. "You must not think of yourself man, or your wife. It will be most unseemly, her being engaged to be married and living in the same house as a boy of Adam's years."

Samuel bristled at this statement and his own face took on an angry expression. "Just what are 'e suggestin' Reverend?" He retorted.

Reverend Siley-Pratt looked more than a little uncomfortable. As he fingered his collar a rosy glow spread upwards from his neck and he averted his eyes. "I wasn't suggesting anything." He stammered uncertainly. "I was only thinking of the girl's good name and her future of course."

"Hannah's name is quite safe in my 'ouse, as ye well know Reverend. And as for 'er future, that will be Hannah's decision alone." Samuel was angry, so he added by way of appeasement. "But I shall inform Hannah of your kind offer." And, as an afterthought. "Thank 'e." Sam waited no more and turned hastily away, leaving a baffled James Tyler to deal with the aftermath of the rebuttal. Village gossip rarely reached James Tyler's ears for he kept himself apart from the servants and, besides, he wasn't local.

Adam did not return until sunset, and with him he brought the message that Doc Thomas would ride over on the morrow to see Maud. Meanwhile she was to be kept rested and warm, and should try to take some weak broth. Samuel took the message over to Netty, who tried to carry out the good doctor's instructions. But old Maud either couldn't, or wouldn't, take the broth. It just dribbled down her pointed chin to be wiped away by Netty. It wasn't that she turned her head, or refused it in any other way, she just did not swallow. Her eyes continued to stare at the ceiling, quite unnerving poor Netty.

Doctor Thomas arrived around noon the following day, shortly before Mr. Franks, the authorities from Tregony and the coroner. Of course there was no body to identify and the staff had to all bear witness to the fact that the Master had indeed been in bed at the time of the fire. It was believed that Maud always lit the lamp in Squire Durance's bedroom, when she took him his supper. Since his wife died he made it a habit of retiring to his room early, and taking his supper at a small table there. It was assumed that the lamp must have fallen over, or been knocked off the table, and that it was this that had caused the fire. The fact that Squire Durance had not called for help gave cause for concern but, when Doctor Thomas explained that he had been treating him for problems relating to the heart, it was recorded that he had probably died of heart failure and there was no blame to the staff of Tremanyon.

The Doctor pronounced that Maud was suffering from shock. He did not bleed her and produced a tonic that Netty was told to give her, which she did without success, and informed them that he would return in a few days time to reassess the situation. But Maud's condition deteriorated rapidly, and when he did return he informed them all that she probably did not have long to live and that they should notify any relatives of her condition.

After the authorities had left, Mr Franks asked Mr Tyler to assemble the staff. They all crowded into the one tiny room of Garden Cottage. There was standing room only, except for Mr. Franks who sat at the small table set into the doorway to the scullery. When all was quiet he spoke out clearly, so that all could hear him. He pronounced that Squire Durance had left the majority of his estate to his sister's only son. However, it was always the intention that on Squire Durance death the estate would be sold. There were a few glum faces at this information. "However." Mr. Franks looked up from the table, the room seemed even smaller with it so crowded. "Squire Durance must have held each of you in high esteem. For each and every one of you are mentioned in his will."

James Tyler was amazed to learn that he had been left the princely sum of £50, as had Maud. Netty was overwhelmed to hear that she and Tom were to share £25, and when Sam and Adam learned that he had left them £20 and £10 respectively, they were speechless. Simon was also the happy recipient of £50 for his loyal service and for his wife's devotion to Mrs. Durance, before Sara's untimely death. Ted and Charlie were each left £20, Hannah, the twins and the under gardeners £5 each. For the first time since the fire a happy smile lit Hannah's face. Now she would be able to set up home in style when she married her Billie.

But all their real worries were for their jobs and homes, and now Mr Franks turned to this subject.

James Tyler's services, of course, were no longer required, and it appeared that Maud would not be with them for much longer. Tom and Netty could remain in the Garden Cottage and Mr Franks hoped that they would continue to care for Maud until her end. Hannah and the twins would have to return to their homes until further employment could be found for them. Mr Franks informed them that he would arrange for their transport home, and would personally endeavour to find them new positions. Although the horses were to be sold immediately, Mr Franks wished for Samuel and Adam to stay on until a buyer was found for the estate. They were to help Tom maintain the gardens and grounds, Tom was the head gardener and the services of the under gardeners were to be dispensed with. He also asked Simon to continue managing the fish cellar and, for the time being, the wood and the game. Mr Franks would make arrangements to pay the crews of the two boats, Elizabeth Ann and Louisa Clare, which were named after Squire Durance's wife and daughter. Ted was asked to stay on at the Mill. However, Charlie and his wife would need to find new employment but could stay on, temporarily, in Primrose Bank Cottage. He gave Simon, Tom and Netty, Samuel and Adam, and Ted, time to talk it through. If they agreed to stay until a new owner was found they would continue on full pay until then. If the new owner decided to dispense with their services, then they would receive a bonus on the termination of their employment and Mr Franks would endeavour to find new employment for them. They all agreed to stay until a new owner for Tremanyon was found for, in truth, they were wise enough to realise that there was little alternative. Both Tremanyon and the headland was their home, and work was not easy to come by in the locality. They would have to take their chances, and hope that the new master would find them suitable.

Maud passed away peacefully in her sleep a few days before Christmas.

1748 – *Tremanyon*

THE RIDE OUT to the headland had not been a long one and the mount that he had hired for this, the final part of his journey, was a fine example of horseflesh, knew the terrain, and was sure footed.

Richard Tremayne had travelled for five days from London, spending the nights at various Inns and Hostels on route. Most of them had been dirty and with poor food, but the last night he had slept well in an excellent hostelry at Ruan Lanihorne, just a stones throw from the ruins of the castle. After breaking his fast on a good selection of home cooked fare, served by the Innkeeper's wife, he was informed that arrangements had been made for the use of a horse from the stables of a local doctor.

As Richard left the Inn to make his way down to the bottom of the hill, he skirted the castle ruins. Large gaps appeared in the stonework and it was quite evident that many of the stones had already been removed from the destroyed walls. A young lad of six or seven was, at this very moment, rolling a sizeable block of stone down the slope towards the road that ran beside the river. Probably it would be used to help to extend their small and no doubt overcrowded cottage, Richard thought with a smile. Above him stood the small Church of Ruan. Below, and to the left and right, the road hugged the small tributary of the Fal River, which wound its way all the way to Tregony. A few shallow draft boats still traded this far up the river, but the rapidly silting river was becoming more un-navigable with every passing year. Once large boats traded all the way to Tregony, now it was becoming little more than a creek and, as well as Falmouth, Truro wharf was growing in importance to shipping. On the other side of the road the cottages nestled into the hillside.

Just before Richard reached the bottom of the hill he came to the set of large iron gates, which stood open. He recognised them from the directions that he had been given, and entering between them he turned towards the stables. From a wonderful selection Richard had made his choice, and was well pleased. As he rode out of Ruan, on to the rising ground of the headland, he acknowledged that Dr Thomas was justifiably renowned for his knowledge of horse breeding. His profession, no doubt, required a reliable means of transport and the means of accessibility to areas often not yet served by roads.

Richard reined in the horse, as he recalled Harris beckoning him as he left the chamber.

* * *

"Tremayne! How are you, old boy?" Martin Harris was one of the members for Tregony. Neighbours in a loose term, as Richard's family owned an estate on the outskirts of Mevagissey. Not far as the crow flies. The estate was now run, and the house occupied, by Richard's eldest brother. As the youngest, Richard, who had too little to occupy his youthful energy, had joined the services where he had risen to the rank of Captain in the Cornish Regiment. At his request Richard had been released after the battle of '45 and returned to Cornwall to recover from his injuries, the horrors of the fighting and the aftermath of war. With the backing and encouragement of his father Richard sought to enter parliament and had been successfully selected as a member to represent the St Austell area. At first he had found it both interesting and exciting. The demands of parliament, the bustle of city life in the capital, the entertainment, the social whirl, and being at the heart of government, all the things that once were new and exciting were now less appealing. Increasingly, he noticed the noise and the dirt, and the longing for clean air and open spaces was becoming harder to ignore. A longing for home.

"Hello Martin, I didn't see you in the house." Richard smiled disarmingly. "How is Daphne?"

"She is fine Richard, thank you for asking, and your family?"

"We are all well, but longing to return to the country again at the end of the session." In truth Annabelle was, yet again, unwell. A malaise that the doctors could find no reason for, but which left her both exhausted and distressed. Richard hoped that she would improve as soon as they arrived home, and that the fresh Cornish air would revive her spirit and bring the colour back to her pale cheeks.

Richard and Martin walked companionably along the panelled corridors chatting amiably, avoiding here and there groups in earnest discussion. Shortly they had made their way towards The Hall where they took an unoccupied table and chairs by the window overlooking the Thames.

Martin Harris beckoned to a manservant, and their pre-ordered food was brought to the table. He glanced at Richard, returning to the conversation of a few moments ago. "Yes. Life is very different here, it suit us. It's pleasant to go home for a while but for me, I have to admit, I am settled into this new life of ours. Are you still residing at St Ewe?"

Richard paused, with a glass in his hand. "Yes, but we are tenants only. Never really intended for it to be a permanent arrangement so we have never really settled there, never felt at home somehow. We both miss the sight of the sea." Twirling the glass between his fingers, he gazed thoughtfully into the amber liquid.

"Hm. Hm. Yes." Martin Harris eyed the selection of cold meats before him and was about to stab at a large slice of juicy York ham. His hand stopped midway to the plate. "Near the sea, you say!"

"Yes." Richard answered simply, with an audible sigh.

Harris dragged his eyes away from the ham and beef on the plate. "Have you heard the news of Tremanyon? Coincidentally, did you know that it is also called the Manor of Tremayne? A branch of your family?" When Richard shook his puzzled head, he continued. "The old boy died in a horrific fire on the night of the big storm. House was gutted. No real heir to speak of. His wife died some years ago, daughter also, his sister's son inherits and the whole estate is now up for sale." His eyes returned to the plate of meat, he speared a slice of the ham and transferred it deftly to the plate in front of him. "Three farms, a mill, various cottages, fishing boats and fish cellar, and the ruins of The Manor of course. On one side the land runs right down to the river and on the other, the sea."

Richard looked out towards the Thames, running swiftly towards the sea. A quiver of anticipation ran down his back as his heart took a sudden flutter. His eyes, looking down on the murky river flowing swiftly by, saw only the sea off the Cornish coast, and in his head he could hear the word Tremanyon . . . Tremanyon. Leaving The House he immediately made an enquiry, sending a letter post haste to the Cornish agents before going home.

On Richard's return home that night, he sat and informed Annabelle that he would have to leave at first light on urgent business. He didn't know how long he would be absent but he promised that he would return as soon as possible. Weak as she was she met it with a laugh. Annabelle had grown used to

Richard's sudden exits, and chided him that one day she would tie him down so that she would know exactly where he was.

* * *

The ground rose before Richard now, and he took the winding lane past the farm and up into the village perched on the top of the hill. Passing through the sleepy village, and beyond the Church, he stopped at the Blacksmiths for directions, leaving behind him a knot of curious villagers all wanting to know where the fine fellow was going. They would see few strangers here, Richard thought as he rode round the slight bend at a junction in the lane. Further down the hill he passed a cottage and some low farm buildings beside the lane and then, as he turned the bend in the lane, before him was evidence of the once tree lined avenue. The Cornish elms were now only a semblance of their past glory, almost demolished by the gale force winds that had ripped them apart with its force and fury. The skeletal arms of the few remaining trees were trying hard to make their presence felt, reaching over, touching here and there, in an endeavour to create the lost mystical passage which, when clothed with the green leaves of summer, would have formed a wonderful arched tunnel.

Slowly he rode the length of the avenue. Now and then a sharp ring would shatter the still quiet, as the stallion's hoof would connect with an exposed piece of stone or granite which had been used to make up the lane. Gateways to the left afforded him glimpses of the coast and the sea beyond and it seemed that they were both only a stones throw away.

Finally Richard arrived at his destination. The lane here suddenly turned to the left, sweeping on down the hill. But now, straight ahead of him, stood the large imposing set of iron gates. On either side, white walls curved to the left and right, and at each side of the hinged open gates, a carved figure of a Cornish Chough topped a stone pillar to be repeated at the ends of each wall. Each bird was standing erect, wings wide spread, and their eyes were cast haughtily downwards as if wishing to inspect and give approval to those who had the audacity to enter through the gates.

A young lad appeared from behind the wall. "Can I be of 'elp t'ye, Sir?"

Richard sat motionless upon his horse. Suddenly he was engulfed with apprehension. Fear rose within him, and with it the certainty that this long and arduous journey was to end in disappointment. He had not realised, at any time during his journey, what store he had put in this expedition. The white pebbled drive beyond the gates, curved gently to the right. What was beyond was hidden from view.

"Sir!" The lad was beside him now, level with his stirrup. "Sir! Can I be of 'elp t' ye."

Richard looked down. "Tremayne." He told the boy. "Captain Richard Tremayne. I have an appointment to meet the agent and Mr Franks, together with Mr Pascoe from Pascoe's Bank in Truro."

The young lad touched the unruly lock of hair that fell over his forehead. "Yes Sir. Mr Franks be up at the 'ouse, Sir. Shall I guide ye, Sir?"

Richard glanced once more beyond the gates. The white pebbled drive beckoned to him. "No lad, thank you, I should like to walk from here. Is there anyone to look after my horse? Do you have stables?"

"Yes Sir." The youth replied uncertainly. "We 'ave stables Sir, only there be no 'orses in 'em no more." He shuffled his feet nervously, looking down at them as he did so. Then plucking up courage and taking a deep breath, he added. "But I can do it Sir. I'll walk 'n slowly like for a whiles, then I'll rub 'n down and give 'n some water 'n feed. e'll be good as new, and ready for ye when ye want 'n Sir." Eagerly he looked up at this fine gentleman sitting so confident and assured above him.

Adam Sawle looked up into the deep blue eyes that returned his steady gaze. They were eyes that were kind, but studying him also, assessing what they saw. Richard had removed his hat, and Adam noted the almost black hair, which was pulled back over and behind his ears and was secured with a simple band of leather, the ends of which were trimmed with turquoise beads of some kind. This man wore no wig, his hair was clean, and his dress was expensive but not flamboyant. Yes, it was clear to Adam that this man was a gentleman.

Richard had also been assessing Adam and having made up his mind he shook his feet free of the stirrups, swung one leg forward over the saddle and slipped deftly to the ground. He was a tall man. Head and shoulders above the youth standing before him, whom he judged to be around sixteen or seventeen years of age. A smile crossed his lips. "What is your name boy?"

"Sawle, Sir. Adam Sawle."

"Well young Adam Sawle. Do what you have just promised and I shall be well pleased." He held out the reins in one hand, his hat still held in the other.

"I will Sir, I will." And Adam, taking the reins from Richard, put his hand out to the stallions head without fear, talking to him, gentling him, before leading him through the gates at the back which Richard had not noticed until this moment.

Richard was left looking at the open iron gates. The hair on the back of his neck rose, sending a quiver of anticipation down his spine. Slowly he turned to look through the field gateway behind him, and across the fields to the view of the bay beyond. A scene set in early spring sunshine, and the sea clear and shimmering. Beyond the bay, and behind the headland, was another such wide bay and beyond that, the bay that could be seen from the house outside Mevagissey.

Turning again, Richard faced the gates and took the first step towards Tremanyon and the unknown house at the end of the drive. Now, at each side of the drive, the trees had survived the full force of the storm and showed only minimal damage. The tall pine trees, mixed with stately beech trees, rose high above the lower specimens of evergreen trees and shrubs such as holly, laurel, rhododendron and camellias. Drifts of late bright yellow daffodils flowed beside the immaculately kept walks that meandered through the large shrubbery. The scent of wild violets filled the air with heady perfume, and primroses showed the first flush of flowers. Early bluebell leaves thrust upwards, giving a hint of the rich carpet that would be spread in a few weeks time. Slowly but surely Richard proceeded towards the curve in the drive, his heart in his mouth.

Suddenly the drive broadened. The shrubbery came gradually to an end, where it finished with a wide expanse of drive before him. A raised lawn to the right lay in front of a low, slate roofed and ivy clad cottage, and this was attached by a tall arched wall to the remains of what must have once been a beautiful dwelling.

Standing in the centre amidst the rubble and burned beams, rising proudly above it all, were the remains of a staircase and the half landing, still intact, with a beautiful arched window at the back of a gabled half landing. The once exquisite window was shattered and open to the elements, splinters of coloured glass hung tenaciously to the frame. The stairs turned and rose again from this point, to finish high above the devastation below. Such destruction, such a total waste.

Sadly, Richard turned away and the ugly scene of charred wood, fire blackened timbers amidst the stone, rubble and slate was dispelled from his mind in an instant.

Before him, sloping gently downwards, as if melting into the natural landscape beyond, was a wide expanse of ornamental gardens, cradled within the half circular sweep of the stone pebbled drive. Opposite him, where he stood at the foot of the steps to the house, a large ornate urn stood at each side of the wide granite steps that stretched down through the centre of the lawn. The steps were in a series of fives and, to each side, a low ornate wall. At the foot of the steps the level box edged garden contained, within it, a round flowerbed. This was divided into segments, each segment divided by another clipped box hedge. The lawns at either side of the flight of steps were bordered with well-stocked flowerbeds, flowing back until they reached the shrubbery and the trees that sheltered the gardens from the elements of wind and rain from the east.

Below, and beyond these ornamental gardens, the lower lawn melted into the landscape of farmland until it dipped into the valley. And there, cradled between two hills, was the one eventuality of a Cornish coastal scene. A sea of Lapis Blue and Jade.

A voice from behind caused him to turn. Two men walked purposefully towards him from the cottage. The slimmer and taller of the two held out his hand in greeting. "Captain Tremayne? I am Edward Franks." Richard took his hand briefly and for a moment he remained looking up at the flight of steps before him. He no longer saw the scared shell and the blackened remains. He looked up and saw only the cut granite steps, rising to an open door in a tall and proud Georgian Manor House. Once again Richard was to feel the shiver run up and down his spine. He knew at this moment that he had come home. Yes, this was to be his home. This was Tremanyon, the Manor of Tremayne. This was to be the home of his family, and all the families that were to follow.

* * *

Edward Franks unrolled the map and laid it out on the table. Glancing about the room to find something to weight down the corners, he reached for the brass candlesticks and placed them at the top, whilst holding down the bottom with one hand and indicating the estate with the other. "As you can see, Captain Tremayne, the estate encompasses the whole of the headland. From this point, at the bottom of the avenue, the boundary is with Rosvarron. That is this large house here, to the east, and their land runs down to the coast here, to the east of Kylyn Cove. In total, there are some 900 acres. Tremanyon itself lies within 35 acres. The Home Farm 210 acres, Kylyn Farm 170 acres, Rhossinnis 295 acres and the Mill comes with just over 100. Then of course, there are the woods here and here and here. Primrose Cottage and the spinney here, and Quay Cottage and the fish cellar here." Richard nodded as he studied the map, but said nothing. "The Home Farm is in hand, of course, as is the Mill, but Kylyn and Rhosinnis Farms are tenanted. You will find all the financial details in the report."

Richard continued to study the map. "What staff have been retained?" He asked before looking up.

"Simon Retallick, he manages the fish cellar at Quay and, of course the boats. He lives in the single storey cottage on the quay, with his daughter Ginifur. His wife died some years back now. Simon has also been acting as the gamekeeper at Tremanyon and the Home Farm since his father retired. John and Annie Retallick own the Well Cottage here, opposite the Mill. Harry Polaughan is the bailiff for the Home Farm. Edward Chaffin runs the Mill, the land that goes with it is farmed by Harry Polaughan and the income is included in the figures for Home Farm. We have kept Samuel Sawle and his son Adam on as well. Sam manages the stables, and Adam helped with the horses, they live in the Coach Cottage at the end of the stable block. We have also retained Tom and Netty Teague, the Head Gardener and the Cook. Charlie and Lilly May have been given time to find alternative work and accommodation, but at present are still living in Primrose Bank. The house staff, other than the cook Netty, have all gone. Tom and Netty you have met, they are living in this cottage for the time being." Richard nodded again, biting the inside of his lip as he gave the matter some thought. "Of course." Continued Edward Franks. "None of the staff have been given any guarantees of employment. The previous owner provided very generously for them all, and there will be a bonus due should you not wish to keep them on, or should they decide to seek employment elsewhere."

"I see." Richard glanced out of the low window. "How long will it take me to tour the estate?" He asked.

Edward Franks released the pressure on the map and it rolled up with a snap. "If you are seriously considering the purchase, and I believe that you are, I would recommend that you spend at least today and tomorrow here. That would give you ample time to meet with the tenants, and the retained staff, as well as see the whole of the estate. Where are you staying?"

Richard turned away from the window. "I lodged at the Inn at Ruan last night, and hired a horse from the local doctor. I could return there or take lodgings for the night in Porthcarrow, if there is an Inn. I told the landlord at Ruan that I might not return for a couple of days."

"Splendid." Edward Franks beamed, he liked this young man. Mr. Pascoe smiled. As many bankers did he said very little, but learned a lot from listening and observing. "We hoped you might." Edward continued, "I have provisionally reserved a room for you at the Inn in the village. It's simple, but clean, and Netty will be happy to cook for you whilst you are here." He stretched his back and pulled at the gold chain attached to his waistcoat to reveal the gold hunter watch. Snapping open the lid he glanced at the time. "Well it is past noon. You have seen over the immediate grounds, how about we go to see Samuel Sawle and his son Adam. You can see the stables etc. whilst Netty rustles up a bite to eat and then we will start a tour of the estate.

* * *

Richard relaxed on the low sill of the open window. From this position he could see over the roofs of the cottages on the other side of the narrow lane, and he had a clear view of the bay. The night was still and very quiet. The sea was glassy calm and he could just make out the gentle lap of the tiny waves as they broke upon the sand, only yards away at the base of the cottages, and a murmur of voices that rose from the room in the Inn below.

The moon sailed out from behind the billowing black cloud as it drifted lazily across the midnight sky, casting a silver trail across the inky water and lighting up the mysterious rock that struck up from the sea on the far side of the bay. The cottages below him clustered haphazardly together around the sheltered cove, whilst small boats bobbed up and down on the high tide. Everything was bathed in the strange moonlight that seemed to turn them into an unbelievable range of blues. Shades of dark navy shadows contrasted sharply with cottages washed in pale blue light, and the night was chilled with the tang of salt hanging on the air.

Richard couldn't sleep, mulling over the events of the last two days. He had covered every inch of the estate, met with the tenants of Kylyn and Rhosinnis, and spoken at great length with Simon and his young daughter Ginny, Samuel and Adam, Edward Chaffin and, of course, Tom and Netty.

He had been greatly impressed by Simon. He managed the boats and the cellars extremely well, was unusually literate and maintained well detailed records. At the same time Simon managed the job as acting gamekeeper for the Estate. But this could not continue, for the work involved in the boats and the cellar was very demanding. Ginifur, Simon's daughter, was a bright and intelligent girl and may well be considered for a position in the house as a personal maid for Annabelle, or perhaps the girls. At sixteen many girls had been in service for a number of years, but Ginifur had stayed at home with her father's blessing and helped him at the cottage. Rachel and Rebecca were growing fast and, besides soon needing a tutor or governess, they would require an additional maid themselves.

Edward Chaffin was doing a good job at the Mill, it would be pointless to think of replacing him, and Samuel was an excellent choice to manage the stables with his son Adam. Richard had taken special note of the care that had been given to the stables themselves, and Adam's attention to the doctor's stallion was far greater than that expected of the stable lad at Heligan, and he was good. Father and son had a natural affinity with horses, that was quite obvious, and Samuel was also a carpenter and wheelwright, thus explaining the attention to the carriages which for some reason had not been sold.

Tom had quite clearly managed the gardens and grounds to a high standard. The immediate gardens were beautifully maintained. Paths and drives were neat and weed free, flower borders clean and tidy, shrubs pruned and the grass kept short. In the walled garden the box hedging was neatly trimmed and vegetables and herbaceous plants in tidy rows. The glass houses were well maintained, with Samuel's assistance no doubt, and the potting shed kept clean and tidy, tools hung in their allotted space, clean pots in neat rows and the cold frames full of young tender plants. The orchards too were well kept. Trees had been pruned to a manageable height, espalier pear trees forming a neat walk to the western door of the walled garden and mature palms lined the drive to the wood. Tom also helped with the management of the woods. The Big Wood consisted of young beech trees, now nearly twenty foot in height. Lerryn Wood, which contained mature hard woods and conifers, and Fern Wood which was also a mixed mature wood, all were part of the main estate including Home Farm. Samuel and Adam had been helping Tom through the winter but now that spring was here he would need extra labour. Edward Franks had assured Richard that there was plenty of local labour available, and he hoped that he was right for it would be necessary to employ a number of people to maintain the high standard and also run the boats and cellar at Quay Cottage.

That only left Netty. Netty had already proved herself a more than adequate cook, equally able to cater for entertaining as well as providing simpler family fare. Richard and Edward had taken all their meals in the cottage, with the exception of breakfast, and Netty had taken this opportunity to show off her skills.

All in all, Richard thought, he couldn't find better staff.

There only remained one question. Would Annabelle like it here? For Richard, there was nothing to decide, he loved it and he believed that he had finally found his home. Richard already knew to the minutest detail what the house would be like, he could see it in his minds eye. What better place could he raise his family?

In his heart he was confident that Annabelle would love it, and yet there was always the chance that she would not.

Richard blinked. The cloud had moved away. The whole of the bay was bathed in silver light, and he knew, at this very moment, that this beautiful peninsular was surely to become his home.

Richard continued to juggle with the problem night and day, throughout the journey back to London. Should he tell Annabelle, or should he surprise her?

Richard and his family returned from London, to St Ewe, for the summer. Annabelle was still unwell. The doctors couldn't, or wouldn't, give a satisfactory explanation for her sudden bouts of illness. Their only inadequate explanation was that she did not have a very strong constitution.

Annabelle hated the foul air of London, and longed for the clear air of Cornwall. The children too were pale and listless, for Annabelle would rarely allow them to go outside, afraid that they would catch some awful disease.

It was probably this that made Richard keep the secret to himself, and it was the spring of 1750 before the family would learn of their new home.

1750 – *Beyond Tregony*

ANNABELLE WAS SITTING in the summerhouse at St. Ewe, watching Rosie helping the girls to make daisy chains on the lawn.

Rosie's head was uncovered, her little cap, normally worn on the back of her head, discarded on the grass. Her straight brown hair was pulled back from her face and the warm summer sun had added a golden glow to her skin, but the two small girl's faces were shielded with bonnets. In contrast their faces were pale, though flushed with the heat. They longed to toss the bonnets away, or perhaps just push them back a little, so that they could feel the warmth of the sun on their faces too. But Mama was watching and firmly believed that a young lady should always keep her head covered, and she should never let the sun colour her face.

Rachel and Rebecca didn't particularly want to be young ladies. They wanted to be like their cousin Wesley. Wesley didn't have to wear a hat. Wesley was allowed to ride out on his own pony. Wesley could climb trees. Wesley was allowed to strip off his clothes and swim in the sea; he could climb rocks and row a boat. But not Rachel and Rebecca for they were, as their mother insisted, young ladies.

The rattle of stones on the path caused the children's eyes to light up as they focused their attention on the wrought iron gate at the side of the house. The familiar figure of Richard, resplendent in his riding clothes, placed his hand upon the latch and the two little girls let out a cry of delight as they leapt to their feet.

Rachel, the older of the two by just twelve months, gathered up her skirts in her tiny hands and ran as fast as her sturdy legs would carry her. Rachel was dark haired, like her father, and tall for her age. Rebecca was slight of build and fair, like Annabelle, her mother. Her tight curly hair framed her face in an unruly fashion Annabelle tried vainly to curtail it with ribbons, but the curls escaped time after time, as if controlled by a life of their very own.

"Papa!" Rachel reached the gate as Richard closed it behind him, and she threw herself into his arms. "Where have you been? You have been gone all today and yesterday too." She admonished him sternly.

Richard threw back his head with a laugh. "That's for me to know, and you to find out, little one." And with this he threw her high above his head, catching her easily and swinging her around whilst she squealed with delight.

As Rebecca toddled steadily nearer Richard placed Rachel on the grass and bent to greet his youngest daughter. Rebecca was quiet and shy, where Rachel was talkative, bright and bubbly like the best Champagne. Richard wondered what he would liken Rebecca to. It would have to be sweet, delicate and perhaps a little understated. He feared for his youngest daughter, hoping upon hope that she was not going to inherit her Mother's ill health. "Hello Becky. Have you come to greet your Papa?" He held out his hands and lifted her gently as she reached out to him.

"Mama says that we must call her Rebecca, not Becky." Rachel informed him.

"But I like Becky best, don't you?" Added his youngest daughter, to which he gave an amused smile.

"Rebecca is a lovely name, that's why we chose it. A perfect name for the lovely young lady that you will one day be." He assured her. "But Becky is just the right name for a Father to call his little girl, I am sure Mama will agree." He held out his hand to Rachel. "Come, let us go and find your Mama. How is she today?"

"Oh, she's much better this afternoon." Rachel informed him. "She came down late, but she has been sitting in the summerhouse this afternoon, while we have been making daisy chains with Rosie."

"Where's Rosie now?" Asked Richard as he glanced across the empty lawn.

"She has gone to let Mrs Hoskins know that you have arrived home. She told Rosie to let her know the minute you arrived because Mama told her that she didn't know when to expect you. Where have you been Papa?" She asked again.

Richard loosened his grip on her hand and ruffled her hair. "You don't give up do you?"

Rachel stopped abruptly and stamped her tiny foot. She creased her forehead into a frown, and waggled a finger at him. "You are changing the subject again Papa. You think I don't notice, but I do. Where do you keep going?"

Richard's immediate reaction was to laugh, she was so much older than her years, seeming to know so much more of what was going on around her than any adult would give her credit for. Instead he adopted an expression of the required seriousness, and answered. "Yes I have been absent a lot haven't I? What does your Mama say?"

"Mama doesn't say much. If I ask her she just says, 'Your Papa has business to attend to.' She also says that you have to make reports on what happens to Parliament when we go back to London. But I don't think she really believes that."

Richard raised his eyebrows. "Oh, don't you?" He exclaimed.

"No I don't." Rachel looked down at the grass. "Her smile goes away when I ask her where you are. She doesn't know either does she?" Richard didn't answer as he considered her words. Rachel didn't look up, but continued to twiddle her foot round and round as she continued to stare at the ground. "Mr Hoskins left Mrs Hoskins, and went away with one of the maids before we came here." Richard grimaced, so that was what it was all about. "Are you going to leave us too?"

Richard was almost too shocked to speak. He bent down, placing the silent Rebecca on the grass, and gripped Rachel's shoulders. "Rachel! What on earth made you say that?"

Rachel looked deep into his eyes, searching for the truth. "Well! You are never at home when we come here now. You go out early and come back late, and sometimes you don't come back for days. And I don't think Mama knows where you are either." Her voice trailed off.

This time Richard was speechless as he took the girls hands and walked around the side lawn towards the summerhouse. Annabelle was watching the path, but did not mask the worried expression quite quickly enough. Richard felt a tightening in his chest, as he realised that he had been so absorbed with his task that he hadn't given a thought to what might be crossing her mind.

The worried expression was erased from Annabelle's face, as she smiled in delight at her husband. Richard was tall and slim at the hips, with broad shoulders, and he looked so handsome in his tight fitting cream riding breeches and dark green velvet jacket with the ruffles of lace at his neck. As always, when they were at home in Cornwall Richard's hair was not powdered, he never wore a wig, and his clean dark hair was secured at the nape of his neck with a thin piece of leather as usual. His riding boots were polished until they shone and they were trimmed with silver buckles. But the boots now looked a little dusty after his ride. Annabelle believed that she was so very lucky that it was she, shy Annabelle Bennett, who had been chosen to marry the handsome Richard Tremayne. Out of all the beautiful and interesting young women available to him, the Tremayne's had chosen her. Annabelle had always feared that Richard would tire of her in time, never believing that she could possibly provide him with everything that he deserved in a wife. She was a good hostess, when her health allowed, Annabelle knew that. She was a good wife, loving and caring, and a good mother to his daughters. But was that enough? She hadn't given him a son. This was the greatest sadness in her life, she would love to have given Richard the son that she believed he so wanted.

Richard stepped through the open doors to the summerhouse and smiled down upon Annabelle. "You look as pretty as a picture sitting here." He told her "And you are looking a little brighter today, but how are you really feeling?" He bent to kiss her cheek.

Annabelle smiled as he patted the children on their heads and sent them out into the garden before taking her hand. Annabelle's eyes shone with adoration and this only served to make Richard feel his guilt even greater. "I am so much better Richard. It is all the fresh clean air in Cornwall that is reviving me." The smile suddenly faded as she realised that he might think this a reproach. "Forgive me Richard, I didn't mean to blame my ill health on spending our lives in London. You have your work to do . . ." Poor Annabelle left the sentence unfinished, not knowing how to continue.

Richard patted her hand comfortingly. "The foul air of London is enough to offend even the strongest constitution, mine included." He tried to reassure her, "I can't understand what Martin Harris and his wife find so wonderful in all that noise and dirt." A tentative smile crept into her eyes, and her rosy lips turned up at the corners, as she understood that he did, indeed, speak the truth. "Do you feel well enough to undertake a short trip tomorrow?" A look of surprise crossed her face. "I would like to take you and the girls to visit some nice people that I have had the fortune to meet."

The smile was replaced with an expression of extreme pleasure, as Annabelle nodded eagerly. "We would love to Richard. Where will we be going?"

"Just a short way along the coast, but we will need to stay overnight. The house is not quite as large as this, nor perhaps as grand, but quite pleasant. Will you be able to manage with just Rose to attend you?"

Annabelle's heart leapt. If Richard wanted to take her and the children with him then she would have managed alone had he asked her to. "Oh yes, Richard. Of course I can. I shall not need to take much with me if it is only for a nights stay, but what clothes will we need? And it does not matter that the house is not grand, as you say, surely it is the people that matter. I have not always lived so graciously, remember?"

Richard smiled his comforting smile. "Wear your travelling clothes, the claret outfit. I like you in that. Take that lovely blue silk dress for the evening, I like its simplicity, a day dress, and nightclothes of course. Travelling clothes for the girls, and those pretty cotton lawn dresses, with the striped overskirts should do well. We'll get Bertha to pack a trunk whilst we have dinner." Annabelle looked so happy that he almost blurted out his news there and then. He wanted so much to tell her that he was home early, because today was one of the happiest days in his life.

* * *

The family set off very early. Annabelle had hardly had a wink of sleep all night, and she was wide-awake at dawn. Richard finally gave in to her and pulled the bell to call for hot water to be brought then, having hastily dressed, he went to check that the carriage and horses were being made ready.

It was a beautiful morning, the air was crisp and clean and the dew lay wet and shiny upon the short grass. A light breeze fluttered the leaves on the trees along the drive and the wispy high clouds were scattering away to the east. It foretold a bright, warm and sunny day.

There was much chattering at the breakfast table, even the usually silent Rebecca couldn't conceal her excitement at the surprise outing and, for once, Annabelle didn't reprimand them for talking at the table. This was to be a very special day, Annabelle was sure of it, and she didn't want anything to spoil it. Annabelle forced herself to eat a slice of ham and a spoonful of scrambled eggs, with a small piece of freshly baked bread, thinking to herself that Cook must have been up very early to prepare the food. Mrs Hoskins had also packed a basket of food, at the request of Richard, and this was waiting at the door when they were ready to depart.

Rose was waiting patiently by the basket, dressed in the travelling outfit that Captain Tremayne had bought for her when she went to London to help with the children. The small trunk at her feet contained her day clothes and nightwear.

Richard glanced enquiringly around the hall as Annabelle and the children followed him down the stairs, his eyes finally fell on Rose. "The trunk?"

"Mr Pellow has strapped it on the carriage, Sir." Then remembering that she hadn't greeted the Master and the Mistress that morning she bobbed a light curtsey. "Good mornin' Sir, Ma'am."

Richard smiled good-naturedly. "Good morning Rose. If you will take Rebecca and Rachel out and settle them in the carriage, I will send Mr Collins in for the basket and the trunk. You will ride inside with us Rose, so don't go suggesting that you ride on top."

Rose's surprise was quite evident by her open mouthed expression. "Are you quite sure Sir?" She exclaimed. Travelling inside the coach to and from London was quite one thing, but she hadn't expected to ride inside on a family outing.

Richard laughed. "Yes Rose, I am quite sure. Mrs Tremayne is sure, and Rachel and Rebecca will be delighted that you are travelling with them. You will be able to keep them amused with your stories and travelling games and, besides, today is not an ordinary day." He turned to take Annabelle's arm as they stepped out into the glorious day. Annabelle was as happy as she had been on her wedding day.

The road between St Austell and Tregony was a good one in summer. Hard and dry, it carried a fair amount of traffic and was wide enough, in most places, for two carriages to pass in comfort. It ran over hills and through valleys for a while, and then rose to follow high ground before dropping down through Tregony to follow the river.

Tregony was no longer a busy inland port, but still a thriving Stanary Town and today was market day. The main street, at the top of the hill, was crowded as the driver made a slow and careful passage through the throng. Rose pointed out the Town Crier as he rang his bell before calling out a proclamation in his powerful voice. She pointed out the organ grinder with his monkey on his shoulder, the bear with a collar being led through the crowd to perform for the onlookers, and the rope that was being hastily erected to create a temporary ring for the Cornish Wrestlers who would compete in the matches that would take place later in the day. More often than not the people would crowd around without a rope, but today was a special day and wrestlers would come from all over the county for their sport. For this wasn't any market day, this was the Mid Summer Fair. The highlight of summer. The girls were out and about dressed in their Sunday best dresses, with combs and ribbons in their hair, or pretty bonnets tied carefully beneath their chins. The boys had combed their hair, styled it as best they could, and strutted like fighting cocks in an attempt to impress the girl of their choice. Gypsies were selling pegs, made from local hazel sticks, or baskets woven from the willows which grew upon the moors, and sprigs of lucky heather. Woe betides anyone who didn't offer a coin or two for their wares, for a gypsy could be quick with a curse if they took a dislike to you. In her brightly painted caravan the Gypsy Queen would tell your fortune if you crossed her palm with a silver coin. She would look deep into her crystal ball and see the future, it was said, or if she studied your hand she could tell you if you would marry and how many children you would have. Artisans offered wares for sale at stalls beside the wide road. There were stalls selling shepherd's crooks made from local coppiced wood, tin-ware such as liquid measures for milk in quarter, half and one pint or quart measures for the dairymen and cook alike. Willow baskets for carrying food, laundry or even potatoes from the field. The travelling doctor extolled the virtues of his concoctions from the steps of his wagon. He had cures for the ague, and potions for fertility. He had powders for headaches and toothaches. Oils to rejuvenate the hair, or heal a wound on any man or beast. If his powder wouldn't work on the toothache, he would even pull out the offending tooth for a fee. Young women were selling flowers, or eggs, or honey. Others seemed to have nothing to sell but were, nevertheless, surrounded by admirers. They were dressed even more gaudily than the others, with bright ribbons in their hair and low cut blouses showing a little more than was necessary.

Richard cast an inquisitive eye about the crowds, wondering whether Martin Harris was in Tregony for the Summer Fair. He made a mental note to make enquiries, for he would especially like to see him and extend an invitation to visit.

At the bottom of the steep hill the river ran under the narrow stone bridge, the old warehouses stood alongside. Here the carriage followed the road beside the narrowing river, where once cargo ships set sail on the turn of the tide to make the journey past Ruan and down the River Fal to the sea. Now the river had silted up and was no longer navigable.

The leafy lane which ran beside the river was in stark contrast to the open fields west of Tregony. Here and there, in the wooded valley, they caught glimpses of the wide calm river glittering in the bright sunshine. A kingfisher sat atop a pole at the edge of the water, searching the river for its lunch, and a brown woodpecker tapped happily at a tree in an attempt to bring out some grubs to eat. Birds sang, pidgeons cooed, and squirrels scuttled across the leafy lane to the safety of a tree. Annabelle was enchanted by the change of scenery. It was all so very different from the open moorlands above St Austell, from the rugged coast of the north, and even the coastline of Looe and the countryside around the east of Cornwall. "It is all so pretty!" She exclaimed. "It is so wooded; I can hardly believe that we are still in Cornwall."

Richard smiled and took her hand. "I thought so too, when I first visited here. But just wait until we rise out of the valley and head out towards the coast." He watched her as she drank in the sweet air, whilst gazing in rapture and awe at the gentle countryside, and it pleased him greatly to see the pleasure and appreciation in her eyes.

They paused for refreshments at Ruan Lanihorne, leaving the coach for a few minutes to stretch their legs and unpack the carefully prepared food basket. After they had eaten Rose led the children into the castle ruins to explore, and Richard and Annabelle watched and waited until the horses were watered and the coach was ready for them to continue their journey. A few ships still pulled into the shores at Ruan but the river was silting up here also Falmouth had now become the centre for shipping and the main port for the Falmouth Packet ships. Any boats wanting to travel further inland now made their way to Truro.

"How much longer Papa? When will we be there?" Asked Rachel as Richard handed her up into the carriage.

"Not long now. Have patience little one." He placed a rug about Annabelle's lap and climbed in beside her, calling out to the driver as he did so, and the horses stepped out once more.

Soon they rose out of the wooded valleys, through the small hamlet of Ruan, and now there were open fields on either side of the rough highway. Yet still the countryside was well wooded. High stone hedge boundaries were planted with Cornish Elms, their light, delicate leaves fluttering in the breeze. Tiny cottages, surrounded by small patches of tilled earth, interspersed the farmsteads where larger houses stood. Sheep and cattle grazed in the grass fields, men worked at rebuilding stone walls, and boys and girls helped to gather in a crop of potatoes from the fields. Finally they dipped down into a valley before rising to the crest of a hill.

Suddenly an excited Rachel called out. "Look Becky, the sea!" And she reached across Rose for her younger sister's hand. As she did so she caught a fleeting glimpse of her Mother's face. Too late, Annabelle disguised her look of reproach and Rachel hesitated before correcting herself. "Look Rebecca. I can see the sea." Then added a little fearfully. "Look Mama, can you see it?"

Rachel was pointing to the sea, cradled in the valley to the left. Richard watched as Rebecca and Rachel continued to study their mother's face, afraid that Rachel had spoilt their wonderful day out.

Annabelle smiled happily back at them, and made a quick though difficult decision. "Quick Becky." She said. "Look, the sea." And she too pointed out of the window. Rachel and Rebecca's faces were a picture of astonishment, and Becky almost missed the opportunity of seeing the sea before it vanished once more behind some trees.

A few moments later they passed through the village of Porth-carrow, and Annabelle was astonished as she saw a young man take off his hat and cheer as they passed by, and a little girl at his side called out excitedly.

"What did she say, Mama?" Asked Rachel.

"I don't know my pet. I didn't hear her. Did you Richard?" Richard didn't answer, hiding his amusement he waved back.

Soon they left the village behind them and came to a bend in the road where the storm damaged trees that once created 'The Avenue' had been cut down and cleared. Young trees had now been planted in their place, Cornish elm on one side and wych elm on the other.

In no time at all they were at the wide gates of Tremanyon. Slowly the horses pulled the carriage through the entrance and along the drive. Annabelle and her daughters sat in silence and anticipation, until the carriage drew up in front of the tall Georgian Manor House.

"Oh it's beautiful!" Whispered Annabelle as she gazed up the steps to the open door. "It must be very new." She ventured as she took in the clean-cut granite walls.

Rachel was gazing out of the opposite window. "Oh Mama! Look, you can see the sea from here as well."

But Richard was alighting from the carriage, and the appearance of a servant kept Annabelle's eyes firmly fixed on the door for sight of their hosts. She placed the rug upon the seat as Richard took her hand, and she stepped down beside him. "Rose, bring the children." Richard instructed as he took Annabelle's arm to guide her up the steps and into the house.

In the large airy hall, waiting for them, were a stocky woman with a ruddy face and a cheery smile beneath her white cap and beside her a man of similar age with a swarthy complexion. Next a tall man with his hat in his hands, and a young girl of similar age to Rose. Behind them, stood the manservant who had let down the carriage steps. The three men bowed respectfully and, as the stocky woman bobbed awkwardly, the young girl dropped a graceful curtsey whilst boldly keeping her head held high. Annabelle was confused as they greeted her.

"We are pleased to meet you Ma'am." Welcomed the tall man.

"Thank you." Annabelle smiled at his greeting.

"My dear." Richard explained. "This is Simon Retallick and his daughter Ginifur, Samuel Sawle, and Tom and Netty Teague." Ginifur smiled at the children as Richard spoke to her. "Ginifur, take Rose and the children to the kitchen with you please. I think Mrs Teague has hot buns and milk for them, isn't that right Netty?"

"Yes Sir, indeed I have." Netty turned to lead the way and Ginifur put a hand out to take Rebecca's.

"Come." She said. And with a swift backward glance to Annabelle, they followed.

Richard turned to the men, still standing smartly in the hall. "Please carry the luggage to the bedroom suite Tom. And Simon, and Sam, If you will see to the horses and the carriage please." They acknowledged the requests, bowed briefly and turned to do the tasks allotted to them. Richard put out a hand to open the door nearest them and Annabelle drew a sharp intake of breath as she saw the plaster decorations adorning the large fireplace before noticing the chandelier hanging from the matching decorations on the ceiling. The room was sparsely furnished, but each piece had been chosen with care and Annabelle admired the blue and white colour scheme with coral velvet drapes at the tall windows.

Richard led Annabelle to a high backed chair. "But who lives here, Richard? Who owns this lovely house?" She asked, refusing to take a seat until her hosts had arrived.

Richard's eyes sparkled with humour as he said. "Someone you know very well, Annabelle."

"Then why aren't they here to greet us? And surely it is not quite correct to issue instructions to someone else's staff members." A frown creased her puzzled brow as Richard stood before her wondering if his decision to surprise her in this way was the right one. "Richard!" Annabelle was becoming concerned at his silence.

"It is a lovely house, isn't it Annabelle?"

"It is indeed a lovely house." She agreed.

"Did you see the view?" He asked, indicating the two tall windows at the front of the house. She shook her head and looked across the room to where the window looked out over the beautiful gardens that sloped down toward the valley, and once again she viewed the sight of the lapis blue sea off the Cornish coast. "Have you ever seen such a view?"

Annabelle shook her head slowly. "No. I don't think I have. It even surpasses the view from my father's house at Looe." She agreed. "But Richard!" Annabelle's eyes were full of unanswered questions as he drew her into his arms.

"Would you like to live here Annabelle? Could you be happy here, you and the children?" His eyes weren't laughing now; they were searching hers for an answer.

"Oh, Richard! What a question." The frown returned. "Whose house is this Richard?" Annabelle's eyes, searching the room for a clue to the occupants of the house, fell upon a portrait at the end of the room. Tentatively she stepped towards it. The face in the picture smiled back at her. Golden curls fell gently about her shoulders, and she wore a silk dress of blue with white lace at the neck and cuffs. "But, Richard, surely this is me? What would a picture of me be doing here?" Slowly she turned. "Richard! Whose house is this? Please tell me." She entreated.

Richard stepped quickly to her side. "It is yours Annabelle. Ours. Our very own home. A home for our children to grow up in and for you to gain your strength. A home for the families that will follow in our footsteps." Annabelle stared at him in wonder, wanting to believe that it was indeed true. "Does it please you Annabelle?" Richard waited for the answer he wanted to hear as Annabelle gazed about the room. "It isn't fully furnished, it awaits your feminine touch."

"Oh Richard! Is it really true?" Tears filled her eyes.

He gathered her once more into his arms. "It is indeed true, my love. This is Tremanyon, the Manor of Tremayne. This house was built for us . . . for you and me Annabelle. A home for Rachel and Rebecca."

Annabelle could not speak. Her heart was too full with love for him as she gazed into his face. Finally she said the words that he wanted to hear. "It is truly wonderful. We will indeed be happy here."

* * *

Two days turned into four and four into seven, and Richard had to send the carriage over to St Ewe to fetch more clothes for them all. Leisurely he showed Annabelle and his daughters over the estate, and proudly introduced them to the tenants and employees

47

alike. On Sunday they attended Church, where they were shown to the reserved pew at the front. The pretty Church, with its curious pointed tower, was unusually full. It seemed that the entire population of the village had turned out to welcome them, and the Reverend Siley-Pratt took great delight in making the most of their captive ears, for he would probably have to wait until Harvest Thanksgiving or Christmas for a congregation of this size again.

As the family left the Church, and stepped out into the sunshine, a tall gentleman walked towards them and bowed gracefully. Annabelle noted that he was not as tall as Richard, his face was thin, and he had a long narrow nose that separated a pair of dark brown eyes set in sallow skin. His mouth was wide, but his lips were thin, and his eyebrows were raised in an arch as he lifted his face. It was a strange, but not an unpleasant face, she thought to herself and she wasn't in the least bit surprised when he introduced himself in a heavily accented voice.

"Monsieur." He addressed Richard. "It is my pleasure to welcome you and your lovely family to Porthcarrow. I am Jean-Paul de Varron, and reside at Rosvarron. We are to be neighbours I believe."

Richard smiled as he accepted his greeting and introduced him to Annabelle and the children and then, without more ado, Jean-Paul introduced them to his wife, Catherine and to the few, more prominent, members of the congregation before escorting them to their carriage which was waiting for them at the gate. Here they were greeted by excited children, crowded about the wall and calling out their own welcome to the new Squire and his family.

* * *

After such a happy interlude, it was with a great deal of reluctance that Annabelle returned to St Ewe, she would have been quite happy if Richard had left her at Tremanyon. But Richard had to return to London before the opening of parliament. This Christmas would be their last at St Ewe. The family would move into their new home for the summer of 1751, and it would be left to Annabelle to supervise the packing of their personal belongings. They would move into their new home when Parliament broke up for the long summer recess.

Christmas was spent at Heligan and, with the coming of spring, it was a happy Annabelle who set about instructing the packing of their belongings, whilst Richard had much to do in London. Time passed quickly, and soon it was the day of departure.

1751 – *A New Home*

THE CARRIAGE WOULD take Richard, Annabelle, Rachel and Rebecca to Tremanyon, and the older coach would bring their personal belongings on at a slower pace. Furniture would follow, and arrangements had been made for the transport of these more bulky items.

The staff lined the hall as the family bade their farewells, and it was a red eyed Rose, stifling back the tears, who waved until they were out of sight before bursting into sobs once more.

Annabelle had made the decision to leave Rose behind, at the request of the owners of the house. For Richard had only rented the house at St. Ewe until they could find a permanent home, and the staff came with it. Richard had assured Annabelle that they would quickly find a replacement, and secretly she was hoping that they would be able to persuade Ginifur Retallick to fill the position. The children liked her, and since Annabelle's old governess had died two years ago, they had continued with Rose's help alone. Annabelle loved her daughters and, when in good health, played a major role in their upbringing. She hated the thought of handing over this responsibility to others. Of course, she knew that soon they would have to enrol the services of a governess, but she kept avoiding this decision. Richard had indulged her until now, but had insisted that by next spring they must make a selection of possibilities. But next spring was still a long way off, Annabelle could only think of today, and settling into her new home.

The change in Annabelle was remarkable. Richard had not seen his wife so animated, her cheeks flushed a rosie pink and her china blue eyes were bright with excitement. He had had to urge her to rest, in order that she didn't over excite herself, so fearful was he for her health, and she had indulged him by resting in the afternoons. But even then she had spent the time planning and ordering furniture and ornaments for their new home.

The journey from St Ewe to Porthcarrow was uneventful, stopping as they did once more at Ruan Lanihorne, this time arriving late in the afternoon.

Mrs Teague had prepared an excellent dinner for Richard and Annabelle, with a lighter meal for Rachel and Rebecca, and they sat down to dine together. This was an unusual event for the girls, who normally took their meal at this time of the day in the nursery at St. Ewe with Rose. But this was an unusual day.

After dinner, whilst Mrs Teague amused the girls in the kitchen, Richard asked Ginifur to join them in the drawing room. The heavy curtains were drawn across the windows, Annabelle was seated comfortably in the high backed chair and Richard standing at ease with his back to the fireplace as a light knock on the door announced Ginifur's arrival.

"Come in." Richard raised his voice a little in order to make himself heard, and Ginifur entered the room with a decanter of port and two glasses together with a small glass of water upon a silver tray.

Carefully she set them down on the table before Annabelle and then stepped back. Nervously she glanced from the master to the mistress, unsure of what was expected of her. Richard recognised her nervousness and endeavoured to put her at her ease. "Take a seat Ginifur." He indicated a chair, set apart from the fireplace, and took the one opposite Annabelle for himself. Ginifur sat awkwardly on the edge of the chair and waited. Richard cleared his throat before continueing. "You will obviously be aware that we have left Annabelle's maid, Rose, back at St Ewe, and that Rachel and Rebecca do not have a nursery maid. We will, in time, be appointing a governess for Rachel and Rebecca but, until then, we will need to employ someone to assist Mrs Tremayne and to help with the children's day-to-day routine. I am fully aware that you have had no training in this area, however, Mrs Tremayne and I were wondering whether you would be interested in being considered for the position." Ginifur did not know what to say. She had wondered, in fact, if they were going to dispense with her services, for it had only been a temporary position until the family took up permanent residence. She enjoyed looking after the cottage by the river, and her father, but she was really now of an age when she should be looking for employment. Richard thought that he understood her hesitation. "Mrs Tremayne and I have been greatly impressed with you during our brief visits. Rachel and Rebecca like you and, if everything works out as well as I believe it will then, even after a governess has been appointed, we would ask you to continue to assist with the girls' daily life."

Ginifur, who had been studying her hands lying in her lap, looked up at the man who was to be her new master. He was tall and dark, and his deep blue eyes looked back at her in a kindly way. His lips were neither thin and tight, nor full and petulant. They hinted at a man with a pleasant disposition and Ginifur, glancing at Annabelle, found herself thinking that she was indeed a lucky lady to have such a handsome husband and pretty children.

Annabelle mistook her silence as lack of enthusiasm towards the suggestion. Perhaps she did not want to leave her father! Annabelle could understand that. It had been a wrench for her to leave home, even though she was going to marry Richard. "Is it that you are afraid of living in, Ginifur?" She ventured. "You would be able to visit your father regularly, for I am sure that we could arrange your hours to be such that you will be able to retain your links with your home."

"Oh no, Ma'am!" Ginifur answered quickly. "It's not Da. He's quite able to look after himself. It's my grandmother." She explained. "Grandmother is ill and I help my grandfather to attend to her daily needs. He is frail himself and can not lift her alone."

Annabelle glanced quickly at Richard. He hadn't told her of this. It was also a surprise to Richard who hadn't been informed of this turn of events. "How long has she been ill, Ginifur?" He asked.

"A couple of months or more now, Sir. Grandmother fell down shortly after you left Tremanyon last. Then she caught a chill and by the time the doctor came she was proper poorly. She doesn't seem to be making any real improvement, and Grandfather is quite distraught. He needs my help, Sir."

Richard nodded his head thoughtfully. "How much time each day do you spend with your grandmother?" He asked.

"I've been doing my chores here, help Mrs. Teague with anything else, and then go down to the cottage around noon. I wash Gran, change the bedding or wash any clothes and then get them a bite to eat. After that I come back here. When I am finished I go back to the cottage to help settle her for the night, before I go home." She explained.

Richard considered the problem. One glance at Annabelle's face told him how much she had planned around Ginifur. "If I allow you to continue to assist your grandparents whilst your grandmother is ill, would you be interested in helping Mrs Tremayne and the girls? It would mean taking on an extra pair of hands in the house and you would, of course, be required to sleep here in the house. You would have your own room, the one that adjoins the children's, so that Mrs Tremayne will get her much needed rest."

Ginifur turned her attention to Annabelle. She was a pretty, but frail lady. Her complexion was fair, her hair a pale blonde, and her eyes were china blue. That she loved her husband and children there was no doubt in Ginifur's mind. For Ginifur had studied her on their visits to Tremanyon. But she suffered with ill health, Ginifur was sure of it. Mrs Tremayne needed help with the children, she certainly couldn't cope alone and Ginifur was very surprised that she had not brought her maid with her. Ginifur made a quick decision. "I would be pleased to work for you Sir, for as long as you find me suitable. But of course I would need my father's consent."

Annabelle let out a sigh of relief, and Richard relaxed his shoulders. "Then that is settled." He said. "Ask your father to come and see me in the morning, and we will ask for his permission to employ you before discussing your wages and conditions of employments. Tonight the children will sleep in the bedroom with us, they are exhausted and will sleep well I have no doubt." He took out his watch. "Now get off with you and see to your grandmother, and wish her a speedy return to good health."

Ginifur stood up, gripping her hands tightly in front of her. "Thank you, Sir." She turned to Annabelle and bobbed a curtsey. "Ma'am."

"Goodnight Ginifur." Annabelle smiled at her. "I am so pleased that you would like to stay on at Tremanyon."

* * *

The first year passed quickly and uneventfully. Extra staff were easily found and employed, Richard and Annabelle made a few new friends, and were welcomed by the locals. Both the employees on the Tremanyon estate and villagers alike soon took to the new Squire and his young family, for Richard took an active interest in all that happened on the headland.

From her first moments at Tremanyon Annabelle showed signs of improvement, and during that first summer she gained a little weight and her face was less tightly drawn. Colour returned to her cheeks as she enjoyed the fresh air. She walked a little in the gardens, when the sun was passed its height, with a parasol to shield her complexion from the sun and Ginifur to keep her company.

This year the family spent Christmas with Richard's family at the family home outside Mevagissey and the New Year with the Bennett family, at Looe.

Chapter Two
1752 – *The Wind of Change*

GINIFUR JUGGLED HER time between her work at the Manor and assisting her grandparents at Well Cottage, for although her grandmother had improved she had not regained full health. She also helped her father to keep the tiny cottage tidy at the quay on her day off. Ginny was a tireless and conscientious worker, and the girls adored her and they were both happy and obedient in her charge. Not that they weren't obedient at other times, for they were fully aware of their mother's continued bouts of ill health.

The improvement to Annabelle's health was short lived, and her sickness returned in the New Year. At Richard's insistence she rested between the hours of two and four, after Ginifur had returned from her mid day visit to Well Cottage. Ginifur tried hard to care for both the children and Annabelle but, although they had taken on Lucy Tucket to help Mrs Teague in the kitchen, and Pearl Craske to help with the cleaning of the house under the watchful eye of Ginifur, it became inevitable that they needed more help. Annabelle had been finding it increasingly difficult to keep the household accounts and Ginifur, who had proved a quick learner and was adept with figures, was soon doing these on a daily basis.

Dr Thomas arranged for Jane Pollard to help nurse Annabelle. Jane came from Flushing, and had nursed the mother of Lord Falmouth through a long illness last winter. She came very highly recommended and Annabelle liked her, which was more to the point. This arrangement worked well and it took some of the pressure off Ginifur.

The days were still short, and it was dark before Ginifur headed out on her evening visit to Well Cottage. She wouldn't admit it to anyone, even to herself, but she hated walking down the tree-covered lane in winter.

This particular evening the wind had risen, blowing in from the east, and buffeting the side of the house. The side door was creaking eerily as Ginifur made ready to leave the house. She pushed her feet into the sturdy pair of shoes that Annabelle had given her and, pulling the hood over her head, she clasped the cloak tightly about her as she opened the door. She knew that it would be dark, for the moon was hidden by clouds, and for a moment she could see nothing at all, not even the steps down to the path.

Suddenly a light appeared around the corner, at the end of the Garden Cottage. It swung dangerously in the wind, but held securely by someone that she couldn't see behind the light. "Hello Ginny." A voice came out of the dark. "'ave 'e forgotten me?"

"Oh hello Adam. I couldn't see who it was behind the storm lamp." Ginifur recognised his voice and explained quickly.

Adam reached the foot of the steps, and she could see him clearly now. He also was wrapped up against the cold. "Father say's there'll be snow by mornin'." He said.

"It certainly feels cold enough." Ginifur agreed, and then noticed a sour expression creep onto Adam's face. "Is anything the matter?" She asked.

The lamp swung violently in a strong gust of wind, the light flickered and Adam steadied the lamp with his other hand. "The matter! No. I just don' like t' think of 'e walkin' down the lane on yer own like, 'specially in the dark." Adam was a quiet and serious young man, just two years older than Ginifur. He was now twenty-two years of age, but not courting. He was popular with the girls in the village, but Ginifur had not heard his name linked with any girl in particular.

"Thank you Adam." Ginifur stepped down to the path, very happy to have someone to accompany her to Well Cottage and back. "Gramps will be pleased to see a familiar face whilst I settle Gran for the night." Clutching the basket tightly, Mrs Teague had packed up a meat pie and some heavy cake for Ginifur to take with her; she stepped out with Adam beside her. For a while they walked in silence, for the wind in their faces made conversation difficult but after leaving the drive they turned down hill. Here the high hedges on either side of the lane, and the trees above, shielded them from the worst of the chill east wind and, although the moon was not fully uncovered by the clouds, the sky appeared to be a little lighter. Above them the skeletal shapes of branches and twigs were etched against the sky, creaking and cracking in the wind.

"We don' see much of 'e these days Ginny. Time was when ye used t' stop by the cottage for a yarn. It seems ages since we've been able to talk." Adam bemoaned.

Ginifur didn't answer immediately, remembering when Adam used to walk down to Well Cottage with her when she went for her lessons with Gran. Then Adam would help her grandfather in the vegetable plot, and enjoy one of Gran's cakes before walking back with her to Quay Cottage. Ginifur never mixed with the girls in the village. As soon as she was old enough to push a broom she had kept house for her Da, and was happy to do so. She was never short of company, for there were always women and girls working in the fish cellar, and fishermen coming and going from the quay. Adam had always been around when she needed him; they had grown up together on the estate. He was almost like a brother. "Yes." She agreed." There seems to be so little time left at the end of the day, and by the time I get back from Gran and organise everything for the morning, done any mending or spent a few minutes reading, I am so tired I usually fall asleep. On my afternoon off I go and help Da at the cottage, prepare him a meal and tend the vegetable plot." She paused before continuing. "But I wouldn't change anything I am lucky to be working for such a wonderful family."

In the darkness Adam's expression was grim. Since the Tremaynes had taken up residence, it appeared to him that they had commanded all of Ginifur's time. He glanced at her, walking beside him. The flickering light filtered through the overhead branches casting dark shadows about them, her face was hidden by the hood which fell over her forehead. Adam couldn't see her face or her eyes, but he knew only too well how green her eyes were and how pretty she was when she smiled. Why was it that she couldn't see the adoration in his eyes, or hear how fast his heart beat whenever he saw her? But Ginifur was blind to Adam's love for her. She felt as a sister might feel for a brother, no more. "They ask too much of 'e!" Adam blurted out angrily.

"No Adam!" Ginifur protested. "They don't. If I work late, it is my own doing. The mistress is ill, and her children miss her company dreadfully, especially with Captain Tremayne away in London. If Mrs Tremayne is to get better, she must not worry about the welfare of her daughters, and she must get better, she has to get better." Then quietly, and to herself, she added. "I know what it is like to be without a mother."

Adam wasn't placated. "The Master should get more 'elp. Where's that governess they was goin' t' employ?"

Ginifur rushed to her employers defence. "Don't you think he has enough on his mind Adam? A sick wife and the doctor not knowing what's wrong with her! Two little girls to look after is nothing compared with his worry. You should be ashamed of yourself Adam. You have been lucky to have a mother who has never had a day in bed, save for the days when she berthed you and your brothers and sisters." Adam didn't reply, and they continued in silence until they arrived at the gate to Well Cottage. "Are you coming in Adam?" Ginifur stopped just inside the gate as Adam paused, his hand still holding it open, then he stepped up onto the path and followed her into the garden.

* * *

With the coming of spring, Annabelle showed the first signs of progress, and by Easter she was spending the afternoons down stairs. Rachel and Rebecca were pleased to be allowed to spend time with her at last, and it was whilst they were with her in the drawing room that Richard arrived home to surprise them on a sunny day in May.

Quietly he opened the door, inch by inch, until he could peep into the room. The afternoon sunlight slipped through the west window and fell across Annabelle who was resting upon the chaise lounge with Rachel squeezed up beside her, whilst Rebecca sat on the floor as she read from an illustrated book. Richard watched and waited for some moments, until Rebecca paused, and as the door creaked a little on its hinges, both mother and daughters looked up in delight.

Annabelle smiled as Rachel and Rebecca flew to their father's side.

"Steady on!" He cried in mock horror as he lifted them easily into his arms. Then, placing them back on the floor beside Annabelle, he knelt and took her hand. "You are looking better than I dared hope, my dearest." He said as he took in her appearance. Her eyes were brighter and she didn't look quite so thin and frail.

"What brings you home?" Annabelle asked. "Can parliament spare you in mid term?"

Richard laughed. "I have to see Lord Falmouth on a matter of some urgency, a convenient excuse to see my girls."

"Do you have to return straight away?" Annabelle hardly dared hope he would be able to spend some time with them.

"I shall have three whole days with you all. Then I shall go to Tregothnan to see Admiral Edward Boscawen and travel back to London from there." Richard told her. "Will that please you?"

"That will please me greatly." Annabelle agreed. "Shall I send for refreshments?"

Richard straightened himself. "It won't be necessary, Annabelle. I saw Ginifur returning from the cottage, she has gone to arrange it with Mrs Teague. Now . . ." He turned his attention to his daughters. "One of you was reading to Mama, which one of you was that?" Of course he knew that it was Rebecca, but waited for their response. "It was Rebecca Papa." Rachel informed him.

"But Rachel can read too." Her sister added quickly.

Richard took the book, turning the pages slowly and carefully. "You have instructed the children well my dear, but you must not tire yourself. You must have worked hard for them to reach this standard." Puzzled, he caught the fleeting glance between mother and daughters. "Annabelle!" Rachel and Rebecca glanced quickly at the floor. "Annabelle!" Richard repeated.

Annabelle lent back against the pillows. "Oh Richard . . . please don't be angry"

Richard's expression softened. "Of course I am not angry that the girls can read. I just don't want you to tire yourself out by the effort of teaching them. We really must discuss a governess for them." Still Rachel and Rebecca kept their eyes averted. "What are you hiding from me?" Richard kept his tone even.

Annabelle raised her eyes to his. "I didn't teach the girls to read." She informed him. "Ginifur did."

"Ginifur!" Richard's puzzled look re-appeared. "You mean, our Ginifur? Ginifur Retallick?" Richard pulled a chair nearer to Annabelle and sat down so that he was level with his wife before continuing. "How on earth could Ginifur teach them to read?" He asked.

Annabelle looked perplexed. "I hadn't thought to ask her." She said. "But when she asked if I minded if the children learned to read, of course I said no I didn't mind." Annabelle was uncertain. "Did I do wrong? They enjoy it so much."

"Of course not." Richard assured her, but he couldn't push the subject to the back of his mind and when Ginifur appeared with tea and Cornish splits with jam and cream, he told the children to go to the kitchen and ask Mrs. Teague to find some for them. As

Ginifur turned to accompany them he spoke again. "Ginifur. Please, stay a moment. I wish to talk to you." Rachel and Rebecca paused anxiously at the door before he shushed them away and closed the door behind them.

With his hand in the small of Ginifur's back he guided her to the centre of the room. She could feel the warmth of his strong hand through the thin fabric of her dress. They were strong hands, strong yet gentle. Ginifur knew this, for she had watched him when he went to see the catch come in at Quay Cottage, where he had taken part in the unloading of the boats. He had lifted the fish baskets single-handed and with ease, as he kept the pace set by the crew, until the catch was safely stowed in the cellar. She had also watched him as he tended a newly born foal, carefully supporting it whilst it took its first faltering steps, and she knew just how gently he stroked his children's hair as he kissed them goodnight. Nevertheless she was nervous. Sure in her mind that she was to be reprimanded for some misdemeanour, she knew not what. Therefore, when she came to a standstill she looked fearfully at her shoes, peeping out from beneath the hem of the blue dress that Mrs Tremayne had ordered for her to wear for work. The two blue dresses, and the wool cape, were the first new clothes that Ginifur had possessed. All her previous clothes had been 'hand me downs' or made from her mother's old dresses. Mrs. Tremayne had also provided the high-buttoned boots that Ginifur was staring at. Each evening Ginifur polished the boots until she could see her face in them. Until she had come to work at the big house, she rarely wore shoes at all. Now she not only had new clothes and shoes, but she enjoyed the benefits that came with her position in the house. She had a room of her own, next to the one shared by Rachel and Rebecca. It was furnished simply. A bed, a chair, a rug on the floor, a small chest to keep her clothes in, and a mirror to check that she was tidy before reporting for work. There were pretty curtains at the window, two warm blankets for the bed, and a further coverlet for cold nights. All these things flashed through Ginifur's mind as she waited to hear her fate.

"Ginifur?" Richard repeated her name, realising that she had possibly not heard a word that he had said.

Ginifur's head shot up. "I'm sorry Sir."

Richard smiled, realising that she was looking at him warily. She was standing stiffly. Uncomfortable, ill at ease. "I'm not angry Ginifur. I only asked how it was that the children had learned to read so well, and in such a short time."

Ginifur's finely arched eyebrows drew together as though puzzled by the question. "I taught them Sir. I did ask Mrs Tremayne for her permission first, Sir."

"Yes Ginifur. But where did you learn to read? Who taught you?"

Ginifur began to hope that perhaps she was not in trouble after all and relaxed her shoulders. "My grandmother taught me Sir. She taught my father, and she taught me." She recognised the scepticism creeping into his face. "They said that my grandmother married beneath her. She was the governess and tutor to the children on a large estate near Exeter when she fell in love with Grandfather. He was the gamekeeper there. When they married they were dismissed, no one else would even consider Grandmother as a tutor after that, for they would give her no reference. My great grandfather was gamekeeper here and, when he died, Gramps returned to Tremanyon to take his place as gamekeeper to Squire Durance. They've been at Well Cottage ever since. Grandmother taught Da to read and write, mathematics, Latin, and history. She taught me also."

Richard laughed. "That explains a lot." He turned to Annabelle. "Simons accounts are incredibly detailed, I would defy any one to keep better records." Richard studied Ginifur, and she in her turn returned his steady gaze. She was growing up, he thought to himself. She wasn't the slip of a girl that he had met when he paid his first visit to Tremanyon. Now she was quite tall, almost to his shoulders. She had filled out, the dress with its starched white pinafore tied about her waist hinted at a shapely figure. Her dark hair was long, but neatly secured away from her face, and those eyes . . ! Her eyes were an incredible shade of green, fringed with long black lashes and framed by neat arched brows above a small and shapely nose. Ginifur was a young woman now, and Richard wondered how it was that he had not noticed this before. "How old are you Ginifur?" He asked.

"I shall be twenty on Sunday Captain Tremayne." She hesitated. "Are you going to dismiss me Sir?" Her tremulous voice added.

"Of course not!! What on earth made you think that?" Richard was astonished that she even thought such a thing. "No. But I would like to consider your position here. It is time we thought more seriously about the future. Now run along, and see if Mrs Teague has any splits left for you to take to your grandparents when you go, and I shall see you in the morning."

When Ginifur left the room, Richard wandered to the window. "Ginifur is a little young to be expected to take so much responsibility." He said, more to himself than to Annabelle.

"But she is so capable." Annabelle hastened to add. "Ginifur keeps the housekeeping books, far better than Mrs Murdock ever did at St Ewe. She and Mrs Teague produce a budget for the week, and Ginifur demands the best meat and provisions from the tradesmen. I even think that they are a little in awe of her." Richard listened attentively, and didn't interrupt as she continued. "She has Pearl organised beautifully, and keeps the linen room in perfect order. She is incredible with a needle and has altered Rachel's old dresses for Rebecca in such a way that you would think that they were different dresses altogether. I allow her to keep the oddments, which she washes and irons, and she has made a beautiful patchwork counterpane for her bed." She paused to let Richard speak if he wished to, but he stayed silent. "She cares for the girls, and they love her. They have gained so much knowledge in her company, not only reading but numbers also. She takes them on walks, where they learn about the countryside and the animals, and she even teaches them about the history of England. I swear she has learned far more than I ever did. She is so industrious Richard. She is cheerful, a pleasure to have around. And I would miss her if you replaced her. I really would."

Richard finally spoke. "I have no intention of replacing her Annabelle. But what you have said has only confirmed what I thought. She is doing too much. You heard her Annabelle. She is barely twenty, yet she runs this house, keeps the books, and cares for the children . . . and you in the past. And she still finds time to teach the children to read and write by all accounts."

"I don't take up so much of her time now that Jane is with us." Annabelle intervened meekly.

"But Jane's position here is only temporary." He reminded her.

This was Annabelle's chance. "But Jane would like to stay Richard, I am sure she would. Would it be possible for her to stay with us? She has nowhere else to go, and it would ease the work for Ginifur too,"

Richard smiled and shook his head. "If it is indeed so, then I would be pleased for Jane to stay on. But it still leaves too much on Ginifur's young shoulders. I think we should consider a housekeeper or a governess."

"Oh No!!" Annabelle was aghast. "That would infer that Ginifur had not been doing the work satisfactorily, and that just would not be true."

"So what would you suggest my dear?" Richard was sure that she had a proposition to put to him.

"Why don't we get a girl to help Ginifur with the menial chores for the girls? Seeing to their bathing and dressing. Supervise their mealtimes. This would then enable Ginifur to continue with the housekeeping duties."

"And act as tutor for Rachel and Rebecca I presume." Added Richard.

"For the time being Richard, please. Let us see how we get on before we add too many more members of staff to our household." Annabelle pleaded.

Richard knew that he would agree to her wishes, but concluded. "Let us sleep on it tonight dearest, and we will see what Ginifur has to say for herself tomorrow." Annabelle knew when to remain silent, and smiled inwardly. She was sure that Ginifur would agree to the suggestion.

Ginifur did indeed agree. Richard more than doubled her wages and offered her a larger room in the attic. But she declined the spacious room, saying that she preferred to stay near the children if it was acceptable to the master and mistress. Better still, she even suggested a girl who would be suitable to assist her with the children, Solly Billings oldest daughter, Peggy. Peggy was fourteen years of age and had all but brought up her younger brothers and sisters, but it was time that she went into service. Richard said that he would see her before he left for London and left Ginifur to make the arrangements.

During the interview Richard had delved into Ginifur's academic knowledge, and he was amazed at the extent of her learning. He almost felt guilty at retaining her in his employ, for she had the ability to go far.

However, Ginifur was more than happy with the new arrangements, for she loved the children, felt a great deal of affection for Annabelle, and was devoted to Richard. Rachel and Rebecca were dubious about the suggestion of a new maid, but when they learned that it was only to enable Ginifur to continue their lessons, and that she was not vacating her room, they came around to the idea.

The new arrangement worked well, and by the time that Richard returned to Tremanyon for the long summer recess, the household was running smoothly.

A Summer Day

WHEN GINIFUR GREETED Captain Tremayne at the door, waiting to take his coat and hat, he noticed that she had grown taller in the last couple of months. She had discarded the white starched pinafore and wore a new dress of deep emerald green. It had a high collar and long sleeves. It fitted neatly at the waist, and flared gently over her hips. Long enough to cover her ankles, but not the toes of her shoes that peeped out from beneath the hem. Pinned above her rounded breast was the silver watch and chain that he and Annabelle had given her for her twentieth birthday. She had cried when she opened the tiny parcel, and said that she had never owned anything so beautiful. The green of her dress accentuated the green of her eyes, and highlighted her flawless complexion. Ginifur had never used powder or rouge, she didn't need to. It would be a lucky man who won her heart, thought Richard as he smiled at her greeting.

"Welcome home Captain Tremayne." She said.

"Thank you Ginifur. I am pleased to be home. How is your mistress?"

"She is well Sir. Mrs Tremayne has improved since the last time you were home. She takes a walk daily with Jane, and the colour has returned to her cheeks." She informed him as he handed her his gloves.

"And my daughters?"

"They have grown Sir, I am sure you will agree. I have had to let down Rachel's dresses so that there is no more spare fabric left, and bound the hems. She will need some new clothes before the winter. Rebecca too is growing, but not at such a rate."

Richard noticed how beautifully Ginifur held herself. "And their lessons?"

"They learn well Sir, and are model pupils. Perhaps you would like to see some of their work whilst you are home. With Mrs Tremayne's permission I have taken over the staff dining room as a schoolroom. The staff eat their meals in the kitchen anyway, and they don't mind for they still have their sitting room.

Richard didn't answer immediately, and Ginifur began to consider that he didn't like the arrangement. But all he said was.

"I didn't really consider the aspect of a growing family, I should have thought of that."

Annabelle was indeed in good health. She was looking almost as well as she did during the early months of their marriage. In fact, that night, as he crept into bed beside her, she turned her slender body towards him, drawing him close to her and into her with all the ardour of those early days. He was afraid that the next morning she would suffer for it, but no, she was awake bright and early, telling him all the things that she had forgotten the night before.

In all the months that she had been indisposed, at no time had he considered being unfaithful. No other woman attracted him, caused him to turn his head or make his pulse race. Richard loved his wife, and that was enough. He would always wait until her health allowed him to make love to her as he had last night.

It was an idyllic summer. The days were long; the sun was warm, and the weather dry. The hay harvest was good, and in the fields the corn ripened to gold.

Richard divided his time equally between the estate and his family. He would rise at dawn to be either at the Home Farm, as Billy Harding brought in the cows, or at the Quay when the boats came in on a high tide.

He worked in order to experience everything that contributed to the financial success of the estate. He helped with turning the hay with the long forks, and stacking the sheaves after the corn had been cut and bound. He helped to pitch the sheaves onto the wagons and build the round ricks in the mowhay. He even tried his hand at milking, much to the amusement of Harry Polaughan and Billy.

Richard carried baskets of fish to the cellar below Quay Cottage, keeping pace with the regular fishermen on a basket for basket basis, and he watched in amazement at the speed the women and girls gutted and baulked the pilchards. The fish were built into a solid wall of fish, three feet high and two feet wide, and each layer was covered with salt. It was hard work and continued throughout the day and into the night until all the fish were baulked. The fish stayed thus for thirty days, but whilst those women worked at baulking the fresh fish at one end of the cellar, others were working on those to be barrelled. First they were washed and then placed into the casks, layer upon layer in a rose pattern, with their tails to the centre. When the barrel was full, a buckler was placed on top and this was forced down by way of long poles. One end of the pole was fixed into a hole in the cellar wall and the other, which rested on the buckler, was weighed with stones. As the fish were pressed down, more fish would be added until the barrel reached its proper weight and held about three thousand fish – a 'hogs head'. The oil and salt ran out of the barrels along the channels or gullies in the cellar floor, to a pit at the bottom. From here it was collected and separated, the oil was sold for many purposes, but particularly for lighting the smelly oil lamps called 'pilchard chills' which lit most of the Cornish cottages in the dark winter nights. When the pilchards were ready, they were transferred to Falmouth or Fowey where merchants shipped them to the ready markets of Spain or Italy.

On these days Richard returned exhausted, and smelling of either fish or animals, and he would go to the stables and strip all his clothes off where Adam would pump the water up from the well and fill the leather horse buckets to the brim. Then, standing on the mounting block, he would tip them over Richard as he scrubbed himself clean and washed the fish scales from his hair or farm animal scent from his body and hands. Even so, the fishy smell always remained, and he would splash cologne over his head and body before he dressed in fresh clothes and went to find his family.

On one such day he found Ginifur reading to Annabelle and the children in the summerhouse at the edge of the side lawn. Ginifur closed the book and rose to leave, but not before Richard noted the rising colour in her cheeks. It occurred to him that he might frighten her and it saddened him, for he thought that they had a good understanding of each other. The following day he went to the schoolroom, during the hours of the children's lessons. Ginifur had persuaded Samuel to make desks for the children, and a board for Ginifur, which she had painted black and wrote their lessons in chalk. Somehow she had managed to acquire books and papers, quills and ink. Rachel and Rebecca had books for writing, books for maths and books for Latin and French. Richard was amazed that they had learned so much in such a short time. "How do you do it?" He asked.

"It's not difficult." Was Ginifur's reply? "You just make it fun to learn, and then they don't really know that they are working at all. Rachel and Rebecca are especially easy. They are like little sponges; they just soak it all up."

It was obvious to Richard that Rachel was the more academic of the two. Rebecca was a dreamer, the artistic one. She had illustrated her nature book with life like pictures of delicate primroses and campion, bluebells and wild orchids, stately foxgloves and wild iris. All looked as though he could pick them right off the page.

Richard commended Rachel on her use of French verbs and then turned to his youngest daughter as she bent her head over her painting. "These pictures are beautiful Becky, Ginifur has taught you well."

"Oh no, Sir," Ginifur exclaimed. "Becky's talent is a God given gift. It is something that cannot be taught."

Richard stared incredulously at his daughter's book and nodded thoughtfully. "May be it is. May be it is. But it is you who has seen her potential and given her the encouragement." He glanced about the room. "Do I recognise Samuel's work?"

"Yes Sir." Then Ginifur hastened to add. "But it was with Mrs Tremayne's permission."

Richard smiled and picked up a reference book. "And all these books Ginifur. Where on earth have they all come from?"

"My grandmother Sir."

"Did they indeed." Richard raised an eyebrow in surprise as he handled another. Studying those on a higher shelf of the bookcase he selected one, browsing through the pages. "These are excellent books, and some quite adequate for a child of more advanced years than your two charges." He glanced at Ginifur.

"They are Sir. I believe I did explain to you that Grandmother was a governess." Was her only reply, he nodded as he remembered and replaced the book with a thoughtful expression.

"We must recompense your grandmother, Ginifur." He said firmly.

Ginifur was horrified. "Oh no Captain Tremayne! She would be mortally offended. It pleased her so much to know that they are being used again. They are old, of course, and out of date. But the basic knowledge is still there."

"They are excellent books indeed Ginifur." Richard agreed. "I am in your grandmother's debt." Ginifur remained silent, shaking her head imperceptibly as Richard patted the girls' heads. "I am pleased with you both." He told them "Work hard for Ginifur." Then, bidding them all farewell, he left the room.

There were warm afternoons, when Richard would get Adam to bring the trap to the front door, a small open carriage they used to collect stores from the village. Netty would send Tom up from the kitchen with a hamper, Ginifur would bring rugs, and they would set off for Rhosinnis Head or Kylyn Cove to enjoy a sheltered tea party in the open air. When their jaunt included the beach, after they had eaten, Richard would lay back on the rug, his head on his hands, and rest. Annabelle would sit on a cane seat, carried especially for her, with a parasol to protect her from the sun, and the children would sit on the rug where Ginifur would read to them quietly whilst Richard enjoyed his short sleep. When Richard awoke, he stretched and yawned, then walked to the rocks at the end of the cove where he would disrobe and dive into the cool water.

Ginifur envied him, for if she were alone she would have been tempted to do the same thing. But she had to contend herself with walking along the water's edge, or dabbling her hands in the rock pools as she and the children searched for limpets and crabs.

One day, when Richard returned refreshed by his swim, Ginifur walked back up the beach with the children, they were both hot and sticky, their faces flushed beneath their bonnets. Richard looked down at them with a puzzled look and said "Do they really have to wear all those clothes in this heat?" Ginifur just looked up the beach towards Mrs Tremayne. Richard nodded thoughtfully to himself and made his way to his wife where he plumped himself down on the rug beside her. A few moments later Annabelle returned to her book and Richard to Ginifur and the girls, where he instructed that their overdresses be removed, their pantaloons were rolled up and their bonnets were discarded temporarily. A few moments later they ran in the shallows with Richard splashing them and their cries of delight rang out along the beach.

To appease Annabelle, who was convinced that her daughters would either suffer with sunstroke, or at the very least catch a chill from being splashed with all that cold water, Ginifur was waiting with their bonnets at the ready, a towel to dry their legs and arms, and shawls to wrap about them when they had finished. She smiled apologetically at Richard's scowl of disapproval, and he laughed as he shook his head, realising the difficulty of her position.

Rachel looked abjectly at her bonnet. "Ginny! I don't want to put my bonnet on. Please, Papa!" She looked at Richard, appealing to him to intervene.

"Put on your Bonnet Rachel." He said with a severity he did not feel and glanced at Rebecca standing obediently still as Ginifur tied the ribbons under her chin. Poor little mites, he thought, if he had sons instead of daughters they would be swimming off the rocks with him. Why should it be so very different for Rachel and Rebecca?

Ginifur had seen the girls covered up, and as they played safely she lifted her skirt with one hand as she stepped into the shallows and scooped up a little of the cold water in her other hand to splash on her face. Richard recognised the look of longing in her eyes as she looked out over the water in the cove. "Have you ever bathed in the sea Ginifur?" He smiled as the blood rushed into her face, bringing a rosy glow to her cheeks as she nodded.

"I have Sir."

"Then why shouldn't they?" Ginifur didn't answer. It wasn't her place to comment on their family life, and she guided her charges up the beach to their mother.

* * *

Since Annabelle's return to good health and the increased staffing at the Manor, the relationship between Adam and Ginifur had returned, more or less, to normal.

With the improvement to her grandmother's health, though she was still weak and frail, Ginifur's visits were now not so necessary. Even so, she would continue to walk down the hill to see her grandparents every other evening, after the children were washed or bathed and ready for bed.

Bath times were twice a week, quite an event. On one of Richard's visits to the Tin Mines he had been impressed with the pumping system that cleared the water from the tunnels. He had spent countless hours planning on paper, and finally come up with the idea of a bathing room. This he had included in his plans for Tremanyon. The bathing room was along the corridor at the back of the house. The linen room was next to it.

It wasn't that Richard had a fetish for cleanliness, but he did like to feel clean. Living in London only served to accentuate his longing for cleanliness. The dirt seemed to be greater in the city where farm livestock was regularly driven along the streets, their dung mixing with that of the horses, which were either ridden or pulling carriages. And drains were more like open sewers, carrying the foul smelling concoction of effluent, which finally made its way into the Thames. Street urchins, smelling no better than the drains, were clad in rags and begged for food. Their grimy faces and bodies had probably never been clean, let alone felt clean water. Clean water, if they could get it, was for drinking and there wasn't a lot of water clean enough to drink. Society was not much better. Body odour was disguised with eau de cologne or rose water. Dirty hair, or bald heads, were covered by exaggerated wigs, which were worn by men and women alike. Too much bathing was feared. It was believed that too much exposure to water removed the necessary body oils, resulting in chills and colds, and that this would lead to pneumonia and ultimately death.

At Tremanyon Richard insisted that the staff in the house maintained a higher standard of attention to personal hygiene than they had previously accustomed to. The staff soon got used to the regular use of hot or cold water, most of them bathed at least once a month anyway! However, now it had to be weekly and a small room in the basement was fitted out with a tin bath which was emptied into a drain in the floor when they had finished bathing.

With more free time Ginifur still spent one afternoon a week at Quay Cottage. Ginifur had lived in this cottage all her life and she had grown up with the pilchards below her in the cellar. Fresh, baulked or barrelled they still smelled the same. The aroma of fresh and salted fish permeated every corner, nook and cranny of the cottage. It's not that she thought it an unpleasant smell; it's just that she had never noticed it before. It clung to the curtains and the bedding, and it hung on the air. Inside or out, it was all the same.

The cottage was furnished more comfortably now. Annabelle had tried to include some of the furniture that they brought with them from St Ewe but they had decided that most of it didn't suit their new home. Some of it was put into store, but Annabelle had offered Ginifur a small round table and a comfortable high backed wooden chair, which she had kept in her room at the manor, a chest of drawers, a side table with a cupboard underneath, a large square carpet, three pairs of curtains and some old but good sheets and bedding. Sam and Adam had helped by carting the items down to the cottage, where she quickly instructed them to move the furniture about for her. Her truckle bed was removed and her father's large bed left in the far corner, hidden behind long curtains. The carpet was almost big enough to cover half the area of the cottage floor. The table she moved away from the draught and nearer to the window to the right of the front door. It was small, just big enough for two to eat off. This was the area she decided to lay the carpet on. The wall the other side of the door was just long enough to take the side table, and the chest of drawers went at the foot of her father's bed. Simon already had a wooden easy chair, and a low nursing chair that he had brought for Ginny's mother. These she placed on the carpet and picked a posy of flowers for a vase on the table.

Having dismissed Simon, Samuel and Adam, Ginifur checked the curtains thoroughly and chose the one with the most wear. Then she measured and cut the fabric to make cushions. She had already washed and pressed the curtains and two pairs she hung at the windows on either side of the front door. The only other window overlooked the cellar. They were old, but they still had plenty of wear in them, and they were a little too long, but she would soon put that right. She set to work. She swept the floors, and polished the furniture lovingly, she had asked Mrs. Tremayne if she might take a little beeswax from the house. Ginifur made her father's bed up with the clean linen, one of the blankets, and finally she covered it with her mother's counterpane. Screwing up her face she tested the old sheet, it gave way with ease. The threads pulled apart. So she went outside, to the stone sink by the back door, and washed it before tearing in into pieces of various sizes for cleaning or drying. Then she washed her father's clothes, prepared a meal for him and, having surveyed the cottage with satisfaction, she bade him farewell.

* * *

Now Ginifur also found time to see Adam. Sometimes she would call at the cottage to bide a while with the family and, at others, she would go and find him at the stables.

When she was a child Adam had taught her to ride. Ginifur loved the horses. After Mrs. Durance died the Squire never looked at his wife's horse again. One day Adam had been running with the horse to exercise it, afraid to mount it in fear it may displease his master, when Squire Durance suddenly appeared on the drive in front of him.

Squire Durance had glanced at Adam, and then took a long hard look at the chestnut mare before he spoke. He drew his eyebrows together, creasing his forehead even more than usual. "If she needs exercise Adam, why aren't you riding her?"

"The mistress never allowed it Sir." Adam answered, his voice barely above a whisper.

Squire Durance gave a quick glance at the mare, not noticing the sadness in her eyes. "I don't expect it will worry her now." He said finally. "I shan't ride her, I can't get rid of her, so you ride her Adam." A second thought came to his mind. "Does Retallick's daughter ride?" Adam nodded. It wasn't quite the truth, but she had ridden astride the old nag when they went into the fields at hay time. "Let her ride the horse then. She's a woman's horse. Too fine boned for a man. Yes, let the Retallick girl ride her, I don't like to see a horse out of condition." And with this, he turned abruptly away.

From that day on Ginifur rode regularly. She owned no riding clothes, but she asked her father if she could slit one of her old skirts. Then with needle and thread, she had fashioned a fair imitation of a riding skirt. Ginifur proved a competent rider, but chose to ride astride the horse, as a man would ride, not sidesaddle as a lady should. This all came to an abrupt end when Squire Durance died and the horses were sold.

To Ginifur's relief, it appeared that Adam's churlish attitude to his employers had only been a temporary spark of anger on a cold winter's night. It had upset Ginifur for a while, as she thought that their friendship would be spoiled.

This particular afternoon it was raining. In fact it had rained none stop for three days and nights. The persistent rain swept in across the Lizard and the Manacles, hiding the whole of the bay in its thick impenetrable blanket. It dripped from the trees in great drops and formed large puddles along the drive.

Ginifur pulled the cape around her shoulders as she darted from the side door of the Manor to the stables. Beneath the cape she wore one of her old dresses. It was really too small for her now and it was very tight across her breasts, and short enough to show her ankles. But she was only going to the stables to help Adam and Sam, no one else would see her, and it really wouldn't matter if it got dirty

Ginifur threw off her cape and hung it on the peg by the stable door. "Adam!" She called out. "Are you there?"

"We'm in 'ere Ginny." Adam's voice came from the tack room at the end of the stable block.

Talking to each of the horses as she passed by, giving each a fallen apple from the orchard, she made her way down the passage.

"Hello Ginny." Samuel looked up from the bench where Adam was helping him. He didn't miss the undisguised look of admiration in Adam's eyes as he stared at Ginifur. Samuel shook his head. Ginifur had no intention of leading Adam on, she was totally unaware of the affect she was having on him.

"Oh. You're busy." Ginifur took in the leather and buckles. "Can I do anything for the horses?"

Samuel thought for a moment as he poised the bradawl over the leather. "Come t' think of it, there is Ginny." He pushed the bradawl through the leather and positioned the bright and shiny brass buckle. "Adam had to leave the grooming of Lanhoose t' 'elp me 'ere. D'ye think ye could finish 'im off?"

Lanhoose was Richard's new stallion. Ginifur had fondled him but never groomed him. "I don't see why not." She laughed, and added. "He can only kick me out, can't he?"

"Da . . !" Adam looked up from the bench.

"She'll be fine Adam." Sam nodded at Ginifur, if he didn't get her out of the tack room Adam was not going to keep his mind on his work. He let out a sigh. So that be the way of it, he thought, it had never crossed his mind that anything would develop between them. They had been like brother and sister. But those weren't brotherly thoughts hiding behind Adam's eyes. How was he to tell his son that he was on a hiding for nothing? For Samuel knew in his heart that Ginifur only saw Adam as the boy she had grown up with, nothing more.

"What's the matter Father?" Adam was holding the leather, waiting for him to finish.

"Tis naught." Snapped Sam. "Stop moonin' about 'n keep yer mind on yer job me son." Adam's eyes opened wide, could his father read his mind? "I'm not blind lad. Give 'er space, 'n don' 'e pin yer 'opes too high." At the sign of fear in Adam's eyes Samuel hated himself for saying it. But Ginifur Retallick wasn't like other girls. Ginifur was different. Ginifur was meant for someone very special. Samuel knew in his heart that this would not be Adam. He threaded the leather needle and handed it to his son. "There! Ye do it son." He picked up the halter they had nearly finished and turned away. As he cleaned and polished the saddle, he could hear Ginifur talking quietly as she worked. Out of the corner of his eye he watched as she used long, steady strokes to brush Lanhoose's shining black coat.

Sam recognised the familiar crunch of boots upon the stones before the voice called out his name, and he was half way up the passage by the time Captain Tremayne walked through the open door.

"Oh! There you are Samuel. I've been thinking about getting a pony for the girls." Richard was dressed for riding, and carried a short whip in his hand. Thoughtfully he tapped his high leather boot. "Doctor Thomas has a pony that he says he might consider selling. His children learned to ride on her but now they have grown she is too small. What do you think? I would like you to come with me and see it."

Samuel knew that Richard had a fine eye for a horse, he didn't need Samuel's advice, but it was his way of showing respect for the master of his stables. "Of course, Sir. When?"

"As soon as this damned rain stops." Richard stared morosely at the open door before grinning. "And I thought I would go for a ride! You were quick enough to forecast this rain; would you care to forecast its end?"

Samuel gave an all-knowing smile. "It'll be just fine by mornin'. Ye'll see Sir."

"I'll hold you to that. Have Lanhoose and Nero saddled and ready by ten o'clock tomorrow will you?" He glanced along the stables. "How is my latest addition to the stables?"

"A fine stallion 'e is, Sir, strong willed mind, but 'andles like a baby in the stall, 'as a magnificent 'ead, strong shoulders 'n legs. All things taken into account, I think your suggestion t' cover Star with 'im is a good'n." Samuel knew that it was what Richard wanted to hear but, nevertheless, it was the truth.

"He also has a sweet tooth." Richard produced a lump of sugar. "Has he been groomed today?"

"Ginny's with 'im now Sir. She took over from Adam who is 'elping me with the new 'arnesses."

"Ginny!!" Richard raised his eyebrows. "Ginifur Retallick?"

"Yes Cap'n. I 'ope I aven't done wrong. Ginny loves the 'orses, 'n she be a frequent visitor t' the stables when she 'as free time. I would'n let 'er 'andle 'im if she weren't capable Sir."

Ginifur had heard Richard arrive, and sent up a silent plea that he would leave the stable without visiting his new horse. Lanhoose sensed her unease and nuzzling into her shoulder he let out a low whinny. She ran a steady hand along his neck and gently breathed into his nose to settle him. His large black eyes never left her serious face as Richard's and Sam's voices came nearer and nearer.

"Ginifur!" Richard opened the lower door of the stall and stepped inside. "Do you have any more surprises in store for me?"

In spite of her unease Ginifur smiled. "I don't think so Sir." She replied gently stroking the horses withers.

"Do you ride, as well as you teach lessons in mathematics and English?" He asked

"After a fashion, Sir, yes I do. Rather, I should say, I did. Squire Durance allowed me to ride his wife's horse, Damson. I really do miss her." Ginifur tried vainly to position the stallion between herself and Richard, suddenly aware of the tightness of her bodice, which was forcing her breasts into a cleavage in the low neck of the dress and, only now aware of the shortness of her dress, she picked up one foot, trying to hide it behind the other leg. The skirt was well short, showing off her dainty feet and trim ankles, and a glimpse of a well shaped leg above the high-buttoned boots.

Richard studied her tense body, the angle of her head, her shoulders set and defensive. He recognised her discomfort and smiled. "And what would be your opinion of my daughters learning to ride?" He asked.

Ginifur bridled, misreading his smile for amusement at her apparel. "It isn't my place to pass an opinion on that Sir. But I understand that many ladies of quality ride, and some have made fine horsewomen too I believe."

"I am sure that you stand correct." Richard was sad that Ginifur had obviously thought that he was teasing her. Wishing to cause her no more embarrassment, he turned away. "Tomorrow then Sam. I'll see you in the morn."

Richard and Samuel returned from their visit to Ruan, bringing with them the pony and a stable mate.

When Richard went to fetch Rachel and Rebecca he found them with Ginifur. "Perhaps you would like to come too Ginifur." He suggested. He was pleased to see that she had regained her composure and hoped that she had forgotten any embarrassment that he might have caused.

The first stall inside the stable was a large one, big enough for two small horses. Samuel led out a white pony, barely twelve hands high and just the right size for the girl's first pony.

Rachel's mouth fell wide open and Rebecca's eyes were twice their normal size.

"She is beautiful. What is her name?" Asked Rachel.

"Stardust. But I don't expect she will mind if you wish to choose another."

"Oh no!" Exclaimed Rebecca. "Stardust is just right. It's a beautiful name."

Meanwhile Adam was leading out a chestnut mare. His face was set in a grim expression as he took his place beside his father.

Richard watched as Ginifur glanced at the mare. "The mare and pony were stable companions." He informed her.

Ginifur stared hard at the mare, which was standing with her head held low and her eyes downcast. "Damson?" She ventured, her voice uncertain until the mare raised her head and whickered happily. "Oh Damson!" Ginifur ran towards her. "I never thought I would see you again." With tears in her eyes she turned to Richard. "Oh, Captain Tremayne." Words failed her. Adam let go of the halter and, without a word, stomped his way back into the stables.

"Doc Thomas felt sorry for her, brought her as a stable mate for the pony. It didn't seem right to part them. The only sensible thing to do was to bring them both back." Richard informed them. "Anyway, you will need to have a suitable horse for yourself to ride if you are to teach the girls." Richard added matter of factly. "For I am afraid, Annabelle cannot ride."

"What are you crying for? Why are you unhappy?" Rebecca slipped her hand into Ginifur's.

"I'm not crying sweetheart." Ginifur brushed the tears away with her hand. "I'm very, very happy."

"Good." Richard found his voice a little strangled. "Then that's settled. I can leave you to arrange suitable clothes for the girls I assume . . . and you had better have something made for yourself. I shall arrange for Annabelle's dress maker to call." With that he turned swiftly away before he himself became embarrassed. It had touched him more that he had imagined it would to see Ginifur's pleasure at being reunited with Damson.

The dressmaker was instructed that the clothes should be a priority and that Ginifur should have a complete riding outfit made for her, with smaller versions for Rachel and Rebecca. She and her seamstresses worked hard and within the week she was back to make final adjustments. On the following week the garments arrived. They were the finest clothes that Ginifur had ever worn, made of pure wool, died forest green, they were sleek and fitting her perfect figure, she looked stunning. The girls were a miniature copy. Adam was not around when Ginifur took the girls for their first lesson, but Sam complemented her on her outfit. "A bit different to that skirt ye sewed for yerself, eh Ginny?"

"It is Sam. I don't know what I have done to deserve all this." She shook her head. "I am so lucky. The Tremayne's are so good to me."

"No more'n ye deserve maid. No more'n ye deserve." Sam returned to the stables, wondering where Adam was hiding.

Tregothnan

AT THE END of August Richard returned to London, and the warmth of summer continued into a fine autumn. Annabelle had retained her good health and he left with his mind at ease, informing her that he would be home at the end of September to attend a ball at Tregothnan.

Annabelle had ordered a new dress and was very excited at the prospect of meeting people from further afield in the county. Even though it was only for a one-night visit the large trunk was packed. The ball gown alone took up a large part of the space and Jane had folded it carefully with plenty of padding to stop it creasing. Then there was the new morning dress for her to wear the following day, and she was to wear her new travelling clothes for the return journey. Annabelle knew that she was being a little extravagant, but she was adamant that she would make the right impression on Richard's friends. Of course, Richard's evening clothes had to be packed, and his new riding habit for the hunting next morning. Dainty evening shoes for Annabelle, day shoes and her new travelling boots. Shoes and riding boots for Richard, and then everything that Jane would need to make Annabelle ready for the ball. Arrangements had been made for Jane and Robert to accompany them. This pleased Annabelle for she would be happier being attended by her own maid. Robert was Richard's manservant, and usually stayed behind to look after the house in Hampstead when Richard returned to Cornwall, but had travelled down with Richard to attend him on this visit.

They were to arrive around midday for the reception, and Annabelle was flushed with pleasure as Jane helped her to dress in new finery for the journey to Tregothnan, on the banks of the River Fal. It was a very excited Annabelle who waved goodbye to the children.

It promised to be a fine day, and on the journey Richard described Tregothnan in great detail. The gardens, he said, were a sight to behold. And on a fine day such as this, the 'Falmouths' would hold a reception on the terrace, facing the gardens that melted into the park and woodland. The woodlands rolled down to the boathouses situated beside the very edge of the River Fal.

From the terraces, he told her, away in the distance you could see the river and on a fine day, beyond it, Falmouth Bay.

Tregothnan was indeed a magnificent sight, situated at the end of a very long private drive, which started at the small hamlet of Tresillian and seemed to go on and on forever. Annabelle had never seen a private house of this size before. It was indeed as Richard had described, but Annabelle was totally unprepared for the 'Falmouths', Edward and Fanny Boscawen.

Richard had always referred to Admiral Boscawen, Lord Falmouth, as 'Old Dreadnaught'. So when an impressive gentleman in his early forties approached them on their arrival, with his elegant young wife at his side, Annabelle was still awaiting their host and hostess.

"Richard! Wonderful, you are the first to arrive." Edward Boscawen didn't wait for Richard's reply, continuing. "And this, this enchanting young woman, must be your wife." He took her hand in his and kissed her gloved fingertips. "Annabelle I believe. I hope you do not mind me using your given name, Richard has told us so much about you we feel that we know you already. Allow me to introduce my wife, Francis." He winked at Richard. "Fanny to our friends."

Francis Boscawen, Lady Falmouth, gave Annabelle a brilliant smile. "Welcome to Tregothnan my dear. We will have to form an alliance for this evening to keep these two from talking shop. If they aren't discussing politics they are talking ships or soldiering. Frankly, I don't know which I find the most interesting. How about you?"

Richard recognised Annabelle's surprise, and silently reprimanded himself for not describing Edward and Francis more accurately, he rescued her from answering immediately. "I am afraid if it isn't politics, or fishing boats, it's the estate. And I have to admit that between them they do seem to monopolise our lives somewhat. But for you, my dear Fanny, I will give you my solemn vow to keep conversation light, frivolous and strictly on a social level."

Francis tilted her head charmingly to one side, and fluttered her eyelashes at Richard. "La." She tapped his shoulder with her fan. "Be careful Richard. That is almost an impossibility. I know my husband, and I have seen the two of you in action too many times. Well Annabelle! Is your husbands vow acceptable to us?" She turned her attention to Annabelle and, trying to put her at her ease she linked arms with her and Richard, speaking over her shoulder to her husband. "Come on Edward; let us make the most of the short time we have with these two delightful people before the hordes arrive." Returning her attention to Annabelle she continued. "It is so refreshing to have the company of people that you really like at this kind of function. For myself, I believe that we have many acquaintances, but very few true friends. Both Edward and I count Richard as a very dear friend, and I feel quite sure that you and I will become real friends too, Annabelle."

Annabelle at last found her tongue. "I hope so Lady Falmouth." She managed.

"Fanny, my dear. You must call me Fanny. Let all those social climbers bow and curtsy, and use our titles, but not you or Richard. Now, what do you think of that view?"

Annabelle gazed at the view that Richard had described in such detail, thinking to herself that even if he hadn't adequately described her host and hostess he certainly had painted a true picture of the house and gardens, for over the trees she could indeed glimpse the Falmouth Bay.

* * *

Richard and Annabelle were shown to a suite of rooms with windows to the west and the south. "Did you ever see rooms this size before?" Annabelle asked as Jane unpacked the trunk.

Jane smiled. Old Lady Falmouth's room was twice this size, almost big enough to swallow the house that Jane had been brought up in. Carefully she unfolded the dress and smoothed out the creases. "Tea will be served in the drawing room Ma'am. So let's freshen you up and tidy your hair and then, after tea, you should rest. For the evening will be long and very tiring."

"Rest! How could I possibly rest?" Annabelle's eyes were bright with excitement.

Jane paused in her un-packing. "I don't know Ma'am, but rest you will for the Captain has ordered it."

Annabelle laughed. "Oh well! If the Captain has ordered it." And indeed she did rest to please Richard, and awoke refreshed.

The evening was indeed long, but Annabelle thought that it flew by. Dressed in her hooped gown of heavenly blue silk with an overskirt of a deeper shade, which matched her eyes exactly, and was trimmed with the finest Belgium lace that money could buy, she danced every dance of the night, with the exception of the ones when Richard insisted that she stopped to eat a little saying that if she didn't she would surely faint with hunger. Richard stepped out once or twice, but was otherwise continually engaged in conversation. Lord Falmouth wanted him to meet every one of his invited guests. Richard's fears that it would prove too much for Annabelle appeared to be unfounded. She radiated happiness, as she was taken under Fanny's capable wing and introduced to local society. The Falmouths' declared that it was a pleasure and an honour, that theirs was the first large social event in the district that Richard and Annabelle had attended.

The ball was a great success, as all Tregothnan Balls were, and it was in the very early hours of the morning that the guests wandered to their appointed rooms. A number of guests were staying over, all except those who lived, more or less, on the door step that is. When they finally returned to their room, where Jane and Robert had everything in readiness for them, Annabelle was full of excitement.

"Shall I call for Jane to attend you?" Richard asked as he watched her sitting before the mirror, removing pins from her own hair. Neither of them wore wigs that were still the height of fashion, or powdered their hair white, discarding both of these for their own healthy heads of hair.

"No Richard, it is late . . . and I can manage." Annabelle's long curls had been coaxed, pinned and dressed with fresh flowers and rivalled any false creation. Richard's own strong wavy hair was secured quite simply at the nape of his neck. The thought of wearing a stiff, hot and uncomfortable wig again appalled him. It had caused some mild amusement in the beginning but it was to the most part now accepted, and it was only strangers who commented on their eccentricity.

When all the pins had been removed Annabelle fluffed up her hair with her long fingers and asked. "Would you help me with these tiny buttons Richard? I can manage the lower ones." Richard smiled as his clumsy fingers struggled with the tiny pearl buttons and hand made loops and, when the last one was undone, he looked up into the mirror as he slipped the dress over her perfectly formed shoulders to reveal her milk white flesh. Annabelle's eyes were shining brightly as she gazed back into his. Her lips parted with a sigh as he lifted her and carried her to the large bed in the centre of the room.

When Jane entered the room the following morning Annabelle was alone in the bed, her hair spread out across the fine linen pillowcase. As Jane poured the jug of warm water into the bowl Annabelle's eyelids flickered and opened. For a moment she was puzzled by her surroundings but then, remembering, she said. "Good morning Jane. Where is Captain Tremayne?"

"Good morning, Ma'am. The Captain rose earlier, the gentlemen have gone riding. They won't be back till noon, or later." With a heave Jane drew the heavy brocade curtains back from the tall windows and the sun streamed in.

Annabelle blinked at the sudden brightness. "Goodness gracious me, Jane! What hour is it?"

"It's gone ten Ma'am, but the master ordered me to leave you to rest."

"What about the other ladies?"

"Some have ridden out with the gentlemen Ma'am, some are sitting on the terrace, and others still haven't arisen. You are not alone."

Annabelle hurriedly slipped her legs over the edge of the bed. "We must make haste Jane. I don't want to be the last lady to make her presence." She laughed as she put a hand to her belly. "My goodness, I'm hungry."

"There is a buffet laid in the dining hall, Ma'am. Fresh ham and cold meats, fried bacon, smoked fish and variety of egg dishes, with a selection of cheeses and fresh fruit. There's warm bread, freshly baked in the kitchens and fresh milk and cream straight from the dairy." Jane informed her.

Annabelle's nose wrinkled as she smiled. "You are well informed Jane."

"I was in the kitchens when they were preparing it Ma'am. Five or six times the size of Tremanyon's they are, and they have two ranges and four clome ovens for baking. Florrie Griffin is still the cook. She was here when I nursed old Lady Falmouth, back along. Besides her, there are two under cooks, Gwen and Ann, four scullery maids to fetch and carry and to prepare vegetables and the like, and two young girls to wash and clean. Two maids to wait at table, besides two men and Mr. Gilbert, who oversees the hall."

"It must take an army to clean the house." Annabelle murmured as she let Jane slip the dress over her head.

"There's the housekeeper, Mrs Mellor, of course. The downstairs maids, and George, who does the heavy work. Four upstairs maids, and the laundry mistress and two helpers. It takes the two girls from the dining hall all morning to clean and polish the silver. The family usually break their fast in the small salon, next to the dining hall."

"I can well believe it. You could almost float the whole of the Spanish Armada in that soup tureen." Annabelle laughed and sat very still as Jane quickly arranged her hair, pinning it neatly into place. "I don't know what I would do without you Jane! I hope that they fed you well this morning."

"They did indeed Ma'am. Florrie looked after our needs and did us proud, Robert and me. She did too 'n that's a fact. There, you're finished." She pushed in the last pin and teased out the curls to frame her face. "Now you can face the world again Mrs Tremayne. And I reckon we did that in record time 'n all, don't you?"

"You certainly have indeed Jane. Thank you." Annabelle studied her reflection before smoothing out her skirts. "Will you see to the packing Jane?"

"Yes Ma'am, don't you worry your pretty self about that. Robert and I will see that it's all safely packed and aboard the coach by the time you are ready to leave.

To Annabelle's surprise they did not depart with the remainder of the guests. Edward and Francis asked them to stay over for an extra day, and a message was sent home to Tremanyon to expect their return a day later. Edward Boscawen said that as Fanny had expressly ordered that they were not to discuss business at the ball, then they would have to stay another day as he and Richard had much to discuss.

As it turned out they discussed very little business, but Edward declared that Annabelle had told Fanny of their new bathing room that Richard had installed in their new home and insisted that Richard went into great detail on this installation. "I must come over and see it for myself Richard. All these baths that have to be brought out and filled with jugs each time that you wish to take a bath and then emptied again. There has to be a better way."

"Of course, any time. Perhaps you and Fanny would care to visit us in the spring . . . when the daffodils are out."

"Indeed, indeed, we should like that very much. Talking of bathing, it has been in my mind for some time now that there is too much sickness on board ship. We loose too much manpower due to dysentery, sickness and the like. If we could improve the cleanliness on board, encourage the men to adopt a modicum of hygiene and improve their diet, I am sure that the improvement to fitness will far outweigh the cost. Our Cornish seamen are the best in the world, and our ships are fully manned without resorting to press gangs. We live in a time that our Maritime force is expanding, and we need the finest Captains and healthy crewmen with British expansion overseas. Biased as I may be, I have yet to find an English sailor who compares to a Cornishman who is born to the sea."

"Edward!" Francis attention was drawn away from her conversation with Annabelle. "I do believe that you are in danger of constructing a little Navy of your own making."

"That isn't so Fanny!" Edward declared. "You mustn't assume that the men crewing my ships are overwhelmingly Cornish, they are not."

"No Edward, of course not."

"You do approve, I believe, of my taking and encouraging good men from this part of the world Fanny." Admiral Boscawen frowned at his wife.

"I do Edward, I do indeed." She agreed. "But beware; others may see this encouragement as an unfair display of favouritism."

"Bah! What rot!" Edward exploded. "Have you ever heard such nonsense Richard?"

Richard smiled. "Unfortunately we fight a great battle as Cornishmen, and I fear it will be one continued for many generations. It is as though the English fear our separateness, and our strengths created by our forefathers."

Christmas at Tremanyon

THE FINE AUTUMN came to an abrupt halt and a cold easterly wind welcomed in the month of November. Large logs crackled and flared in the magnificent fireplace in the drawing room, and coal fed the tiny fireplaces in all the bedrooms, including Ginifur's. The coal barge arrived just in time. The pre-ordered coal was delivered by boat to the Quay, and Samuel and Adam hauled it up to the house with the horse and cart.

Netty was kept busy preparing for the family's first Christmas at Tremanyon, and she was going to make it a Christmas they would remember. Dried fruits were cleaned and soaked in the best brandy, mixed with precious herbs and spices and turned into rich fruit puddings and cakes. Nuts and suet were added before baking between sheets of crisp, light pastry. Autumn fruits had been added to the stone jars, already half filled with summer fruits from the garden and preserved in brandy, and the peaches were already turning to a rich golden colour in the sweet liquor.

The pantry was well stocked with preserved foods to last the winter, and the last of the beans had been salted in the largest earthenware jars, the lids sealed with fat to keep out the air.

Outside, logs were cut and stacked in the shed by the kennels. Carrots, potatoes and beets were regularly checked for frost damage and the onions were moved to hang in a dry place for storage. Manure was dug into the garden being prepared for spring planting and the fire kept burning to heat the glasshouses.

Richard was detained in London, and because Annabelle wished to purchase some presents, she organised an outing to Truro, taking Jane and Ginifur with her.

Samuel and Adam had the coach ready by six in the morning, extremely early for Annabelle, and they took the long windy road via Tregony.

It was Ginifur's first visit to Truro. She had been to Tregony once in her life, and that was when she was quite small when Simon had taken her to the Mid Summer Fair. As the carriage rolled down the long wide hill she was amazed at the number of carriages and carts that were struggling to make their way up and down. Samuel expertly manoeuvred the carriage through the traffic of the narrow streets, making his way safely to the Red Lion

Coaching Inn in the centre of the town. Here the ostler unhitched the horses and led them away to the stables at the end of the mews. "The Squire not with 'e t'day, Sam?" He commented.

"No Charlie, 'e be 'eld up in London. Mrs Tremayne wanted to make a visit 'erself. And the young'n; well tis 'er very first visit t' Truro." Sam smiled as he watched Ginifur, her eyes darting back and forth, afraid that she might miss something. What a change there was to the child that he had watched growing up. Gone the little girl in her hand me downs, or dresses made out of her dead mothers few clothes. In her place stood a young woman on the brink of life, a young woman, with the poise equal to those of higher birth. A rare beauty. Samuel sighed and turned to his employer's wife. "When would ye like me to 'ave the carriage ready t' return to Tremanyon, Ma'am?"

"We will come back to the Red Lion for something to eat around two, I would think." Annabelle informed him." We ought to leave no later than three did we?"

"Not really Ma'am. Even then, twill be dark long afore us gets 'ome."

"Very well, Samuel. No later than three then." She agreed before turning to Ginifur. "Ginny, are you going to come with me, or do you wish to wander alone?" She asked.

Ginifur looked startled. "Oh no Mrs Tremayne, I'd rather stay with you, if I may?"

This said Annabelle led them out into the bustling throng and the noise of the street outside the coaching inn. Threading their way through the crowds they headed towards the river. Market stalls were set up along the quay with the backdrop of the ships tied up against the wharf. Traders, wrapped up against the cold, were selling their wares whilst stamping their feet in an effort to keep warm. A young countrywoman selling hedgerow preserves was shivering, clad only in a threadbare dress with a sack pulled tightly around her shoulders. The baby lying in a basket at her feet fared little better, but was covered with rabbit skins that had been carefully cured and sewn together, by his mother most likely Ginifur thought. Besides the preserves there were tiny purses, and small bags made from scraps of fine leather. It was hard work no doubt, for Ginifur noticed the woman's fingers, hard and calloused where she had pushed the needles through the skins without a thimble to protect them.

There was a wood carver from Port Holland, a blacksmith from Tregony selling his hand crafted tools and lady with a strange accent selling bales of fine woollen cloth from Lancashire she said. Ginifur knew that Lancashire was up north, for she had learned a lot about the woollen industry in her studies with her grandmother. Opposite the lady from Lancashire was a couple from Tregony. They were selling their own warm tweed, spun and woven in the district and washed in the streams. It was a coarse woollen cloth, known locally as Tregony Cloth, sturdy and long lasting. Their trade was mostly with the fishermen and farmers. The fine woollen cloths were brought by the gentry, as were the velvets and silks, from France, and the Belgium lace sold under the bright awnings further along the quay. There was silver jewellery and cheap trinkets, cooking pots, copper kettles, and horsebrasses, leather bags and saddlery. Basket ware and walking sticks, novelties for the children and boiled sweets with fancy names like Wintergreen, flavoured with warm herbs and spices, and Summer Fruits, tasting like blackberries and raspberries. There was soft fudge and chocolate from France, Turkish delight that melted in your mouth and crunchy honeycomb, and chestnuts being roasted on an open brazier.

After a great deal of thought Ginifur settled on some pretty hair ribbons and a tortoiseshell comb for Rachel, and a drawing book and paints for Rebecca. For her Da she chose a shirt for Sunday best, a warm shawl for her grandmother and a carved walking stick for her grandfather. This was the very first time that she had ever been able to buy presents for those she loved. But she didn't know what to get for Adam.

Having wandered through the market stalls they then went to look at the shops in the main street. Ginifur watched as Annabelle carefully selected a gold pin from the goldsmith, for Richard no doubt, a locket for Rachel, and a tiny gold cross on a fine chain for Rebecca. Ginifur wished that there was something that she could give to Annabelle and Richard. But what could she possibly give, that they didn't have? Ginifur mentioned her quandary to Jane.

"With your skills with a needle I'm sure that you could make something that they would appreciate more than anything that you could buy Ginny".

Ginifur was sceptical, but she decided to give it some thought. Returning to the Market stalls, she purchased some pure silk embroidery threads and some pieces of fine linen and, finally, she settled on a pocketknife with an inlaid handle for Adam

"Who is the knife for?" Enquired Jane.

"It's a Christmas give for Adam . . . why?"

"Give a knife, cut a friendship." Jane said firmly.

"Oh, Jane! You don't believe all those old wives tales do you?" Scoffed Ginifur.

"Don't you?"

"Of course not." Retorted Ginifur.

"Then I suppose it'll be alright then." But Jane pulled a wry face as she turned away.

"Ginifur!" Annabelle's voice broke into the conversation. "Ginifur, the girls need new capes. Do you think they should have the same colour? How about that shade of blue?"

"That would suit Rebecca admirably Ma'am, but do you not think that the claret would compliment Rachel's colouring better."

Annabelle studied the bolts of cloth. "I'm sure you are right. How much do you think we will need? Oh, you see to it will you? I will choose some trimmings."

"Of course Ma'am. Would it help you if I chose the trimmings also?" Ginifur offered.

Annabelle discarded the lace that she was fingering uncertainly. "I think that is a far better idea. While you arrange that, I shall go and pick out some sugar comfits for Christmas. Ask them to send the packages around to the Red Lion by two thirty. No later or we will be gone. Here, there should be plenty in here." She handed a small bag of coins over.

Ginifur chose the fabric and trimmings with great care, knowing the girls preferences it was easy. The bag contained a good handful of sovereigns and silver and Ginny felt honoured that Annabelle trusted her enough to handle the purchases on her own. "You will deliver them in time, won't you?" She asked the stallholder.

"Of course Ma'am. Young Joe 'ere, e'll take it round, soon as I cuts it off the bolt."

Young Jo stamped his feet, blowing on his fingers at the same time to warm them, and Ginifur noticed that he wore no shoes. His only protection from the wet and cold were the off cuts of old leather tied about his ankles with a piece of discarded string. His trousers had been carefully patched by someone, but he wore no coat. There was only an old sack pulled over his shoulders with no more than mended rags beneath. But never the less, she noticed, he was clean. Someone cared for him. She glanced down at her own clothes, and felt very privileged indeed beside this poor lad. She could easily be mistaken for a lady. "Deliver the packages safely Joe and ask for me, Ginny Retallick. Don't go giving it to anyone else mind."

A pair of big eyes looked up at her. "I won't Miss. I'll ask for 'e. Miss Retallick did 'e say?"

"That's right Joe." She laughed at the title Miss Retallick and gave him a brilliant smile before turning to find Annabelle who was taking delivery of a large box of sweetmeats. Consulting her watch she said. "It's already half past one Mrs Tremayne. Shall I carry that for you?"

"Is it that time already?" Annabelle handed her the beautifully packaged box. "Well come to think of it, I'm hungry, how about you Jane? Ginny?" Jane and Ginifur agreed. "Have you both made your purchases? Then let us retire to the Red Lion for refreshments."

Slowly they made their way back through the crowded passages between the stalls, Ginifur making one final purchase from the young woman with the baby in the basket. She purchased two tiny leather draw string bags, sewn with the neatest of stitches. She didn't know why she purchased them, but she felt compelled to. The gratefulness on the woman's face made Ginifur feel very humble indeed. "Is the baby your first?" She asked to cover her embarrassment.

"No Ma'am. 'e be my third cheeld."

In spite of her thin weary face Ginifur didn't think she was old enough. "Surely you are too young to have a family of that size? How old are you, if you don't mind me asking?" The words were uttered before she realised that she had been very rude.

But the girl didn't seem to mind the question. "I don' really know Ma'am. Me Ma never seemed to know when I was born, sometime in the summer she would say, if pushed. Seven of us there was, Sue says. She be the eldest, 'n she reckons she'm twenty-seven. Then there's Charlie, Will, Fred and Ann. Then there's me and then Joe. Joe's the baby, though 'e wouldn' like to 'ear me say so 'im being thirteen now. I remember 'is age, 'avin' 'im killed me Ma, or so they d'say."

Ginifur looked back along the stalls. "Joe? Is he working here too?"

"Yes Ma'am. Mr Tiddy d' use 'im t' run errands. E's a good lad, and lives with me and Liam now both me Ma and Pa are dead."

Ginifur took a small coin from her own purse, it was now nearly empty. "Please get something for the babies."

"God Bless ye Ma'am. God Bless ye." A tear appeared in the corner of the young woman's eye and Ginifur turned quickly away to hurry and catch up with Annabelle and Jane.

At the Red Lion she followed Annabelle up the ornately carved wooden staircase to the bar and dining room above. Jane had taken the parcels to the coach and Ginny left instructions that she should be called immediately a lad came with some parcels for her. They were led to a table overlooking the main street. Samuel had instructed the staff that Mrs Tremayne and her companions would be returning for refreshments and they were brought plates of cheeses and cold meats, a basket full of warm fresh bread, another of fruit and a large pewter jug of mulled wine.

Ginifur had only been seated for a few minutes when Sam beckoned to her from across the room.

"There's a lad with parcels for 'e Ginny. Won't let go of 'em till ye come, 'e won't." He led the way back to the courtyard, continuing the conversation as he went. "Poor mite. Did 'e see 'ow 'e was dressed? 'ow 'e 'aven't died of cold is a wonder t' me, with 'is clothes in tatters as they be. Yet e's clean Ginny! In all those rags, 'n e's clean.

"I know Sam. His Pa and Ma are both dead, and he lives with his sister and her husband. She's no more that a girl herself, with three children. And poorer than Church mice, I wouldn't be surprised. Is there anything we can do for them?"

Sam looked puzzled. "Like what Ginny?

Ginifur frowned. "I don't know Sam. I just wish that we could do something for them. I don't know about you, but I've not seen such poverty around home, have you?"

Sam had to agree that there was no one that he knew in or around Porthcarrow who appeared to have so little. "I'll find out where 'em lives first. Then us'll 'ave t' get our thinkin' caps on. I'll bring some of the boys' clothes for 'im next time I come in with the Cap'n. The worst of 'em be better than what 'e be wearing right now."

Ginifur's face broke into a smile. "Oh thank you Sam. I'll find some things for the girl and her children too."

"Let's find out where 'em d' live first Ginny." He placed a hand on her arm. "They may be too proud to accept charity Ginny, ye must remember that."

Ginifur nodded. "I'd like to give him a tip for bringing the parcel though Sam."

"Ye leave that to me Ginny. Just take the parcels from 'im and leave it t'me."

"OK Sam, if you think that it's best." Ginifur agreed.

"I do Ginny. I'll see 'im right, don' 'e worry none."

Sam opened the side door that led out into the coach yard. There Ginifur took the parcels and thanked Joe, telling him that he was to listen to what Sam had to say. She turned away, but aware of his eyes still on her back she turned. "What's your sisters name Joe?"

Joe looked warily back at her. "Me sister, 'ow does 'e know I 'ave a sister? Anyways, which sister? I got three of 'em." He fidgeted uncomfortably.

"The sister you live with Joe. The one in the market with the baby."

Joe's eyes opened wide. " 'ow do 'e know she's me sister?"

"She told me Joe." Ginifur laughed. "Don't look like a scared rabbit; nothing is going to happen to her, or you."

Joe looked easier. "You sure Miss?"

"I'm sure Joe. I promise."

" 'er name's Kate, Miss. Kate Fierney. She married Liam Fierney when they found she was avin' 'is baby. She'v 'ad one a year since. The first was Lorna, the next Poppy and the baby is Aiden.

"Where are the others? She only had the baby with her at the stall." Ginifur asked curiously.

"No, the others was there Miss. They was under the table tryin' t' keep warm."

Ginifur closed her eyes briefly. "And Liam, where was he? What does he do?"

"'e were a fisherman, come over from Ireland 'e did. Didn' go back after 'e married Kate, but no boat would take un on. Now 'e cuts willows 'n makes baskets, crab pots and the like. 'e was selling 'em on the Quay, but 'e don' make much money, and Kate does what she can." Joe explained.

Ginifur sighed. "OK Joe. Go and find Sam will you?"

"Yes Miss." His eyes lingered on her face for a moment before he turned to go. Ginifur watched until he went out into the yard before making her way back to the dining room.

True to his word, Samuel did find out where the Fierney family was living. It was little more than a stock-house. A tiny barn that would barely provide adequate shelter for animals in winter. Ginifur's fears that Samuel may be right in his belief that they may be too proud to accept help were unfounded. There was little that could be done to improve their habitation or living conditions, but the family were appreciative of their concern and readily accepted the offer of warm clothing and boots for themselves and the children. For old and worn as they were, they were a vast improvement to their own tattered garments.

Samuel learned the whole story of the sad plight of the young family. He took an instant liking to Liam, a sensible hard working

91

lad, and for the first time in his life he felt anger at his own countrymen for not giving the boy a chance. Of course, he knew that fishing was a family business, that's the way it had always been.

On his second visit, just before Christmas, Ginifur demanded that Sam take her with him. No amount of persuasion would deter her, she went with Annabelle's blessing and, on her instructions, taking with them a hamper of food made up by Netty. By a genuine consideration the contents had been kept simple, but there was an adequate supply of food to carry them through the next few days, with some special treats for the children for Christmas Day.

Kate sat down on the wooden stool and cried when Ginifur arrived with yet more parcels. Being as she was, considerably shorter than Ginifur, and undernourished in the bargain, Ginny's old dress fitted her well and gave ample room for growth.

Lorna and Poppy huddled together in a corner. They were shy and apprehensive on her arrival, but Ginny's natural ability to captivate a child's interest soon overcame this hurdle. In no time at all they had conquered their fear and were soon sitting on her knees looking at the pictures in the book that she had brought with her.

There was an instant friendship between the two young women, and Liam showed no sign of jealousy, mistrust or envy. Only genuine gratitude for the first sign of help and understanding for them and their circumstances.

They asked for no help to alleviate their plight. No promises were made, and no false hopes were raised.

But Ginifur and Samuel vowed that they would find some way to help this young family.

* * *

Ginifur hesitated, before knocking on the door. Captain Tremayne had only returned home a few days ago and there were only four days to Christmas Eve. She had only seen him briefly, on his arrival, and he had been employed constantly on the Estate business since. She wondered why he had called for her. Perhaps he wished for a progress report on Rachel and Rebecca's education. Of course It could be about the Housekeeping accounts, but she was quite confident that they were accurate and all in order. She drew a deep breath. Well it wasn't worth worrying about! There was only one way to find out. She smoothed out her skirts, checked the white cuffs at her wrists and pushed a wayward lock of hair into place, and then she knocked firmly on the door.

"Come in." Richard's familiar voice called out, and Ginifur entered the room to find him seated at one side of the fireplace. The logs crackled and flamed in the open grate and the weak winter sun sent a beam of light across the polished table at his side. Richard was alone in the room. "Good morning Ginifur." Richard signalled towards the chair on the other side of the fireplace. "Please, take a seat."

Ginifur did as he bid her, but still she sat uneasily on the edge of the chair, her back stiff and straight. When Richard didn't continue Ginifur's eyes wandered to the fireplace.

"It's lovely isn't it?" Richard broke the silence as if he had read her thoughts.

Ginifur smiled. "It is. I was just remembering when the gentleman was here to make sure they fitted it correctly. He had all those Italians wrapped round his little finger didn't he?"

Richard laughed. "He did indeed. Grindlin Gibbons is a master craftsman, equal in my opinion to Adams, and those men recognised a true artist when they met one." Richard looked up at the ceiling. "Between them they did a proper job didn't they?" Ginifur was amused by his use of the Cornish terminology. "I don't think that I will ever be able to thank them enough." He paused, and Ginifur waited for him to continue. "I believed that I had thought of everything when we designed Tremanyon. But it took you to make me see that I hadn't."

Ginifur looked both shocked and puzzled. "I'm sorry Sir!"

"Well, I didn't think of a schoolroom did I? In fact I didn't really think of my daughters at all. I really should have made a nursery suite a priority. There isn't room for the girls to have their own rooms, let alone a place for them to take their lessons or relax in their own way."

"The school room works quite well Sir." Ginifur attempted. "And Rachel and Rebecca love sharing a room, but if necessary one of them could have mine and I could move up to the top floor . . . if you are agreeable Sir."

Richard's eyes crinkled at the corners, as something amused him. "I don't think that will be necessary Ginny. We have decided that a West Wing will be added to the house. Four bedrooms, a nursery and a schoolroom on the first floor, and a dining hall and serving rooms below. Do you think that you will be able to cope with three children and the housekeeping position?" He asked with the amused smile still hovering on his lips.

Ginifur's eyes opened wide. "Three children, Sir?"

"Three Ginifur." He said with emphasis on three.

"Do you mean . . ?"

"Yes Ginny. Annabelle, my wife, Mrs Tremayne is expecting another child."

Ginifur beamed. "I am so pleased for you all, Sir." She said, and meant every word.

A more serious expression replaced Richard's amused one. "Thank you Ginifur. She is convinced that the child that she is carrying is a boy. I hope that it won't take too much out of her." The first sign of concern crossed his face. "I am glad that she has Jane to assist her, but I would be grateful if you will keep a special eye on her during the coming months of her confinement. She is especially fond of you Ginny, and will listen to you. If you have any fears, then you must send word to me in London, at once. You do understand?"

Indeed Ginifur did understand Richard's concern for her mistress. Although her health had improved lately, she was still very delicate. "Of course Sir. I will be happy to help Mrs Tremayne in any way that I can."

Richard smiled. "Then I will be able to return to London, after the Christmas break, relatively happy. But you must remember to send word immediately if there is any fear for her health." He impressed upon her.

"I will Sir. I promise." Ginifur assured him again. Then thinking that the interview was over she made to rise

"No. I haven't finished yet Ginifur." He indicated that she should remain seated. "Oh yes. The builders will be starting work after Christmas, and the new wing should be ready for occupation well before the birth of the new baby. I would like you, when the time comes, to arrange for the curtains, decoration and such like. Mrs Tremayne will not be able to undertake that responsibility in her condition, and we both agree that if she is well enough then, needless to say, you will consult with her and then make the final arrangements for her." Ginifur was taken aback at the trust they put in her, but nodded her agreement. "You know the tradesmen, Ginifur." Richard explained. "And I shall give you a letter of authority in this matter. Now, on my wife's instructions . . ." Richard smiled. "I have been talking to Samuel." He changed the subject suddenly. "What do you know of this young family that seem to be causing you all such concern?"

Ginifur had not been expecting this, and stumbled. "What family is that Sir?"

"A young woman named Kate, I believe, and her husband Liam and young brother Joe."

"Oh! That family, Sir!"

"Yes Ginifur. That family." Richard adopted a suitably serious expression.

Ginifur took a deep breath, drew herself up in the chair, straightened her skirts and looked down at her hands before raising her eyes to meet his. "What, in particular, do you wish to know Sir?" She asked meekly.

"I would like to hear, from you, your version of the events that prompted the desire for my wife to ask me to consider aiding this family that I know nothing, whatsoever, about."

"I see, Sir." Actually Ginifur had no idea that Annabelle had given a second thought to the family, let alone asked her husband to consider aiding them. She gave a slight cough to clear her throat. "Well. It all began when Mrs. Tremayne took us to Truro to do some Christmas shopping . . ." Ginifur went into great detail about the events of the day and how she and Samuel had become acquainted with Kate and her young brother Joe. She told him of the circumstances that the young family were living under, of Liam's failure to be accepted by the local fishing families, and his subsequent efforts to support his family by basket making. She described the industrious Kate and her brood of clean, though undernourished children, the windowless hovel, with barely a stick of furniture, and she completed the picture with a description of young Joe. When she had finished Ginifur relaxed her shoulders, as though she had cast off a great burden.

Richard remained silent, deep in his own thoughts, and Ginifur wondered what Samuel had had to say on the subject. The silence seemed to go on an on for ever, then Richard spoke.

"So, Ginifur! What is it that you would like me to do for this family of yours?"

Ginifur was aghast. She had made no suggestion to Mrs Tremayne, or Samuel for that matter, that she wished her employer to offer the family any help or for him to accept any responsibility for them in any way at all. She jumped to her feet. "Sir! It had never crossed my mind that you should become personally involved in this families misfortune. Truly, Captain Tremayne, I only wish to help in any way that I can to alleviate their hardship."

Richard smiled. "Sit down Ginny. I am fully aware of the fact that you are not asking me for help for this young family. But now that the subject has arisen, if I should consider it, what is it that you, my wife and Samuel, would like me to do? I can get no satisfactory suggestion from either my wife or Samuel; in fact I get no suggestion whatsoever. And . . . if I am to consider the possibility of assisting this young couple, I need some help. I haven't met Liam and Kate, or Joe. It is only you who can give me any idea of the help that I can offer."

Ginifur sank back into the chair. She supposed that she had secretly pinned her hopes on this moment, but never dared allow herself to think of the possibility. "Would it be possible for you to visit them, Sir? Perhaps, sometime, during your stay."

Richard rubbed his cleanly shaven chin. "Would I be welcome?" He asked. "Or would I be viewed as a member of the nosy upper class?" Richard paused before continuing. "Then, having met them, if I were to consider offering some form of employment, would it be thought of as an offer of unacceptable charity by the misguided gentry? We, including you Ginifur, have to be sure that what we offer is not confused as misguided interference."

"I understand Sir. I really do. But I have to help them; I have lost my mother too. But I have my father and I have my grandparents." Ginifur tried to explain her feelings. "And I have employment and a roof over my head, provided for me by, if you don't mind me saying so Sir, a gentleman of great principles and understanding."

At this Richard burst out laughing. "Good grief Ginifur, you make me sound like a very pompous prig indeed."

"Oh no, Sir!" Ginifur apologised profusely. "I don't agree, and I meant no disrespect Sir."

Still laughing, Richard reached out and patted her hand. "OK Ginifur, you win. Get Samuel to inform your little family of my wish to visit them. If, and only if they wish it, then you and Samuel will accompany me on a visit after Christmas."

* * *

Christmas was a very jolly affair. All the staff, both outdoors and in, were invited to a Christmas Eve Party in the staff quarters below stairs. The schoolroom was cleared to increase the space to accommodate them all and Richard and Annabelle and the children arrived to dispense the very generous Christmas boxes.

Ginifur accompanied the family to the Church service on Christmas

96

morning, and had been surprised when Richard and Annabelle insisted that she join them at their Christmas celebrations after dinner. Simon called at the Big House to walk with her to her grandparent's home at Well Cottage, where Ginifur had previously made all the preparations for their family celebrations. After they had eaten their dinner, and their few personal gifts were exchanged, Simon walked back with her to Tremanyon in order that she could continue her duties to the family.

Chapter Three
1753 – *Liam and Kate*

WITH THE START of the New Year came an unusually cold spell. Snow fell, not only on the moors, but even on the peninsular betwixt river and sea. Nevertheless, Richard ordered the carriage to be prepared, and made the promised visit to Ginifur's adopted family, as he referred to them. He too was appalled at the degradation that had been forced upon them by circumstances beyond their control. He knew of no one on his patch that had been forced to live as they were attempting to live. Richard, as Ginifur and Sam had, took an instant liking to young Liam. "We Celts should stick together." He declared and, taking the offered stool, he sat down and was immediately in deep conversation with Liam.

They had taken with them some tea and brandy. Ginifur and Kate had soon boiled some water, brewed the tea and added some brandy to warm them all, and then Ginifur opened the tin of cakes and biscuits that Netty had made that morning. Dusk was drawing in before they took their leave and, before their departure, Richard had made the necessary arrangements for Samuel to collect them and bring them over to Tremanyon to discuss the possibility of work and a new home.

Before Richard returned to London, Liam, Kate, Joe, and the children Lorna, Poppy and Aiden, were installed in the tiny cottage behind the kennels. It had a bedroom, a living room and a kitchen, with a 'lean to' out back. Kate was ecstatic, and declared that Ginny was a fairy godmother. For Ginifur it was like having a sister and brother, her happiness seemed to be complete.

There was only one thing to mar Ginifur's happiness. During the cold, wet weather the children's riding lessons were curtailed. But Ginifur continued to ride Damson at least once or twice a week. She had fashioned herself some riding clothes to wear in wet weather refusing, stubbornly, to wear her beautiful riding habit that Richard and Annabelle had ordered for her. Besides, her own home made split skirt allowed her the freedom to ride either side saddle or astride, as she wished. Often she would leave the side-saddle in a safe, dry place and continue her ride over the headland on bareback. Countless times she would ask Sam if

99

Adam was free to join her, but Adam was rarely around the stables when Ginifur was present, and it was left to Sam to explain his absence. Ginifur was puzzled. She knew that he was around the stables at other times, for she had seen him from her bedroom window in the Big House.

Liam proved himself to be able to turn his hand to anything, and when the building work commenced his strength and stamina were praised by the local builders employed on the job. He could dig out twice the amount of soil for the foundations as anyone else on the site, and without pausing for rest. He could carry more, and work for longer hours. He had a happy nature, a smile always lurking beneath the surface, and a whistle always on his lips. His willingness could easily have been misconstrued as ingratiating himself with his new employer, but it wasn't. Liam's rejection by those employed in the only industry he knew was soon forgotten. When he wasn't working on the new building, he would take Joe and the children to the willow garden, and Richard told him that when he purchased another boat to ply from the quay, he would be given the opportunity to go back to sea.

The willow garden, situated in the damp valley between Tremanyon and Rosvarron, had been neglected and was very overgrown. Slowly but surely Liam began to coppice the willows, trimming any useable whips and tossing them to one side where Jo would sort them into sizes and tie them into bundles. Later, Liam would fashion these whips into crab pots and fishing baskets and one day surprised Netty by turning up at the cellar door with a large basket he had made for her and a vegetable trug for Tom. But to say that he didn't miss the sea would be untrue.

When Joe wasn't helping Liam, he would help Sam to muck out the stables, and was shortly undertaking all the menial jobs that had once been Adams.

It had been the intention that Peggy Billing would help Ginifur with the children, but she and Pearl were kept fully occupied as housemaids to maintain Ginifur's high standards. So it was with Richard's blessing that Ginny employed Peggy's young sister Lizzie to help look after Kate's children. Ginifur then took Kate under her wing to guide her in the aspects of life in the house in readiness for the arrival of the new baby. Ginifur had great faith in Kate's ability to be able to assist Rachel and Rebecca, leaving her to concentrate on her other jobs and with the preparations in the new nursery wing. Kate was provided with a set of clothes to wear whilst in the house and Richard had insisted that the whole family be provided with a set of inexpensive but serviceable clothes, for their own were nought but rags.

The cold January was followed by a wet February, but the building work continued at a pace. March saw the start of an early spring and the green shoots that had been held back in January and February sprang upwards in the warm sunshine and lengthening days.

In spite of the building work being carried out at Tremanyon, news came that the 'Falmouths' would still pay their visit at the end of April, putting the staff at Tremanyon into a flat spin. The weeks before the expected arrival brought a flurry of activity in both the house and the gardens. Ginifur ordered the chimney's to be swept, and then organised a thorough spring cleaning of the house. Ginifur took on extra temporary staff from the village and curtains were taken down and either washed or brushed and hung in the air to freshen. Carpets and rugs were taken out of doors for a beating and the rooms washed and cleaned from ceiling to floor.

Ginifur and Netty worked out a menu for the three day visit, and Samuel and Adam were sent to Truro for the extra provisions. Ginifur checked and rechecked her lists, to ensure that nothing was forgotten.

* * *

The spring was warm and sunny. The fruit trees in the orchards blossomed early, and there were no late frosts to damage the early buds. The last of the daffodils nodded their heads in the woodland and primroses and bluebells covered the floors of the woods, and under the trees and shrubs along the drive. The weekend of Edward and Fanny Boscawen's visit was perfect. The sun shone, there was no wind, and it was like early summer.

It was to be a purely private visit, there were no plans for a large assembly of people to meet them. Having ridden around the estate Edward declared that the views indeed rivalled anything that Tregothnan had to offer. Annabelle and Fanny renewed their acquaintance, walking in the gardens whilst Richard and Edward were out riding. The long evenings, the four of them spent around the roaring fire in animated conversation.

Edward was fascinated with the bathing rooms for Richard was now including one, with modifications, in the new West Wing.

This brought the return to the conversation of health aboard ship, and Edward was pleased to hear that Richard too agreed with him that any improvement in cleanliness, and diet, must improve the overall health of the crew. The difficulty, of course, would be to implement compulsory washing and personal hygiene. Edward already insisted on hosing down his seamen once they had left shore, each man was then issued with a set of worn but clean seaman's clothes. Also the diet of those on board was particularly controlled by food rations that would, and could, be stored safely for the major part of a long voyage at sea. When landing on foreign shores dry rations were always supplemented by whatever could be found fresh ashore. Be it meat or fruit.

Ginifur and Netty, and indeed the whole of the household, had worked hard to make the visit a success, and they were gratified that the 'Falmouths' declared that it had been truly a memorable visit. "The food!" Proclaimed Edward. "Is equal to the standard in any fashionable London Residence of high society. In fact it was better than most, and I should know" He declared, for he had visited most of them.

* * *

Annabelle confounded them all by her good health throughout her confinement, taking a great interest in the new West Wing and helping Ginifur to choose furnishings and drapes for the new rooms from samples that Ginifur arranged to have brought to the house.

Dr Thomas visited her regularly, instructing her in the latter weeks to rest a little more. She suffered with little or no morning sickness, and she never lost her appetite. She put on a little weight regularly, but did not become too heavy. Rachel and Rebecca were thrilled at the prospect of a new baby in the house, and would take it in turns to read to Annabelle when she rested in the afternoons.

Richard came home as often as was possible and he had returned, quite by chance, at the end of June when Annabelle went into premature labour.

A Shadow Falls

THE FULL MOON sailed low above the horizon as the sky began to streak with light from the east. Dawn was near. The hour of the birth was imminent, and Annabelle hung on tenaciously to the last minutes of her young life. She had been in labour for three long days. Annabelle believed that she was going to die, but she was determined that it would not be before she had given birth to her precious son and held him in her arms. It was a boy; Annabelle was convinced that she carried a boy child. A son for Richard. It was her life's ambition, to give Richard a son.

A drop of bright red blood appeared as Annabelle's pure white teeth bit into her lower lip, and her eyes closed tightly as the pain tore through her frail body. She was even too tired now to cry out in anguish, for Annabelle had been in the last throes of childbirth for the last twenty-four hours.

Jane stirred up the fire as Ginny bathed her mistress's head with cold water, for she was both hot and cold with fever at the same time.

"How much more can Mrs Tremayne take?" Ginifur asked Dr Thomas. James Thomas mopped his brow with the damp handkerchief. "The moment is near. I have finally managed to turn the baby, but it will be a struggle and I don't know if she has the strength to push anymore."

With a sudden gasp of anguish Annabelle opened her mouth and let out a blood curdling wail. It carried and filled every corner of the house, stopping Richard in his tracks as he paced up and down the hall. Terrified, he ran up the stairs three at a time, and drew to a frantic halt at the bedroom door. His hand gripped the handle, afraid of what he would find, and let it loose as he felt it turn beneath his grasp. As the door opened, Ginifur stepped out of the room closing the door behind her. Her face was drawn and tired. Dark circles about her eyes were a testament to her faithful and sleepless vigil.

"Annabelle! My wife, I heard her scream. Is she alright? Has the baby been born yet?" Richard was frantic with worry.

"It is a boy, Sir." Ginifur informed him, without looking up into his face. The baby had been born with the final push that produced Annabelle's dreadful cry of agony. "Mrs Tremayne has fallen into an exhausted sleep and Jane is washing her now. I am sure that as soon as Dr Thomas has seen to your son, you will be able to see Mrs Tremayne."

Richard stared unseeing at the closed door. His fear was etched in the lines about his dark burning eyes, his grim expression and his tight lips. Glancing up at him Ginifur wished that she could offer him some comfort, for she knew that the worst wasn't over yet. "Annabelle! My wife! That cry, I thought that she was dying." A veil of sadness flitted across Ginifur's eyes, and she turned away quickly. "My son! Is he alright? It has taken so long, why hasn't he cried?"

Ginifur was spared from having to answer as Dr Thomas opened the door and stepped onto the landing. "Richard, I was just coming to find you." Richard stared at him as James Thomas studied the pattern on the carpet, before raising his eyes to meet his.

"My wife? My child?" Richard's heartfelt plea was like a knife in Ginifur's heart.

"Your wife has been delivered of a son Richard. There is no easy way for me to say this. I am afraid that he was stillborn. I tried everything I could. Believe me, I did."

"Annabelle?" Her name was a whisper on Richard's lips.

James Thomas ran his fingers through the fine cropped hair on his head; his wig had been discarded long ago. It was hard enough that he should loose a baby, but to have to impart further sad news to Richard was worse. "Annabelle has been through a prolonged childbirth. Her heart has never been strong, you know that Richard."

"What are you saying?" Richard's eyes blazed out of dark sockets. Dr Thomas put out a hand to touch Richard's arm, but he shrugged it off angrily. "What are you trying to tell me man?"

"Annabelle has fallen into an exhausted sleep, from which she might not wake."

"No!" Richard tried to push him aside.

"Richard!" James Thomas barred his way. "I said that she might not, but if she does I believe that she will have, at the most, only a few hours of life left. She has fought long and bravely, in the belief that she would bear you a son. It was the one gift that she longed to give you."

"I didn't want a son if it meant that her life was in danger, I am quite happy with my two daughters. Why did you let it continue, if her life was in the balance? You could have stopped it, I know you could."

"May be I could. Maybe I couldn't. I did warn her Richard, but she begged me not to tell you. If it was to be the last thing she was to do in her life, she wanted to do it. She believed from the first moment that she was carrying a boy; nothing was going to stand in her way. Nothing." He nodded to Ginifur and, as she opened the door, Annabelle's faint voice was heard from within.

"Richard! Where's Richard?" She asked Jane, who was smoothing the pillows behind her head.

"He'll be here in a minute, Ma'am. Rest now, you've worked so hard. You must rest now."

"Where's my baby? It is a boy, isn't it? Where is he?"

Jane watched Ginifur as she approached the crib. "He's with Ginny Ma'am. He's sleeping too, for he's had a long hard struggle into this world."

Richard glanced through the crack in the door. "You said he was dead! You said he was stillborn!" He exploded angrily.

James Thomas closed the door. "I told you the truth Richard. Now, you have to be strong. Annabelle must not learn that her effort has all been in vain. Don't let her leave this life thinking that she has failed you. Do you love her enough to do this for her Richard? Do you?" Richard stared in disbelief at the closed door. How was he to face life without his wife beside him? How was he to tell his daughters? "Richard!" Dr Thomas gripped his shoulder. "You must do this for her . . . We can't wait, time is of the essence, and we have to go in."

Richard watched in a daze as the door slowly opened again. All signs of the activities in the room over the last three days had been miraculously removed.

Annabelle lay in the four poster bed, her fair curls spread out upon the fine linen covered pillow. The gold of her hair was accentuated by her pale, pretty face, drained of any colour. Her eyes were dull, and she was finding it difficult to focus.

"I have sedated her. She has been given laudanum for the pain" James Thomas whispered in Richard's ear.

Richard glanced about the room. Everything looked so normal. But it wasn't, was it? Jane had placed a chair by the bed and left the room by way of the adjacent dressing room. Only Ginifur remained in the far corner, by the crib, nursing a tiny bundle of clothes.

Richard stepped towards the bed and Annabelle, sensing him, turned her head towards him. "You have a son, Richard. Are you pleased? He is so good, he is sleeping already. Not like Rachel. Do you remember how she cried? She made enough noise for two didn't she?"

Richard gulped down the large lump that had risen in his throat. "She did indeed." He agreed as he reached the chair and sat down on it to take her hand in his. "How are you feeling, my dearest? "

"I'm tired." She whispered. "What day is it?"

"Wednesday." Richard replied.

She looked at him incredulously. Her eyes, seeming too large for her tiny face, were set deep within purple sockets. Her skin was transparent, tinged a fragile blue. A vein pulsed irregularly on her temple. "I've been here for three whole days?" She asked.

"You must rest now, you are tired, my dearest. You have worked very hard and must sleep." Richard was finding it hard to focus his eyes on her face, and blinked back the tears that threatened to fall.

"Where's my baby? Where is our son?" She moved her head to search the room. Her eyes finally settled on Ginifur.

"He is asleep Annabelle. Ginifur has him safe." Richard tried to assure her.

"Please Richard, bring me my baby." She pleaded.

Richard glanced fearfully at James Thomas, who beckoned Ginifur forward. The baby was tightly wrapped in white linen and a fine shawl. Only a small portion of his face was showing above his mouth and nose. He looked for all the world as though he was, indeed, asleep. Ginifur settled the tiny bundle in Richard's arms, arranging the clothing carefully around the babies face. He stared at the tiny bundle lying in his arms. It was almost weightless, this son of his.

"What is he like Richard?" Annabelle asked.

"He is a little like you, but he has a mop of dark hair." He told her.

"Is he alright?" She asked fearfully.

"Ginifur says that he has all his fingers and toes, and his little extras." He attempted a feeble joke, which brought a brief smile to her face, and he prayed silently that she wouldn't ask to hold him.

"What name shall we give him?"

"What name would you like to give him?"

106

"Richard would be nice, but would you mind if we named him after my father?"

Richard smiled as he looked down at her. "Of course not; Henry is a fine name for a lad."

Annabelle's eyes wandered about the room. "It's getting dark, what time is it?"

Richard shot a startled glance at Dr Thomas who nodded his head with a sigh. The early morning sun was shining brightly, filling the room with light. Richard turned back to his wife. "It is nearly eight o'clock." He told her.

"The night is drawing in early." She said. "May I hold my baby Richard?" James Thomas indicated that he should hand the baby to his wife, and in fear and trepidation, he laid the tiny scrap of humanity in her arms.

Annabelle peered down at the tiny bundle of clothes. "Will you light the lamp Richard? It is almost too dark to see him." Richard looked bleakly at the oil lamp on the side table, and taking the tinder he lit it. Annabelle's eyes focused slowly on the light. "That's better. I am so tired Richard, will you stay with me till I sleep?"

Tears welled up into Richard's eyes; his vision was blurred as he took her hand again. "Of course I will my dearest." He bent over to kiss her gently on her mouth.

"I love you so much Richard." Annabelle whispered.

There was a tight constriction in Richard's throat. How was he to answer her when he feared his own voice would break with the raw emotion that was welling inside him? Somehow he found the strength, and in an unwavering voice, that he felt was not his own he replied. "And I love you too my darling. Now sleep and dream sweet dreams."

Annabelle smiled sweetly as her eye lids slowly closed for the very last time. She slipped silently away as she heard him speak his last words to her. Richard bowed his head, and his salty tears fell upon Annabelle's hand.

At the signal from Dr Thomas Ginifur lifted the lifeless babe out of Annabelle's arms. She paused as she looked down at Richard's bowed head, and her heart ached for him. Her eyes swam with tears as she left the room and paused for a brief moment as she tried to stem their flow. Feeling the tiny babe through the covers, and blinded by salty tears, Ginifur stumbled towards her bedroom. Sobbing inconsolably she dropped into her chair, grasping the baby tightly in her aching arms.

As the sun rose above the trees outside her room, the flood of tears slowly diminished and Ginifur's eyes alighted upon the china figurine upon the windowsill. It was a much cherished gift to her from Annabelle, and depicted a mother and child. The deep rose pink shade of the mother's dress was paled in the bright sunlight, yet Ginifur hardly noticed this as she studied the shadow that the ornament created upon the sill. The shadow was long, and thin, and dark. In no way did the shadow resemble the model of its creator.

Straight backed in the chair, Ginifur was mesmerised by the shadow. Her eyes never left it, hardly blinking, and she was as rigid as the china figurine itself. Ginifur didn't feel the tiny body as it grew colder and colder within the protective shawl. She didn't notice the sun move higher into the blue sky until it was about to slip over the roof and take the sunshine from her room. Although she was studying the shadow so hard, she didn't even notice it getting smaller and smaller, until her ears picked up the light knock on her door. Ginifur drew a deep breath as, with a sigh, she noticed that the shadow form of the figurine had almost disappeared. There was just a small pool of grey at the feet of the beautiful mother who gazed down upon her child. In another moment the sun had passed over the roof and the shadow vanished completely. In the absence of sunlight the colour returned to the figurine.

Ginifur blinked and, oblivious to the presence of Dr Thomas who had entered unbidden, she spoke aloud. "Life's just like that." She whispered.

James Thomas laid a gentle hand upon her shoulder. "What did you say Ginifur?"

Dark circles surrounded the pair of dull green eyes that looked up at him. Ginifur's face was drawn with exhaustion and her creamy white skin contrasted dramatically with dark circles surrounding the bloodshot whites of the eyes. "Life . . ." She repeated, nodding towards the figurine. "It's there one minute, solid, real, casting a shadow. Then suddenly it's gone, like the shadow, but never to return. Yet an unseen shadow remains in its place." She added. "It was like that when my mother died. Her shadow remained. In the daytime it was like you had two shadows instead of one. You couldn't see it, but you knew it was there. And at night, even in the darkness it was still there, hiding in the corners. Until the shadow fades, the sadness and grief remain. It was along time before Da laughed again." For the first time she glanced down at the tiny bundle in her arms. "But what about him?" She asked of no one in particular. "He didn't even live long enough to cast a shadow. But the shadow he will leave will be a very long one indeed."

Dr Thomas stared down at Ginifur's uncovered head. The cap that he had given her to wear during Annabelle's birthing had been discarded during her long vigil. Her dishevelled hair was pulled away from her face, unruly strands falling across her shoulders. He thought to himself that Ginifur was wise beyond her years. It came from the responsibility thrust upon her at such a young age, and spending all her time around adults. He wanted to comfort her, for he knew of her affection for her mistress. But if he did he felt sure that it would only unleash a fresh flood of tears. Instead he spoke more harshly than he intended. "Ginifur! Captain Tremayne wishes to see you." Ginifur glanced up. "Rachel and Rebecca. They do not know of their Mother's death, Ginifur. They will need you. They will all need you."

Ginifur's eyes opened wide as she quickly pushed herself up from the chair. "Oh! Those poor babes!" She glanced briefly at the bundle in her arms. "Where are they?"

"They are with Kate. Liam is with Captain Tremayne. Give me the baby Ginifur, then wash your face and freshen yourself up." He added more gently.

Ginifur pulled the shawl away from the babe's face. Peaceful in death, his skin was smooth and unblemished for he hadn't had to struggle into this world. He had given up his life before his birth and it had been left to Annabelle to bear the struggle alone. "Poor little lamb. What a waste. She wanted him so much." Her lips trembled as she turned to face the Doctor. "Why?" She demanded of him. James Thomas held out his hands, and with one final glance she handed him over. "How do you explain that to two little girls who are excitedly awaiting the arrival of a new baby brother or sister? How do you tell them that there is no baby, and what's more they have no mother either?" She stared up at him, and for one brief moment there was a spark of anger and accusation in her eyes and James Thomas looked away. "I was Rachel's age when my mother died. A child needs a mother. Oh God!" Ginifur's voice broke. "How could he do this? Why? What does it achieve? You tell me, Dr Thomas. Do you have the answer?" She brushed her eyes angrily.

James Thomas swallowed the lump in his throat. It was never easy. "I have no answer Ginifur. But I do know this. The children will need you. Captain Tremayne will need you. And for their sake you have to be strong." He pulled the shawl over the baby's head.

"And him!! What will happen to him?" She pleaded in desperation. "He hasn't even been baptised!"

James Thomas looked at the lifeless boy child held in his arms. "He will lay with his mother." He assured her.

"The reverend will never allow that!!" Ginifur exclaimed angrily.

"You leave the parson to me." James Thomas stated firmly. "I can handle the Reverend Siley-Pratt, don't you worry. Now go and freshen up Ginifur. Change your dress and comb your hair, and put a brave face on it for the family's sake. Captain Tremayne will be in the drawing room . . . But take your time." He turned to leave her gazing past the figurine in the window, beyond the window pane and the trees, and even beyond the bay that could be glimpsed through the fluttering leaves.

Tearing her eyes away from the window Ginifur slowly undid the row of tiny buttons that fastened the front of her dress. She stared at the stains of blood, Annabelle's blood, before letting it fall to her feet. Stepping out of the dress she picked it up, laying it upon the bed. Carefully she poured some water into the decorated china bowl. When Annabelle had learned that she only had a tin bowl and jug, she had immediately sent in the china set. Not only were there a matching jug and bowl, but a soap dish, trinket dish, and a pair of tall candlesticks. Annabelle had also insisted that Richard ordered a mahogany corner unit especially designed to hold these utensils, with a cupboard underneath to hold the matching chamber pot. It had saddened Annabelle to learn that Ginifur had been left at an early age without a mother, and they had developed a very special relationship. It was a relationship closer than that of Mistress and servant, an indefinable friendship.

Ginifur splashed the cold water on her face and then, picking up the soap she rubbed it thoroughly on the piece of flannelette she used as a face cloth, and scrubbed her face roughly, bringing a little colour back into her face.

* * *

Richard stood with his back to the fireplace, his head turned to the windows gazing unseeing into the distance. In a daze, with Liam's quiet assistance, he had washed and shaved the black stubble that had appeared during the last few days. His face showed his exhaustion, his eyes appeared more black than their usual bright blue, as if they themselves were in mourning.

Jane was upstairs, attending to Annabelle's body. She washed her tenderly and dressed her in a fine lawn gown. Jane knew exactly what to do in the laying out of a body, and this time she took very special care so that Annabelle would look as though she was peacefully sleeping. Jane brushed Annabelle's curls out to frame her delicate face and applied an almost invisible touch of rouge to her cheeks and lips.

The house was quiet. Even the garden was silent beyond the open window. The lavender bushes, in the beds at the front of the house, that on any other summer's day would be alive with the hum of bees, were empty and quiet. In fact there wasn't a bee in the garden. As folklore dictated, Tom had gone to the hives immediately to inform them of the death of the mistress. Neither were the birds singing in the trees. They were there, but they didn't chirp merrily as they usually did, they sat silently on the boughs amongst the leaves. The lone birds that were on the wing were those with young to feed, and they did this hurriedly and silently. Even the normally energetic squirrels were unusually inactive. The world seemed to be asleep.

Richard sensed, rather than heard Ginifur's soft tread upon the stairs, and had turned to face the door moments before the light tap.

Ginifur hesitated, straightened a fold in her skirt. The cold water had reduced the puffiness around her eyes, induced by tiredness and tears, even so her normally bright eyes were unusually dull and misty. She had sponged herself from head to toe, trying to erase the memories of the night. She had splashed some of her precious Rosewater on her hair and brushed it vigorously, bringing some blood back into her head and helping to clear her mind. With a final quick inspection she satisfied herself that she was well presented. She straightened her shoulders and, holding her head high to give the illusion of composure; she knocked on the door and waited.

Richard didn't call out for her to enter; he glanced thoughtfully at the door and then opened it himself. "Come in Ginny. You have had a long few days. Dr Thomas and Jane have told me how tirelessly you have worked, and what comfort you gave to . . . to my wife during her ordeal." He paused, glancing at the portrait at the end of the room. "Thank you, for all you have done. I don't know what she would have done with out you being there for her."

Ginifur blinked hard. She had to control her emotions. For the sake of her departed mistress she must, and for Rachel and Rebecca. But most of all for the master. She would be able to comfort the children, but who was to give comfort to him? "Oh Sir! I only did what anyone would have done, and . . ." Her voice trailed off. For what else could she possibly say? What should she say?

But Richard seemed to hear the unspoken words. "I know Ginifur. You don't need to say any more, for I know." He bit his lip and turned away for a moment, before continuing. "I haven't told the girls yet. I should do it myself, alone." He turned quickly, his eyes searching hers. "But they are only children, such little girls. I am not sure how they will react. I don't know that I will be able to give them the necessary comfort. I might let Annabelle down."

"Oh no, Sir!" Ginifur exclaimed. "You would never do that."

"Will you stay with me whilst I tell them? Will you help me Ginifur? I can not do this alone. They love you, and you will be able help to ease them through this tragic event."

Ginifur wanted to put out a hand to offer him some comfort. But how could she? She a mere servant to this man of high birth. Instead she nodded her head in agreement.

The semblance of a smile hovered briefly on his lips. "I was sure that you would, so I asked Liam to fetch Kate and the girls as soon as he heard you enter the room." And he turned to face the door as the chatter of young voices drew closer and the door burst open.

"Papa! Papa!" Rachel ran to her father. "Kate won't tell us about the baby." She burst out angrily. "What is it? Have we got a brother or a sister? Becky says that she wants a sister, but I think it's time we had a brother or there will be too many women in the house. Don't you agree Papa?"

Rebecca paused by the door, watching her father and Ginifur. A sensitive child, she knew that something was wrong. Ginifur stepped towards her, and held out her hand to encourage her into the room. Becky took the outstretched hand and her eyes vainly searched Ginifur's for an answer to the unasked question. Finally she put it into words. "Where's Mama? Why is everything so quiet?"

Ginifur led her towards Richard. What was he going to say? How was he going to tell them?

The Darkest Hours

THE WHOLE OF the household was in shock. In fact it would be true to say that not only the whole of the household, or even the workers on the estate, but the whole of the district was in shock. In the short time that the Tremaynes' had lived at Tremanyon, they had been taken into the hearts of the employees, tenants, tradesmen, gentry and the villagers.

In the ornate coffin, the baby that Annabelle had given her life for was cradled within his mother's arms. Richard walked behind the coffin all the way from the gates of Tremanyon, followed by Ginifur with Rachel and Rebecca holding her hands on either side. The family from Mevagissey joined the procession at the Church, then the 'Falmouths', Dr Thomas and his wife, Monsieur de Varron and Lady Catherine (who was herself with child), and then the local gentry. Martin Harris had returned to Tregony especially to be present and offer his condolences and respects. Never before had there been such a funeral in Porthcarrow Church.

The Church was overflowing for the funeral. The only spare pews in the church were reserved for the family and friends, the remainder would be filled with members of the staff of Tremanyon. The churchyard and the road beyond were thronged with villagers, farm workers, fishermen and their wives and children. The high windows and the doors of the Church were left open and, in utter silence they all listened to the words and music that flowed from the church.

When the coffin, and the family, left the Church for the return trip to Tremanyon and the tiny chapel of rest that Richard had ordered to be built, never for one moment expecting it to be used so quickly, there was a stunned silence. Mothers and children silently wept as the horse drawn carriage made its progress back along the narrow street lined with villagers. No fishing boats had put to sea, farm workers had been given the day off, and tradesmen had closed up for the day as a mark of respect.

* * *

For a few weeks Rachel and Rebecca were quieter than usual, but other than their first natural tears, and the immediate awkward questions, they seemed to be accepting a life without their mother.

But Richard! It was different for Richard.

Richard spent every waking hour, of every day, at work. He left the house before dawn to work alongside Simon. Sometimes he would even go out on the boats overnight, pulling in the nets and lines with the crew. Or he would spend long hours at the farm. His only relaxation was when he rode out on Lanhoose. He would ride at a ferocious pace until both he and the horse were spent, and on his return he would dismiss Sam or Adam, insisting that it should be he who rub the horse down and see to his needs before his own.

In his grief Richard would sometimes forget his daughters; until he would come upon them, by chance, if he was in the house during daylight hours. Then he would be full of remorse and give them his undivided attention for a while, wearing a mask to cover his own grief he would even manage to laugh and play games on occasions. If he was at home in the evenings he would dine alone in the library, and then drink into the long night.

Ginifur would lie awake in her room at the top of the stairs until she could hear him stumble up the stairs in the early hours of the morning. Her heart would ache for him, for Rachel and Rebecca, and for herself. Annabelle's sudden death had left a great hole in all their lives. Ginifur hadn't realised how much she had grown to love her mistress, Rachel and Rebecca, or Richard. They had become her family. What affected them affected her. If they were happy, then she was happy. If they hurt, then Ginifur hurts also.

Ginifur was hurting now!

* * *

The pilchards that should have started to arrive during July, were noticeable by their absence, and by the middle of August the whole neighbourhood had one ear listening for the call of hevva from the lookouts posted at strategic points along the cliffs. But the long awaited familiar boiling of the sea, as the shoals of fish came near to the shore, never came. The lookouts remained silent. If the seining from the beaches was bad, those with boats fared no better. It was said that the pilchards arrived at Looe and were to be caught as near as Mevagissey to the east, and they were aplenty in the west from the Lizard to Penzance. But in Dingerien Bay and Falmouth Bay there were none to be found. Boats went farther out along the coast, but if they strayed too far east, or west, they were in danger of being set upon by the owners of boats who usually fished these waters. They came back with a few mackerel, maybe a skate or two and a handful of flat fish, but little else. Barely enough to feed the family let alone have enough to sell.

As if this wasn't enough, the corn in the fields, that had looked so promising in the early summer, started to die on ear. It wasn't that the grains were small; they just didn't develop at all. There was nothing but empty, dry husks. To make matters worse, the potato plants that they all relied on for the winter were one minute healthy, lush and green, and the next wilted and brown. When they dug up the potatoes they were rotten, black and foul smelling. Potato blight had hit the peninsular.

More than one person was heard to say, in the silence of their homes, that it was as though Annabelle's death and her still borne child had cast a curse on the neighbourhood. Betsy, the white witch who lived in the shady valley just outside of the village, confirmed it, and she prophesied that it would take another birth to lift the curse. Not any birth, she pointed out, but a special birth.

Richard was the only person unaware of the gossip and rumours. Ginny had heard them, Tom and Netty had heard them, and everyone on the estate had heard them. But, as one, they vowed that this gossip would not reach Richard's ears.

The food shortages forced Richard to push his grief to one side for a while. He covered every inch of the estate, both Home Farm and tenanted lands at Rhossinnis and Kylyn. The hay that had been cut would never be enough to feed the animals through the winter and they needed the dredge corn to give the cows a balanced diet if they were to continue to yield milk. There would be no gleaning for the villagers. No fallen grain to pick up for their own consumption or to feed the few chickens they kept in their back yards.

The fact that there were no potatoes was even worse! It was the staple food of the country folk. Scrubbed and boiled in their skins, they were eaten alone, or with fish or meat if they were lucky enough to have any. Now there was neither and even the rabbits appeared to have left the district for pastures new.

As the summer drifted by and the days grew shorter, Richard struggled with the problems raised by the food shortages. It wasn't only his own personal problems that gave him concern; it was also the plight of those who lived and worked on the estate, and of those in the village and surrounding areas too.

Food shortages were not unknown in Cornwall, but it had never happened on this peninsular before, not on this scale. Not here, where they always had an abundance of food from the land and the sea. There had been food riots in the past, the last in forty seven when the tin miners had roamed the countryside, breaking into corn stores and demanding action from the government. None came then, and Richard knew that none would come now. If they were to survive this famine, they would have to find the answers themselves.

Chapter Four
1753 – *The Messenger*

IT WAS ONE day in late August that a horseman rode in, quite un-announced, and with a letter for Captain Tremayne. He was under instructions to deliver the sealed letter to Richard personally and, whilst Adam went in search of his master, Ginifur led the messenger to the kitchens for refreshments. The rider was exhausted, having ridden with very little rest since he had left London, only using the time that it had taken to change horses and grab a bite to eat. As Netty bustled about the kitchen, getting him some food, he dropped his head forward upon his arms and fell fast asleep at the table. Netty put her shawl across his shoulders and left him. Who knew where the master was? It might take some time before Adam found him.

It did.

First Adam tried the Home Farm, but when he found Harry Polaughan he said that he hadn't seen him. Then Adam went to the Quay. The boats were moored up and in the cellar they were barrelling the last of the salted pilchards. The Captain had been down at the quay earlier, Simon told him, but he had left taking Liam with him. Adam scowled and rode off along the river path towards the mill. Ed had seen Richard and Liam cross the stepping stones at the end of the mill pond and head out across the headland towards Rhossinnis. Adam took off down Well Lane, towards Kylyn Farm, and then followed the coastal path out to the headland where he met Richard and Liam heading back home. By the time the party had returned, the rider was a little refreshed and tucking into a plateful of rabbit stew and potatoes. The only potatoes to survive the blight were those in the walled garden at Tremanyon. Tom was convinced that they had been spared the worse in the garden by the bees, for as country lore demanded Tom had informed the bees immediately he heard that Annabelle had lost her young life giving birth to the Captain's son. The young messenger jumped up as Richard strode into the kitchen, and pulled out a letter from inside his jacket.

Richard took the letter and waved his hand. "Eat up, eat up man. You have earned it, you must be hungry." The rider nodded.

"I will see you once I have read this." He glanced briefly at the contents of the letter and, as he left the kitchen, he added over his shoulder. "Netty, get someone to find Ginifur. I will be only a few moments."

Pearl scuttled off to find Ginifur, and she was waiting for Richard in the kitchen on his return. "There will be no reply." Richard told the messenger.

"No Sir. I was told to make sure that you got the letter, and read it. Then I was to go straight to Tregothnan to deliver a letter to Admiral Boscawen."

"Not tonight you aren't" Stated Richard.

"But, Sir!" The young rider attempted to protest.

Richard shook his head. "But Sir, nothing. What ever is in the letter can wait until the morning. In any case, I have the feeling that Lord Falmouth won't be at all surprised by its contents. Tonight you will rest. Ginny, get Pearl or Peggy to bring down some blankets so that he can sleep in the school room for the night."

"Yes Sir." Ginny made a move towards the door.

"I'll be all right Sir." The rider assured him. "I'll bed down with the horse, in the stables. It won't be the first time, I don't expect it will be the last."

Richard shook his head. "Listen Man, I won't hear of it. Do I make myself clear? You will get a good nights sleep, and in this house. I'll hear no more on the subject. Just make sure that you see me before you leave in the morning. I have decided that I will send a letter to Admiral Boscawen and it will give me ample time to pen it."

The rider gracefully gave in to his superior. "I understand Sir." He acknowledged.

Richard grinned. "Good man." Then he turned to Ginifur. "When you have settled things here Ginifur, I would like to see you in the library." Richard waited only long enough to hear her acknowledgement before leaving the basement with his mind racing.

When Ginifur opened the library door, Richard was writing at his desk. "Come in, come in." He looked up briefly and beckoned her into the room. Finishing his writing he put down the quill, ushered her to one of the high backed leather chairs by the fireplace and proceeded to pace about the room. He paused for a moment as he took the letter that had just been delivered from his pocket. "This letter is from London Ginifur. It contains information of national interest, and it is necessary that I take you into my confidence." Ginifur, though puzzled, showed no sign of it. "I know that I can trust you implicitly."

This time she did answer him. "Of course, Sir."

Richard continued. "In the next few days we will be receiving visitors of great importance, and it is essential that their presence here is kept in the utmost secrecy. We will need all the bedrooms made up for visitors, including my own room. Yours and the children's will be needed for the few servants that they will bring with them. We will have to sleep in the new wing, if you can get it habitable enough for a few nights."

"The west wing is all ready, Sir. I just haven't moved the girl's things over. There was . . . I was . . ." Annabelle hadn't been around to instruct her to make the move, and she hadn't dared broach the subject with Richard.

Richard looked surprised. "You mean that it is furnished?"

"Yes Sir. You asked me to organise it Captain Tremayne, and with Mrs. Tremayne's agreement it was finished before . . ."

Richard frowned. "Yes. Of course, I suppose I just stopped thinking about it. You never told me it was ready."

Ginifur lowered her head. "I'm sorry Captain Tremayne. I thought, I thought that you had other things on your mind."

"Yes." Richard mused. "I have been somewhat pre-occupied." He brightened. "Well, that will make your job a little easier. Now, Lord Falmouth will be the first to arrive, he has been before so it should not cause any unusual comment in the village, but the rest of the visitors would. I must stress that news of their presence here must not get out. Once the rooms are made up I don't want Pearl or Peggy or Lizzie in the main house until the visitors are in the dining room. That will be your responsibility. Another thing." He continued. "I know it is a tall order, but I would like you to instruct Liam at waiting at table and, although it is not your province, I should like you to assist as well. There may be conversation that must be forgotten. Liam can keep a still tongue in his head, and he is quick to learn. I don't think it will be too difficult for you, and if you think it helpful use Kate too." He paused. "Liam is similar in build to Robert. There is a spare set of clothes in the store room. Fetch them out and see if they fit. Is there anything that you wish to ask me now?"

"How long do I have to prepare everything, Sir?" Ginifur was already working out a time table in her head.

"Three days. Including tomorrow, three days. Lord Falmouth will arrive on Friday. You will have time?"

Ginifur wondered briefly if this last was a question or a statement, but nodded. "Yes Sir. We will make a start first thing in the morning. May I ask how many we will be catering for?"

"There will be six visitors, and myself, to cater for in the dining room. The servants can all eat in the old staff dining room if you can vacate the school room. In any case, you might as well move into the new rooms. It will be brighter and much better for you and the girls. The servants can also use the staff sitting room, but there is to be no fraternising between servants Ginny. Make that very clear to Tom and Netty; it will be for them to keep an eye on Pearl, Peggy and Lizzie."

Yes Sir." Ginifur made a mental note of the requests. "Is there anything else Sir?"

Richard shook his head and smiled. "No, there is nothing else Ginifur, for the moment. Are you not going to enquire as to who the visitors are?"

"No Sir. If you think that it is necessary to inform me, then I know that you will. I shall do my best to carry out your wishes Sir." She paused as something crossed her mind.

"The household arrangements I shall leave to you, Ginifur. You can work it out. But there must be complete secrecy . . . if anything should get out." His words hung on the air. "If there is anything you find that you need, just ask. Send Sam and Adam to Truro for provisions, but impress upon them the urgency to keep a still tongue in their heads."

"Is that all, Sir?"

Richard laughed. It was the first time that Ginifur had heard him laugh properly since Annabelle's death, and she smiled. "Is that all, Sir? Does nothing faze you, Ginifur?" He smiled back at her. "Yes Ginifur that is all, for now."

"Then, if you will excuse me, Sir. I must begin to make arrangements before Pearl and Peggy start on the bedrooms."

Richard smiled again and, holding out his hand, he took hers as she rose out of the chair. "Thank you Ginifur. What would I do without you?" He said and, as he felt her hand tremble in his, he let it loose.

"Goodnight Sir."

"Goodnight Ginifur." Richard watched thoughtfully as she left the room without a backward glance.

The next few days flew by in a flurry of activity, and by Thursday Netty was busy in her improved kitchen with preparations for the visitors. Richard had completed an inspection of the new bedrooms in the west wing and opened the kitchen door to find her in the midst of pastry making. "Well Netty! How are you getting on?"

"Tis grand Cap'n, just grand. They big cupboards'll do just a treat, and the new range does a proper job I can tell 'e. It can cope with anything. That poor ol' dumb waiter will be really put to the test I'm a thinkin'."

Richard thought for a moment." You will have enough staff to help you?" He suddenly thought to ask.

Netty laughed "That's all been taken care of Sir. Ginifur has employed Mary Lobb and Kitty Pellow to 'elp me with the vegetables and washing up. Truth is, Cap'n Sir, tis 'elped a great deal, d'ye see?

Richard nodded. "I do see indeed, Netty. In fact I think that you could do with a little more help on an ordinary day, I'll speak to Ginifur about giving you more help in the kitchen. Have you settled on a menu with Ginifur?" Richard asked.

Netty grinned from ear to ear. "Oh aye, Sir. We've worked out a menu fit for the King 'iself. Sam 'n Adam have fetched everything on the list from Truro, and all we need is them visitors Sir."

Richard laughed. "Lord Falmouth will be pleased. I only hope that he doesn't offer you a new position at Tregothnan Netty."

Netty beamed at her employer. "No chance of that Sir. Oh no. Besides, my Tom would never leave Tremanyon."

"I'm pleased to hear it Netty." Richard paused at the door. "Anyway. I'd never let either of you go." Netty's laugh followed him along the corridor and for the first time he realised that the sound of laughter had been missing from the house for too long.

Richard was alone when he inspected the new nursery wing. Although Sam and Liam had been greatly involved in the work, he could easily recognise Ginifur's inspiration and attention to detail. His own things had been moved into the room intended for Ginifur, and he stood for a few moments in the light and airy room. Large windows to the west and the north flooded the room with light. In place of the more usual heavy drapes there was a light rose flowered material at the windows, with plain muslin gathered and pleated to accentuate the delicate pastel colours. In the centre of the room was the big bed that had been stored in the sheds since their arrival. The ironwork was freshly blackened, the brass work polished till it shone and gossamer curtains fell in folds from the half canopy above. There was no heavy, dark furniture in the room, with the exception of the kneehole dressing table holding the treasured candlesticks and trinket dish. Samuel had built cupboards into the chimney alcoves for Ginifur's few clothes. It made his own room look stuffy, and over furnished. Everything about the room was fresh, and clean, and bright. Just like Ginifur, he thought. And for one brief moment he pictured her at the dressing table.

The Proposition

ADMIRAL BOSCAWEN WAS indeed the first to arrive. He rode over with only his manservant to accompany him, and arrived after dark. Ginifur directed him to the drawing room before informing Richard of his arrival. Showing the manservant to the room reserved for his master, with the baggage that had been strapped behind him on the horse, she then took him to the rooms prepared for the visitor's attendants before returning to the drawing room.

She was surprised to find that Lord Falmouth was still there alone, and she was glad that she had had the presence of mind to get Tom to light the fire, for the evening was cool and the Admiral was standing before it warming his hands. "Would you care for refreshments, Lord Falmouth, Sir?" She asked.

Edward Boscawen turned and smiled. "Hello young Ginifur. Yes. Yes, please. I ate a while ago, but I wouldn't say no to a glass of port, or one of that fine cognac that Richard keeps well hidden." He winked mischievously.

Ginifur was surprised by his attire. Quite sober and unimpressive, not as she had seen him in the spring, but she quickly dropped a curtsey. "I shall attend to it at once, Sir." She turned towards the door.

"No! Stay a moment. How are the girls? Missing their mother no doubt?" He asked.

Ginifur was surprised at the turn of conversation. "They do, Sir. But they are being exceedingly brave about it and, on the whole, are coping well."

"No doubt due to your care and attention. Richard is lucky to have you to watch over them. He has said so himself, to Fanny, on more than one occasion. Annabelle also held you in high regard, said that she would trust you with her life."

A shadow passed across Ginifur's face. "She was a wonderful mistress Lord Falmouth, I miss her dreadfully."

"Yes, a sad loss. Very sad indeed. A sweet, charming, delicate little thing she was. Richard took it bad, he idolised her. How is Captain Tremayne, Ginifur?"

Ginifur was taken aback. "It's not for me to pass comment on my master Sir. It wouldn't be seemly, it wouldn't be right."

Edwards's solemn expression softened. "Very honourable of you Ginny. But in truth, it would help me to know how he is bearing up. It wouldn't be disloyal, I assure you."

Ginifur's eyes searched his for assurance. "He is, I believe, learning to adjust to life Sir. He has spent the summer on the land, or at sea, working himself till he almost dropped at times. But it's early days yet, time is the only healer. Time and work, and the children too I hope."

"You have a wise head on those young shoulders of yours young Ginifur." She smiled as the colour rose in her cheeks at the praise. "I am glad that they have got you to watch over them. Both the girls, and Captain Tremayne."

"Thank you Sir. I shall do my best." She dropped a curtsey. "Now, if you will excuse me Sir, I will arrange for your refreshments."

Admiral Boscawen nodded his assent, and watched thoughtfully as she left the room.

No sooner had the door closed behind her than it flew open again, as Richard burst in. "Edward! Good to see you. Ginny said that you rode over, with only a manservant for company. Did anyone see you arrive?"

"The village was quiet as a grave, no one saw me ride through. How are you my dear friend?"

"Keep myself busy. That helps. Well now! What is all this about, Edward? I am sure that you know something about this visit. Come in." He called as there was a knock on the door. Liam entered, carrying a tray with Port, Brandy and two glasses, and a plate of pastries and sweetmeats. Richard smiled to himself. Ginifur had instructed Liam well, he looked as though he had done it for years. "This is Liam, Edward. Liam and his wife are a valuable addition to my household."

Liam didn't smile, Ginifur had drummed it into him that he should never show any expression on his face. But, nevertheless, his eyes twinkled with pleasure at the remark.

Edward was impressed. He had heard of Ginifur's little family, and Richard's philanthropic gesture. "I am quite sure that you won't find a better employer in the south west, Liam." Liam bowed his head in acknowledgement. "You are from Ireland I hear?"

Liam glanced uncertainly at Richard, and he indicated that he should reply. Ginifur hadn't told him what to do in this circumstance. "I am Sir. My family live outside the city of Kilkenny, but

I have been sailing with my uncle's boats, from the south coast, since I was fourteen. We traded with people in Newlyn and Falmouth."

"A son of the sea! It must be difficult to come to terms with your feet on dry land!"

"It's not so difficult, Sir. At least I can see the sea."

"Liam, leave the tray." Richard rescued him. "We will serve ourselves." Liam placed the tray on the table. "Are the men in place Liam?"

"Yes. Sir. Samuel and Adam will take turns at the main gates. Ed and his sons will watch over the lower drive, and Simon and I will take it in turns to keep watch around the house."

"Thank you, Liam. You may go."

Liam bowed and left the room.

"I thought you had gone off your head when you told me about Ginny's little family. I have to say, I was wrong. I am most impressed." Edward Boscawen admitted.

"Liam is a good lad. He has been brought up in a good household, but won't speak of it. And Kate, his wife, well there is more to her than meets the eye. She is quick, hardworking and honest. They are both am asset to my household. I can't tell you why, but I trust them as I've trusted few people I know. With the exception of Ginifur, of course. I don't know what the girls would have done if they hadn't had Ginifur." He paused. "So, Edward, what is all this about, and where do you fit in?"

Richard lifted the decanter of brandy, and when Edward nodded, he filled the glasses and took a seat by the fireplace.

Edward frowned into his glass. "You know that I wasn't happy at the handing over of Louisburg in forty eight." Richard nodded. "I told them that this war with the French wasn't over. There are constant skirmishes on the frontiers, Indian and French war parties are attacking our settlers, and our trading posts are being attacked and burned to the ground. And so it starts all over again. William Pitt needs to be in government, we need his leadership or we will loose the colony. He wants someone to go behind the scenes, find out what is going on out there. But it needs someone with experience in land warfare and one who understands military operations, but also someone who will be able to pass himself off as a settler perhaps. We need to know the situation in Quebec, and how well they can withstand a siege. I believe that Pitt will be voted in, and then we will be able to defend the colony. But we won't be able to do this without first hand information. I shall be sailing for Boston in a few week's time, we need to find the right man for the job by then. We are hoping that he will sail with me."

Richard raised his eyebrows. "And the right man is . . ?"

Edward sipped his brandy before answering. "Damn fine brandy, Richard, damned fine. I suppose you are not going to tell me where you get it from."

Richard grinned. "You're damned right, I'm not. And you are avoiding the question."

Edward cleared his throat. "Yes, well!"

"Just who, in your mind, is the right person, Edward?"

"Of course, there has been no decision. Pitt asked if I could recommend someone who would meet all the requirements. It cannot be anyone who will be readily recognised, but it has to be someone who understands the situation."

"And your recommendation was . . ?" Richard continued to press the question.

"It had to be you Richard. You have the military experience. You understand the political implications, having been closely involved in the issues arising in our colony, and yet you are not too widely known personally and not at all along the frontier. You are fluent in French, with little or no English accent, and in my opinion, you are the man who is most likely to succeed. But it was only a recommendation Richard. Only a recommendation."

Richard stared into the golden liquid as he swirled it around the glass. "I have the girls to consider now."

"Yes, you do. But you can't shut yourself away at Tremanyon forever, Richard, pretending that the world is not still going round. You still have responsibilities to the people that you represent." Edward reminded him.

Richard's eyes flashed with anger. "I know my responsibilities Edward. I have responsibilities to my family too. I'm no fool either, Edward. A venture, such as you describe, will be fraught with danger. The risk's enormous. My children have no mother, Edward. What would they do if they had no father either? What you suggest is out of the question."

"Listen to Pitt, Richard. Before you dismiss it, Richard please listen to Pitt." Edward pleaded. "I do understand your reasons. I gave it a great deal of consideration before putting your name forward. But there are really very few men, if any, capable of pulling this off. And, besides . . ."

"Besides?" Richard asked

"I have a personal interest in this issue."

"You? How?"

"Louisburg should never have been included in the settlement. Strategically it is too important. If an attempt is made to recapture it in the future, the mission will be undertaken by me and my crew. I know that a journey from Quebec to Louisburg will be a long one, but I have to know the situation in Louisburg as well . . . There is only one person that I can trust to get that information and bring it home."

Richard bit the inside of his lip and shook his head. "Surely you have an alternative choice, Edward? I can not believe that I am the only man in England today who can attempt this, this escapade to the New World. I know nothing of the terrain; surely you have someone out there who can undertake this for you?"

Edward looked up with troubled eyes. "Why do you think it has come to this?"

"If your men on the spot can't succeed then what chance is there for me?" Richard exploded angrily.

Edward whirled the last of his brandy around the glass before answering. He rose slowly from the chair, poured himself another drink and then took the decanter to Richard. "This venture will be different."

Richard gave an undisguised sigh. "Of course. This time it will be different! How often I have heard that statement in wartime?" He held out his glass for Edward to refill. "Forgive me for being facetious Edward. Enlighten me, please. What makes you think that this time it will be so different?"

Edward gave a lift of his shoulders. "Perhaps 'it will be different' is not quite the right way to put it. And, perhaps 'it may be different' would be more correct. But the circumstances will indeed be different this time." He agreed.

"Ah! Now we come to it!"

Edward grimaced, and took another sip of brandy. "The venture will be different, that is true. Of course I can give no guarantees of the outcome, but we will have two great advantages."

Richard was sceptical, and the expression on his face showed it clearly. "And they are?"

"Firstly, if you were to accept the assignment, you have far greater experience in the field. Both in combat and behind the lines." Edward paused.

"Secondly?"

"Secondly." Edward nodded knowingly. "Secondly, you will not be alone. You will have a Frenchman with you who has knowledge of the frontier, and of course the French. There was no stigma attached to his leaving the Colony and he has many connections in Quebec."

"A Frenchman! Edward we are all but at war with the French!" Richard nearly exploded. "And you will trust a Frenchman to lead an Englishman to spy on his compatriots. Come on Edward!" Richard shook his head in disbelief.

"This is no ordinary Frenchman." Edward declared.

"No. Of course not!" Richard laughed.

"No Richard. Hear me out." Edward looked into his empty brandy glass. "This particular Frenchman left his homeland many years ago. He says, now, that he believes his country is on the brink of a revolution, and he is emphatically against the way that he thinks France is heading, and he wants no part of it. He first went to the New World and traded with the Indians and the frontiersmen and then, when the skirmishes on the frontier increased he came to England. He is a genuine man Richard, and I believe him."

"So. Who is this remarkable Frenchman, Edward?"

"I am not at liberty to tell you at this moment in time. Listen to William Pitt and his companions. Ask them all your questions. We can only reveal the Frenchman's name to the person who undertakes the mission. You must understand that."

"Yes, of course Edward. Of course I understand." Richard stared at the log, as it flared brightly sending sparks flying up the chimney. "I'll listen, Edward. I owe you that much. But I promise no more than that."

The tension eased on Edward's face. "I can ask no more of you, than that Richard. I will put no more pressure on you, I give you my word. If you listen to what Pitt has to say, take note of his advisers, and then give due consideration, I can ask no more of you."

Richard took a deep breath. "Even if I say no?"

Edward nodded. "Even if you say no. I would be disappointed of course but no, I will accept your decision." Richard's slow smile gave away his doubts, but Edward chose to ignore it and relaxed back into his chair, pushed his feet nearer the fire and glanced at the empty glass in his hand. "Damn fine brandy, indeed, damn fine." He concluded.

Richard reached for the decanter and refilled their glasses before continuing the conversation. "When do you expect William Pitt and his entourage?"

Edward saluted Richard with his glass before answering. "I sent my coach to Plymouth three days hence; Pitt's advisors have been arriving there over the past week or so to avoid suspicion. A second coach has been sent to Boconnoc where I am supposed to be making a visit, Fanny and I have visited before so there will be no surprise at yet another visit. It will arrive in the evening with the shades drawn down and will depart with them in the same position. The coaches will meet up in Fraddon and the advisors will transfer to my main coach. Neither coach will make any rest stops that may arouse interest or speculation, only for a change of horses. They should arrive at Tremanyon tomorrow, in the coach that Fanny and I used in the spring. It shouldn't cause too much comment. The menservants and the luggage have come on ahead, and I have arranged their collection. They will arrive in a tradesman's coach tomorrow."

"You have given all this a great deal of thought Edward." Richard commended him

"If there should be speculation the consequences could be enormous. Pitt is watched night and day in London. Who he speaks to, who visits his house, who accompanies him at meetings or social gatherings. The only time he feels he is left alone is when he is visiting his family at Boconnoc. He very rarely leaves the estate during his stay, and entertainment is purely a family affair. If he had met you in London, then there would be no way of keeping it a secret, they have eyes everywhere. Then you would have been watched and, if indeed you did accept the challenge, assumptions could be made and the mission placed in jeopardy. Pitt has enemies, as you well know, but not only that, there are those who would hand over the colony to the French and leave our countrymen's fate in their hands." He scowled angrily. "Fate! All our information leads us to believe it will be their death."

Richard's curiosity had been aroused. "It is a hard country I hear."

Edward nodded, and smiled. "Yes, it is. But quite beautiful in its own way. Mountains and trees, so many trees, and so many rivers. A wild continent. The winters are cold and long, the summers hot. It is a hard life for the settlers, who hack a new life for themselves out of the wilderness."

"I thought that it was said that the New World was a land full of opportunity?"

"Opportunity for the rich yes, in Virginia where the land is good. But there is no opportunity for the poor to own their own land, so they have travelled northwards to the frontier and into Canada. There they cut timber, build their own log cabins, usually a single room only, and slowly clear the land to eke out a miserable living. They survive, just. But they are scattered over a wide area. There are virtually no communities, no towns, and no law. They live on what they can grow or shoot. They trap for food, and the fur they trade at the trading posts that are days and sometimes weeks away, leaving their families with little or no protection. At first the native Indians were no problem. They watched, were even a little curious, but the settlers did them no harm and, in point of fact, some even traded with the Indians. But in the last months we have received disturbing reports that war parties have been attacking the British Settlers."

Richard's eyes widened at this. "Only the British?"

Edward paused a moment and sipped at his brandy. "It does seem that way. Most of the British settlers are widely scattered. The French settlers, as yet, are few but they stay close to each other . . . But . . ."

Richard waited. "But . . !" He repeated, reminding Edward that he was waiting.

Edward did not continue immediately, choosing his words carefully "We believe that it is more than just an isolated incident. It seems that they are well orchestrated. They kill everyone, man, woman or child, young or old. However, a report reached Pitt last month. The last known massacre left a survivor." Richard said nothing. "The last settlers had received warning of an advancing war party, and had hidden their teenage daughter in an under-ground bunker a short way from the homestead. Thank God the child saw none of the atrocities; she was still in hiding when the nearest neighbours arrived. Luckily one of them knew of the hiding place, just big enough for one, and when they lifted the hatch she was still quaking with fright."

Richard looked puzzled. "So what was so different about this war party? There would have been no survivors if they had found her."

Edward nodded in agreement. "The girl said that she heard someone giving orders in French. And there was more than one, for she heard another acting as an interpreter, and others blaspheming at the Indians."

"How did she know it was French?"

Edward smiled. "How did I know that you were going to ask me that question? The answer to that is that one day her father had taken her to the Trading Post, and they were trapped there by a freak blizzard for a week. There was a French fur trapper and his son there also, and they struck up a friendship. The trapper spoke no English and the man and his daughter spoke no French, but the girl was bright and intelligent, she learned well. The following year the Frenchman and his son called at their homestead on his way to the trading post, and they renewed their acquaintance. Not all Frenchmen are bad, Richard. Neither are all Englishmen good, I hasten to add. Anyway, as a consequence she knew enough French to understand it when she heard it. She understood it enough to know that they knew that she was missing and that was why she didn't dare to come out of hiding, fearing that they may be waiting for her."

"Dear God!!" Richard exclaimed in horror. "What sort of mental state must the poor child be in after an event like that?" He didn't wait for an answer and continued. "Where is the girl now?"

"Boston." Edward replied "It would appear that there are no living relatives out there, or at home in England. She is being cared for by a good family until her future can be decided for her."

"It would appear that you are extremely well informed, Edward."

Edward nodded once more. "Perhaps! If you remember, I sailed to Boston with replacements for Fort Edward and Fort St. John. We stayed in Boston expecting to bring home an up to date account of the position of the French along the frontier.

"And . . ?" Richard encouraged him.

A frown creased Edwards's brow. "The Mohawk tracker, who had accompanied our man, returned to Fort Deerfield alone. But he carried with him the notes made by our man, who was killed by a stray marksman from a raiding party. Before he died he charged the Indian to return to Fort Deerfield with his incomplete notes."

Richard eyed Edward warily. "Was the tracker trustworthy?"

"Oh yes." Edward assured him. "I myself travelled to Fort Deerfield to interview him. The Mohawk are indeed our allies, unlike the Huron who are making war on the settlers, aided and abetted by the French."

Richard's scepticism returned. "What makes you so sure that it was not this Indian who killed him?"

Edward shrugged his shoulders. "I have to admit it is only intuition. As a race they show very little in their expressions and death, to them, is not to be mourned. But the Mohawk, by their very nature, in peace they are just, hospitable and generous. The Huron are their sworn enemy. He spoke of our man as his companion, as a man of great courage, who died an honourable death. He had travelled night and day to return with his book of notes, and the news of his companion's death. He was almost at the point of exhaustion himself."

Richard nodded thoughtfully. "I assume that you did not get the information that you required."

"I am afraid that we didn't." Edward agreed. "It is a hard country to traverse. It is necessary to combat not only the French and their allied Indian tribe, but it is necessary to combat a hostile climate in winter and rugged countryside both afforested and mountainous, with fast running rivers and waterfalls. To top it all there are bears, wolves and bison to be wary of."

Richard almost laughed. "You paint a very pretty picture, Edward. It would seem that you not only require a man with both knowledge and courage, but a small miracle as well."

Edward did manage a smile. "You may be right . . ." and was about to continue when there was a knock on the door.

"Come in." Richard called out, and Ginifur appeared in the doorway. "Yes Ginny?"

"I was about to lock up, Sir. Is there anything else that you require before I retire to my room?"

"Is it that time already? He glanced at the grandfather clock in the corner of the room. He had heard it chiming on the hour, but had not recalled the number of strokes. "No. We will require nothing more. Leave the front door Ginny, I will see to it." He smiled briefly. "Goodnight Ginifur."

"Goodnight Sir." Ginifur answered, and then dropped her eyes as she curtseyed to Edward Boscawen. "Goodnight to you also, my Lord Falmouth."

Edward smiled pleasantly as he bid her goodnight, and when the door had closed behind her turned to Richard. "You have indeed found a treasure there Richard, whether you are aware of it or not."

Richard did not reply, but gazed at the door briefly before leaving the room to lock the outer doors. When he returned he extinguished the candles, burning in the sconces upon the walls and together they made their way to the stairs where Edward turned to Richard. "You will think on what we have spoken of, Richard?"

"I will bear it in mind, Edward."

Edward placed a friendly hand upon his shoulder. "I am sure that whatever your decision, you will make the right one."

"And if I say no?"

Edward nodded his head. "If you say no, Richard, having listened to what Pitt and his advisors have to say, I will accept your decision and assure you that it will not affect our friendship."

Richard laughed. "If you say so, Edward. If you say so."

The Delegation

IT HAPPENED AS Edward Boscawen had predicted. The servants arrived around mid morning, and dusk had fallen for quite a while before horses and a carriage was heard approaching the house along the shingle drive.

Richard and Edward were waiting to greet the guests. The house was bright with candles burning in every room, and torches burning in their sconces by the front door. The dining hall was prepared, the table laid with the best silver and china, the centre of the table decorated with an arrangement of fresh fruit and flowers. Netty was tipped off by Ginifur, and made the last minute preparations for the banquet. Tom put extra logs beside the fireplace, and Kate and Pearl quickly took jugs of hot water to the bedrooms for the guests to freshen themselves after a long journey. Liam walked slowly round the dining table, repeating to himself Ginifur's instructions, and familiarising himself with the unfamiliar.

Ginifur, dressed impeccably in her emerald green dress with the starched white lawn collar and cuffs, her hair brushed until it shone and secured for the first time in a chignon, her only adornment the dainty silver watch and chain, stood quietly waiting at the foot of the stairs ready to direct the visitors to their rooms.

As the carriage drew to a halt at the foot of the steps, Richard himself leaped forward, with Edward immediately behind him. Richard opened the door and pulled down the steps. "Welcome to Cornwall and Tremanyon, Gentlemen."

A thin man dressed all in black, save for a white cravat at his neck and white silk stockings on his legs, alighted from the carriage. He wore a black tricorn hat, black fine wool jacket, black breeches, and black shoes trimmed with large silver buckles. He made a slight bow to both Richard and Edward before answering. "Thank you Captain Tremayne, thank you indeed." He gripped Richard's hand firmly before turning to Edward. "Edward. Good to see you. Come Gentlemen, get out and stretch your legs." He indicated for Richard to lead them up the wide steps to the hall and towards Ginifur, in her position at the bottom of the stairs. "There is hot water in your rooms, Gentlemen. Ginifur will show you the way, when you are refreshed we will meet in the drawing room for a drink before dinner." Richard indicated the door to his left.

William Pitt murmured his approval as he followed Ginifur up the broad staircase, whilst chatting to the shorter of his companions, rather foppishly dressed in a blue skirted jacket over an embroidered waistcoat and more frills at the neck and wrists than Ginifur imagined a fairy godmother might wear. To make up for his lack of height, he wore a tall white wig, and heeled shoes more suited to a female. In his hand he held a silver topped cane which he appeared to use for effect only. The other gentlemen were less brightly dressed, though fashionable.

When Ginifur had showed the guests to their rooms, she checked that Kate and Liam were ready to assist her with carrying the food to the table. Kate, wearing one of Ginifur's dresses finished off with a white starched apron and cap, was placing the warmed soup dishes in clean cloths whilst Netty was putting the final pastry decoration to the Oyster and Beef Pie, which would be the third course. Making a final visit to the dining room, she gave Liam a quick reassuring smile and happy that all was in order she returned to the drawing room. "Excuse me, Sir." The door was left wide open and Richard and Edward were standing with their backs to the fire.

"Yes Ginny." Richard smiled at her. "Is everything ready?"

"Oh yes, Sir." She assured him. "Netty has just made the final touches to the pie, the soup is almost at boiling point, and we will be ready to serve dinner whenever it suits you. Shall I get Liam to bring in the sherry?" The last consignment from Jean-Paul had contained a few bottles of 'Jerez fino' from Portugal.

Richard smiled as he nodded, pondering Edwards reaction to this fine wine. "Certainly, as soon as everyone is assembled we will come along to the dining room."

"Thank you, Sir." Ginifur left to organise Liam to carry the decanters and glasses to the drawing room, where he set them on a small table before returning to the kitchen to be ready to carry the soup tureen to the table when required.

Richard was pleased to see that Robert's spare clothes looked so well on Liam. Ginifur had assured him she had had to do very little in order to make them fit. Thanks to Ginifur's diligent instructions, and Liam's quick mind, Richard's guests would never know that they weren't made for him, let alone that forty eight hours ago he had not waited on the gentry. It had indeed been fortunate for him that Ginifur had such a warm heart and taken pity on the family.

When the guests had assembled, and enjoyed a glass of the fine wine, Richard led them to the new dining room.

"This is a fine room indeed." William Pitt complemented him. "In fact, it's a fine house altogether. Well proportioned. Spacious, without being overlarge, a nice family house."

Richard acknowledged the compliment. "Thank you, Sir. I am well pleased with it, although I have to admit that I had to add this wing because I had omitted to think of the children, and our original dining room was really too small for entertaining."

Liam arrived and placed the soup tureen on the serving table, before pulling Richard's chair out for him to be seated at the head of the table, then doing the same for Lord Falmouth who was to be seated on Richard's right. Ginifur directed William Pitt to the chair on Richard's left and, when they were all seated, she indicated that Liam and Kate should start to serve the soup. When they had withdrawn, Richard said grace before they tucked into the soup with relish.

"Excellent game soup, Richard!" Pit remarked. "Did you bring your cook with you from London?"

"Indeed he didn't." Edward spoke before Richard could tend and answer. "And a finer cook you won't find in the whole of London. I'll wager that you will all agree with me by the end of your visit. If Richard wasn't a friend, I swear I would find a way to tempt her to Tregothnan."

Richard laughed, good humouredly. "She wouldn't go without Tom."

Edward wasn't put off. "I'm sure I could find room for Tom too, if he could keep my kitchen gardens to the standard of yours."

William Pitt smiled at the repartee. "Well if this game soup is a sample of her culinary skills then we shall at least be able to agree that there has been some pleasure amidst the main aim of our visit to Cornwall." He turned to his host. "I have never been this far west, Richard, although I have to admit that it hasn't been for the lack of invitations. In truth Boconnoc is as far west as I have travelled until today. Edward is constantly beleaguering me to travel further into his Celtic nation. I swear that he believes that England stops at the Tamar."

"But of course it does." Enjoined Edward. "We are virtually an Island nation too. The Tamar is only yards short of dissecting the land from South to North after all."

Richard noticed that although William Pitt laughed loudly at this joke, his eyes didn't. There were those who thought the Cornish people were unruly, a law unto themselves. He indicated to Ginifur to instruct Liam and Kate to remove the plates and bring on the second course.

After the third course was served, as previously instructed, Ginifur retired from the room to enable the conversation to flow more easily.

Horace Percival had been studying Ginifur, as she confidently and expertly instructed the staff. "Your housekeeper is exceedingly young in years, is she not Richard? Not that I am faulting her at all, in fact she is to be commended for her attention to detail."

Richard gave the point some thought before answering. He also had thought that Ginifur was exceedingly young when they first came to Tremanyon, but now he never gave it a passing thought. "You are quite correct Horace; I believe Ginifur would be around twenty one years old. Annabelle never wanted a large household, she had great faith in Ginifur's abilities, and Ginifur never let her down. She has managed the house and staff almost since the very day we arrived here. The question of her age never occurs to me now."

"A trim little figure and a pretty head on those shoulders too." Remarked Claude Bunting.

"I don't think my wife would agree to employ a housekeeper as attractive as that in my house." Added Frederick Harmsworth.

Richard frowned, was it possible that he had taken Ginifur for granted. Twenty one years old! She was barely more than a child when they had come to Tremanyon. Now he thought of it, she had grown into a beautiful young woman. She induced a peaceful and calm influence within the house, had gained in quiet confidence, was always immaculate in her dress, and instructed the staff politely and firmly. In fact, never was a house more smoothly run. Twenty one! Yet her life revolved around Tremanyon. Her time off was spent either at Quay Cottage or Well Cottage. Did she have a young man? Richard wondered. He had once thought that she and young Adam were particularly fond of each other, yet he rarely saw them together nowadays.

"Richard!" Edward brought him out of his contemplation.

"I'm sorry." He apologised.

"We were discussing the information that we have received from our operative on the frontier." Edward prompted him.

"Spy." Corrected Richard, much to Edwards's irritation.

"I wouldn't call it that." Pitt disagreed, his expression showing his displeasure at the use of the ugly word.

Richard checked himself, before asking. "Wouldn't you? Then what would you call it?"

William Pitt needed no time for consideration. "A foreign agent." He explained.

"I see, there is a difference?" Richard found it increasingly difficult to keep the derision from his voice. "I'm sorry Edward." He added, as he noticed the concern on his face. "I meant no offence."

"No. I understand." Said William Pitt, who didn't, and wondered if Edward had been right in suggesting that Richard might consider the assignment.

"So, as you can see, our information is incomplete." Edward addressed the rest of the table. "It is essential that we send a new agent to cover the stretch of the St Lawrence River from Quebec to Hudson Bay and, I myself would like some up to date information on Louisburg. We believe that the next few months will prove that we should never have made a settlement with the French. Our Indian tracker is willing to undertake another expedition into the area, and has offered to act as a guide to our operative agent."

"Has anyone offered to undertake this operation?" Asked Percival.

"Colonel Webb has suggested a sergeant in his company, but we would rather bring in someone new. Preferably someone who has never been seen along the frontier. We have a Frenchman who has offered us his assistance but, as you know, the reason we are here is because Edward would like Richard to undertake the challenge." William Pitt looked straight at Richard as he spoke. "So where do you stand in this? I am assuming that Edward has broached to the subject to you?"

"He has." Agreed Richard. "But I would like you to explain the true necessity of such an undertaking. My children would be very much alone in the world, now that their mother has been taken from them. I would have to believe that such a venture was truly essential, before I made up my mind on something as important as this."

William Pitt held up his hand as everyone tried to speak at once. "Gentlemen, gentlemen! One at a time, please."

One by one Pitt and his companions expressed their own views, enlightening Richard on the present situation, indicating their individual reasons why the present government was lacking in it's response to the possibilities of all out war along the borders.

It was William Pitt who gave the final summary of events and added. "The New York Militia has officially offered to back us in an offence against the French. They fear an encroachment on the New York state if the French advance isn't brought to a halt."

A knock on the door brought a halt to the conversation, as Ginifur entered to ascertain whether they were ready to progress with the meal. Richard indicated that she might proceed, and Liam and Kate swiftly cleared the table of dirty dishes. Ginifur brushed up any spilt items of food into a silver scoop, rearranged the centre arrangement and then, standing at Richard's shoulder, watched as Liam and Kate brought in the syllabubs, made with Cornish Mead, together with a large ginger trifle, an apple pie, and a selection of sweetmeats. Ginifur explained the variety of deserts and then one by one she placed their choice in front of them, starting with William Pitt as Richard had requested. Conversation returned to a more general nature. A mixture of politics, religion and pleasure. They all agreed that the formation of the Gentlemen's Clubs in London, a great success where a man may consort with men, where he may deliberate without distraction or interference by the female form. Where he may talk of horses, hunting, riding, gaming and gambling, or deliberate on the King and his court, a subject only talked about in trusted company.

The deserts were followed by a selection of cheeses. Cornish Yarg, Somerset Cheddar and a French soft cheese that Richard said was from the Camembert region"

"The best thing, in fact the only thing, about the frogs is their Brandy and Cheese. How did you come about the cheese Richard?" Asked Claude Bunting.

"Our neighbour is a Frenchman, and a friend. How he obtains it I have never asked, quite legally I presume, but he sends it over to us on occasions, together with an excellent Brandy." Richard offered by way of an explanation, tongue in cheek, as he noticed Edward watching him answer what could have proved a difficult question.

"Excuse me, Sir." Ginifur appeared at Richard's shoulder. "Shall I serve the Port and Brandy in the drawing room?"

"Yes, Ginifur. Thank you." He shot her a brief smile of approval. "We have French coffee also gentlemen. The French coffee isn't to be sniffed at either, another gift from my neighbour." He winked at Edward.

When they were seated comfortably in the drawing room, with their Port and Brandy, conversation soon retuned to the New World and its problems. At times it was heated, at others agreeable, but by the time they retired for the night, Richard was inclined to agree that the undertaking appeared to prove necessary. However, whether he should be the person to undertake it, he was still to be persuaded.

Edward was the last, bar Richard, to leave the room. He settled himself comfortably in the deep chair opposite Richard. "Well my boy!" He finally broached the subject uppermost in their minds. "You are persuaded as to the benefit of such an operation?"

Richard thought about his reply before answering. "I concede that the circumstances lead me to believe so."

"And you?" Edward continued. "Will you not consider undertaking it yourself?"

"I shall sleep on it Edward. I'll say no more than that." He drained his glass, and then placed the guard around the fire. "I'll see you in the morning Edward."

Edward pressed the issue no further. "Goodnight Richard."

Richard gave a mirthless laugh. "I don't think that there is much chance of that, but goodnight Edward."

* * *

Indeed Richard had little sleep that night and the early hours of morning, before dawn broke, found him standing by the beds of his daughters, gazing down on their peaceful sleeping forms.

By mid afternoon of the next day Richard had made his decision. He gave William Pitt and his companions the answer that they had hoped for.

Edward slapped him on the back. "Well I can't disguise the fact that I am pleased at your decision. If anyone can do this, you can."

"Myself and the Frenchman don't forget. By the by, who is this mysterious collaborator?"

Edward frowned. "Collaborator is a bit strong, don't you think?" Richard shrugged his shoulders. "He is in fact a very principled man, as I previously mentioned to you. He is alarmed at the political situation in his country and abroad. By a strange turn of events he met and married an English Lady and I expect that you will be surprised to hear that you are, in fact, acquainted with them both." Richard's puzzled look made Edward laugh. "It is de Varron, Richard. Your neighbour at Rosvarron."

"de Varron?" Richard repeated. "Jean-Paul de Varron?"

"The very same." Edward continued to grin.

"Of course, I knew that he had spent some time in the New World. Come to think of it, it was he who said that he believed that there will be a great future to be found there, once it is opened up. It never became clear to me why he chose to come to England though." Richard frowned.

"Jean-Paul had built up a good business. A Trading Post serving the English, French and Indian communities. A vastly different lifestyle from that he was accustomed to, but he was relatively happy. In France he is in fact a The Comte de Varron of Brittany. The fact that his home in Cornwall is Rosvarron is purely coincidental. It is actually the family home of his wife Lady Catherine. He had made a great deal of friends amongst the English settlers, a regular visitor to their homes and welcomed by their families. Then the French put pressure on him. Expecting him to turn his back on his friends and involve himself by informing them of the happenings along the frontier. This he would not do, and therefore he had no alternative but to leave. He went to Boston, then to Virginia and back again, but found it hard to settle. I met him in Boston and took a liking to the fellow, Frog or no. When he said that he would like to go to England I offered him passage and a temporary home. It was there he met Lady Catherine of Rosvarron. Strange world isn't it?" Edward's eyes searched Richard's face for a clue as to his thoughts. "Strange also the similarity between his name and the house, almost as though it was meant to be." He added.

Richard contemplated his neighbour. "Yes. Although we don't socialise much when I am home, preferring to spend the time quietly, he has joined us with his wife for an occasional informal gathering and, of course, we see them regularly at Church. I gather he was of Roman Catholic religion, but decided to change when he married. Quite a hard decision I would think."

Pitt, who had been listening to the two sided conversation, quietly, now entered it. "So, Richard. How would you feel about de Varron as your partner in this adventure?"

"I would need to discuss it with him first, before passing a final opinion." Richard informed him.

"How do you feel about him joining us for dinner?" For the first time a semblance of a smile lit William Pitt's dark eyes as well as his mouth. "I happen to know that he is hoping to hear from us."

"Then . . ." Said Richard. "I shall send Adam over with an official invitation to Dinner." He reached for the bell pull. "You have certainly thought of everything gentlemen, and must have been very sure of my answer."

Ginifur opened the door. "You rang, Sir?"

"Yes Ginifur. Dinner will be served at six?" He asked.

"Of course, Sir. As you requested."

"Will you arrange for an additional place to be laid at the table, and ask Liam to get a message out to Adam. I would like Adam to ride to Rosvarron immediately to take a message to Monsieur de Varron. I shall be in the library."

"Yes, Sir. I shall send Liam to find Adam right away." Ginifur left the room.

"If you will excuse me gentlemen." Richard bowed his head briefly, before retiring to the library to write the invitation to Jean-Paul de Varron, leaving Edward, Pitt and the others in animated conversation. "Well!" He said aloud to himself, as he pushed his seal into the hot wax to seal the missive. "There's no going back now. I only hope that I have made the right decision."

* * *

Admiral Edward Boscawen was sailing from Falmouth, for Boston in the middle of September; it didn't leave a lot of time. Although it would mean that they would arrive in New England just before the onset of winter, it was decided that Richard and de Varron would sail with him. It would be well into the following year before another voyage could be arranged. Richard told Liam that he would like to take him with him, without divulging the reason for the journey, but giving him the freedom to decide. The Irish were viewed as invaluable allies to the French, as they had not deserted the Old Faith and still encompassed the one true religion, Catholicism. Liam's company should create no difficulties. Liam discussed it at great length with Kate who, knowing that he longed to go made it easy for him.

The pilchards failed to arrive at all. The two fishing boats at Quay faired little better, bringing in some cod, dog fish, mackerel and flat fish, but hardly enough to warrant the keeping on of the

143

crews. All hopes were pinned on the Herring shoals arriving in time.

There was hardship in the village. No pilchards meant no work in the cellars, no spare fish to salt for winter, no oil for the lamps. A failed harvest meant no gleaning in the fields. No grain meant there was no flour; no flour meant that there was no bread. This could have been born if the potato crop hadn't been decimated with blight.

Preparations

THERE WAS BARELY a week to go when Richard called for Ginifur to join him in the drawing room. "Please sit down Ginny." He asked politely. By now she was a little more comfortable when seated in his presence, and she sat a little further back on her seat, not perched on the edge as she had in the beginning. Her back was still ramrod straight, and her hands clasped firmly on her lap. "I have instructed Pascoe's Bank to arrange payment of any of the accounts that you send to them. You will, of course, continue to keep the household books as you have in the past, but you will have to add to this anything that is needed in the stables. Your father, Simon, will manage the boats. As long as the herrings arrive he should have no problems. Home farm is self sufficient, but I have asked Harry Polaughan to bring the books over for you to look at monthly. They have enough dredge corn for the animals for this winter." He shook his head sadly. "It really has been a dreadful year. I hope that you don't think that I am leaving you all in the lurch. It really is important that I go." Ginifur was shocked that he should talk to her on this level, almost as an equal. "Not only will you have responsibilities for the children, but for the whole estate too. There is no one else that I can trust to leave it with Ginny."

"If you feel that I am trustworthy enough, then I can only assure you that I will try not to fail you, Sir." Ginifur assured him, her voice almost failing her.

"Edward, Lord Falmouth, will come to see you on his return. You must always feel free to turn to him or Lady Falmouth for help or advice. They have both assured me that they will always be there for you. I am not doubting you, but he will glance at the books now and then to ensure that all is well for you all.

"Yes, Sir."

Richard took a step towards the window and looked into the garden. "Robert will manage the house, in Hampstead. Separate arrangements have been made for him." He paused, and Ginifur waited. "Anything that you need for the girls, you must get without question they do not seem to be worried unduly. Have they said anything to you?"

145

"No, Sir. They are treating it as though you are going back to London. I have explained to them that you will be away for a lot longer this time, and I have shown them where you are going on the globe."

Richard raised and eyebrow. "Have you indeed? And what was their reaction to that?"

Ginifur gave a little laugh. "They thought that it would be fun to be on a boat for a long journey."

"Yes, they would." He took the seat opposite her. "And you? How do you view this long absence of your employer?" Ginifur's heart skipped a beat. She would never be able to tell of her fears, for she had indeed heard snippets of conversation not intended for her ears. Supposing he was never to return! As if reading her mind he added. "Should anything happen to me, then the girls will be brought up by my family. Details are with my solicitor in Truro. The employees on the estate will be dealt with fairly."

Ginifur was horrified. "Oh, Captain Tremayne, please don't even mention it. Nothing must happen to you. Think of the girls." She wanted to plead with him to take every precaution, to tell him that the thought of a life without him in it was unbearable.

Richard gazed into her eyes. She did have such beautiful green eyes, he found himself thinking. "I shall think of them every day. I promise you. Now, do you have anything worrying you?"

"I don't think so, Sir." Ginifur answered bravely. "Except, perhaps, what my official position is here whilst you are away?"

"You will have complete control over the running of the house, staff and grounds. If there are any problems on the rest of the estate they have been told to contact you, and you will inform Mr. Pascoe or Mr. Franks. They will advise you, or make the decisions in my absence. If Lord Falmouth is at home, then you can contact him for advice. Lady Falmouth will visit you from time to time, don't be afraid to ask her for help." Ginifur stared up at him. "You can do it Ginny. I wouldn't ask it of you if I didn't think that you could."

"Thank you, Sir. I shall look after Rachel and Rebecca as if they were my own." She tried to assure him

"I know you will. You love them too much to allow any harm to come to them." Ginifur felt a tear prickling at the back of her eyes, and lowered them quickly. "We have a few more days yet. Come to me if you have any worries."

Ginifur rose from her chair. "I will, Sir. I will." Richard placed a hand on her waist as he guided her to the door. He had done it automatically, without thought or premeditation, and he found that he was suddenly aware of her tiny waist. He could feel her firm flesh beneath the linen dress, she wore no stays or corset, her figure was perfect and needed no artificial aid.

Ginifur could feel his strong hand guiding her, and her heart leapt at his touch.

* * *

The last few days flew by, with Rachel and Rebecca caught up in the excitement of packing. Ginny was placing the last of Richard's clothes into the open trunk when she turned to see Rebecca standing forlornly by the open door, her thumb stuck firmly in her mouth, and clutching the rag doll that Ginifur had made for her. "Hello Becky. Were you looking for me or for your father?" Becky didn't answer, so Ginifur rocked back on her heals and held out a hand. "Come here little one." Rebecca sidled up to her, until Ginny reached out and placed her hand about her waist to pull her the last few inches. "Are you worried about your father going away? Is that it?"

A tear spilled out of the tiny child's eyes, and trickled down a pale cheek. "Yes." She whispered.

"Your Papa, has been away before, Rebecca. It didn't worry you then." Ginifur tried to reassure her.

"That was before." Rebecca's eyes were fixed firmly on the trunk.

"Before?" Ginifur thought that she knew the cause of the problem. "You are worried that he won't come back, is that it?"

"Mama didn't. She went away and didn't even say goodbye." The tears began to fall and her tiny body was shaking.

Ginifur pulled her into her arms, stroking her hair and whispering comfortingly in her ear, until the sobs subsided. Then, gently, she sat Rebecca on the floor in front of her. "Becky, we have spoken about your Mama often. I thought that you understood that she didn't want to leave you. If she had thought, for one moment, that she was going to leave you, she would have seen you before she went."

"The baby took her away. She didn't have to go with him, we needed her too."

Ginifur wanted to hold her tightly in her arms, but she resisted the temptation. "The baby didn't take her Becky. Mama was always poorly, you must remember how often she was in bed. Not just for a few days, but weeks sometimes. Your dear mama had two babies before. Rachel and you. There was no reason to believe that it would be any different this time." She told the white lie. "It wasn't the baby, Becky. It was her heart. It could have happened any time, and she wouldn't have had time to say goodbye."

"Papa won't come back." Rebecca stated flatly.

"What on earth makes you say that?" Asked a horrified Ginifur.

Rebecca looked uncertain. "Mama didn't." She repeated angrily.

"Your Papa is very different. He is strong and healthy and he loves you dearly. He will always come back." Ginifur said more confidently that she felt.

"You won't go away, will you Ginny? You won't leave me too?" Rebecca's tears trickled down her cheeks once more

"Oh no, Becky!" This time Ginifur did gather her in her arms. "I won't leave you. I'll be with you always, or until you need me no longer." She added more realistically.

"I'll always need you." Rebecca was quite adamant. As her attention was drawn back to the trunk she added. "If I can't go with Papa, can Lilly go?" Lilly was the much loved rag doll.

"Now that is a good idea. She can watch over your Papa, and see that he comes back to us." Us! Ginifur realised immediately that she should have said 'You'. It was a slip of the tongue . . . or was it? She lifted the warm coat that she had packed into the trunk, and slipped the rag doll beneath it. "There! She will be nice and comfy there, and warm, for it will be very cold on the ship."

The Farewell

THE NIGHT BEFORE Richard was to depart; Ginifur had gone to bed leaving him in the Library with his second bottle of red wine and a fresh glass of brandy.

It was a bright moonlit night. The moon was nearly full, and the trees painted black skeleton shapes against the hazy blue of the sky. When Rebecca called out in her sleep, Ginifur didn't need a candle to light her way to the child's bedroom, for a ray of moonlight flooded through the landing window.

Rebecca hadn't woken, but she was tossing restlessly in her sleep and Ginifur woke, and was immediately aware that one of the children needed her. Making her way quickly to the child's room she knelt beside her bed stoking her hair and talking quietly and reassuringly to her until she settled back into a peaceful and hopefully dreamless sleep. Satisfied that Rebecca had finally settled Ginifur rose to her feet, straightened the coverlet and planted a tender kiss on the child's forehead before turning to make her way back to her bedroom. Startled, she stifled a cry of surprise as she saw Richard leaning against the frame of Rebecca's door. His hair was dishevelled and he wore only his breeches and his shirt, the neck undone. Ginifur was very aware of the flimsy nightdress beneath the light shawl that she had thrown about her shoulders as she had left her room, and her dainty feet were bare.

"The child is restless." Was it a question or a statement? Ginifur couldn't be sure, and she wondered how long he had been standing there.

"She sleeps soundly now, Sir." She assured him. "I was just going to return to my room." But Richard didn't move. She would have to squeeze past him if she was to leave Rebecca's room.

Richard gazed down at her perfectly oval face. The moonlight enhanced her flawless complexion, as it gently played across her face and shoulders. Her hair hung in one long, loose braid, tied with a green ribbon and hanging loosely over her shoulder. He studied her, as if seeing her for the very first time. He made no attempt to move, and Ginifur was transfixed. Her heart was beating fast as he slowly raised his hand to her breast and gently pulled at the loose end of the ribbon. Unfastening the bow, he released the braid and pushed the ribbon into his pocket before ruffling her hair and allowing it to fall freely over her shoulders, suiting her much more than the severe look created by it being continually pulled back away from her face. Richard was amazed at the vision before him. Ginifur's flawless complexion was completely natural, a simple beauty. He reached out to touch her face then ran his fingers down her neck and arms until they met with her long slender fingers where they twined together. Then he lifted her hands to his face. Long slender fingers with oval nails, the skin so soft and her nails polished till they shone.

Ginifur looked up at him and he gazed into her eyes for a long moment before taking her hand in his firm grasp. Richard stepped slowly backwards, away from his daughter's bedroom, and led Ginifur from the room along the corridor and across the landing. She followed him willingly as he opened the door to his own room. The wine was gentle on his breath, but he wasn't inebriated for he walked surely and confidently, and his speech was clear not slurred with drink.

Closing the door quietly behind them, and standing at the foot of the large bed, Richard touched her shoulder in wonder. Gently he pulled the shawl aside, revealing her perfect neck and shoulders. He could see the outline of her body beneath the thin nightgown. Slowly he slipped the shawl from her shoulders, dropping it carefully at her feet before running his hand across the soft petal like skin above her firm breasts, and then gently he eased the gown from her shoulders. Ginifur made no attempt to hold it as it fell in loose folds to the floor, leaving her standing naked before him. The sight of her slender body took Richard's breath away. Perfectly formed breasts rose above a slender waist and softly rounded hips. This time his fingers traced her outline, running them through the valley of her breasts and across her flat belly. He paused as she shivered and took a sharp intake of breath, and he gazed into her green eyes, bright and shining, framed by thick dark lashes. Ginifur felt that she was drowning in his gaze. "You have nothing to fear." He whispered

Ginifur found her voice. "I am not afraid." She assured him. Her voice was rich and warm, like honey. It was as though he had never heard it before, and it stirred a feeling deep within his own breast.

One strong arm slipped around her waist as the other lifted her beneath her knees, and carefully he placed her upon the crisp linen sheet of his bed before kissing her tenderly on her lips, not as he would kiss her later with passion. It was the first true kiss of Ginifur's life. She lifted her green eyes to his blue ones and smiled, lost in her love for him. Ginifur's only thought to give him whatever comfort she could offer.

Slowly Richard removed his shirt, without taking his eyes from her beautiful body and, before he removed his breeches, he lay beside her letting his hand rove unhurriedly over her body, feeling the shivers of anticipation as Ginifur's instincts reacted to his experienced hand. Then, without her knowing it, Richard had removed his breeches, and was suddenly lying naked beside her. Ginifur marvelled at the feeling of the touch of his body against her skin and, as his hands increasingly explored her body, she was lifted higher and higher to feelings of unimagined intensity until it felt as though her body was about to explode in delight. Richard too was lost as he explored every intimate part of her. Cupping a firm breast in his hands, he took a small rosy nipple between his lips and caressing it with his tongue he felt her body shiver once more with anticipation. Time and time again he brought her to the point when she felt she must surely burst with love for him. Then, each time, he gently brought her senses back to her. Lying beside her stroking her hair and kissing her lips, face, and neck whilst whispering endearing words into her ears, before embarking once more on his journey of discovery. Finally, running his tongue between her breasts, lingering briefly around her navel Richard continued his travels downwards. Somewhere at the back of her mind, Ginifur wondered at the fact that she could not, and would not pull herself away from this extraordinary experience, feeling that it was the most natural occurrence for her to partake in everything that this man wished to do with her body. But now she could bear it no longer. Ginifur's body arched and rose up towards him, a small cry escaping her lips encouraging him to complete their union and her hands reached out to grip his shoulders. Richard raised his head to look up at her face, filled with love and longing for him. Gently he eased his body upwards until he could once more gaze into her clear green eyes. Guiding himself deftly to the place he most wanted to be, he slid home into the slippery warmth of her body, slowly, carefully, in order not to hurt her as he knew he inevitably would. But Ginifur clung to him, pulling him deeper and deeper within her until she uttered a small cry and hesitated before drawing him further and further, until they both exploded in sheer delight as they reached fulfilment together.

Ginifur felt the explosion within her, transported through a place where the stars shone brightly and she was filled with a feeling of completeness. She gave no thought to herself, or of the consequences that may occur, and not knowing what may be expected of her after this night of wonder. All Ginifur knew was, that at this very moment she finally acknowledged that she was in love with this man who lay beside her. In love with Richard Tremayne . . . her master.

Richard? Richard was too captivated by this young woman he continued to caress, to give any thought to anything at all, only knowing that he needed this woman who lay beside him with a yearning he had never felt before. He enfolded her within his arms, her head resting in the hollow that seemed especially made for her, and as the moon made its way across the sky to make way for the dawn they made love once more before finally falling asleep in each others arms.

Later, as the sun clutched at the very edge of the sea beyond Dingerien Head, Ginifur awoke to find herself still cradled within Richard's arms. He lay with his head supported on the large linen covered pillow, and the covers had slipped down revealing his shoulders and chest. Ginifur had never seen a grown man naked before. Throughout the summer Richard had worked for long hours in the fields without his shirt, his firmly muscled torso was tanned, dark curls of hair licked at his chest as she gazed at his sleeping body. In sleep he was peaceful, and with a happiness upon his face that they hadn't seen for many a month. Ginifur lifted her hand to brush light strokes across his chest, and downwards until her hand rested gently on his firm belly. He gave a low groan of pleasure and his lips parted in a deep sigh. Ginifur held her breath. Was it a sigh? Or was it Annabelle's name that he whispered in his dreams? It seemed as though a dark cloud had passed across her eyes and with it, it dawned on her of the uncompromising position she had put herself in. Carefully she extracted herself from his arms and, mindful not to wake him, she slipped out of the high bed to stand for a moment to take one last look at him lying there. Then gathering up her clothes she fled for her room, before she was found to be missing.

Richard awoke, and automatically his arm reached out, seeking the comfort of a warm body on the other side of the bed. His eyes flashed open as he realised that he was stark naked. He hadn't slept like that since Annabelle had died. He was surprised that the thought of his dead wife hadn't produced the usual gut wrenching pain. He lay on his back and examined his feelings. He still missed her very much, his sadness was real but the pain had diminished. Sitting up in the bed he stared down at the dent in the pillow next to him, the tell tale creasing of the sheets. A frown settled on his forehead, it hadn't been a dream for there, in the middle of the bed, was the tell tale sign of the events of the night before, a dark red stain, and he winced at the feeling of guilt that assaulted him. He could still smell the fragrance of her fresh skin, unadulterated with perfume. He could still feel the silkiness of her hair as it brushed against his face and chest, and the flicker of desire ran once more through his body. Placing his feet on the floor, feeling the thick pile of the Chinese rug beneath his feet, he glanced down at the floor and his eyes were drawn to a bright splash of emerald amongst the reds and blues of the woven colours. Slowly he bent to retrieve a length of silken ribbon. Through the open windows he heard the carriage draw up below his bedroom. Twisting the ribbon thoughtfully between his fingers he walked towards the window. He didn't cover his body as he watched Sam and Adam secure the trunks to the rear of the carriage. Placing the ribbon on the dressing table he reached for his silk gown and made his way towards the bathing room, where he took time over his ablutions. Returning to his bedroom, his eyes were continually drawn to the length of green ribbon lying in front of him. Finally, he picked it up and fingered it briefly before placing it safely in his pocket.

The aroma of frying ham and eggs drifted to greet him as he made his way towards the dining room. Netty herself was laying the dishes on the serving table as he entered the room. "My goodness Netty!" He nudged her playfully with his arm. "That looks like a feast for a dying man, let alone for one who is going to go without your cooking for the next few months or so."

"Get away with 'e Captain." Netty blushed, but he noticed a tear forming in the corner of her eye.

"You make sure that all my girls get fed properly while I am away."

"Oh Cap'n!" Netty fled from the room with her pinny tightly held to her face to hide the tears that flowed.

Richard looked down at his plate. He had been quite hungry when he first came down. Now he wasn't so sure. Nevertheless, for fear of offending Netty, he carefully selected some ham and eggs and took them to the table. Through the tall windows he watched as Liam and Kate, with their young ones, made their way round to the front of the house. He realised that he hadn't seen Ginifur and the children this morning, and found that he was disappointed. He had been hoping that she would be in the dining room when he entered. Perhaps she and the girls had eaten in the nursery and they would be waiting for him to finish to say there goodbyes. He smiled to himself, as his heart beat loudly in his breast.

But it was Kate who was waiting in the hall, with Rachel fidgeting on one side and Rebecca hanging tearfully to her hand on the other side. Richard glanced enquiringly up the stairs. "Where is Ginifur?"

Kate hesitated, uncertain how Captain Tremayne was going to take her answer. "Ginifur left early this morning, Sir. It's her day off. She always goes down to her father on her day off." She explained. "She asked me to . . . tender . . . her . . . apologies . . ." Kate stumbled over the words that she had been instructed to say, and had tried hard to memorise "If she was unable to return before your, departure, she said I was to say that she wished ye God speed, Sir, and she will pray for your safe return to your children and . . ." She grasped for the rest of her words. Richard waited. The unfamiliar cheerfulness that he had woken with, diminishing fast. "She wished to . . . re . . . it . . . er . . . ate her assurance that she will love and care for Rachel and Rebecca as if they was her own." Kate had finished her duty to Ginifur, but added. "Ye must not fear for the girls, Sir. Ginny would never fail them."

Richard placed a hand upon each of the girls' heads, ruffling Rebecca's curls. "Liam!" He called out through the open door.

Liam bounded up the steps. "Sir!"

"Run to the corner of the walled garden. See if you can see Ginifur coming up the track through the woods."

Liam set of to do as he was bidden, hoping that Ginifur would have had a change of heart, yet knowing deep inside that she wouldn't. What on earth could have happened? Ginifur had arrived at the cottage at dawn, with instructions for Kate. They had asked no questions, there was no point. If Ginifur wished Kate to know the reasons she would tell her in her own time. Liam stayed a moment, studying the bend in the track at the beginning of the wood, but he knew in his heart that he wouldn't see her, he wasn't surprised. "I expect she took longer than she had thought." He offered the feeble explanation. "And we are leaving earlier than we had planned." He added lamely.

Richard nodded briefly, reaching into his pocket to finger the length of green ribbon. Once more he glanced expectantly at the corner of the house. Knowingly Rebecca took his hand. "Ginny will be back Papa. She promised. Ginifur always keeps her promises."

"Yes, kitten. She does." He picked her up, holding her tightly in his arms.

"Papa! You're hurting me." She protested.

He laughed ruefully. "Yes, I'm sorry. It's just that I love you so very much, you and Rachel. Don't ever forget that."

Rebecca's lips quivered. "You're not going away for ever and ever, are you Papa? Ginifur promised that you would come back. You are going to come back aren't you?"

Richard forced a carefree smile to his face. "Of course I am coming home. If Ginifur has promised it, then it must be so."

He kissed her forehead before placing her once more on the ground beside Kate and, bending, he planted a kiss on Rachel's cheek. "Be good for Ginifur, and Kate, and Netty. And make sure that you look after them as well as they will look after you." He glanced again at the corner of the house. "Ready Liam?"

Liam took Kate briefly in his arms, they had said their real goodbye before they left the cottage. He kissed each of the children before wordlessly studying Kate. She smiled a sad smile, but held back the tears bravely. Then he turned to open the carriage door and pull down the step.

Netty stood at the top of the steps with Tom, wringing her apron in her hands. "May God go with ye Captain."

"Amen to that." Added Tom

"Thank you Netty. Tom." He put a hand on Adam's shoulder. "Take care of the horses, Adam."

"I will, Sir."

"Tom!" Tom had a comforting arm about Netty's shoulders. "Keep talking to those bees, and watch over the girls." His gaze encompassed Kate, Netty and the children. They all knew that he included Ginifur in this request. Tom nodded, unable to answer.

"Samuel!"

Sam glanced down from his position above them, reins in his hands. "We'm all ready, Sir."

Richard gave one final glance over his shoulder. "Come on the Liam, let us away." He turned to Kate. "Tell Ginny . . ." Tell

Ginny what? "Tell Ginny, I understand, and I leave in the knowledge that Tremanyon and the family will be safe in her hands until I return. You all know my wishes?" They nodded in unison. Ginifur's word was to be final, in all matters relating to the manor. Lord and Lady Falmouth would visit regularly and, if in doubt, Ginifur would look to them for advice. "Then I bid you all farewell. We will return. I know not when, but we will return sometime. Soon I hope. But return we will." He smiled. "Ginifur says that it will be so." He leapt up the steps and with one final wave to his children the carriage moved forward and was soon hidden by the bend in the drive

* * *

Ginifur arrived at Quay Cottage even before Simon was awake. He found her sitting on the quay wall, staring down at the water lapping below her feet. She wore a cotton shirt tucked into a simple woollen skirt, and a tweed shawl about her shoulders. She hadn't worn anything so simple since she had started work up at the Big House. Simon realised, of course, that they had been her mother's, and they now fitted her perfectly. But he did wonder where she had been keeping them all this time.

Simon had first seen Ginifur from the window, above the cellar and he watched a while to see if she was waiting until she saw movement in the cottage. But she didn't turn round; she didn't glance up at the cottage once. Her shoulders were hunched forlornly, her head hung low, and there was a sadness about her that he couldn't define.

After a while of watching and waiting, Simon opened the unlocked door and made his way down the grassy slope. Their own small boat, Sandpiper, was lying at her mooring. He realised now that, although her head hung low, she was in fact studying the boat. Ginifur was a competent sailor; she was almost born on water. It was a natural element for her. She swam like Kiara, the mermaid that was believed to live in the bay. She could sail close to the wind, and navigate the most dangerous channel along the south coast.

"Mornin' Ginny." Simon sat down casually beside her. "You're about early." She glanced up but didn't answer. "Is somethin' amiss, child?"

Ginifur shook her head, but it was an answer in itself. He could read her like a book. "Can I take Sandpiper out into the Roads? I would like to go fishing." She asked.

156

He hid the surprise from his voice. "Doesn't Captain Tremayne leave this mornin'?"

"Yes." She answered flatly. "Kate is looking after the children till I get back."

Simon knew better than to press her on the subject, but asked. "Will you be out all day?"

"Maybe . . . I don't know."

Simon waited a few more moments, in quiet thought, before going to the short flight of steps at the side of the quay. He vanished for a moment before reappearing with a rope in his hand, to which was attached a small dinghy. Slowly he guided the dinghy along the wall to the larger set of steps, where it lay a few feet below the lowest step. "I'll row ye out, shall I?"

"Thank you Da." In those three words she had said so much more. Icy fingers clutched at Simon's heart as he felt the sadness within her.

Clutching the shawl about her shoulders, Ginifur sat on the bottom step and confidently stepped into the centre of the dinghy. Her balance was so perfect that the boat hardly rocked or swayed. She sat down in the stern as Simon joined her, watching as he methodically slipped the rowlocks in place, pushed them away from the wall, and then placed the oars in the rowlocks. With a few swift strokes the little dinghy had reached the sailing boat. Simon grasped the side of Sandpiper and watched for Ginifur to make her move. The tide was coming in, but the north easterly wind would make it easy for her to leave the river.

Ginifur's eyes met his loving gaze. "I should be back by mid afternoon, Da." She informed him "Please do not worry. I just need to be alone for a while."

Simon nodded. He wished he knew what was the matter, something was very wrong. He could not believe that she would absent herself from the house, on this day of all days. On the very day that Captain Tremayne was leaving for what appeared to be a long absence, and to a land far away. He raised a smile, as she glanced back at him from Sandpiper. She would tell him when she was ready, she always did. He pushed the dinghy away, lifted his hand in farewell, and rowed slowly back to the quay, the flowing tide doing the job for him. Once more on the quay, he watched as Ginifur made ready, but not waiting to see her leave. She wouldn't want that.

Ginifur crossed the shawl over her breasts, and tied it securely behind her back. She checked the tiller and rudder . . . it was in place. Expertly she loosened the sheets and unfurled the sail. She raised the fore sail, and secured the sheet in the clamp before making ready the mainsail and untying the mooring rope from the anchored buoy. Taking her place at the tiller, she swiftly pulled the mainsail up the mast and Sandpiper slid away from the mooring and headed out of the river.

It was, in fact, a beautiful day, with a good light breeze. Ideal for sailing, and fishing. Ginifur spent the morning sailing up and down Falmouth Bay with the long line trailing behind her. As her haul increased, and the pile of fish grew steadily at her feet, the miserable feeling in the pit of her stomach receded. She began to feel more like her usual self, and she laughed aloud at the antics of two Cormorants as they dived in and out of the water. She didn't feel the least bit lonely. Seagulls wheeled overhead, calling out to her, and Shag followed the shoal of fish guiding her into their midst. She glanced about her. No sign of any other boats. Why, oh why were they not out here to benefit from this massive shoal? She thought about heading for home, but by the time she could raise the men, the fish would be way past the Lizard. A cry escaped her lips. She had committed the sin of not concentrating as she removed the fish, one by one, from the long line and she had caught her finger on the barb of a hook. Luckily the barb had only gone in a short way and, having carefully removed it, she sucked her finger as she gazed up to the top of the mast. It must be nearly noon, she thought. So engrossed she had been in her fishing, that for the time she had completely forgotten why she was out there. She turned her attention to Pendennis Castle. Beyond the castle Richard and Liam were probably already aboard the frigate, making ready to sail on the high tide.

Ginifur's attention was now fully focussed on hauling in the fish, her nimble fingers quickly clearing them from the line. What a catch there was! Plenty for everyone on the estate, a few for Netty to salt or for Tom to smoke, and some left over for the folks in the village. She set sail for the headland on the other side of the estuary and, just as she made it to the point where she could see right up the river to Penryn, she saw the frigate, in full sail, steadily nudging it's way out of harbour.

Within a short space of time she had the boat in position, just below the cliff on the other side of the river. Quickly she pushed over the tiller, bringing the little boat quickly about and, dropping the mainsail, she loosened the foresail to flap in the wind. Ginifur threw out the anchor, although Sandpiper held steady in the sheltered spot. The tide was at the point where it was doing neither one thing nor the other. It neither washed her towards the shore, nor pushed her towards the horizon.

With her heart in her mouth, Ginifur watched the ship edging closer; until it was so near that she felt that she could almost touch it. It was so big! Ginifur had never been this close to a large boat before, let alone a ship of His Majesty's Navy. As it sailed slowly by she caught sight of the name on her bows, The White Rose, and she heard an appreciative whistle from the rigging which brought a figure to the rail at the back of the aft deck.

The sight of this figure brought her swiftly to her feet, it was Liam.

* * *

Richard and Liam stopped at Rosvarron to pick up Jean-Paul but, even with this detour the carriage arrived at the docks with plenty of time to spare where Richard supervised the unloading of the trunks, leaving Liam to see them safely aboard. He gave his last orders to Samuel, bidding him farewell and watching until the carriage was out of view before climbing the gang plank to board the ship.

Edward Boscawen had given orders that Richard and Liam were to have the Captains own quarters, Jean-Paul in the smaller cabin allotted to one of the Officers. All three had tried to assure him that they were happy to sling a hammock somewhere aboard ship, but none of the officers would hear of it. Edward Boscawen kept his own quarters, of course, and the Captain moved his belongings into the next cabin.

Spying Liam amidships, watching the comings and goings of the crew, Richard beckoned him to follow him to the poop deck. High in the aft they watched as Edward's Captain directed the preparations for sea, last minute loading of fresh foodstuffs in the main, for most of the loading had been done the day before. As the last consignment came aboard the gangway was drawn back on to the harbour. Harbour men stood by the capstans to release the mooring ropes, The Captain took his place beside the helmsman and Edward stood a little way to his rear watching operations with

Richard and Liam beside him. "Let loose aft" Instructed Captain Trethewey, echoed immediately by the louder voice of the first officer, and the shrill sound of a whistle sent the crew scurrying up the rigging like a pack of monkeys. Sure footed, they scampered bare foot along the spars, taking up their positions in readiness to let loose the sails. It was the largest vessel that Liam had ever been on, and he was totally absorbed by all that he saw.

"All set, Sir." The Boson informed Captain Trethewey, who was standing beside the helmsman at the wheel and glanced at his Admiral for his acknowledgement that he had heard.

Admiral Boscawen surveyed to scene below him, casting his eyes aloft and running his eyes over the crew. "Let us get under weigh then, Captain Trethewey. Set sail."

With the precision of a crew well rehearsed, the aft ropes were released and the White Rose edged away from the dock. The six boats that towed them away from the dockside, released the lines when they were in mid river and Richard and Liam watched as the sails unfurled, slapped and filled, taking them across the river to Flushing before heading out into the Carrick Roads. With his feet squarely planted on the deck, Richard adjusted to the movement of the ship and, slipping his hand inside the pocket of his jacket, he felt the length of silk ribbon brush his fingers.

As the frigate slipped slowly past Pendennis Castle, a sailor let out an appreciative whistle and all eyes followed the direction he indicated.

Liam took the few short strides to the railing of the aft deck. He stared down at the tiny boat bobbing up and down in the water, and at the tiny figure within it. Suddenly the figure leapt to her feet, the boat rocking dangerously for a moment. "It's Ginny! Captain Tremayne. It's Ginifur. She's come all the way out 'ere to see us off." He waved frantically at the slight figure standing up in the boat.

Richard was taken aback by the extent of the pleasure that engulfed him. He hadn't realised, or cared to admit, the disappointment that he had felt when he found that Ginifur was not at home to see him depart. He stepped swiftly to the aft rail. Sandpiper was now astern, but he could see Ginifur's face clearly as she braced herself against the motion of the boat, rocking in the wash of such a large vessel.

Briefly Ginifur stopped waving as she stared up at Richard. What was he thinking?

Richard reached into his pocket and, on instinct, withdrew the length of ribbon. In an impulsive gesture he raised it up at arms length. "Goodbye Ginny." His voice flew away on the wind, but he could still see the uncertainty in the expression on her face. What had he done? Would she ever forgive him?

Ginifur caught a brief glimpse of a flash of emerald green that fluttered in Richards's hand. A tear fell unhindered down Ginifur's cheek. Why should she worry, there was no one about to see or hear her. "God speed my love." She called out, "May the good Lord watch over you and Liam, and the Frenchman. May he bring you all safely home to Cornwall." Ginifur watched until she could no longer see the figures on board. Then she brushed any remaining tears away, and concentrated on hoisting the square sail for her homeward tack.

On the aft deck of the White Rose a lone figure watched from his vantage point, as the little sail was hauled up, and he waited until the tiny craft vanished into the mouth of the river between the castle and the headland.

The noise of the wind in the sails and the rigging stopped anyone from hearing him as he glanced up to the sky above. "Dear God, take care of her and my daughters. They are dearer to me this day than my own life." For the first time he acknowledged that Ginifur had reached into his heart and found a corner of her own. He tried to examine his feelings, and failed. How large a space she now commandeered he could not, or would not, admit to. He glanced at the ribbon in his hand and frowned. He stayed there for some time, staring at the receding coastline.

Chapter Five
1753 - *The White Rose*

LIAM STUDIED HIS master's face, as he stared at the spit of land that was their home before they slipped behind the Lizard Point, and then left him to his thoughts.

It was sometime later when Richard found Liam on the floor of the cabin unpacking their clothes. Liam looked up as he entered the low doorway. "I'll soon have it stowed away, Sir. Then I'll stash the trunk in the hold." Richard glanced around the cabin, it would do them fine. There were two bunks, a writing table and storage space for clothes. In the corner was a folding table that would convert into a wash stand. Richard was impressed. Edward really was trying to put into practice what he preached. "Well! Would you believe it?" Liam exclaimed. "How did you get here?" He turned round to face Richard. "Look Cap'n. We have a stowaway." He held aloft Rebecca's rag doll. Richard recognised it immediately. He well remembered the day that he had caught Ginifur unawares, as she stitched away at the shapeless head of the doll, forming a pert nose and a pretty rosebud mouth before embroidering china blue eyes in silk thread.

Richard reached out, and took the doll from Liam's grasp. Carefully he removed the length of ribbon from his pocket and tied it about the dolls neck. "I am not usually given to superstition Liam, but wherever we go this baby and ribbon go with us. I charge you to ensure that neither of them is lost. They are the first thing you will pack wherever we may go. If anything has to be left behind, it is never to be this doll and ribbon. You understand." He glanced at Liam, defying him to mock him.

But how could Liam possibly mock him. If Captain Tremayne felt that this was in some way a form of lucky charm, far be it for him to comment. Didn't Liam himself have a stone from the river in Kilkenny about his neck? Liam's mother had found the stone with a hole in it, polished from it's tumbling in the river, and had threaded it on to a long leather thong when he had first gone to sea. Kate had fished it out of the box at the back of the cottage this very morning.

Liam took back the proffered doll and placed it upon the shelf, he would take as much care of the doll as he did the stone. When he turned, Richard had left the cabin, and Liam continued to unpack the trunk, but all the time his eyes kept returning to the length of emerald green ribbon. Didn't Ginifur wear a ribbon of that very same shade of emerald green?

By the time Liam returned to the deck they had travelled quite a distance. As the tide had turned the wind had increased, filling the sails and straining the canvas. Ahead of them he could already see St. Michael's Mount, beyond that was Penzance and Mousehole. It was at Mousehole that he had left his family to return to Ireland without him. The White Rose would be round Lands End and heading out into the Atlantic by nightfall. Liam wondered if he would catch a glimpse of his homeland on this journey and, for the first time since he had been at Tremanyon, felt the pangs of homesickness reaching into the pit of his stomach. Oh how he would love to take his wife and children to meet the family.

"Missing Kate already, Liam?" Richard appeared at his shoulder. "The first time you have been apart?" Liam nodded in answer to both the first and second part of the question. Richard continued. "The first time is the hardest. Hopefully, for you, there won't be a second." He glanced around the decks. "Have you seen Jean-Paul?"

"Yes, Sir. It's in the Admiral's cabin he is. Studyin' the maps that he brought with him. Lord Falmouth said, if ye had a moment to spare Sir, perhaps ye'd care to join them."

Richard nodded thoughtfully. "I might just do that" He drew himself to his full height and took a deep breath of salty air. "Are you alright lad? There's still time to change your mind. We meet up with the rest of the fleet in Mounts Bay and can send you in to Penzance by longboat if you wish, but that will be your last chance."

Liam shook his head fiercely. "Oh no, Sir! It's not changing my mind I am, there be no fear o' that. Ye can't imagine how good it feels to be back on the sea again.

Richard pulled a rueful expression. "No, I don't expect I can. I like the sea, it's true, but I prefer to be on land. Preferably my own land at Tremanyon. What on earth made me entertain this escapade? I must have been truly out of my mind." He glanced at the straining sails. "But she's fine ship, I'll give Edward that, and at this speed we will be in the New World in record time."

They were indeed making good time. The following morning they woke to be welcomed by a clear blue sky and a fair wind. To

Liam's delight, on the horizon could be seen the feint outline of Ireland.

"Ireland, Liam." Richard breathed in the pure clean air as he came up on deck.

"Yes, Sir. Tis Dungarven Bay, I'm thinking. That's where my uncles' boats sail from." He searched the sea around them in the vain hope that he might catch sight of a boat from his homeland.

"Hm . . ." Richard thought for a moment. "Liam. I think it would be a good time for you to get used to calling me by my name, instead of Sir or Captain."

Liam looked horrified. "But Captain Tremayne!"

"There are no buts about it, Liam. The success of this mission depends on us not being discovered. And if you keep calling me Sir that will certainly give the game away. The next few weeks we have on board will give you good time to get used to calling me by name."

"But . . ." Liam screwed up his face as Richard frowned. "But what name shall I be callin' ye?"

Richard laughed. "How do you feel about calling me Richard? It is my name after all!"

Liam smiled while he pondered the question. "Back home, I have a cousin called Dickon. T'would be a form of Richard I'm thinkin'."

Richard grinned. "Dickon! Dickon! I like that." Then he screwed up his face in a thoughtful expression and added. "In fact, I like the sound of it very much. It has given me an idea" He rubbed his top lip as he mulled it over in his mind. "I was never very happy with the idea of passing myself off as a Frenchie. But a sympathetic Irishman sounds quite plausible. As your older brother, I could well have been sent to serve in the English Army from an early age. In fact we had some young lads from Ireland in my own regiment. Hence the difference in our accents. Yes, I like that idea. Well done Liam." Liam looked puzzled, wondering how he figured in the decision but said nothing. "Now." Richard continued. "Are you sure you still want to go on with this adventure?" He glanced out at the coast, seeing quite clearly the entrance to the harbour. "I could throw you overboard and let you swim to Ireland."

"Oh no, Sir." Liam hesitated as Richard scowled. "No . . . Dickon. T' be sure I am wantin' to see this New World everyone is talking about."

Richard smiled. "So near yet so far, eh?" He laid a hand on Liam's shoulder and could feel the tension, sense the yearning for home, for he had felt this himself when away from Cornwall. "I'll tell you what Liam; I hear they have fine horses in Ireland."

"Indeed they do S . . . Dickon. The finest horses ye have ever seen." Liam agreed.

"If we return from this venture, I promise you that I will make sure that you see your home and family once more. We'll take a trip and see those fine horses of yours."

"If?" Liam searched Richard Tremayne's face for an honest answer.

"God willing, Liam. I never promised that it would be an easy venture."

"No, C . . . No you didn't." Liam's eyes were drawn back to the figure of Jean-Paul as he emerged form below. "I can't make him out Sir . . . Dickon. To be sure, I can't." Then with a shrill whistle, and a command from the Captain, the ship changed course and put Ireland to her stern. The fresh easterly wind filled and stretched the canvas, the timbers creaked, and the White Rose ploughed steadily through the Atlantic swell.

"With a good following wind, such as this, we shall make good time. But I expect the snows will have spread down the coast ere we land." Jean- Paul joined them.

"Do they really come as early as this?" Questioned Liam.

Jean-Paul nodded. "Yes. Sometimes even in early October, yet it can come later. But it always comes, believe me." He smiled at Liam. "Yes, it always comes, and it is colder than anything you have ever known. Cold enough to freeze a man into a block of ice."

Liam shivered.

"Don't frighten the lad." Richard had heard the exchange.

"I don't mean to frighten him. Just make sure he knows what will be awaiting him at the end of this voyage. It's a harsh climate in winter, mon ami. Harsher than anything you can imagine." He stared up at the sky, his face set in a grim expression, and Richard wondered why he had agreed to accompany them.

* * *

It was an uneventful crossing. The winds did remain favourable, and the weather unusually fine for the time of the year.

The sun was just slipping beyond the horizon when the call "Land to Starboard" brought Richard, Liam and Jean-Paul to the side of the ship and there, just visible in the fading light, they could discern the thin purple line that foretold the end of their six week voyage. It was indeed a record breaking trip, when this journey was rarely accomplished in under eight weeks.

"With luck we shall be in sight of harbour by dawn." Jean-Paul read their thoughts, as they watched as the light faded, and the first land that they had seen since leaving the coast of Ireland vanished once more.

Long before dawn Richard retuned to the deck, to watch the stars dim as pale fingers of light edged over the deep purple mountains in the far distance, lightening the sky to shades of lilac and yellow before clearing to a pale watery blue and bathing the land in misty shades. As the sun edged its way above the distant mountains they became a dark and mysterious back drop against a cloudless sky of bright blue. The sun dazzled him, and Richard shielded his eyes to study the nearing land, wondering what the future held in store for them as he turned the collar of his jacket up against the chill of the morning. The weather had indeed been growing increasingly colder throughout their journey.

"The snows are late this year." Jean-Paul joined him at the ship rail. "Unusual. It rarely comes later than the beginning of November; I hope that we won't have to pay for it with a late spring."

Richard watched with interest as the coast became clearer, and he could see the small inlets, groups of dwellings clustered together to form tiny fishing communities. He knew instinctively that they were fishing villages and, as if in confirmation of his thoughts, the first fishing boats appeared, edging their way out to sea. "How long will we be in Boston?" He asked.

"Only as long as it takes to fit you and Liam out with warm clothing fit for the winter out here. We'll take advantage of this unseasonable weather and get a good start." He too looked at the nearing land mass. "Fort Deerworthy is further North than Fort Edward, a long enough trip even in fine weather."

Liam appeared beside them, shivering in the sharp wind that penetrated his inadequate clothing. "I've packed the chest . . . Dickon." Even after six weeks he found it hard to use the name, and tried not to use any name at all if possible.

"Then unpack my other cape, Liam, and put it on yourself." Richard ordered.

Liam stamped his feet, to get the circulation moving in his legs. "I'll be all right, soon as I get movin'" He said.

"You'll be no use to either of us if you die of cold Liam, and believe me this is only a foretaste of what is to come." Instructed Jean-Paul. "Do as Richard says. When we get ashore, we'll fix you up in clothes suitable to keep you alive in blizzards and snow."

"It will get colder than this?" Liam asked in wonder.

Jean-Paul laughed. "Mon Dieu, mes enfant, this is as nothing. Believe me. This is nothing at all. Now get that cape." He gave him a playful push towards the open hatch to the lower deck, and turned his attention to Richard. "When we reach harbour, I shall go straight to the Fort; I want to find out if there have been any messages left. Do you wish to stay here and find accommodation?"

"No. We will leave our luggage on board for the moment, and Liam and I will come with you, Jean-Paul. We are all in this together; I want to know everything that happens from here on in."

Jean-Paul lifted his eyebrows and shoulders in unison. "There is one thing, Richard." His voice was heavily accented, and his pronunciation of his name came out as Reechard. "We have to trust each other implicitly."

"Yes, yes. I know." Agreed Richard

The two of them watched as the ship edged slowly towards the ever nearing mainland, until the wharf was now quite clear, ahead of them. The White Rose was alive with activity. Canvas sails were furled to order, sailors aloft awaiting orders, sailors readying mooring ropes, sailors positioning fenders level with the wharf. With great skill, and under Edward Boscawen's observation, the Captain and the helmsman guided the slowly moving vessel to the long wharf. Harbour boats raced towards them to take them in tow and finally on the shrill blast of the whistle the ropes were thrown from fore and aft, skilfully caught and wrapped around the capstans on the dock side.

The long timber wharf was bustling with activity. Ships that had berthed before nightfall were already unloading their cargoes of settlers, their tools and livestock, and the few personal belongings that they had brought with them. They had left behind them furniture, in favour of the implements that they thought would be necessary for their future life in the New World. Richard glanced at the settlers huddled together on the dock. Few of them possessed suitable clothing for these temperatures, let alone anything worse. He shook his head in wonder at the risks they were undertaking. What had driven them to leave all they had ever known? How many of them would even survive the first winter?"

Settlers, traders, merchants, shopkeepers, all jostled together with sailors and men in uniform. Hand carts loaded with baggage wove precariously between carts and carriages, making their way towards other boats making ready for departure. Horse drawn carriages and coaches waited on the coach line for the passengers to disembark from the newly arrived ships to Boston. Richard, Liam and Jean-Paul watched in silence as the ship was made secure, and the gang planks finally secured to the wharf, before Edward joined them and stared down at the melee of humanity on the wharf below. "Boston." He announced. "Gateway to the New World." And then glancing at the throng on the wharf added, more soberly and echoing Richard's own thoughts. "I wonder what the future holds in store for them? For some, at best, a new life and some land to call their own. For others the dream will remain a dream. I wonder how many of them will even survive this first winter?" Turning away from the dock he added. "I expect that you will want to go to the Fort right away, your luggage I will take with me to Widow Barnes boarding house on Church Street. She is a fine lady, and will have enough rooms I am sure for us all. I shall meet you there later, when I have finalised things here."

Richard thanked his friend, and Edward grinned. "Don't thank me. I was the one who got you into this mess, remember?"

"I am sure I will, before many days are passed." Richard turned to his companions. "Come on then. Let's get this venture on the road." He indicated for Jean-Paul to lead the way, and gripped Edward firmly by the hand, before following Liam.

A New World

ON THE WHARF they had to shoulder their way between the mass of bodies. Voices were raised in order to make themselves heard, creating a babble of sound. A multitude of languages and accents assailed their ears. Liam's eyes darted hither and thither as, amongst the English and continental languages, he picked up some Irish accents here and there, and even some Gaelic. It was so long since he had heard his mother tongue, he felt his heart leap and he was in danger of being left behind and lost, but Richard took a firm grip of his arm, and steered him before him until they finally made it to the carriage line and the carriage secured by Mr. Coggins.

At the fort they learned that the Indian tracker, Running Bear, had arranged to be at Fort Deerfield at the full moon. This gave them ten whole days to arrange their clothing and supplies for the journey. It would take five, possibly six days to travel to Fort Deerfield, and from there they would head on north into the borderlands, hopefully before the worst of the winter weather set in.

The next few days hurried by in a flurry of purchases. Warm clothing was the first priority, along with the food stuffs. The Commander of the fort had supplied them with horses, guns and ammunition, and Richard had spent any spare time instructing Liam in the loading and firing of the rifle provided for him. Liam had never held a gun, let alone fired one. But as always he proved a quick learner, he had a good eye and a steady hand. In no time at all he was hitting the targets that Richard and Jean-Paul had set up for him, and reloading almost as quickly as they did. Jean-Paul was well pleased, and any doubts that he had regarding the wisdom of bringing him with them quickly faded.

These last days were also spent in long hours of discussion with Edward and Major Warren-Clarke. Richard had committed to memory Pitt's requests, and with seven days in hand they made ready to leave Boston.

"Promise me you will call in at Tremanyon." Richard asked for the umpteenth time as he bade farewell to Edward.

"Of course. Of course. It will be the first thing I do on my return." He assured Richard. "Don't worry about your family Richard, I promise that Fanny and I will keep an eye on all of them"

All three were good horsemen, and had been provided with the best mounts available, and unmarked with the army brand. From Boston Jean-Paul would guide them to Fort Deerfield and their meeting with the Indian guide. Then he was to make a return to Boston and would find passage on a French ship to Quebec.

The track was wide as they left the town behind them, allowing Richard and Jean-Paul to ride side by side. Liam followed with the furs, food, utensils, water and their few personal items re-packed and strapped securely to the two pack horses.

Their first night under the stars was spent in the foothills, they had made good progress on their first day. Jean-Paul shot a rabbit, which they roasted on a stick over the fire, before spreading their bedrolls around the glowing embers and covering themselves with the cured fur skins.

In spite of the excitement, and the strange surroundings, Liam was the first to close his eyes, hearing the crackle and snap in the woods about them, quite sure that he would never be able to sleep in the wild. Of course he had slept under the stars before, however that was always on board the fishing boat with the water lapping gently against the hull. But soon enough his eyelids became heavy, and the long hours in the saddle had wearied him enough for his tiredness to overcome his fears, and soon he drifted into a dream-less sleep. Richard took longer, his mind dwelling on his daughters, and Ginifur, and although Jean-Paul appeared to have drifted off to sleep immediately he slept the sleep of the hunter, with one eye open and his mind alert for any unusual sounds in the night.

By the time Liam opened his eyes Jean-Paul had rekindled the fire and Richard had made a can of thick dark coffee. Cupping the tin mugs in their hands, they sipped the sweet strong liquid and shared a loaf of bread as their breath formed mist clouds in the chill of the early dawn. The ground was white with frost; the fur skins too were white and stiff from their exposure to the night air.

Richard tipped the dregs of the coffee into a square of muslin, squeezed it dry and slipped it back into the can. It would serve to make another can of coffee; they didn't have enough to waste. He scooped up some dust and wet leaves, scattering them amongst the dyeing embers and then, satisfied that there would be no sparks to burst into fresh life, placed some stones upon the ashes. When the horses were saddled, and the pack horses ready, the threesome re-mounted and headed for the edge of the clearing. Jean-Paul studied the eastern sky. "The snow is coming. It will not be many days more before it falls." He said to no one in particular.

A puzzled Richard pondered on the clear blue sky. The moon that had been late in arriving the night before, still hung there. "Snow!!! Surely not. It is so clear, it couldn't possibly snow."

Jean-Paul turned in the saddle. "It's in the air, mon ami. Not today, but it's coming."

Richard remembered the snow clouds as they backed up along the horizon at home, and wondered how his family was fairing without him. He took one last look at the moon before entering the tree belt. The day would be well under way at home, and he thought of his two daughters. Ginifur would never let any harm befall them. As her name came into his mind the picture of her standing in the boat, waving goodbye flashed before his eyes. She had looked so young, and so small for such a large responsibility. Yet she had matured far beyond her years. No, he had no doubts that she would not fail him, for what could possibly go wrong in the few months that he would be away? By next summer he would be home in Cornwall. Home, with his family at Tremanyon.

* * *

Ginifur stirred in her sleep, and opened her eyes. She rose from the chair where she had fallen asleep, and went to stand at the window of the children's day room in the nursery wing. Kate had taken all the children for a walk.

Ginifur's time of the month was due again. It had caused her no great concern when she had missed her last one. She had heard that it did happen from time to time, and pushed the memory of Richard's last night at Tremanyon firmly to the back of her mind, as if it had never happened. But it had. And Netty! She had been giving her some queer looks of late, on the point of asking her a question, then tuning away. What if . . ?

* * *

Richard gave an involuntary shiver. Icy fingers clutched at his heart, causing him to reign in his horse. He stared at the track in front of him, and Jean-Paul's receding back.

"Are you all right . . . Dickon?" Liam's concerned voice broke through his thoughts from behind.

Richard mustered a smile, shaking off the strange feeling that had washed over him. "It must be the cold. I felt a chill wind wash over me."

Liam frowned. Now that the sun had risen it had warmed considerably. And there was no breeze at all. The air was still.

Jean-Paul turned in his saddle. "We'll stop for a while before we put the horses to the next rise. Are you all right Richard?" He echoed Liam's own question.

"Of course I'm all right." Richard snapped angrily, pushing away the dull ache in the pit of his stomach and trying vainly to rid himself of the feeling of foreboding that had risen for no apparent reason.

Jean-Paul pulled a pocket watch from his jacket. They had been riding for over two hours. He considered stopping in this clearing to give themselves a rest but, glancing at Richard, he saw the colour had retuned to his face, and his eyes had lost the vacant expression, he decided to push on to the river.

They had stopped as planned, forded the river, and made good progress before nightfall. Although both Liam and Jean-Paul kept an eye on him Richard gave no hint of whatever ailed him on the second day and they continued to make good time, reaching Fort Deerfield on the sixth day. The next evening would be the night of the full moon.

* * *

Richard glanced out of the window of Major Webb's office. In front of him was a large open space before two large gates in a wooden stockade. To the left a row of log cabins, where the officers and their families were quartered, behind them, the long buildings that housed the soldiers. To the right were the stables and the fodder store, and behind that the arsenal. He knew it was the arsenal, for the small window apertures were barred, the door bolted and barred and a guard at the door. Beyond this was the general store. Everything that was needed in the fort was available here. From needles and thread, through flour and salt, to guns and powder. For the merchant would also supply the settlers who were within travelling distance of the fort. Liam had thought it an Aladdin's cave. Jars of sticky sweets, a rare treat for the few children who had to live along these harsh borders, resided on the counter next to a jar of buttons of all shapes and sizes. Shovels, forks, buckets and tools hung from the beams. Sacks of flour, buckwheat, cornmeal and dried beans crowded the floor with barrels of treacle, boxes of nails, cooking utensils and pot bellied stoves. Tin plates and mugs, pots and pans were crammed together with jugs and bowls. Rugs and blankets and coarse linen jostled for space on the shelves with lengths of fabrics. Rough woollen tweeds, hard wearing and in dull colours for serviceable winter clothes, bright cotton gingham to brighten cabin windows and plain cotton fabrics for summer wear for the women and girls. A few cards of lace and ribbons, for which there was little call in this harsh country where there were few, if any, social gatherings.

Richard was listening to the conversation between Major Webb, his lieutenant and Jean-Paul, but was watching the tall figure approaching the building. The man's long, straight, dark hair fell below his shoulders, a band of leather about his forehead kept it from his face which was dark skinned over a fine bone structure. He had a long straight nose separating wide, deep set eyes, hollow cheeks, a wide mouth and narrow lips. Skin that was taught over strong bones and his dark eyebrows were raised with lines creasing his forehead, accentuating the deep thoughtful expression. He wore only moccasins on his feet, buckskin leggings laced at the sides, and a square beaded type of apron. About his shoulders was a Buffalo skin, beneath which he wore a fringed buckskin top, embroidered with a beaded design. He painted a fine picture as he strode confidently beside the uniformed soldier, and a firm knock on the door preceded their entrance.

"O.K Hammond, you can leave us." Major Webb gave the soldier permission to leave them. "Welcome, Running Bear." He greeted the Indian, raising his hand in salute.

The Indian's nod was his only answer as he stepped into the room. "I have come." He said finally. "The Englishman has arrived?"

Richard watched from the window. The Indian was tall, taller than both Jean-Paul and Liam. As tall, if not taller than himself. He noticed the Indian take in the two strangers beside the desk, assessing what he saw. At that instant he was not aware of Richard, standing quietly as he was in the shadow beside the window.

"Greetings, my brother." Jean-Paul spoke in the Indians own tongue, but he wasn't fooled.

The Indian's eyebrows drew closer together, his expression wary, his lips compressed into a fine line. His eyes narrowed and the muscle in the side of his neck contracted and twitched. All this Richard noticed. "You are not English. You are French." The Indian made the accusation, his voice was controlled, but ice cold as he spoke in almost perfect French.

"Mai oui. Je suis Francais." Jean-Paul agreed.

Running Bear turned angrily to Major Webb. "It is not what we agreed." He stated angrily. "What is a Frenchman doing in an English fort? I go." He ended, and was about to turn away.

"Running Bear." Major Webb's voice halted him before he turned and saw Richard. "Your Englishman is over there. Jean-Paul is his friend; he lives in the land of the Englishman." He indicated Richard by the window.

Running Bear turned quickly, angry that his sixth sense had not made him aware of the stranger earlier. Richard stepped out of the shadow, unlike Running Bear, he had had time to observe the man who was to accompany them and be his guide. He didn't know why, but he felt quite sure that he could trust this man. There was directness in his speech and in his walk, and in his manner. Now that they were face to face he saw that, although his eyes were dark, almost black even, there was honesty within them. His face was long and lean, with sharply carved features, and he showed no signs of deviousness in his mannerisms. Richard was usually a good judge of character. "I am Richard. Richard Tremayne. It is me that you have been asked to guide through your country and I would like to thank you, in advance, for any danger that you may be placing yourself in."

Running Bear did not answer. He studied Richard from head to toe and then back to his face, where his eyes never wavered for a second as he stared deep into his eyes. Richard felt that they saw into his very soul. But he must have liked what he saw, for Richard saw a smile hover at the corners of his wide mouth as he inclined his head in a sign of acceptance. "The boy? He is your son?"

Richard shook his head. "No. He is my brother."

Running Bear seemed to accept this. "And he is your friend? This Frenchman?"

"Yes, he is."

"They come with you?"

"Only my brother. Jean-Paul will meet us in Quebec, in the spring.

Running Bear nodded thoughtfully. "And you trust him, this Frenchman." He added scornfully.

Richards answer was instantaneous. "I do Running Bear. I would trust him with my life."

Jean-Paul held his council. The Indian, no doubt, had reason enough to distrust the French, and Richard would need his help to make it through the high country to meet him in Quebec,

"And you Major? Do you trust this Frenchman?" Running Bear pressed further.

The Major looked straight into the Indian's eyes. "I do. He is no stranger to this country and well known to my countrymen. Before the troubles he traded with Indian, English and French alike. He had a profitable Trading Post, and only left when he was asked to renege on his friends along the borders.

Running Bear's eyes narrowed again as he searched his memory. "There was a Frenchman, my people traded with him. He was a friend to the Indian, he treated them fairly, as equals. He was a friend to the English too, this Frenchman. When he left the troubles began. Raiders killed many settlers, and my people were blamed." He fixed his eyes on Jean-Paul. "His name was Jean, this Frenchman, and another took over his Trading Post."

"A Scotsman. You are wrong, he was from Scotland." Corrected Jean-Paul.

"John Smith." Suggested the Indian.

"No. Andy MacDonald."

The Indian paused, whilst he pondered the man in front of him. "His wife and daughter died of the fever. He has only one son."

Jean-Paul smiled. "Maggie and her daughter Mary, were alive and well when I left twin Forks and, unless they have died since, there were two sons, Ned and Ewan.

For the first time Running Bear smiled at Jean-Paul. "This is indeed a friend of the Indian and the Englishman. But can you truly turn your back on you own people?"

The evidence of Jean-Paul's concern was quite clear in the expression on his face. "These men who issue these orders are not my countrymen. My own family in France fear that there are forces working to undermine our government and King. I feel that those elements are already at work here in Canada."

"When do you leave Fort Deerfield?" Asked Running Bear.

"On the morrow. I have a few matters to settle around here."

"And the Englishman?" He turned to look at Richard. "Where do you want him to go?"

"To my friends homestead, Will Travis. Near Twin Forks. Andy MacDonald will direct you."

"I know of this Will, and his wife and daughter. They too are friends of my people." Running Bear acknowledge.

Jean-Paul showed his relief. "That is good. They will give Richard and Liam shelter for the winter. Give them time to acclimatise to the country and its ways, so that they will not be obvious strangers to this country when we meet up in the spring. I will get word to Andy MacDonald when the time is nearer, and arrange a meeting point."

Running Bear gave every impression that he was happy with the arrangement, and Major Webb breathed more easily. "When will you leave, Running Bear?" He asked.

"As soon as the Englishman and his brother are ready." He looked quizzically at Richard.

"We can be ready to leave right away. Liam and I will load up the pack horses, that is all there is to do. We ourselves are ready right now." Richard assured him.

The Indian nodded to himself. "Then we will be gone in the hour." He stated finally.

Running Bear

BY NOON THEY had left the Fort behind them, and Richard and Liam were on the next leg of their long journey. Although Major Webb had offered them another unbranded horse, for Running Bear, the guide preferred to go on foot. However Richard refused to leave the animal behind, saying that he would rather take it with them for an emergency.

Richard was amazed at the stamina and pace of the Indian as he ran, unchecked, ahead of them. Leading them unerringly through the forest that grew closer around them as they headed north. He appeared to need no rest, or food, or water, but kept up his steady pace, pausing only to glance at the sky or check for some signs that he alone understood, as they passed through what appeared to be unpopulated land. Richard found himself wondering what on earth it was that the settlers thought that they would find out here. There were few clearings large enough to build a homestead let alone create a farm. Slowly but surely they climbed steadily higher, through the lower slopes of the brooding mountains that loomed ahead of them. Tall firs mixed with the bare, skeletal forms of deciduous trees that grew all around them. The first four nights were spent in the open, as they had done with Jean-Paul, and Richard was beginning to forget the weather warning that Jean-Paul had given.

On the fifth day they proceeded more slowly. The ground was becoming uneven, stony, and they were climbing higher now, the horses not so surefooted. The trees towered above them, allowing only brief glimpses of the sky and a few pink tinged clouds that were racing across it.

Dusk came early, and Jean-Paul's snow began to fall. Lightly at first, a few tiny flakes began to find their way between the branches of fir. So dry they were, and the ground already frozen, that they settled and stayed to make a light frosted carpet that twinkled in the fast fading light. Running Bear slowed his pace and paused as they came to a fast flowing stream. "Soon the snow will be harder. We must make camp." He glanced at Richard for his agreement.

Richard nodded. "Whatever you suggest."

Running Bear indicated the way forward. "We follow the stream. There is a waterfall beyond the next bend. Above it there is a cave. It will make a good shelter till the storm ends."

"Storm!" Richard listened. There was hardly a breath of wind.

"Snow storm." The Indian explained. "There will be much snow, it is very late coming." He held out his hands to the reins. "You will lead the horses."

Eyeing the terrain beside the stream, Richard nodded his agreement. "Liam! Dismount and lead the horses. We are following the stream to a cave for the night. Be careful, it will be slippery I fear."

"Yes, Dickon." The form of address was becoming easier now. Liam dismounted, checked that the pack horses and the riding horse were securely fastened together, took the reins of his own horse and that of the leading pack horse and followed Richard and Running Bear on foot. The stream was fast running, and tumbled merrily over the shallow stony bed, reminding Liam of the brook back home in Kilkenny. There were fish swimming in the shallows, against the flow, and he thought how good it would be to catch one.

The earlier tiny flakes of snow fast turned fat and fluffy, clinging to the fur hats covering their heads. In no time at all it had created a thick blanket at their feet and crunched with every step, until it began to fall so fast that Liam feared he would even loose sight of Richard, who was only a few feet ahead of him. As if aware of his sudden fear Richard called out. "Keep close, Liam. Don't fall behind. It would be too easy to get separated in the snow especially with this visibility. Dear God, I've never seen snow like it." He added, in wonder. "And it's so dry, not like the wet mush we get at home." Within minutes the boughs of the trees were heavy with snow, bearing down upon the travellers beneath and forcing them to leave the edge of the stream where the branches were lower. But Running Bear never faltered in his step, kept them at a steady pace away from the stream where there was more cover from the trees and better visibility, following a path that was only known to him, but much steeper now.

Richard marvelled at the silence created by the snow, it was as though all life had stopped. The only sound that he could hear was made by their passing. The birds had stopped singing, nothing moved about them. No rabbits, no squirrels, not even a mouse. But as they made their way, more slowly now, there came to his ears a sound that he hadn't heard before. It reminded him of the waves pounding upon the shore during an easterly gale at home in Cornwall. A kind of roaring sound that grew with every step.

Running Bear glanced around to make sure that they were still following him. "The waterfall." He announced. "It is the waterfall that you hear." Richard smiled. Was the Indian also psychic, could he even read ones thoughts?

As the trees thinned, the noise grew louder and louder until, suddenly, they appeared on a rocky ledge above the stream that had only been an offshoot that was formed from this torrent of water that rushed it's way down from the mountains. Here it turned into this foaming mass that cascaded some fifty feet or more into a large pool which then split into three or four rivers and streams. The ground was slippery where the snow could take no hold, ice formed on the outer rocks and they kept to the bank. Still the snow fell, bigger flakes now and heavier still. "We are nearly there." The Indian assured them. "Do not loose sight of me, it would be hard to find you if we separated." Richard had no intention of loosing sight of him. When they paused at the waterfall he had made certain that a leading rein had been secured between his own horse and Liam's and, even with the snow flakes clinging to his eye lashes, not for one moment did his concentration waver or his pace slow. He kept Running Bear firmly in his sight and only a few feet away.

Suddenly they came to a rocky escarpment, their route blocked, but Running Bear turned sharply to his right, picking out a narrow track leading upwards. It was only just wide enough for them and the animals to negotiate. Twenty or thirty feet further on the track came to a sudden end and a small clearing surrounded by a stand of giant fir trees. Their shelter would provide them with some cover from the worse of the snow, but would not be enough shelter for the night, Richard thought as he shook the snow from his head and face.

Running Bear headed straight for the rock face. "Come." He beckoned. "Come, bring horses, come."

Richard glanced at Liam. His face was blue with cold, they had to get him warm, the boy was freezing to death. Where on earth was that cave? "Come on Liam. We are nearly there." He assured him, and reaching back to take the leading reins of the horses he pushed Liam before him until they stood beside a large rock.

181

"Come, see? The Cave." Running Bear pulled Liam to one side and beckoned for Richard to follow. The large rock sheltered an opening in the escarpment. A cave, large enough to hold them all, and the horses too.

Richard let out a great sigh of relief. "Thank God, and thank you Running Bear. I don't think Liam would have lasted much longer in this weather. Here lad, get the furs off the horses and wrap yourself in them quickly." Liam struggled with the straps, but his fingers were too cold. Richard soon had them released and Liam, wrapped in furs, leaned back exhausted against the wall of the cave. Running Bear pointed to a pile of wood. "There are dry sticks. You can light a fire?"

Richard laughed, in spite of the cold. "Yes . . ." He assured his companion. "I can light a fire."

The corners of Running Bears mouth lifted slightly. "You light fire. I get food." Before Richard could open his mouth, to stop him from going out into the storm, he had vanished, leaving him quietly wondering to him self whether they would ever see the Indian again. However, he busied himself lighting the fire, there was plenty of wood that someone had stored in the past, and he soon had boiling water to make some coffee. Richard need not have worried. He had just handed a steaming mug to Liam, whose colour was now returning to normal, when Running Bear re-appeared at the entrance to the cave with a small deer that he had shot with an arrow from his bow. "Food." He declared. "Soon you will feel better." Then he fired a question at Richard. "You. You think I leave you here to die?"

"No." Richard lied. "Not for one moment."

Now the Indian did smile, a real smile, a knowing smile. "You must trust me, my brother. We must trust each other." Richard said nothing as he gave a hand to drag the carcase of the deer into the cave. "The snow will fall for many days. This will feed us well and we will dry some strips to carry with us when we leave." He glanced at Liam. "Your brother is looking better." Richard stared into the fire wondering at the wisdom of starting out on such a venture at this time of the year. Surely it would have been better to make the journey in the spring, after the snows had melted. "Believe me, my brother; the time will be well spent. I will teach you both to hunt and survive in the mountains, in case we have to part. When we arrive at the settlement that your Frenchman speaks of, you will both feel as though you belong to this land of mine.

You will learn to track like my people, hide like my people and think like my people. And I will learn about you and your land across the sea and, maybe, I will begin to understand why your people flow into my land like the waters flooding the shore."

Richard looked up. "Can you really read my thoughts so well?" He asked

Running Bear gave one of his rare smiles. "No. It is your face. The white man's face is easy to read. We learn, from a young age, to keep our feelings behind our eyes. Now, did you learn to skin a deer in your country?"

Richard shook his head. "I have to admit, I did not. I have shot a deer on more than one occasion over the years. But no, the skinning was left to others."

"Here it will be necessary to kill and prepare your own food, so you must learn." He beckoned to Liam. "Come little brother, this time you watch. Next time I shall watch."

Liam's face tingled as the blood brought life back into it, and the coffee brought warmth to his belly, but his limbs were stiff as he struggled towards the fire. "I have skinned deer before. At home in Ireland." He laughed. "Perhaps it wasn't as wild or free as this fine animal, but we skinned, cut it up and buried the skin long before it was missed."

"You mean poached!" Richard smiled.

"Now did I say that?" Liam gave an air of mock offence.

"Poached!" Running Bear repeated.

"In England, or Ireland or Scotland for that matter, few deer are truly free or wild. The herds run upon the hills or in the forests, but they are claimed to belong either to the King in London or the Lords of the Manors. No one may freely shoot a deer." Richard explained.

Running Bear was puzzled. "Then how do you feed your families?"

Richard laughed. "I said that they weren't allowed to shoot deer. Some people do, and it is called poaching. But if they are caught the sentence is severe."

Running Bear was not convinced that he would like this land across the sea. He made a neat incision and guided the knife in a long straight line. "The Major, he said your name was Richard, No? Why does your brother call you Dickon?"

Richard was angry with himself. He should have realised that this question was bound to arise. "Dickon is a pet name. A name close members of your family use."

Running Bear understood this. "My brother used to call me 'Runs like the wind', for I ran faster than all the rest. How large is your family?" Luckily he turned this question to Liam.

"My father and mother, then Richard is the eldest, then my . . . our sisters Aileen and Caitlin then Aiden then me and Nora, and last there is Sowra."

"Sowra!" Running Bear repeated. "Sarah?"

"No, Sowra. It means summer. It suits her; mother says she is like a ray of sunshine. Dickon is the oldest by some years." He explained. Richard made a mental note of 'his' sibling's names and order of birth, for it was possible this might come up again. "We have a farm, but only father and Aiden work on it. Dickon was already a Captain in the Army when I went to sea. Aileen and Nora are married and Sowra is the baby. She and Caitlin are still at home." Liam's eyes misted over. "Well, they were. It is so long since I was . . . we were at home, and neither of us has had word."

"You have a wife?" This question to Richard.

"I had. She died, in childbirth." Richard explained.

For once Running Bear's eyes did show his feelings. "I am sorry." He said. "The child? Did it live?"

Richard shook his head vigorously. "He died too. But I have two daughters."

"No son?" The Indian pressed.

"No son."

The Indian pondered on this reply. "A man should have a son." It was as though he spoke to himself

"And you? Are you married?" Richard turned the question to Running Bear.

"My wife is also dead. At the hands of the French."

"I see." Said Richard thoughtfully. That explained the man's feelings towards the French. "You have a son."

The Indian's face was a blank sheet of paper. "He also was killed. I had no more children, but they would have killed them all."

Now it was Richard's turn to feel sorry, and thought how lucky he was to have his daughters.

It snowed off and on for the next five days. When it began to ease Running Bear took them on forages around the cave and waterfall. He taught them to look through his eyes, to notice broken twigs, the lie of the snow that showed a path, the fish under the overhanging grasses, and the way the wind blew. He taught them to listen with his ears, to hear the rustle of a hidden animal, the flight of a bird, the wind in the trees and the stream that babbled over nearby rocks. He taught them to walk on the snow, using strips of pliable wood strapped together with strips of hide to form platforms to strap to their boots and to find places where the snow was not so thick and therefore easier for animals to reach the grasses beneath. Running Bear taught them to track and trap the animals whose meat would keep them alive during the winter and produce the much sought after furs to trade. He taught them to skin and treat the furs that they would take with them to back up the story that they were fur trappers. He taught them to find or make shelter for the night, to move unseen, and to hide their tracks. In truth he taught them all he could. And they became close, as close as brothers.

When the snow clouds finally cleared, the sky became so blue that Richard could hardly believe the colour. And in the sunshine, in spite of the snow, it was incredibly warm. It was only in the wind that the cold was really apparent, and Running Bear told them how dangerous the wind and cold were. He had known people lose their noses, he said, for their faces had frozen without them knowing. From that moment on they covered their faces with the woollen scarves that they had brought with them.

Now it was time to head further north. To Twin Forks.

* * *

This part of their journey was uneventful and at this time of the year the French soldiers were dug in behind the shelter of the fort in Quebec. The few French that were about were trappers, and even these were mostly found further north. In this border area it was mostly English and Scots settlers who cut the timber to make a cabin and claw a meagre existence from the small plot of land that they had carved out of the wilderness. The cabins were few and far between, and they gave each of them a wide circle, for they wanted no chance that word of their presence would go before them.

And so it was not until a week before Christmas that they arrived at Twin Forks.

As they approached, it looked a peaceful sight. There was barely a breath of air to stir the trees as they paused on top of a rise that gave them a view of the settlement. The settlement lay serenely in a hollow of this large valley, nestling between the mountains. Smoke, rising slowly from the blacksmiths forge, hung in the air. Somewhere nearby someone was chopping wood and, not far away, a dog barked as it chased a rabbit across the snow.

The settlement consisted of the Trading Post, with a primitive local bar for the sale of liquor, a blacksmith and a few cabins. The Trading Post was the first building that they came to and Richard and Liam tied their horses to the rail in front before following Running Bear up the steps.

The interior of the Trading Post was dark, for the windows were few and small. As at the fort, it was crammed with every manner of items that would or could be needed and, in addition, to one side, was evidence that the owner also traded in the purchase of furs. As their eyes became accustomed to the gloom, Richard noticed the beaded curtain, behind which burned a light, and it was towards this that they were heading. A chair scraped upon bare boards, and the curtain parted with a jangle as a tall, red bearded man appeared.

"Running Bear!" Exclaimed the man in obvious delight. "You haven't passed this way in a long time, what brings you to this neck of the woods?" He gripped Running Bear firmly by the shoulders.

"Greetings Mac, my friend. Your family are well?"

"Indeed they are, and you are in time for supper." He became aware of the strangers behind Running Bear. "Your friends?"

"I came upon them on my journey. They were trying to find the cabin of Will Travis; I said I would show them."

The cheerful smile faded from Andy MacDonald's face. "Then you haven't heard?"

The Indian looked puzzled. "Heard! Heard what?"

"Will's cabin was raided. Burned to the ground. They were all killed. Will, his wife, young Fiona and even little Sally, only a babe in arms.

"No. It's not possible. When was this?" Running Bear was dismayed, and showed it. "Who did this thing?

"It's true, I saw it for myself. Will was going to come in for supplies for the winter, he was overdue. Thinking that maybe they was all taken ill, I loaded up some bits and rode out there. Back in early October it was, before the snows came."

"Who did this thing?" Running Bear demanded to know.

A hard look came into Andy MacDonald's face. "I know it was the French, the bastards. True they hid their tracks well, made it look like the Indians. But no, it was the French all right" He looked at Richard. "I'm sorry to be the bearer of this news. A friend of yourn?" He asked suspiciously. "Will never spoke of anyone who might call."

"No." Richard told him. "A friend of a friend, so to speak. When my friend heard we were heading north he said that he thought that they might be able to put us up until the spring. He was going to get word to him. I didn't know the family, but I am sorry nevertheless."

"Trappers are you?" Andy MacDonald eyed their clothing, their wind and sun burned complexion, their rough hands.

Richard recognised his appraisal and gave silent thanks to Running Bear and his teaching. "Yes. We have furs outside if you are interested. We will certainly need further supplies, for now it looks as though we will have to continue our journey."

"Hm." Andy rubbed his bewhiskered face. "Let's take a look."

Outside they gathered about the pack horses, and Richard noticed the man's eyes as he inspected the furs, he was also taking stock of the horses. "Nice Pack horses." He ran his hands down the neck of Richards mount and lifted the saddle leather before turning to Richard. "Nice horse."

Richard's face showed nothing, and he smiled inwardly as he remembered insisting that the horses showed no branding that could identify them as army stock. "They are not for sale."

"Pity." Andy returned his attention to the furs and gave a silent whistle. "These are good furs. In excellent condition. You been trapping long?"

"Long enough, and not round here." Richard informed him.

"Well . . ." Andy drawled." I will admit that they are as good as any that this renegade ever brought in." He inclined his head towards Running Bear. "And I can tell you, his skins were always the best. You sure you didn't have a hand in this, my friend?"

Running Bear had turned away and was inspecting the hooves of one of the horses. "This animal needs a new shoe." He countered.

Andy MacDonald didn't notice that he had not received an answer to his question. "Let's go in and have a drink. Then we'll trade. You comin' in Running Bear."

Running Bear had taught them the art of haggling. He had told them to ask high and how much to accept for each fur. He watched and was pleased with his pupils; they would fare well till the spring. But where were they to go now? While he watched the haggling he was pondering the question when Andy suddenly said.

"You remember Donny? He was a friend of yourn weren't he? Over the hill, in that valley by the stream. Fell off the roof, last fortnight, and broke his neck he did. Elly won't leave the place. Says she and the kids are staying put, it were his dream to own his own land so she says she won't leave it. God alone knows how she'll survive the winter."

"You are indeed the bearer of bad tidings, my friend." Running Bear was visibly moved but his thoughts were moving on. "Elly will need a man around to help her through the winter."

Andy MacDonald had had the same thought. "Yes." He scrutinised the newcomers. "You look honest enough."

Running Bear answered for Richard. "I believe they are. I trust this man and his brother."

"Your word will be good enough for Elly." Andy pulled a face. "It's young Tuck who might kick up a fuss. Thinks he has to take the place of his dad he does. Just thirteen and going on thirty all in just a couple of weeks."

They did their trade and, guided by Andy MacDonald they stocked up with flour, sugar, salt and dried goods for Elly and her family, leaving the balance of the trade on account for anything they would need before setting off at the end of winter. Accepting the offer of a meal and place to unroll their bedding, they spent the night with Andy and his family, before setting of to meet Elly the following morning.

Elly greeted Running Bear with obvious delight, and held out her hand to Richard. "It is pleased to meet you, I am." She said in her lilting Irish Brogue. "Aileen O'Donnell, but Elly to all my friends. This is Kiery, and here is Kathleen, my daughters seven and nine. And this is Tuck, on account that he tucks in to all he can eat."

Both Elly and Liam were delighted that fortune had brought them to her door, and it provided them with a good start to the relationship. Tuck worshipped Running Bear, and Liam and Richard soon won him over when they took him hunting whilst Running Bear stayed behind to talk to Elly. On Christmas Eve, Running Bear took his leave, with the promise that he would return when the snows began to thaw.

The Shipwreck

AS RICHARD AND Liam spent the night on the Trading Post's floor, Ginifur was rising. The wind had howled all night long and from the window, through the pale dawn, she cast her eyes out over the sea. The sea was whipped into frenzy and, on the wind, the spray carried as far as the house turning into salt crystals upon the glass panes. Ginifur shivered and pulled the shawl tightly about her shoulders, but didn't move away from the window as she watched the birds fighting to reach shelter away from the coast. Suddenly her eyes settled on a point out in the bay. As desperate as folks were, surely no one would have put out to sea the night before such a storm, for they all knew that it was coming. For the last two days the omens had predicted the coming storm. Ginifur rubbed the mist from the glass, and concentrated harder at the spot in the middle of the bay. No, it wasn't a fishing boat. It was much larger, and listing badly. There was a ship in trouble, and there would be no time to loose.

Quickly she dressed in old clothes, the warmest that she could find, and then calling up the servants stairs she ran down to the kitchen where Netty was already tending the range. "There's a boat in the bay and it's going to go on to the rocks. Look after the girls Netty; I'm going to raise help."

Netty sent up a silent prayer for the people on board the ill fated ship, put the kettle on the range and went to see to the children.

Ginny ran as fast as she could to the stable block. Banging on the coach cottage she told Sam to send Adam to get her father, and anyone else that he could find. Then she haltered Damson, throwing herself upon her bare back and galloped off towards Porthcarrow. At the bottom of the avenue of trees she turned Damson into the sanding lane that lead to the beach. The horse was already spooked by the wind in the trees, and the little lane was more sheltered than the high ground to the church, but as she neared the beach she realised that she should have gone through the village to raise more help.

At the beach her fears were realised, she was alone. Just her and Damson. But at the precise moment she was going to turn Damson's head; she caught sight of a knot of villagers scurrying across the cliff top. The first to reach the beach was Big John, carrying a huge coil of thick rope and another of thinner rope. Behind him others carried smaller lengths, anything that they could lay their hands on. Ginifur fastened Damsons halter to a tree, in the lee of the hedge that lined the path to the beach and ran to meet him. "At first I thought she would flounder off the rocks off Dingerien Head." She shouted above the groaning of the wind. "But the wind is driving her this way. Where do you think she'll end up?

"Tis 'ard t' tell Ginny." They all stared out over the boiling waters. Huge waves crashed upon the rocky cove. "Tis fer certin she won't be able t' make it t' safety on Pendarves beach, listing like she be. Must 'av taken on some water! No, twill be between 'ere 'n Kylyn Cove I reckon. God 'elp 'em." He turned and shouted to one of the men behind him. "Get up the cliff. Iffen she looks like she be movin' nearer Kylyn send the boy t'let we know." The man set off at a run, with the boy behind him, others crowded under the rocky cliff as they all stared helplessly at the ship struggling to keep upright in the dangerous sea. "Are'em comin' from the Big House?" John's question was torn away in the wind, and Ginifur was hard pushed to answer.

"Adam has gone to get them. They should be here soon." As if in answer, Sam, Simon and Adam appeared on the beach followed by all the farm hands that they could muster in a short space of time. They arrived just as Ginny's voice pierced the wind. "Look, she's listing harder. It's being driven onto the rocks at Wreckers Point."

"You'm right Ginny, come on." Big John shouted, beckoning for them all to follow as he and Ginny set off, battling against the wind, sand and spray. Within seconds Ginifur's shawl was torn away from her body but she didn't falter or turn, giving no thought to herself she struggled on behind Big John. At the end of the tiny cove they clambered up the rocky point, until they could see the ship reel and roll in the turbulent sea. It was so close that they could see people on board, pleading for help, but there was nothing that they could do. The ship was too far out. Then one wave, larger than the rest, rose beyond the helpless craft, rolling unrelentingly forward it urged itself beneath the hull, heaving it upwards and impelling it with tremendous force onto the nearest rock. The sound of angry shattered timbers filled the air, drowning the sound of the wind, and Big John was galvanised into action. "Quick Ginny, take the rope. Secure it to a rock. I'm goin' in."

Ginny grabbed the end of the thinner line, but tried to stop him. "You can't" She cried out.

"Just do as I say maid, 'n do it now or I'll be a gonna fer certin. Ye know what t' do." With steady hands he tied one end of the rope about his waist and clambered out over the rocks until he was in danger of being washed in. With one final look back, to make sure that Ginny had done as he instructed, he waited for the next wave to recede and then dived beneath the foaming surf.

Ginny stared out at the black, angry seas as Simon covered the ground between them. As she had been instructed she let the thin line run through her hands as the slack was taken up by Big Johns slow progress through the angry sea. "He'll never make it, Da." She voiced her fears as she glanced back to see how much rope was left.

"If any one can, it will be Big John." Simon assured her as he gathered the men around him, in an effort to organise a rescue attempt if John was able to get a line to the ship. With each surge the broken ship moaned and groaned. Sails and rigging, masts and spars crashed and swirled in the seas about it, and even Simon had to admit that if Big John did indeed survive the swim to the ill fated ship it would be a miracle in itself.

Suddenly, from the cliff, came the cry. "e's made it, Big John, e's made it. Look."

All eyes were riveted on the doomed ship and they were all greatly relieved to see Big Johns broad back as he climbed a rope dangling over the side. A tremendous cry went up from the beach and they rallied, as near to the waters edge as they dared. On the stricken craft Big John hauled in the thinner line to which Ginny had now attached the strong rope. When he had hauled it all on to the boat he secured it to the remnants of the mast and vanished below to appear with a woman hanging tightly to his hand. Ginifur watched in awe as he tied her to him, and then lowered himself, and the woman, back into the sea. It seemed to Ginifur an eternity before they both appeared above the waves, washed this way and that by the currents. Hand over hand Big John felt his way along the rope, finally making it to the comparative safety of the rocks where they all waited. Willing hands helped them ashore, and carried the young woman up to the beach where she was tended by the women from the village.

By this time others were struggling along the life line. More of the men on shore had attached safety lines to their waist and were struggling in the water to help them ashore, oblivious to the rocks tearing at their clothes and limbs. Under the cliff the women tended the wounded, and it appeared that most of the passengers and crew would be saved when the young woman let out a terrible scream. One of the women rushed across the beach with the information that there had been a young child on board. The mother had thought that someone would bring her with them, but no child had come ashore. Ginifur scrambled over the slippery rocks to Big John who received the appalling news with alarm. Then, without another thought for his own safety, he gripped the rope once more for a return journey to the floundering ship.

There were only a few more of the crew to attempt to make the safety of the shore, one was already on the line and with difficulty Big John managed to pass him through the raging sea, until he once again made the uncertain safety of the vessel. Hasty words were passed with the two remaining men on deck and Big John vanished below once more. Eyes were glued to the spot where Big John vanished, and a sigh of relief was expelled as he appeared with the missing child. Holding their breaths, everyone on shore watched the hazardous attempt to save the child, and Big John was only an arms length from help when the child was snatched from his arms by yet another surge of water. Big John had been in the freezing water so long that his hands and arms were numb. He could barely hold onto the rope to save himself.

With no thought of the danger, and her father's voice ringing in her ears, Ginifur hesitated briefly as she assessed the swell of the sea, just inches away from her. As the next swell rose up over the rocks Ginifur jumped into the boiling sea. She was a strong swimmer, for a girl, they said. In fact some said that there was none stronger.

Ginifur's head appeared above the raging water and she opened her eyes just in time to see the figure of the child, dressed in red, floating not far from her. Ginifur bravely struck out and was just a stroke or two from reaching her when the child was engulfed by the next large wave and vanished beneath the turbulent water and debris from the stricken vessel. Taking a deep breath, Ginny pushed herself out of the water, pointed her head downwards and dived beneath the waves. In the dark green gloom the currents, swirling this way and that, were filled with flotsam and seaweeds. It was almost an impossible task to see anything at all but, as the pain in her chest became almost unbearable, she caught sight of a tiny red garment billowing out behind an even smaller body as it spiralled downwards. With a final desperate effort, Ginifur thrust herself forwards and, with one mighty stroke, she caught the cloth in her hand and struggled to the surface. Gasping for air she shook the hair from her eyes as she searched around her. She was only a few yards from where willing hands waited to drag her to safety. Taking a firm grip under the child's arm she struggled to reach her terrified father and friends. She was going to make it, everyone was sure. But just as they reached out to give her aid she pushed the child towards them and vanished beneath the next wave. Simon quickly passed the child backwards as he searched the surging water for any sign of his daughter and, oblivious to the pleading of others, was about to dive in when Ginifur was lifted up by the next wave and thrown upon the rocks. Big John caught Simon's coat just in time, pulling him back to safety, and Simon bent over the battered and inert body of his daughter as tears burned down his face.

All those gathered on the rocks and beach thought that young Ginifur Retallick had perished in her attempt to save the child from the sea but miraculously, when it seemed that all hope had passed, she suddenly coughed and spluttered, spewing salt water from her lungs, and opened her swollen eyes.

Amazingly only two people were lost in the shipwreck. Many were injured, including Ginifur, but all these survived. The mother was elated at the rescue of her child, and said that words would never be able to express her undying gratitude. She would never forget Ginifur or Big John, for the part that they had played in rescuing her daughter from certain death in the sea.

Ginifur was carried back to Tremanyon where Netty undressed her, bathed the salt from her body, and treated the numerous cuts and bruises with her own special remedies. Having applied the salve to her tender body, Netty sent Adam to get the Doctor.

For the next three days Ginifur slipped in and out of consciousness. Kate took the full control of the children, whilst Netty fussed over the injured Ginny. As little as they had, the villagers sent gifts of herbs and remedies and wishes for her speedy recovery. And slowly, each day she improved.

On the fourth day Doctor Thomas arrived to check up on his patient. Ginifur had been all but oblivious to his previous visits, and smiled at him weekly from her chair by the fire. Dressing herself had been an effort, and she appeared very small and frail wrapped in the large paisley shawl. "Hello Doctor. It's kind of you to call." She greeted him.

Doctor Thomas smiled graciously. "Not at all. I am honoured to call on the local heroin."

"They make too much of it, they really do. It was only what anyone would have done." Insisted Ginifur

"But they didn't" He pointed out.

"Only because I was the nearest." Ginifur dismissed any attempt at bravery.

"Be that as it may, others see things quite differently." He looked her up and down. "How are you feeling today?

Ginifur smiled weakly. "Pampered and spoiled for no reason. I cannot stay here being fussed over, I have got responsibilities and work to attend to. And the sooner I get back to it the better I will be."

James Thomas laughed. "Well that is fighting spirit. We'll see how you feel in a few days time. I can assure you that Netty has everything well under her control. Now, I think we have another matter to discuss. Don't we?"

Ginifur blushed. "I don't know what you mean."

James Thomas pulled a chair near to her and sat down. "Don't make this harder for me than it already is Ginny. Netty undressed you and bathed your body after the soaking and battering you had in the sea. When she called me in to see you, she expressed her own natural concern. Do I make myself clear?"

If Ginifur could have turned whiter, she would have. Her eyes became so large that she appeared to be almost all eyes. Then tears formed in the corners of her eyes and, in a very short time, she was engulfed with anguished sobbing.

Doctor Thomas took her hand gently in his, and waited patiently for the sobs to diminish, then he handed her a handkerchief for her to wipe her face. "Who is the father Ginny?"

Looking at her hands in her lap he just heard her muffled reply. "I'm not saying."

"Is it Adam?"

"No." Ginifur said in a flash. "What does he know about this? How many people have been told?"

"Calm yourself Ginifur. You are not well enough to get your-self distressed. It's only a wonder to me that you haven't lost the child after such an ordeal as you have been through." James Thomas patted her hand gently. Giving her reassurance. "No one but myself and Netty know of your condition. Netty informs me that she has been having nagging doubts at the back of her mind, but has voiced them to no one, not even Tom. You have hidden it well, for you must be at least ten weeks gone. Am I correct?" Ginifur nodded forlornly. "But this has to be spoken of Ginifur. You know the consequences of not informing the authorities of the father of your child. Who ever it is, he would not want you to go to prison for their misdemeanours."

"It was my misdemeanour too. I am equally guilty. I could have said no, but I didn't, did I? No. I won't say who the father is." Ginifur declared.

"If you won't tell me, then have you told him of the consequences of his actions? For if he has any honour in him, he will marry you and put an end to all this grief that you must be harbouring."

"No."

"No?" James Thomas frowned.

"No, I haven't told him. No I cannot tell him, and no I am not going to tell him. I shall bring the child up on my own." She said with finality.

"Ginifur, child! If only life were that simple. But you know that this cannot be. When your condition becomes apparent, as it must in the due course of time, the authorities will doubtless be informed by some well intentioned busy body. I give you my word it won't be me. Think hard on this Ginifur, talk to Netty, for she will guard your secret, tell your father of your predicament and ask guidance, and come to me if you think that I can be of assistance in any way."

Ginifur's eyes softened. "You are a good man Doctor. But my answer will be the same."

Doctor Thomas pondered the dilemma for a moment. "You and young Adam were always close. Time was when everyone thought it a certainty that you two would be wed. He is a good lad, kind hearted and generous. Perhaps . . ?"

"What on earth are you suggesting? That I ask Adam to marry me for the sake of someone else's child?" Ginifur was appalled at the suggestion.

"No Ginifur. For your sake. To keep you from being interned, jailed. For that is a very real possibility if you do not marry, or at least give the name of the father of your child to the authorities."

Ginifur buried her head in her lap. "I can't tell, I just can't." She sobbed.

James Thomas continued to pat her hand. "There, there. We still have time. You disguise your condition extremely well. No doubt due to your unusually good health and firm young muscles, your body shows hardly any evidence of your pregnancy at the moment. But that will change Ginny; you do have time to consider the consequences of your refusal to name the father of your child, but not long, no not long. Promise me that you will reflect on what I have said?"

Ginifur raised her bloodshot eyes, and his heart went out to her. He searched and searched his mind, but he could think of no one whom had been closer to Ginifur that young Adam. But if the child said that he was not the father, then it must be so. "I want you to take this physic that I am leaving, and continue to cover the cuts with the salve that I gave Netty. The lacerations are healing well, you are lucky that your face was only bruised and not cut. You have too pretty a face to have disfigured with scars."

This last comment brought a smile to Ginifur's face. "Thank you again. I will think about all that you said. I know that I have to, I just kept refusing to believe what I knew to be true." She said bravely.

"Then we shall say no more, for now. I shall call again, in a few days, but don't rush to get back to work Ginny. You still need rest, believe me." He removed a small bottle from his bag. "One drop in a glass of water on rising, and two drops before you go to sleep. It will help your body to rest and heal, and will not harm the infant that you carry." With one final pat of her hand he rose, closed the bag and left the room.

Ginifur stared into the flames, flickering in the hearth, and her eyes had not moved from the fireplace when Netty arrived with some tea and warm splits spread with thick clotted cream and jam. "My goodness, the fire is nearly out." She exclaimed. "What on earth is Tom thinking about?" She took a log from the basket and very quickly the fire was flaming brightly again.

"I expect he came when Doctor Thomas was here." Explained Ginifur. "He probably didn't want to disturb us."

There was truth in that statement. For Tom indeed had been to stoke up the fire, but turned away when he heard Ginifur's sobs. "Don' know what's amiss." He had said to Netty. "But the poor cheeld is sobbin' 'er 'eart out, that she be." Netty kept her secret, but she was glad that it was now out, even if not in the open. She had feared for some time that this was what it was going to be. God help the poor child, she is going to need it, she thought fearfully.

* * *

For the next few days Ginifur sat quietly in the large lounge. Netty said that the master would have insisted. Ginifur wasn't so sure, but did as she was bidden. Finally, she confided her secret to Netty, without telling her of the father of her child, and they talked long into the night with no ultimate decision, but it was comforting for Ginifur to talk of her fears. It was Netty who persuaded her to talk to Kate, nearer her own age; Netty hoped that she might confide in her. Perhaps Kate could persuade her of the wisdom in disclosing the name of the babe's father. But Ginifur was resolute; nothing would entice her to see reason, as they saw it.

Ginifur persuaded Kate to fetch some of Rachel's outgrown clothes for her to refashion for Rebecca, for the child was growing so fast that nothing fitted her. On occasions Kate brought the children to her and they played card games or read to her as she sewed. But each day Ginifur grew more restless to return to work. Christmas had come and gone without Ginny being aware of it and there was much to do, she said.

Finally they gave in to her demands, and Ginifur resumed her responsibilities.

The hardship in the community did not really improve, but was lessened considerably when the survivors of the shipwreck heard of their predicament. On New Year's Eve a wagon load of food and presents arrived to be distributed between the rescuers. It brought a much appreciated respite from the burden of living from hand to mouth, struggling to feed their families on a meagre diet of few roots and fish, and there was laughter heard in the village, where none had been heard for many a month. It pleased Ginifur that the villagers had something to smile about, for they still ate well at Tremanyon. Ginifur had done whatever she could to ease their problems, sending spare vegetables and restricting their own meat eating to give to the sick and infirm, or children and the elderly. She knew in her heart that Richard Tremayne would have wished it.

The New Year's Eve celebrations passed quietly enough and Simon, Kate and the children joined them in the manor house. Netty, though, insisted that they would eat in a grand style as they had not celebrated Christmas, and Tom declared it to be a 'right jolly do'. In spite of everything, Ginifur was inclined to agree. Simon had requested that Sam purchase three bottles of wine on his trip into Truro, a turkey, fresh and dried fruits and some sugar comfits as well. Whatever the cost it was worth it to hear Ginifur laugh again and, as they played forfeits and hunt the thimble, for a few hours Ginny forgot her woes.

197

* * *

But it was only a brief respite from the burden of worry that Ginifur carried and she knew that she would have to face her father with the news ere long. He listened with a heavy heart as she told him of her unplanned pregnancy. There were no recriminations, it would have been easier to bear if there had been, she thought afterwards. But he only gave her words of comfort and support, concern for her well being and her future. "Are you not going to ask me who the father is?" She had asked.

"If you wish me to know, then you'll tell me. If you do not, then you have your reasons, and I respect them." Was his reply. "But what of the consequences?"

That was the crux of the matter. What of the consequences? Kate had come up with the suggestion that if Ginny kept confined to the house, then no one would know but themselves, and they could pass the baby off as hers and Liam's. "A baby born as a result of the passion before Liam's leaving." She declared with a cheeky grin, unaware as she was of the events of the night before Captain Tremayne's departure. She could dress accordingly, fashion a bump with some old rags, and walk in an ungainly fashion nearer her time. After all she had had enough practice, she announced with a wry laugh. But could they get away with it? Ginny hopefully brought the subject up with Doctor Thomas, for they would need his support and discretion.

James Thomas laughed at the ingenuity of the plan. But said that it would be impossible to carry out, and as the days passed it would be inevitable that the staff at Tremanyon would learn the truth. Ginifur bravely insisted that she would tell them herself and, with Simon and Netty beside her, she called a meeting of the staff employed in and around the house.

Adam's initial reaction was complete and utter shock. For, like everyone else, he could think of no one who would do this thing to Ginifur and, what is more, anyone whom he thought Ginifur would consider giving her body to. This initial reaction firstly resulted in feelings of rejection, and then finally he seized upon the thought that, in spite of her position, he would offer to take her for his wife. After all, it was what he had always wanted, and he was firmly convinced that it was only Ginny's feelings of duty and obligation that came between them. Once she had the responsibility of a husband and child, this would all come to an end.

198

At first Ginifur rejected the idea. She said that it wasn't right to expect anyone else to shoulder her responsibilities and, besides, although she loved Adam dearly, she didn't love him in the right way to base a marriage upon. Adam was crestfallen, but undeterred. He persevered, saying that he accepted that Ginny had loved someone else, for why else would she be bearing his child, but that he would offer her love and security and in time their love would grow. Ginifur wanted to believe this, but in her heart she knew that this could never be.

"What should I do?" She asked her father.

Simon shook his head. "I cannot tell you, my child. Did you love the man who did this thing to you?"

"I did, and I still do. I always will." Was her honest reply.

Simon was puzzled. "Then tell me, why won't you inform him of your plight?"

"I can't Da. Don't ask me why." And Simon respected her silence.

Finally Adam persuaded her that he would make no demands of her. He said that he was more than willing for time to take its course. That he could, and would, wait for the day that Ginifur gave himself to him freely, and Ginifur's resolve buckled under the strain.

Ginifur and Adam were wed at the Church in the month of March. No one was surprised. Their only wonder was at the lateness of the marriage, for no one doubted that Adam was the father of the unborn child. It appeared to all the villagers that everyone was happy at the outcome.

And so they were, all but Ginifur and perhaps Simon and Samuel.

"They make an 'appy pair." Sam remarked to his son's father in law.

"I hope that they will be truly happy." Was Simon's simple wish for the couple.

"But 'e don' think so?"

Simon sighed, and voiced his doubts for the first time. "Do ye?"

Sam watched the couple as they joined in a jig. "I wish it could be so, but I fear it won't. I love Ginny as a daughter, I could love 'er no more. But I knows in my 'eart that 'er 'appiness will not be found with my son. There be 'eartbreak ahead o' we, Simon. And I believe that this be not only my thought alone. Ye believe this to be the truth also."

Simon had no answer to allay the man's fears, and said nothing as he stepped forward to toast the bride and the groom.

It had previously been decided that there was no room for the couple to live under the roof of coach cottage, it was full to overflowing already, and Ginifur still had the responsibility of caring for the Master's two daughters. Although married they would continue to live under separate roofs, until the Master returned to resume his responsibilities. But Ginifur knew that it was only postponing the inevitable outcome.

* * *

The hopes that the New Year would improve the fortunes of the community were proved false but, with the coming of spring, it was easier to garner food from the hedgerows. Boiled till tender, young nettle leaves were a good replacement for the spring cabbages that failed to mature, and young shoots of sea spinach was found in abundance above the high water mark. There were a few more fish to catch but not in abundance. The spring calves were born, but their mothers produced little milk and there was only enough to feed their young, very little to spare for their owners. What little there was, was given to the children and babes who could not be put to the breast. Everything seemed to be against them. The rabbits had deserted the district and, even if they had gone poaching, they wouldn't have found a partridge, pheasant or even a wood pigeon on the peninsular.

It was a hard time indeed, and everyone wondered when it would end. Old Betsy, the white witch, told them that the time was near. She had read it in the fire, the signs were quite clear, and they all believed her. They had to, for there was precious little hope for them to cling to in their hours of desperation.

Jamie Sawle was born on a bright sunny morning in the middle of June, with Doctor Thomas himself present at the birth. This delighted Rachel and Rebecca for it fell midway between their own birthdays.

Within days the fish returned to Dingerien Bay. The failing crops rallied, the cows mysteriously began to give more milk, and the villagers gave thanks for Jamie's safe delivery.

In their minds it was because the baby had been born to the heroin of the shipwreck. For what other reason could there possibly be?

Chapter Six
1754 – Quebec

PADRAIG O'DONNELL, DONNY, had been a carpenter by trade, but he harboured the dream that he would, one day, have a farm of his own. It was this that had brought him and his family to the New World, chasing a dream, and to the sheltered valley some few miles away from Twin Forks. Here, with Elly by his side, they had cut the timbers to construct the sturdy log cabin. Each log fitted snugly into the next and any tiny gaps were filled with a mixture of mud, moss and dried grass giving them two bedrooms and a large living room. He had built a lathe, and furnished the house himself with timber from the forest. He had made everything from tables to chairs, cupboards for utensils and clothes and bowls and platters for preparing food and eating. Elly had turned the cabin into a warm and welcoming home. In truth, she declared, it was far better than the tiny hovel that they had been forced to live in back in Ireland and, although she admitted that the winters were long and cold the summers, though short, were always dry and sunny. The valley had been sparsely covered with trees when they arrived and decided to make their home here, most of these grew where the hillside rose to meet the mountains and she said that it had been an easy task to create their farm. A small river ran through the centre of the valley, near to the site of the homestead, so they had an abundant supply of water and good soil. Richard asked if she feared that they might be attacked, and she said that she accepted that this did sometimes happen of late. But she and her family had made friends with the Indian population long ago, as soon as they had arrived, and they called in on her in friendship if they were passing near by. Donny had fortified the house as well as he could. Wooden shutters could be placed across the windows, with a slit in them just wide enough to take aim and shoot a gun. A stockade fence surrounded the perimeter, but she realised that this would be quite useless if they should come under attack. Moreover she believed, innocently, that no one would now attack a woman alone with children. Richard hoped that this would be so but, from what he had learned, this was not likely to deter anyone whose eyes were fixed resolutely on wiping out the English settlers. He was beginning to admire the resolve and determination of these settlers in their search for a new life in a New World.

Richard and Liam enjoyed their visit. They taught Tuck all that Running Bear had taught them, and he flourished under their guidance, advancing swiftly into early adulthood. They extended the cabin, even though the outcome was far short of the standard of the original cabin built by Donny. But Elly proclaimed it an outstanding success, and Tuck was pleased that he finally had a room of his own.

The snows finally cleared from the valley in April. Running Bear, true to his promise, returned, and by the time Richard's son struggled to make his appearance on earth they were well within striking distance of Jean-Paul and Quebec.

Richard and Liam had used their time wisely. Whilst teaching Tuck to fend for his family, they had replenished their fur stocks. They now had an excellent assortment of skins and furs to substantiate their claim that they were fur trappers. Running Bear greeted them warmly and, as much as Elly wished that they could stay longer, they departed with the promise to call upon her and the children on their return journey. Tuck too was sad to see them go. But with his shoulders straight and his head held high declared that, due to Dickon and Liam, he was now fit to take care of them all.

It was with a heavy heart that they took their leave, turning to wave before they disappeared in the tree line. Richard declared that it was almost as bad as leaving Tremanyon, and Liam was inclined to agree. For a brief spell they had tasted again the comforts of family life.

With improved weather conditions they now covered the ground more speedily. They had received Jean-Paul's message that he awaited them, and Running Bear knew where to meet him. On their final night, only a day's ride from Quebec, they made camp beside a wide river and waited. It was a clear night, and the stars shone so brightly that Liam felt that he could almost reach out and touch them. They sat in silence as Running Bear brought their attention to a shooting star. "A good omen." He declared. "Your mission is blessed by the Gods."

Suddenly Running Bear held up his hand in a silencing gesture. They listened, but for once they could not hear what he could. Nevertheless, they took up their pre-arranged positions by the fire as they had planned. It looked innocent enough to a passer by, but

Liam and Richard were ready if an unwanted visitor approached, and Running Bear had taken cover nearby.

A lone rider approached them on foot, his horse following on the loose rein as he negotiated the track by the river. "Cest un bonne nuit." He spoke in French as he came nearer the fire. The billy can bubbled on the fire and the Frenchman sniffed appreciatively. "Café . . . non?" Richard lifted the spare cup without speaking, and offered it to the stranger. "Merci." He took it, sipped it, and glanced around about him, noting two neatly tied bedrolls and the pile of furs beside the tethered horses.

"That is a fine collection of furs that you have there my friends." He spoke in English but received no response and returned to French. They were a rough looking couple, he thought, and turned away. He was about to leave the bright circle created by the fire when Richard called out.

"Mon ami!"

Slowly the Frenchman turned, screwing up his eyes as he scrutinised the face of the taller man. He had at first thought the man unkempt, but on further appraisal realised that this was not so. Beneath his fur hat, his hair was long but clean, and his facial hair had been trimmed, not allowed to grow in the wild disorderly fashion more favoured by trappers. And although his complexion was dark and swarthy, caused by long exposure to the elements, it made the whites of his eyes so much brighter. This face, and that of the younger man, was impossible to read. This pair had spent too many months in the forest, estranged from company, their ways had become like those of the Indian. And yet! Those eyes! Bright blue they were, accentuated by the whiteness, and he could swear that they were laughing! Cautiously he stepped nearer to the fire. The younger man looked up from whittling the piece of wood, and smiled through his raggedly trimmed beard. He looked like . . .

"Liam! Liam! Is that really you?" He turned to the stranger with the blue eyes. "It isn't? It isn't? Mon Dieu, I don't believe my eyes."

Richard rose from the log beside the fire, his hands outstretched. "Hello Jean-Paul. Is our disguise truly so good?"

"Good! Cest magnifique. And those furs!! You didn't trap them yourselves!"

"Indeed they did." Running Bear's voice made Jean-Paul jump, for he hadn't heard him coming up on him from behind.

"It is incredible, truly incredible. If you can fool me, then you will fool anyone. Come, my friends, tell me about your adventures since we last met, and I will tell you all my news.

And so it was, around the camp fire, that they exchanged their news. Jean-Paul was sad to hear of the murder of his friend and family, and of the untimely end to Paddy O'Donnell. He listened to the descriptions of their travels, and learning the ways of the wilderness from Running Bear, and marvelled at the change in the man and the boy. They looked as though they had been here for eight years, not just the eight months that they had.

Jean-Paul told them of his arrival in Quebec, and the way that he had managed to wheedle his way into the confidences of the army. "This has turned out to be easier than I expected." He proclaimed jubilantly. "And, would you believe it? They want me to try to find someone who is going back to England, who would be prepared to find out what is in the minds of the English Government. I said that I knew of two Irishmen who wanted to return for a spell, one of whom had spent time in the English army and had connections. But I made no promises. I wanted to know what you thought about it first. Seeing you now, I am confident that having seen you like this there is no way that any one would ever know you when you return to normal life."

Richard laughed. "Normal life! I have forgotten what that was. All I want now is a hot bath and a hair cut."

"A hair cut!" Jean-Paul held his hand up. "Not too much. It's just right as it is, believe me. And you Liam! Well! I can't believe it is the same lad who travelled on ship with us. You're a credit to Richard, and to you Running Bear. Did you ever believe that you would achieve this transformation?

Running Bear smiled. "Of course! I would expect nothing less from my blood brothers." Before their parting in the winter, Running Bear had produced a knife and, making a tiny incision in each of their finger tips, they had solemnly mixed their blood, as was his custom. They were now brothers.

They talked until dawn struggled to push away the early mist clinging to the valley floor and, as Running Bear took his leave, they packed the furs upon the pack horses and set off for Quebec.

* * *

Every entrance to Quebec was guarded by military presence and, as they approached the uniformed guards at the main gates, Richard noticed the strict scrutiny that was being given to the documentations or papers and hoped that their own documents would hold up under scrutiny. As they waited he took the opportunity to study the surrounding countryside, its position would make it difficult to formulate an attack. There was a steady flow of people both in and out of the settlement, papers were only checked on the inward journey and no heed whatsoever was given to those who were only leaving. They passed un-accosted, without so much as a token glance from the soldiers, and he realised that they did have a weakness in their defence if, and only if, it was possible to gain admittance. With this in mind he made a detailed examination of the diversity of apparel worn by those wishing to enter. Most were of the lower order, poorly dressed and with little consideration to personal hygiene. Presuming of course that they had access to such facilities, for obviously some had travelled many miles before they had actually reached this point, as they themselves had. There were a few carts, drawn by a motley collection of animals, but mostly handcarts pushed by their owners. Some wealthier men rode on horseback and there was the occasional carriage needless to say owned by the gentry from Paris or Orleans.

They were no more than a few yards from the post when one of the guards looked down the line. For a moment he stared straight at the threesome, before passing a few words with a companion. Richard's heart skipped a beat. He had thought that they would be quite inconspicuous amongst the throng that pressed forward. The Captain of the guard listened and then followed his gaze before advancing down the line. Perhaps he was approaching someone else; in any case Richard did not want to draw attention to themselves by trying to attract Jean-Paul's attention, which was diverted elsewhere. But no, the soldier was indeed heading towards them and Richard was ready to admit defeat when a broad grin stretched the soldiers face from ear to ear. "Mon ami!" He called out in greeting.

Jean-Paul turned at the sound of the voice. "Bon Jour Maurice. Como ce vas?" He responded as if to an old friend. Richard relaxed, attempting to hide any sign of his previous unease.

"Are these the trapper friends that you were hoping to meet up with again? Welcome to Quebec." The soldier saluted Richard, then continued. "A friend of the Comte de Varron is a friend of mine." He stood to attention, and nodded briefly.

"Merci monsieur, you are most kind." Richard answered in perfect French.

The sergeant expressed his surprise. "You speak French! I thought you were from Ireland?"

Richard kept to the Frenchman's language. "That is true. But I have had many opportunities to visit your beautiful country, and have a good ear for languages. French is a lovely language, so much more expressive than English." He flattered the soldier

The soldier laughed. "I like your friend, Monsieur le Comte. But tell me . . . what on earth are you doing waiting in line with the rest of this rabble? You should have come right past and told me that you were waiting. Come, come. All of you, come." He led the way to the front of the queue and, brushing aside any objections from the guards on duty, he lifted the barrier. "We shall see you at the supper in honour of le General Montreaux, will we?"

Jean-Paul expressed an apology. "I think not. It would be impolite of me to leave my friends to amuse themselves on their first night in Quebec."

"Is that all that is stopping you? Do your friends have suitable clothes for such an occasion?" He asked

"Of course, that would be no problem." Assured Jean-Paul. "But..."

"No. No excuses. I'll send the invitations to your rooms. You are still lodging at the Madam's house on Rue de jardin?"

"I am, but . . . it is too much of an imposition."

"Nonsense, nonsense. Go now. I shall see you later. Adieu my friends, adieu." He hastened them along as they passed without so much as a glance at their papers.

Well out of reach of hearing Richard let out a deep breath and spoke in low tones. "I really thought, for one moment back there, that they had picked us out as spies."

Jean-Paul laughed. "Believe me, mon ami, there is no way anyone is about to consider you a spy. Have you actually seen yourselves?"

Richard and Liam glanced up and down at their apparel. "Well no, to be honest, I don't think I have." Said Richard, as he looked Liam up and down as if for the first time." A broad smile crossed his face. "But now that you bring it to my attention, we do look a little . . . different.

"Different! Well that is an understatement." He laughed as they reached the first street. "Follow me. First we will arrange safe stowage of your furs, stable the horses, and then I shall take you to the bath house. The best bath house in town."

"Then lead on, we are right behind you." Richard placed an affectionate arm about Liam's shoulders as they pressed their way through the narrow passages, thronged with people going about their daily business.

Whilst Richard and Liam luxuriated in the steaming baths, had their backs scrubbed by two delightful Mademoiselles, and smoked two large cigars as scented soapy water was regularly topped up with jugs of hot water, Richard began to feel almost human once more. Jean-Paul efficiently arranged the prompt arrival of the gentleman's outfitter who, after sizing them up declared that he would be able to fit them from his stock. However, he confessed, they must accept that the fit would not be to his usual high standard. Whilst the elegantly dressed gentleman hurried away to arrange for the delivery of evening wear, from top to toe, they availed themselves of a long massage and then, draped securely in bath robes, sat in the barbers chair for a hair cut and a trim for their beards. Mindful of Jean-Paul's bidding; they left their hair quite long and only trimmed their beards, having them tidied. However the end result was altogether quite pleasing and they were confident that they would be presentable for the evening invitation.

* * *

The clothes, when they arrived, fitted perfectly and although Richard declared that they were a little flamboyant for his taste, they were designed to the highest degree of French fashion. With coats of the finest velvet, waistcoats of beautiful brocade, and ruffles of exquisite Flemish lace, they created the illusion of a fine pair of Irish gentlemen abroad. Richard was especially complimentary of Liam's outfit. "Well my fine friend, you look quite dashing. I doubt even your own mother would recognise you." He gave a low laugh. "I wish Ginny and Kate could see you now, they would be as proud of you as I am."

Liam blushed uncomfortably, and pulled at the tight band at his throat. "Do ye think so?"

"I do Liam. I really do." Then he returned to their present circumstances "Now, tonight! Whatever you do, stay as near to me as possible. Try not to be drawn into any conversation that relates to the political position of the English and the French. And, whatever you do, stick to the story that we are here purely as fur trappers. I know that I don't have to tell you all this, but its best that we both understand. I shall continue to speak in French only, partly because my own accent is easily identified, whatever reasons we may give. I don't know, but it may put them at ease and they may be more open about what is going on out here. Keep your ears open, and listen for any information that may be of help, and tell me later, when we are alone. Now, do you have any questions?"

Liam rolled his shoulders to ease the tension. "Surely they're going to recognise I'm not cut out to wear clothes such as these . . . S" Richard raised a wary eyebrow. "Dickon." Liam finished lamely. "It's the clothes. It was alright out there, in the woods." He explained, and Richard smiled.

"These clothes are the least of your worries, but a slip up like that might cost us both our lives." He placed a hand on Liam's shoulder. "Over the last few months Liam, you have almost become the brother you purport to be. Indeed I sometimes find myself thinking of you as such. Things will never be the same for either of us again. It may well be that you will have to continue to use this name that you have now Christened me with, when we return home. So don't let yourself make a slip now Liam, too much rests on your shoulders."

Liam looked into Richard's open face, his eyes agreed with the words from his mouth, and he signalled his acknowledgement with a brief nod. "I won't let ye down, I give ye my word."

"I know you won't Liam" This time he gripped both of his shoulders firmly in his hands. "Now, Let us put our best foot forward. If you don't catch the eyes of some pretty French coquette I will be amazed. Hark. I hear a carriage." Richard moved quickly to the window. "Yes it is Jean-Paul. Are you ready?"

Liam found a nervous laugh. "Be Jesus. They'll not be believin' me, when I tell 'em. Liam Fierney all dressed up as a gentleman, and attending a grand do. They'll think I've gone simple in the head, t' be sure they will. No, tis thinkin' I'd better be keepin' this to meself I am"

"To be honest Liam, I'm finding it hard to believe myself. The two of us here, in the midst of the French Army and being entertained like this. No I'm not finding it easy to accept at all."

Jean-Paul awaited them by the carriage steps. He greeted their approach with a well humoured chuckle as he shook his head. "Mon ami, what can I say?"

"As little as possible" Richard retorted as he leapt into the carriage. "We're both feeling like two over dressed geese, I only hope that no one intends to serve us up for dinner."

"No fear of that, mon ami, believe me. Le General is eager to meet with you, and he has heard that you have brought in some white ermine furs in perfect condition. He is eager to purchase them for his wife." Jean-Paul explained. "To be honest, I find it hard to believe that you really trapped those animals yourselves. Are you sure Running Bear didn't do it for you?"

Richard laughed. "I know. I find it hard to believe myself. But we did, yes. If the truth be known, and circumstances had been different, I would rate it as one of the most wonderful experiences of my life. As it is, well, it certainly is an experience. One I don't think I would like to repeat.

Jean-Paul's face lost its humour. "I agree mon ami, but the end . . ."

"I hope that the end justifies the danger that we are all putting ourselves in." Finished Richard. "And I fear that you will never be able to set foot on French soil again after this."

Jean-Paul did not answer. The only sound was the horses' hooves and the wheels of the carriage, as they rattled towards the barracks.

Richard's fears for the dangers involved in such a venture as theirs were quite reasonable. However, on this occasion, they were unfounded. Their entrance was greeted with great interest. News of the arrival of the Irish trappers had quickly spread, and it was rumoured that they were not mere trappers, but Irish Gentlemen out on an adventure. The inhabitants of Quebec rarely received visitors from France, let alone Ireland, and they were eager to hear news from Europe and to meet the two elegantly dressed gentlemen. Word had quickly spread from the bath-house, and the barbers, that they were both elegant and young, handsome and wealthy. Mother's had no difficulty in coaxing their daughters to pay special attention to their dress and hair, and the interest had ensured a full turn out at the Assembly Room.

As they mounted the stairs, on either side of Jean-Paul, Richard acknowledged their greetings verbally, and Liam with an enchanting smile that was perceived to be the shyness of a younger brother.

Jean-Paul strode confidently into the grand room, which was exquisitely decorated for the occasion with gigantic displays of flowers. Strains of music rose from the discreetly placed musicians, and gave a soft accompaniment to the gay chatter of the assembled to greet the General. The arrival of the newcomers soon caught the eyes of those already present, and a tall gentleman, dressed in a salmon coloured velvet coat and richly embroidered with gold, detached himself from the throng to make his way towards them. "Monsieur le Comte! Delighted that you have joined us. These must be your friends that you speak so highly of. Welcome to Quebec." He said. Then added "Welcome to New France."

Richard bowed briefly. "Merci monsieur. It is most kind of you to invite us to this special occasion."

The fine fellow raised an eyebrow. "Your French is excellent monsieur. You must have spent much time in France to acquire an accent thus. Well, Comte de Varron, are you going to introduce me?"

Jean-Paul smiled briefly. "Monsieur de Crecy, may I introduce my good friends from Eire. Monsieur Dickon Fierney and his brother Liam, from the county of Kilkenny in Ireland."

Monsieur de Crecy bowed low. "I am, pleased to meet you Monsieur. I hope that your stay with us will be a pleasant one, and a profitable one. Let me introduce you to some of my family and friends." He singled out a group not far away. A woman, obviously his wife, dressed in the latest fashion from Paris, and a young woman, divinely pretty, with blonde curls bouncing against her alabaster neck which was emphasised by the low cut of her classical sapphire gown, and the matching gems adorning her neck, ears and hair. "My wife, Madame Marguerite de Crecy, and my daughter Marie."

"Enchanted." In turn, Richard took the extended hands and kissed the tips of the fingers covered in priceless lace. Liam bowed politely, following Richards actions to perfection, and Richard found it hard to disguise his smile of amusement. Liam was truly a quick learner or an adept mimic.

Monsieur de Crecy turned to the gentlemen of the party. "May I introduce Captain Duvaix and Major Gravelle? Both gentlemen being members of the French Army of course."

Captain Duvaix and Major Gravelle bowed stiffly, adding their welcome, and the conversation was aimed at Richard and Liam's visit. Great interest was taken in their accounts of their exploits in the wilderness, and their bravery at facing the wild animals that they had shot, or trapped, for the highly prized furs. The discussion on European politics had arisen when a buzz of excitement filled the room. Their attention was mercifully drawn to the arrival of the General.

General Montreaux made his entrance surrounded by officials in high capacity. A short man in stature, but with an aura of dignity, he moved slowly around the room nodding briefly in acknowledgement to the words of welcome. Richard and Jean-Paul watched from the secluded alcove, their newly found acquaintances having moved forward for a better view. The General's observant eyes flitted about the mass of bodies as though searching out something, or someone."

"Not an easy man to deceive, I fear." Richard commented quietly as the Generals eyes settled on the trio at the furthest point of the room. Jean-Paul's eyes met the Generals, and he bowed his head in acknowledgement of his attendance before passing further down the line to the waiting dignitary.

"Perhaps not. But I have no doubts of the success of this mission." Jean-Paul answered confidently.

"Then if you have no doubts . . ." Richard left the sentence incomplete as Monsieur de Crecy returned to direct them to the tables laden with food for the reception.

"Come, my friends. Come and sample the delights of our country. I expect it will have been many months since you enjoyed the pleasure of a civilised repast."

Richard's laugh was genuine. "Indeed. You would be quite correct in that assumption."

"Then you will much appreciate the gourmet delights on offer."

Richard smiled. "Verily we shall. Liam and I are most grateful to you for such a generous invitation."

This pleased Monsieur de Crecy greatly and, with undisguised delight, he led the party towards the room laid out for the buffet.

The evening passed pleasantly, with few difficult moments. Richard remained faithful to his word and spoke only French. Jean-Paul translated when necessary for Liam, and most could speak a little English to attempt to put him at ease and make him welcome. They showed pleasurable interest in his own country, both being Catholic allies, and on this subject Liam could converse quite happily. It was not until the first guests were making their departure that the official party headed in their direction.

"Comte de Varron!" Major Gravelle hailed him. "General Montreaux wishes you to introduce him to your friends from across the seas.

"Indeed it would be a pleasure." Jean-Paul made the brief introductions.

Richard's bearing impressed the General, and his words of welcome were warm and sincere. He asked briefly about their exploits and said that he had heard that they had brought with them some pure white ermine furs.

"Indeed, that is correct." Richard informed him. "We were extremely lucky, for they are furs of excellent quality and much sought after."

The General smiled knowingly. "Quite so, quite so. I may be interested in them myself, if you do not already have a buyer for them"

"I would be delighted to show them to you, Sir." Richard offered, knowing that this could easily camouflage the real intent for his visit.

"Then perhaps we could discuss the matter?"

"It would indeed be an honour, General." Richard bowed.

General Montreaux beckoned to his attendant. "Make an appointment with Monsieur Fierney for the morrow."

The attendant looked dismayed. "You have a full diary of appointments for the morrow, Sir."

"Then change something." The General growled. "I look forward to the pleasure of renewing our acquaintance Monsieur." The General bade them farewell and turned to leave with his entourage.

The flummoxed attendant consulted his General's diary, shaking his head in dismay. "In the afternoon?"

"We are free all day." Richard assured him.

"Then tomorrow, in the afternoon, at four. I shall send a carriage."

"There is no need." Jean-Paul informed him. "I have my own carriage, it will be a pleasure to escort Monsieur Fierney to the General."

The attendant looked unsure. "I don't know?"

"Don't worry. I will ensure that Monsieur Fierney arrives in good time." He dismissed the General's assistant. "Now mon ami, let us retire to our rooms. I expect that you are looking forward to a good nights rest, in a soft bed."

"You cannot know how much." Richard laughed. "Do you hear that Liam? A real bed!! Soft feathers to lie on and clean sheets to cover us. Absolute luxury. Absolute bliss."

Liam didn't mention the fact that he had never slept on a feather mattress in his whole life. This was an experience he was looking forward to.

The three friends left the elegant surroundings in high spirits. The evening had gone better than expectations and, besides that, had been pleasantly diverting.

* * *

After the evenings entertainment, and assisted by the luxury of lying in the large comfortable beds, Richard and Liam awoke from an excellent night's sleep to find that Jean Paul had organised a spread to break their fast, followed by a tour of their surroundings. As they walked around the fortified town Richard made mental notes of the landmarks and defences that were visible for all to see, but all the while appearing to take an interest in the normal activities of the inhabitants of the bustling community. He was surprised by the height of the cliff that bordered the town from the St Lawrence River, and pondered on the possibility of an assault by this means. He doubted anyone would expect and assault from that position. They moved on, and here and there they stopped to pass the time of day with an acquaintance of Jean-Paul, or sample the taste of food from the stalls in the market. It was apparent that Jean-Paul had become well accepted in the locale, and all doors were open to him. What was left of the morning and afternoon passed quickly and, as the time neared, Jean-Paul led them back to their rooms to make ready for the meeting with the General.

The ride to the General's quarters passed through the military emplacements, giving Richard further valuable insight to the fortifications and weaponry for the occupying army. Assembled within the encampment was a large number of infantrymen parading on the parade ground, attending to military duties and the like. A vast collection of buildings formed the stables where the horses were either being attended to or exercised, and Richard concluded that there was a like number of cavalry in attendance. As a whole it represented a formidable army. Jean-Paul informed him that the troops had been called in from the outposts at the onset of winter, but less than half had returned, for what reason they had remained in the wilderness he had failed to learn. All of this Richard committed to memory, for it was far too dangerous to put on paper.

The carriage drew up in front of the low building, which was the temporary office of General Montreaux. After they had alighted from the carriage, an armed soldier escorted the driver away, together with the horses and carriage, and Jean-Paul led the way up the short flight of steps. The sharp knock on the door was answered immediately and the General's assistant opened the door to give them admittance.

General Montreaux rose from the seat behind the imposing desk, and moved forward to greet them. "Bonjour, I hope you slept well. It was a good evening, don't you think?"

"An excellent evening indeed." Jean-Paul agreed. "Both diverting, interesting and informative."

"Yes indeed. Well Monsieur Fierney, I see that you have brought the ermine pelts with you. May I inspect them?" He indicated the large bundle carefully wrapped and tied in hessian. "You may leave us Renard." He dismissed his assistant. "I shall not require your services for a while." The assistant looked agitated but, nevertheless, obeyed the command.

Liam untied the bundle and carefully spread the furs on the floor.

General Montreaux let out a slow whistle of approval. "Mon Dieu! These are excellent furs indeed, and no doubt will command an equally high price." He bent to examine the pure white fur. "Not a blemish to be seen." He added.

"There are none to be found." Richard assured him.

"Then I shall not haggle with you, for I have set my mind on having them for my wife, for a gift when I return to France."

They quickly agreed on a fair price before Liam carefully packed the furs again and the General wrote a note of authority for payment. To seal the arrangement General Montreaux opened a bottle of French Brandy, offering them each a glass, and for a few moments the talk was of trivial matters. Richard was of the mind that he had mistaken the invitation when suddenly there was a change in the direction that the conversation was taking.

"Do you have the opportunity to visit England?" The general suddenly asked.

If Richard had not been expecting something of this nature, he might have been flummoxed. "I do, on occasions. I was sent to England for my education, it was this that enabled me to spend much of my time in France."

"Where were you educated?"

"In London and Cambridge."

"You have friends there?"

Richard smiled. "Acquaintances rather than friends. There is not much love lost between our two countries."

General Montreaux had acquainted himself with the political position between England and Ireland. "No, I don't expect there is. So you have no loyalties to the King of England?"

"The Irish have no reason to be loyal to the Crown of England." Was as honest an answer that Richard could give.

"Do you have connections in London?" The General felt his way.

"Connections?" Richard knew quite well what he referred to.

"In government. Do you know any persons involved in government?"

"Quite a few, in point of fact." This, at least, was an honest answer. "My English education means that I am acquainted with number of current members of the government who were at Cambridge at the same time I was. We keep in touch now and then to discuss the general way of things."

"Interesting. Interesting. More brandy?" Liam declined the offer, but Richard and Jean-Paul accepted a further glass as the general continued with his conversation. "The British are a land hungry nation, do you not think?" Richard disguised a smile. "I wonder what their position is on Canada?"

"I have been away too long to comment on that I am afraid."

"But you hope to return soon?"

"As soon as Liam and I have made enough money, or find the pangs of homesickness, and the want for a comfier lifestyle become too great." Jested Richard.

"If it is the latter then that won't be much longer I think. Maybe you would be interested in an undertaking of financial benefit which might help you to bring your homecoming forward." The general suggested obliquely.

"An increase in our financial position could certainly aid that. Did you have anything particular in mind?"

"I might. I might." But the General immediately changed the topic of conversation. "What are your immediate plans?"

"As soon as we have secured a good price on the remainder of the furs, we will head west. I have a fancy to visit Nova Scotia. Mon ami, le Comte, has told me how beautiful it is there." Richard told him. "Yes it is." General Montreaux agreed. "I stopped there on the way out here, but a journey overland! That is a great distance to travel on foot. Do you plan to return to Quebec?"

"All being well. Yes. We plan to spend the time making a fine collection of furs to take home with us." Richard placed his glass on the desk. "It has been good doing business with you General."

General Montreaux frowned briefly, then turned to his desk and fingered through a pile of papers. "I believe there is a ship sailing for Louisburg in a few days time. I am sure that I could secure you a passage on board, and provide you with introductions in Nova Scotia."

Richard and Jean-Paul could hardly believe their luck. "In that case general, we would be happy to accept your offer, and it will certainly mean that we will hopefully be able to return to Quebec before the winter sets in next year." Jean-Paul spoke for them both.

The general raised an eyebrow. "You will be joining your friends on the next stage of the adventure? Do you think that you are up to it?" He eyed Jean-Paul's fashionable clothing, in great contrast to the serviceable, though now new apparel of his friends.

"It is too good an opportunity to miss. I am looking forward to it. Something that I will be able to tell my grand children about." Jean-Paul grinned.

General Montreaux smiled doubtfully. "Come and see me when you return. I may be interested in some more furs. For my daughter." His smile suggested there would be another reason.

"It would be a pleasure." Richard indicated to Liam that they were leaving and he turned to the door.

General Montreaux led the way onto the covered veranda. "Merci, le Comte, for your introduction to your friends. Enjoy your trip. It has been a most pleasurable meeting. I shall not forget it."

Jean-Paul smiled warmly, but kept his thoughts behind his dark eyes. He doubted very much that the General would forget the episode in years to come. And if Jean Paul indeed did decide to return to Paris in the future, this incident would more than likely make things very difficult for him indeed.

Back in the carriage, having bade their farewell and safely outside the military compound, Richard gave a deep sigh of relief. "What do you think of that, Jean-Paul?"

Jean-Paul laughed. "Better than I hoped. Far better. You were incredible, so convincing I even found myself believing in you." He punched at the air. "And to then be provided with the means of travelling to Louisburg in less than half the time it will take us overland! Who could ask for more, mon ami? Who could ask for more?"

Their laughter was mixed with relief as they made their way back to the store where they had arranged to discuss the sale of the remainder of the furs.

* * *

Whilst Richard and Jean-Paul made ready for the voyage, Liam, taking his gun with him, to all appearances went hunting for the day. In actual fact he met up with Running Bear to tell him of their plans and arrange for a message to get to him as soon as they returned. Two days later, the trio and their horses boarded a merchant ship bound for Louisburg. The return journey would take them across water and through wild country with plenty of opportunity to hunt and collect furs to take home.

The Hidden Cave

JAMIE DIDN'T CRY as he entered the world on that bright sunny June morning, and Eliza Scott was heard to say that he gurgled merrily as she wrapped him in the sheet before placing him in Ginifur's arms. "I've never seen a baby so happy to come out of the womb." She declared. The corners of the tiny rosebud mouth were turned upwards into a contented smile as his eyelids separated briefly to glimpse at his new surroundings. "If I didn't know better myself, I'd swear that child is smiling already." Eliza puffed up the pillows behind Ginifur's head as she gazed down at the miracle in her arms.

"I can't thank you enough. I don't know how I'll ever pay you Doctor Thomas, or you Miss Scott." She said.

"There's nothing to pay my bird." Eliza told her. "After what you did for that cheeld back along, you certainly deserves this attention. Isn't that so Doctor?"

Doctor Thomas dried his hands. "She's right Ginny. There was a slight chance that there may have been complications. After your heroic deeds I wasn't about to take any chances. You deserved the best attention, and Miss Scott and I both agree on that. I am glad to see that you and your son have both survived the ordeal, he is a lovely baby." He folded the towel and placed it on the nearby cupboard. "Now, make yourself presentable for that young husband of yours, and we'll send Kate to fetch him."

Kate reached out for the baby and handed Ginny a comb and hand mirror from the dresser. "What are you going to call him, Ginny?"

"Jamie." Was Ginifur's instantaneous reply.

Kate stared at the baby, wrapped into a tight bundle in her arms. "Any reason?"

Ginifur screwed up her face and smiled. "No. I just like the name." She had tidied herself to her satisfaction and held out her arms.

From that moment on Jamie was to bring joy to all who were lucky enough to share his life, and to those whose lives touched it in passing. All that is, except one.

For from the moment that Adam entered the room in the Big House, to see the babe snuggled close to Ginifur's breast, the first stirrings of resentment entered his head and found lodging within his heart. He had convinced himself that when the baby arrived it would of course be his and Ginifur's. But seeing the happiness in her eyes, as she gazed lovingly at the tiny scrap of humanity lying in her arms, he knew that he had been deceiving himself all along. This child was Ginifur's. It had never been, and never would be his.

"Come on Adam." Kate pulled at his sleeve. "There's nothin' to be afeared of. Tis only a baby, Adam. Look. Isn't he just like Ginny with all that black hair?"

Adam pushed aside the angry questions that were once more rearing their ugly heads, and affected a smile of cheerfulness. "Are 'e alright Ginny? I hope it wasn't too bad for 'e."

Ginifur tore her eyes away from her son. "No Adam. It was quite easy really. Look." She held him up for Adam to see. "Isn't he beautiful?"

Jamie chose this moment to force his little eyelids apart, and they had a brief glimpse of his bright twinkling eyes. Adam took in the curve of his tiny mouth and firmly convinced himself that Jamie was laughing at him and actually found Adam's situation amusing. From this very moment Adam was resolved that Ginifur should have another baby, another boy, a son. His son.

"Oh look!" Kate exclaimed. "His eyes are the brightest blue I have ever seen."

Ginifur had prepared herself for this possibility. "All baby's eyes are blue at birth." She countered.

"Maybe." Kate agreed. "But I don't think his will change, for I've never seen a pair of eyes as bright a blue as his." Her voice trailed off as if she was remembering something.

"My mother's eyes were blue. Bright blue, Da told me. Da's eyes are green, like mine. Jamie must have inherited them from my mother."

Kate smiled at her. "That explains it then." She agreed.

Minute by minute, hour by hour and day by day Adam's resentment grew. It festered deep inside him, eating away at his insides and turning the once loving and caring young man into one filled with jealousy, bitterness and anger.

In fairness to Ginifur, she did not overly spoil the child, for he received only the attention that was deservedly his and, as soon as she was well enough, she returned to work to continue her responsibilities of running the house and caring for Rachel and Rebecca in Richard's absence. The girls adored the new arrival, and would watch over him carefully as he lay crooning in the bassinette, which had been a gift from Fanny Boscawen which she had brought over from Tregothnan as soon as she had heard the news.

Ginifur knew that Adam's advances could not be avoided for much longer, the day would have to come when they must become man and wife in the truest sense of the word. In truth, she admitted to herself, he had been extremely patient. However much he might have deluded himself into thinking that he could wait until she was ready. Ginifur knew that this was not a realistic objective even though, in all honesty, she admitted to herself that she secretly hoped that moment would never come.

During the first short weeks of their marriage they had little opportunity to be alone, and then, after Jamie's birth, Ginifur had little spare time with the additional work created by a new born child. However, her caring nature ensured that she made every effort to encourage Adam to develop a relationship with Jamie and, although they still had to spend their nights apart, Adam had from the beginning of there marriage taken all his meals with them in the kitchen, and they enjoyed a few brief moments alone in the staff sitting room.

So it was that on a sunny day near the end of August, when Jamie was two months old and could be left for a few hours with Kate and the girls, that Ginifur requested Netty to pack a basket of food and asked Sam if he could spare Adam for the afternoon, suggesting that they take a walk to Kylyn Cove.

Adam's initial half hearted response was soon raised when Ginny informed him that she intended leaving Jamie, Rachel and Rebecca with Kate for a few hours. "It would be good." She declared. "To stretch my legs, paddle my feet in the water and get away from the house for a short while."

Adam couldn't agree more. The sooner he got her away from the house on a permanent basis, the sooner he thought that they would be happy. How he was going to achieve this he didn't know, yet. But there had to be a way, and Adam was determined to find it. However, for the moment, he was prepared to set aside all thoughts for the future, or Jamie for that matter, for the prospect of a whole afternoon with Ginny was a step in the right direction. Surely that was proof enough, if proof be needed, that she wanted to spend time with him and it was only Tremanyon that got in the way. Yet again Adam managed to convince himself that everything would be right if only they had a home of their own.

Adam stepped out beside Ginifur, and felt that he was once more walking upon air. There was a spring in his step and he cheerfully swung the basket as though it were as light as a feather, even though it contained a stone jar of cider, a pork pie, cheese, fresh bread, apples and a cherry pie with a pot of cream. Adam thought that his heart would burst with happiness as Ginifur put her arm through his in an affectionate gesture and chatted away in the close manner of their youth. Only Ginifur was aware of the fact that she deliberately avoided any mention of Jamie, or his progress. She was sensitive to his feelings towards her son, and had more than once found herself wondering whether she had been fair to either herself, Adam or Jamie by agreeing to this marriage of convenience. But she had agreed. Therefore she would try her best to make Adam happy. For that was the least he deserved and, if she could succeed in that, then maybe his attitude to Jamie would improve.

It was a beautiful day. Ginifur had said as much to Sam before they left Tremanyon. Sam had nodded wisely. "Yes, fer now. Enjoy yerselves, fer take my word on it, tis the lull before the storm. Us'll see rain afore night fall." But the day was too beautiful to spoil with thoughts of rain and, as they walked arm in arm down the lane towards the mill, Ginifur's forced bright spirits were replaced with genuine enjoyment and, by the time they turned into Well Lane, it was as if the clocks of time had been turned into reverse and sped back to her childhood. Seeing her grandfather at the gate of Well Cottage she called out a greeting and told him that she would see him later, and by the time they had reached the coastal lane they were laughing at their childhood antics.

Kylyn Farm was situated beside the coastal lane, the yard was empty as they crossed over and entered the tiny track that led to Kylyn Cove. The cove was almost entirely enclosed by a finger of land that attempted to encircle it and was affectionately referred to as The Point. Between the tip of The Point and the cliff on the opposite side was a dangerous unmarked channel, virtually forming the cove into an impenetrable lagoon. At the end of the track the land sloped gently down to reveal a beautiful shell and sand beach. Blue, green water gently lapped upon the sand and seabirds and sand martins flew above. On the cliff perched three tiny cottages, bright with fresh coats of lime wash.

"Look 'ow 'e manages t' get in and out of 'ere. E's some brave."

Ginifur watched Will steering the small craft unerringly through the narrow passage as the water whirled and splashed around submerged rocks. "It's not so difficult when you know the channel." She was purely stating a fact, there was no intention to belittle Wills achievements.

Adam glanced down at her face. "Of course." He remembered. "Ye can sail in and out of that channel too, can't 'e? There can't be that many left that can."

"Oh I don't know." Ginny disagreed. "There's Gramps and Da, and Eddy Pollack, Henry Stevens, Tubby Jack, Billie Carne . . . and Will of course." She didn't mention herself. "Of course there may be others, but they are the only ones that I know of.

"You'm the only girl." It was almost an accusation.

"Only because Da didn't have a son. If he had, he would have taken him out instead of me. The others raised objections, I heard it was said that a secret wasn't safe in a woman's hands. But Da refused to accept it."

"Don' know why 'em keep it a secret, tis bloody daft."

"It's been that way for generations. No one who isn't born into it will learn its secret."

"There 'av been exceptions. Look at your Gramps." Adam pointed out.

"That's not true." Ginifur declared. "His father knew the secret, and Gramps had learned of it before he went away. It was Gramps and his father who tried to warn the smugglers."

"Well, anyways, ye c'n show me, now that we'm married." Adam suggested.

"You know I can't Adam. That would break my vow."

A black shadow flitted across Adam's face, to mar his new found happiness. "No, of course ye can't." But suddenly he brightened. "But I've got a secret of me own." He grinned happily. "If'n I shows 'e, promise ye won't tell?"

Ginifur was relieved that the moment had passed, and would have gladly promised anything, other than the secret of the channel. "Of course I do Adam, what is it?"

"Come on." He grabbed her hand excitedly and almost pulled her along the beach in his hurry. "I'll show 'e." Nearing the end of the beach he placed the basket upon a bed of shingle, smugly placed his hands upon his hips and looked up at the face of the cliff. "There." He said smugly. "Can ye see anythin'?"

Ginifur stared at the rocky cliff face and frowned. What on earth did he expect her to see? It was a rocky cliff face, just as it had always been. There had been a rock fall during the storms back in the winter, but that really was not unusual. Scrubby bushes still managed to find enough earth to hold their roots firmly in the larger crevices and there were still enough ledges for the birds to nest upon. She shook her head. "What am I looking for Adam? I can see nothing unusual."

Adam grinned. "That's just it, ye can't see it."

"Well if I can't see it, why am I looking? What on earth are you gabbing on about Adam?" She added crossly.

"It's 'cos ye can't see it, that it's so special." He tried to explain. "Back in the spring Ma asked me if I could find some gull eggs, so I comes to Kylyn to 'ave a look. Even though the gales 'ad taken away some of the cliff, there was still plenty of room fer nesting sites."

"I can see that Adam."

"Wait a bit. Jest wait a bit." Adam continued. "Anyways, I got t' this spot 'n started up the cliff. Jest there . . . see? Don' look none too easy do it? Tis deceivin', tid'n 'ard at all."

"Yes but . . ."

Adam waved a hand at her. " 'old on Ginny. Remember as when ye was a young maid, 'ow ye used t' 'oist yer skirts up so's ye could climb trees?" She nodded. "Well, can 'e do it now? There be no one about 'cept thee 'n me." He was so happy that Ginifur did not want to spoil his fun, so she hoisted her skirt between her legs and tucked it firmly in her waistband, revealing her trim legs, neat ankles and her feet encased in dainty buttoned boots. Adam gave a cheeky whistle, but showed no evidence that the sight of her legs caused him any discomfort. He took hold of a rock above his head, put his foot in a small crevice, and pulled himself up with ease. Having taken another similar move he turned and reached down his hand. "Put your foot where I did, 'n take a hold of me 'and. That's right." She did as he bid her and, step by step, they climbed about half way up the cliff where they rested on a ledge. "Twas over there I picked up the gulls eggs. Great big 'erring gull it were, by that large rock." Ginny nodded. What on earth was he getting at? "Anyways, I'd picked up the eggs 'n was about t' make me way back down again when, y'see that bush over there, next t' the rock?" He turned to see if she was paying attention. "Well, the bush suddenly started to rustle like!"

"I expect it was just the wind." Suggested Ginny.

"That's what I thought, then I realised it weren't windy. Not a breath. So, I took a step or two nearer and beyond the nest it was easier.

The ledge was wide enough to walk right up to the bolder.

Ginifur was beginning to get impatient. "Adam, what is the point of this? So you collected the eggs, but that is nothing special. We did that as children."

Adam could hardly contain himself. "I know, I know. Come on I'll show 'e." Carefully he led the way until they reached the largest boulder in the cliff, beside which was the bush. "Now close yer eyes Ginny. I'm goin' t' push some branches t' one side. I want to' show 'e some'at be'ind it." Ginifur put her hands over her eyes as she felt the branches tangle in her hair and catch at her clothes, but it was only for one brief moment until she heard Adam say. "There. Ye c'n open yer eyes now."

Ginifur did. And her eyes opened wide in surprise as she found herself at the entrance of a large cave. "It's the secret tunnel isn't it? The one that all those stories were about. Gramps said it had caved in and was lost." She glanced into the opening. "Are you sure that no one else knows about it? It looks to me as though there have been people her. See, here's a piece of tallow candle." She held a fragment out to Adam.

"That's mine. I bin comin' ere all summer. Explorin' it like."

"Exploring it? Adam! It's only a cave."

Adam looked smug. "That's what ye think." He retrieved a tinder box and a candle from a chipped out ledge. Striking the tinder and lighting the candle he stepped further into the flickering shadows of the cave. "Come on, come on." He was child like in his excitement, and Ginifur was caught up in his spell as she followed. Eerie shadows fluttered about the cave as they stepped deeper into the cliff. The cave was large enough to stand up in and it smelt dry, not musty. And at the back was another tall, smooth boulder, similar to the one at the entrance. Ginifur looked around her in amazement. "That's not all, look!" And in the blink of an eye Adam had vanished behind the rock and she was left completely in the dark as his voice echoed around her. "Walk round, be'ind the rock Ginny." Ginifur felt the rock in front of her. Surely it was just a part of the cave wall. But as she felt her way to the side she could see a glimmer of light from Adam's candle illuminating a narrow gap. Pushing easily through the space she found herself in a low tunnel where she was forced to bend her head and shoulders. She wasn't frightened. Adam obviously knew his way around, and it was quite exciting. A few more steps and they arrived at a high roofed underground cavern. Adam now lit more candles to show her where she was.

"Oh Adam! I don't know what to say. It's incredible. I can't believe that you are the only one to know that it is still here."

"I think I am, at the moment. I think they storms dislodged the rocks as was blockin' the entrance. Most of 'em fell t' the beach and I cleared 'em away. The big'n! Well I reckon that just slipped a mite, just enough to let 'e squeeze by. Well!" He exclaimed. Completely satisfied that he had given her a surprise. "Tis some secret, eh?"

Ginifur smiled. "It is that Adam. To be sure it is a wonderful secret. But I wonder how long it will be before someone else finds out?"

"Ye promised not t' tell mind." Adam looked worried.

Ginifur shook her head. "I'm not going to tell anyone Adam. It's your secret and you keep it that way for as long as you can."

"There be tunnels leading off this chamber." He pointed out the carved out entrances running from the main cavern. "Some are small caverns, probably used by smugglers for storin' brandy and the like. Some are blocked by rock falls 'n others go back inland. But I aven't searched 'em all yet. I don' know where they all leads."

"You will be careful won't you Adam? There might be another rock fall and you are trapped down here."

Adam was pleased that she had showed some concern for his safety. "Well, if I don' turn up one day, ye'll know where to start lookin' then won' 'e?" He joked and then struck one large hand across his middle. "My stomach is rumbling! Was there food in that basket ye made me carry, or did 'e jest bring it along t' collect they shells you'm so fond of?"

Ginifur laughed. "Get along with you. All you do is think of your belly."

Adam was about to retort back, but stopped in time and congratulated himself. For once he didn't speak without thinking. He extinguished all but one of the candles, and then led Ginifur back through the tunnel and, after checking that there was no one outside to see them, down on to the beach.

They chose a sheltered spot where there was a dip in the sand, and smooth rocks to lean against. Ginifur pulled the checked cloth from the basket and laid the food out upon it.

Adam licked his lips. "That's a real treat Netty's packed for we, Ginny. We ought t' do this more often." He declared, and Ginifur was inclined to agree.

After they had eaten, Ginifur lent back against the rock and closed her eyes, whilst Adam stretched himself out on the sand, rolled on to his belly, and was soon sound asleep.

It might have been the heat of the sun, or maybe she was more tired than she would let herself believe but, whatever it was, Ginifur must have been lightly dozing. Her mind was lazily drifting, in that peaceful state between sleep and waking. Her body quivered in brief response, to what? Somewhere, deep down inside her a memory stirred and, as she felt a light breeze plucking at her skin, her nipples hardened in anticipation. Silently her heartbeat quickened as his name hovered briefly upon her lips until she abruptly opened her eyes to find Adam straddled across her hips, her blouse was undone, with her breasts revealed, and his hands were fumbling beneath her skirts. Ginifur thrust him angrily away, and, as she jumped to her feet, her eyes flashed with fury. "Adam! What on earth are you doing?" She shouted.

Ginifur's reactions had been so sudden that Adam had stumbled backwards on the sand, and glared up at her angrily. "What d'ye think? Fer God's sake. Ginny, we'm married. Jesus Christ, Ginny what d' ye think I am? A monk?"

Ginifur straightened her skirts and hastily covered her breasts. "Don't speak like that Adam. It's wrong to take the name of the Lord in vain."

Adams face screwed up in anger. "I'll do as I damn well please and, God or no God, I'm gonna take 'e as a man should." He threatened as he recovered and took a step towards her.

Ginifur stepped backwards. "Not here Adam. Not out in the open, where we can be seen. It wouldn't be right, it wouldn't be seemly."

"Seemly!" Adam exploded. "Right! Jest where is it seemly or right? Tell me that Ginny. Where is it seemly, 'n when would it be right?"

"In bed of course. When we have a bed of our own. It won't be long now." She attempted to placate him.

But Adam was in no mood to be placated. His face was red with rage at being spurned. "So, in bed eh! Tid'n seemly or right fer me t' fondle me own wife, even when there' be no one around t' see us. Is that it?" Ginifur didn't answer. "Is that it Ginny?" He shouted. "Tid'n seemly or right eh! Then tell me." Adam's contorted face filled Ginifur with fear; she had never seen him like this. "Tell me then, jest where did ye lie with the misbegotten whoremonger who sired that bastard son of your'n, eh?" Ginifur's face drained of all colour as he berated her. "And ye 'ave the gall t' tell me it id'n seemly!"

Ginifur's hand flew up to his face so fast that she almost wasn't aware of her own actions, and Adam certainly didn't see it coming. Her hand hit his cheek with all the force that she could muster and Adam reeled in shock as he now received the full force of her cold and angry words. "Adam Sawle! Don't you ever, and I mean ever, speak to me like that again. Don't you ever speak of my son in that way, or of his father, whom you know nothing of. It was you who wanted this marriage Adam. In my heart I feared it would lead to this, but I tried to believe you. Of course I know that we must be man and wife in the fullest sense of the words, but not like that Adam. Taking advantage of me whilst I was sleeping. That's not the way."

At the back of Adam's mind he knew that it wasn't but he burst out. "Take advantage!" His temper was still aroused and he struggled vainly to contain it, but failed. "Take advantage of me wife! If I'm takin' advantage, what the hell was that . . ?"

"Don't, Adam." Ginifur's eyes flashed a warning along with her words. "Don't." She bent down and picked up the basket. She took a deep breath and looked him straight in the eyes. "Now, I am going to walk slowly home, and I suggest that you do something to cool down. When we have both had time to think on this we will discuss it like reasonable people." Her arms and legs were trembling with shock, or perhaps anger, yet she managed to hold on to her emotions, not wishing to show how much she was upset by the incident. Ginifur turned away, walking slowly back along the beach. In truth, each step of the way, she expected to feel a hand upon her shoulder which would force her to stop. She refused to turn around and kept her head held high until she reached the track. Then taking the cliff path, she quickly found a sheltered spot where she collapsed and allowed her emotions to run free. As the tears flowed, all Ginifur's grief came rushing to the surface. She cried for Jamie, for Richard, for Adam and finally she cried for herself. When, at last, her tears were spent, Ginifur felt physically drained. She wiped her face with the damp cloth she had put in the basket to wipe her hands before handling the food; she patted her hair into place and straightened her skirts. In spite of her disturbed state she had the presence of mind to realise that if she walked home past Well Cottage she would be seen and called in to see her Grandmother. There was no doubt in her mind whatsoever, that they would immediately recognise that something was amiss. And how would she explain Adam's absence? No, she wouldn't go back to Tremanyon that way, she would have to take the footpath to Rosvarron and then cut down through the willow garden and up through the orchard. She hadn't walked that way for ages, and for a moment she pushed her worries behind her as she looked forward to following the path that led down into the valley behind the Elizabethan house on the seaward side of Tremanyon.

* * *

As Adam watched Ginifur's retreating figure, her back straight and her head held high, her shoulders set square and defiant, Adam's attempt to vent his anger upon the nearest rock gave him no relief and only rewarded him with a painfully stubbed toe to aggravate his condition. In exasperation he picked up a handful of flat stones and, marching to the water, skimmed them out over the calm water of the cove. With each throw his frustration and anger diminished slowly and, reflecting on what had occurred, the first pangs of regret worked their way into his heart. He really shouldn't have said those things about Jamie, but Ginny expected too much of him. Damn it! He was only a red blooded Cornishman after all. It was really her fault. If she would behave towards him as she should, none of this would have happened. But she was right, it had been his idea. He had persuaded her for her own good. For her own good! That really wasn't honest was it? He did it because he wanted to do it. He wanted Ginny for his own, baby or no baby. But Jamie was the hardest part. When they had a child of their own, it would be different. When! The next throw was badly angled, and the stone made a big splash and sank. When? He asked himself again. There wasn't much chance of that when he couldn't even touch her, let alone lay with her. Glancing up Adam saw the small sail of Will Davies boat appear beyond the channel, and slowly he walked along the beach to meet the occupant when he came ashore.

"Did 'e 'av a good catch?" He asked in genuine interest.

"Bit better'n it 'ave bin. 'Bout time too, s'bin some'ard this last year like, 'n I've lost a few of me best customers too. I'll 'ave t' cut me profit t' get em back, I c'n tell 'e. Still, never mind, least ways I've got some'at t' sell at last! Look!" He pulled out a large lobster. "'n this fine beauty'll take some beatin' I'll be bound."

Adam eyed the huge lobster. "Christ, e's some size. Are em all like that?"

"Pretty well. T'be honest, I don' think I ever knowed em t' get so big, 'n the quality of the flesh 'n the flavour don' suffer none either. 'ere, 'ave this'n on me, 'spect Ginny d' like lobster don' she?"

"Yes, she does. Thanks. It's kind of 'e." Ginny did indeed like lobster. At least he would be able to take home a peace offering.

Will Davies lifted a box of crabs out of the boat, and then clambered back in to take off the other one full of lobsters. "Give us 'n 'and will 'e? Tis a bit 'eavier than t'other one." Adam took one side of the box as they lifted it out between them. "Did 'e 'ear about the commotion at Pentire, t'other night?"

"No! What was that?"

"Georgie Jump, Vyv Roberts, Peter Painter 'n Bony Burns, t' name a few. All got caught top side with brandy 'n the likes. There was militia men 'idden in the bushes between the cliff path 'n 'igher Varney. Folks say they was tipped off like, knew jest when t' expect 'em."

"Not all of 'em surely?"

"That's the way I 'eard it. Someone's got a lot t' answer fer, I says. Well, them's the last lot that'll run outa Pentire Cove fer a time, I reckon. They'll 'ave t' find somewhere else t' bring it ashore now."

Will Davies waded into the water and heaving on the stern pushed the little boat a bit further out of the water with Adam pulling on the bow. Satisfied it was safe, Will looked at the boxes. "Care t' give us 'n 'and with these?"

"Sure." Adam, helped carry the boxes to one of the cottages on the cliff, and was about to take his leave when another thought came to him. "Must make 'em wary about takin' it out up Pendarves Valley!"

Will frowned. "What do 'e know about Pendarves Valley?"

"Pendarves Valley? Or them as goes from the beach through Josh Adcock's farm yard. Makes no difference, bet em all are a bit worried."

"You knows about that 'n all? 'ow do 'e know about the 'carrow boys?"

"No more 'n no less 'n most folks here abouts I guess." Adam had guessed correctly. He hadn't known anything for sure, only stories, hints, nothing definite. But Will knew. That was quite obvious. Adam looked down at the cove. "Don' know why 'em don' use Kylyn. There's no one foolish enough t' follow em through the channel."

Will looked at Adam warily, through narrowed eyes. "Them did, once upon a time. But the route out got blocked. Mind you, that were years back now. I 'eard me grandfer talk about it."

"I think there may be a way out now." Adam smiled knowingly.

"What do 'e mean?"

"Thanks fer the lobster Will. Ginny will enjoy it. I'll see 'e around." And leaving Will to think over their conversation he headed for home in a happier frame of mind. If his suspicions were correct Will would be making contact with him soon. Adam smiled happily to himself. At last he believed that he knew of a way to get enough money to take himself and Ginny away from Tremanyon.

With Jamie, Rachel and Rebecca bathed and in bed Ginifur made her way down to the kitchen. "My!! That's a rare smell." She exclaimed as she opened the door.

"Young Will Davies gave Adam a lobster for yer supper." Netty looked up from the bubbling pot. "Mind ye, the size of this'n, ye'll be eatin' it all week."

Ginifur smiled and glanced at Adam, who was chatting to Tom at the end of the table. "Then I guess it would be better if we all enjoyed it, for it's sure to go off if it's that big."

"I thought ye might say that." Netty grinned as she lifted the scalded, bright red lobster from the pan. "Get they plates outa the oven Adam, and ye, Tom, get out they crackers and picks."

Within a few short minutes they were laughing happily as they picked out the meat from the shell, and Adam was showing no sign of anger or resentment. It was as though the events of the afternoon had never happened.

But they had. And Ginifur knew that it was a problem still to be addressed.

* * *

Ginifur was at Well Cottage, helping her grandfather to carry water to the vegetable garden, when the Boscawen's carriage turned into the gates of Tremanyon. She had just filled another pail when she glanced at the dark shadows that filed the granite enclosed space behind the iron gate. "How on earth did you manage to cover the entrance to the tunnel without disturbing the well?" She asked.

The question, out of the blue as it was, momentarily stunned John Retallick. His eyes glazed over as he stared first at the shadows and then at his grand daughter. It was so long ago, what on earth had suddenly opened up the past? He picked up two of the buckets and turned towards the garden. Anne Retallick was podding peas as he paused beside her.

"What's the matter John?" She asked, taking in the puzzled frown as he placed the buckets on the ground and Ginifur joined them.

"I asked about the well, Gran. I didn't realise that it would upset him. Forget I spoke, Gramps. I'm sorry I asked you if it upsets you."

"No, child." Anne said firmly. "If you can be trusted with the secret of the passage into Kylyn Cove then you can be trusted with the secret of the way out. Tell her John. If anyone has a right to know it is Ginifur."

John Retallick sat down on the log he used for chopping wood, as he stared back towards the well. "It was so long ago, maid, that it all seems like a bad dream." He reminisced. "The exit at the well isn't sealed, no more'n the one at Tremanyon." Ginifur wanted to ask questions but held her tongue. "Me 'n father, were on look out, father at the well 'n me at the creek. T'was unnaturally quiet. Always is quiet when the free traders are abroad, but that night yer couldn't put yer finger on it, but it weren't right. Then I 'eard the footsteps on the bridge above me 'ead and Stumpy's voice calling out "Are 'e there John?" "What are 'e doin' 'ere." I asks. "Ye should'n be out ternight." "I know." 'e says. But Widow Bennett's cow was due t' calve down, 'n she was some fat that she thought she'd 'ave trouble pushin' en out. So 'e told 'er e'd stay with the cow till she'd calved down. T'wasn't one calf but two, that's why she were so big. Anyways, 'e was goin' 'ome when 'e 'eard the militia comin' into the village, e'd only got as far as the smithy. They placed guards all round the village so's nobody could leave, 'n then set off t' Rosvarron. We was usin' that exit that night. "Are 'e sure" I asks un. "Course I'm sure." Says 'e. "Then someone must 'ave been got at." Says I. "Got at I don' know 'bout that, but I reckons 'e was paid." Spittin' as 'e said it. "What do 'e mean?" I asks. Then 'e tells me that 'e saw Jonas Johns showin' 'em, the way. "Jonas! 'e should 'ave been christened Judas!"

John Retallick paused, and sighed deeply. "We ran like the devil was snappin' at our 'eals. Father 'ad been watchin' at the well, 'n 'e 'elped we down, hopin' all the while that we'd be in time t' stop em leavin' the tunnel at Rosvarron. We was too late. There was only Wesley and Ben, who had secured the panels that hid the exit at Rosvarron. We could 'ear the shots outside. They put up a fight they did. Those that weren't shot, were 'anged, fer killin' a sergeant and one of the soldiers in the fightin'. Wes, Ben Stumpy 'n me went back to the cave and released the stones that would bring the rocks down over the entrance, and the exit at Rosvarron, if it were in danger of bein' found. Fer the tunnels 'ad t' be kept a secret. There was only the four of us, Father, me Wes, Ben, 'n now Stumpy of course, who knew where it were, 'n we weren't tellin'." John Retallick paused before adding. "Now there be only me, 'n yer gran of course."

"But they must have known at Rosvarron and the Big House, surely?" Ginifur asked.

"Rosvarron, yes. The Big House, no." John told her.

"No!"

John Retallick shook his head. "No. It were built long time ago. It was well hid, 'n the master never knew."

"Where Gramps?"

Ginny's grandfather let out a great sigh. "Be'ind the cold 'ouse. In they cellars." Ginny knew where he meant but found it hard to believe. "You know they old iron rings in the wall? S'pose they'm still there?" Ginifur nodded her head. "Ye takes 'old of the one nearest the door and winds it t' the left like, 'n the wall moves. But why are 'e askin' me these questions? Ye 'aven't found the tunnel 'ave 'e?" Fear filled her grandfather's eyes.

"I didn't. No. But Adam has found the cave. The cliff has slipped and moved the rock, I think." Ginifur explained.

John Retallick grabbed Ginifur's arm. "Stay away Ginny. Tis bad luck that tunnel, believe me. Stay away, promise me now."

"I will Gramps." Ginifur hastened to assure him. "Don't worry yourself. I'll stay away . . . I promise. But . . ." She was about to ask him something else that puzzled her when a cry was heard from the gate.

"Ginny! Ginny! Come quick. It's the Falmouths." Pearl's breathless voice floated up to them.

"The Master! Is Captain Tremayne with them?" Ginifur's face flushed at the thought as she hitched Jamie on to her hip.

"No. No. Just the Falmouths. Oh, hurry up Ginny."

Ginifur bade her grandparents a hasty goodbye and, gathering up her basket, she hurried down the path, asking questions all the time, but Pearl having no answers.

John Retallick watched Ginifur's retreating back then turned to his wife. "I don' like it." He said. "I don' like it a' tall." As Ginny reached the lane she turned and raised her hand in parting. Both waved back as Annie pondered on John's words, but kept her own thoughts to herself. She smiled at the thought of young Jamie, he was turning into a bright babe. It was early days yet, and Jamie certainly did favour his mother, and yet . . ?

* * *

In her room Ginifur hastily changed her dress and tidied her hair. She had sent Pearl to fetch Kate to look after Jamie, and with him safely settled she made her way to the drawing room where Netty had, rightly, served the Falmouth's with tea whilst they waited. Ginifur knocked on the door before opening it and, on entering, bobbed a polite curtsey to the visitors. "I do apologise for not being here to welcome you Lord Falmouth, my Lady." She added in acknowledgement to Fanny Boscawen who smiled in return.

"Don't worry yourself Ginny. Young Rachel and Rebecca have been entertaining us, and telling us how Jamie has grown. I've brought him some clothes for the winter, it will soon be upon us and he will need something to keep him warm." Fanny Boscawen had visited Tremanyon shortly after Jamie was born, bringing a bassinette with her, she was much taken with the baby. She had been over twice since, with gifts of clothes and a beautiful cot for him to sleep in when he was a little older. Ginifur had, at first, been reluctant to accept the gifts. But Fanny Boscawen had a kind heart, and soon made Ginifur realise that it made her happy to give the things that she brought with her. "Besides." Fanny added. "Richard would never forgive me if I didn't watch over you and the babe." Ginifur took the proffered garments and thanked her for her generosity. "Now. Where is young Jamie?" Fanny asked. "I must see him, please."

"He's in the nursery, with Kate." Ginny explained. "Rachel, will you go and ask Kate to bring Jamie down to the drawing room, please?"

Rachel ran eagerly from the room, both of the girls adored the baby and declared that it was far better than having a doll to play with. Edward Boscawen stood indulgently by, as he watched Fanny take Jamie in her arms.

"He is so beautiful, he has positively stolen my heart." Fanny declared. "And those eyes! They are so blue, they . . ." She pondered for a moment. "They remind me of someone." Ginifur's heart almost stopped beating. "Are Adam's eyes this blue?" Fanny asked.

"No, they are brown. But my mother's eyes were blue."

"Then she must have passed them on to her grandchild." Fanny reasoned. "It is so sad that she didn't live to see Jamie. She would have been so proud of him." Fanny beckoned to Rachel and Rebecca. "Come let us take Jamie into the garden whilst my husband talks to Ginifur. Do you mind if I take your son outside?"

"No, Ma'am."

"Then we will see you both in a little while." Fanny gave a parting smile and left the room.

"Well Ginifur. This is a surprise." Edward said.

"Yes, Sir. I expect it is.

"You have known the young man for a long time I gather."

"Since we were children, Sir. We grew up together."

"Richard never said that you were stepping out together." Edward was puzzled.

"Didn't he, Sir?"

Edward glanced at her serious face. There was more to this marriage than she was making out. "I hope that you will be truly happy Ginny."

"Thank you, Sir." She paused, holding back the question uppermost in her mind. "Was that what you wished to see me for Lord Falmouth?"

"Mm. Partly. Netty tells me that you are still sleeping in the house."

"I sleep here alone; I can't leave the girls, Sir, not with their father away. He didn't know, it wouldn't be right, they have no mother you see, and besides I gave my word to Captain Tremayne that I would guard them with my life." Ginny's words tumbled out.

"Ginny, Ginny!" Edward laughed and raised his hands to halt her tirade of words. "I am not suggesting that you leave the children. But you must have some time with your new husband, that is only right also." He studied her frightened face. She was holding something back, he was sure of it. "Now, Netty tells me that the Garden Cottage is still empty, save for the furniture left in it when Richard purchased Tremanyon. In his absence I believe that he would want me to grant you permission to make a temporary home there until a more permanent arrangement can be made on his return."

Ginifur's eyes widened. "I can not leave the girls in the west wing on their own. All the staff sleep in the attic rooms, they would not hear them if they needed help in the night. Adam knows that and he has agreed that I stay with them until their father returns."

"I am not suggesting that you leave the manor on a permanent basis. Only that perhaps Adam would like to feel that you do have somewhere to share a bit of your time together for an odd hour or an evening. Maybe an odd night here or there when perhaps Pearl can sleep in the west wing." He studied her more closely. "I am not forcing you to leave the girls Ginny, just give yourself the opportunity to spend some time with your new husband." What was the girl frightened of? She certainly did not give the impression of a young woman in love.

"But Captain Tremayne.."

"I will deal with Richard when he returns, leave it to me. Richard may well be away for longer than we had first expected. You must be fair to Adam, Ginny. Really, you must."

Ginifur knew that he meant it kindly, and she was also aware that she owed Adam a little of her time. It might not be such a bad idea at that. She smiled shyly.

"Good that's settled. Fanny and I have seen the cottage, it is quite adequately furnished, but if you need anything else just let us know.

"We shan't need anything else, Sir. It will be grand as it is. But... Lord Falmouth! Is there no news of Captain Tremayne?" Her smile faded and was replaced with a worried frown.

"Richard! Ah, yes my dear, of course. No." Edward paused. "No, I am afraid that we have no more news than came back to us that they had seen the winter through and were on their way to meet up with Monsieur de Varron in Quebec. Fanny brought the letters over didn't she?"

"Oh yes, Sir. She did. But I wondered when we would be expecting him home. The children ask for him all the time, Sir, you see."

Edward moved slowly towards the window, watching his wife as she laughed at something the children had said. "The truth is Ginny, I don't know. The White Rose is bound for Boston in October. If Richard arrives before we leave then he should be back by the end of the year. If not, well it won't be until next summer."

Ginifur gasped. "As long as that? I didn't realise that he would be gone for so long."

"It was on the cards. It is a big country young Ginny. Vast compared to our tiny island and they will have to cover much of the way on foot."

Ginifur's voice was only a whisper. "Yes, I do realise that."

"Just tell those little girls that their father is doing a very special job, and that he will be home as soon as he can.

"Yes, Sir."

Edward smiled. "Meanwhile, is everything else alright?"

"Oh yes, Sir." Ginifur assured him. "I send the accounts in monthly, the books are all up to date. Do you wish to inspect them?"

Edward laughed, good humouredly. "Oh dear, no, indeed. I hear that you keep a very detailed account of the expenditure at Tremanyon, that nothing is wasted and that Richard has a house-keeper and bailiff rolled into one. Mr. Franks tells me that your book keeping skills are second to none."

"He exaggerates, I assure you." Ginifur blushed at the compliments. "But I do my best."

Edward smiled. "No one can ask more of you than that, Ginny. Now, where is that wife of mine. You had better watch those children Ginny, for they are in danger of being kidnapped. Especially that young son of yours. I have never known her to be so taken with a child as she is with him, no, never."

"I will, Sir, and thank you. Thank you for everything."

"Don't mention it. I promised Richard that I would keep an eye on things. Glad to help." He opened the door and held it back, beckoning for her to go through. Ginifur hesitated; knowing her position in the household, but Lord Falmouth indicated the door-way and added chivalrously. "After you, my dear. After you."

Ginifur and the children waved to the departing carriage, and her mind returned to the question as to whether Richard would indeed be home by the end of the year. She decided that she would not raise the girl's hopes of seeing their father before then. Better to wait and see.

Adam

ADAM WAS DELIGHTED with the suggestion that he moved into the Garden Cottage and that they would have somewhere private to spend some time together. At first he was quite happy for the odd hour or evening in her company, until the day shortly before Christmas when he returned from Truro a little worse for drink.

Sam smiled grimly as Adam slipped, rather than stepped down from the carriage, quietly saying to Ginifur. "I'm sorry e's come 'ome in this state maid." Maid being a term of affection and not demeaning in any way. "I left 'im t'mind the parcels at the Red Lion and came back t'find e'd almost drunk the tap room dry. Lord knows where 'e got the money, there certainly won't be any left for Christmas."

But Adam had heard him. "Tha's what ye thinks, Father. But I've got more'n that. Besides, there be plenty more where that come from. I've enough t'drink, or t'spend on m' beautiful, lovin' wife, as I wish." He threw an arm about Ginifur's shoulders. "Well, she'm beautiful 'nuff, don' 'e agree father." He glanced over his shoulders to a now angry Samuel.

"She be that, son." Sam agreed

Adam gave a wry grin as he scratched his head. "Yes, but lovin? Do 'e reckon she be that too?"

Sam looked uncomfortable. "A kinder girl ye won't find this side of Truro."

"Kind!" Adam's smile held no humour in it. "Just how kind be that?" He asked angrily flinging his arms wide and nearly falling over with the sudden movement.

"Come on Adam. Let's get you in to the cottage." Ginifur pulled on his sleeve. "I think that I had better get you to bed."

"Bed!" Adam's voice raised in a mirthless laugh. "Get me t'bed! Be that an invitation Ginny?" He stumbled and fell on to his knees. Ginifur reached out to steady him as he pushed himself up, thrusting her roughly aside. "I don' need no invitation, Ginny. You'm me wife. If I want t'bed ye I will, 'n there's damn all ye can do about it."

Ginifur glanced back at the carriage, but Sam had unfastened the horses and led them away, not wishing to be a spectator. As he rubbed down the horses there was a grim expression upon his face as he wished that things could have been different. She followed the haphazard progress of Adam, who was far worse for drink than Ginny had ever seen him, or anyone else for that matter. Where on earth had he got the money? Adam stumbled on the step, and catching hold of the door handle he fell through the door, landing in a heap at the foot of the stairs. Puzzled to find himself at the foot of the stairs he looked up at Ginifur silhouetted in the doorway.

"Well, well, m' lovely wife."

Ginifur shook her head in disbelief. "What on earth have you been doing?" She asked, genuinely concerned for him.

"Tha's obvious in't it? I bin 'avin a drink with m' friends."

"What friends, Adam? What friends do you have in Truro who have enough money to get you into this state?"

"Who says it were their money?"

"It has to be, Adam. You don't have enough money to get drunk on." She countered.

Another wry grin spread across Adam's face. "Oh don' I, Miss Know It All? Well tha's where you'm wrong." He pulled out a handful of sovereigns from his pocket, and thrust them towards her face. "See . . .'n there be plenty more where they comes from."

"Adam!!" Ginfur stared at the golden coins within his grasp. "Where on earth did you get those? What on earth have you been doing?"

"Wouldn' 'e just like t'know, m'bird?" He grinned up at her. "Wouldn't 'e just like t'know?"

"How could you possibly have that amount of gold coin?" Ginifur demanded. "If you saved for ten years you still wouldn't have that much money."

"No, guess I wouldn' at that." He scratched his head as if pondering the problem. "But then, as they d'say, tid'n what ye know, but who ye know. But then again, if'n 'e put what 'e know 'n who 'e know t'gether, well tha's a different story altogether."

"Adam!" You're talking in riddles." Ginny said angrily.

"Hey diddle, diddle, wha's Adam's riddle?" Adam giggled and his head slumped forwards.

Ginifur laid a hand gently on his arm. There really was no point in talking to him whilst he was in this state. She would have to wait until he had sobered up and then get to the bottom of it. "Come on, Adam. Let me help you up the stairs." Adam looked up, and for a brief moment his eyes held the tender look they once held, and Ginifur was filled with remorse for what might have been, and what it had become. Holding out her hand, Adam took it and pulled himself upright then, with Ginny to steady him, they made their way up the narrow winding stairs.

Once in the bedroom Adam sat down heavily upon the bed, and sank back against the pillows. Ginifur gazed down at him. "Adam!" She ventured. But Adam gave no answer. Persuaded that he had sunk into a drunken stupor, she carefully removed his boots and socks and then lifted his legs onto the bed. Then, safe in the knowledge that he was sound asleep, she struggled to remove his coat and thick woollen shirt before staring down at his trousers. There was mud on his knees, where he had fallen more than once. Ginifur was reluctant to cover them with clean sheets. She hesitated. Searching his face for any sign that he would waken. But Adam's eyes remained tightly closed, his breathing deep and steady. She pushed aside her fears and lent forward, gently undoing his buttons, one at a time. Still Adam slept on. When all the buttons were undone, Ginifur positioned herself carefully on the bed, lent over Adam's inert body, took a grip at each side of his trousers and tugged.

Adam's eyes flew open. His face only inches from hers. And in them she saw, with certainty, that she had made a fatal error. All signs of drink, bar the smell, had evaporated away. Adam now appeared to be stone cold sober. His eyes were full of lust and hunger for her body, there was no sign of love or pity In that split second of time it was too late to run. Adam's hands pinned her arms in his vice like grip as she mouthed one whispering plea. "Please Adam, not like this." But she knew there would be no stopping him this time. This was to be how her marriage to Adam would be consummated. Not with tenderness and love. Not as she remembered it to be, with love and gentleness, but with something more akin to hate and anger. Her first instinct to fight gave way to resignation. There was no point. The drink had taken away all his reason, and only added to his strength. Adam tore at her clothes, ripping her dress from neck to hem, and then proceeded to do the same to her under garments, until she lay naked before him, upon the bed.

Ginifur turned her face away, pulling the torn clothes over her, not wanting to see the devouring look in Adam's eyes. Angrily he grabbed her arms, and tore the clothes from her grasp. "Ye are mine. Mine t'see when I want, mine t' take me pleasure with, 'n I've waited for that pleasure long enough." He pulled his trousers to the floor and with one last hungry look fell upon her trembling body. His rough, weathered hands tore at her body, scratching the tender skin at the top of her thighs, searching for her most intimate parts. His mouth searched hungrily for hers and, when she averted her face, he grabbed a handful of hair and forced her face towards his. "Were 'e so reluctant with yer lover?" Ginny closed her eyes, not wishing to see the lust glowing in his own. "No, I did'n think so. Well I'm all 'e 'ave now Ginny." His legs forced hers apart as he thrust his body towards hers. His mouth was hard upon hers, bruising her lips, and she wanted to cry out for help. Her struggles weakened until she finally submitted to the inevitability of her situation. Angrily he spread her legs apart and roughly thrust his swollen member at her lower body and Ginny gave a low cry of despair. Once she had given in, it was soon over. Adam was spent and slumped heavily forward upon her slight body. As heavy as he was she didn't try to move him and very soon his heavy breathing convinced her that he had finally fallen asleep.

Now that he had spent himself, it was not hard for Ginifur to roll him over and struggle out from underneath him. Her body hurt with the abuse she had received, her eyes burned with unshed tears, and her heart ached with the memory of the only night of love that she would ever know. She stood beside the bed for a moment, glancing down unemotionally at the inert body of her husband. She didn't hate him. She hated herself for allowing herself to be persuaded into a loveless marriage from which there would be no escape. Looking out of the window, she saw a light appear at the back of the house. Netty would be wondering what was keeping her.

There was a jug of water and a bowl on the small table. Slowly she poured the water into the bowl and shed herself of the torn clothing. Soaking the cloth in the water, she freshened up her face, before scrubbing angrily at the areas between her legs. Then, satisfied that she was partially clean, she looked down at her slim body and pressed her hands against her taught belly. A tear struggled to escape as she fought away the fear that this night might well have produced new seeds of life within her. She didn't want another baby. She glanced back at Adam, peaceful now in sleep. No, she didn't want Adam's baby, and that was the truth of

242

the matter. With tears clouding her eyes Ginifur stumbled naked from the room into the smaller bedroom next to it. Here, in a cupboard, she had kept a change of clothing. There had been no reason to keep then there, but she was glad that she had. Her fingers fumbled clumsily with the tiny buttons, her hands shaking, her body trembling as the shock set in. Finally, when she was clothed once more, she attempted to tidy her dishevelled hair, and calm her outward appearance before descending the stairs and making her way to the Big House.

Pleading a headache, Ginifur retired to her room soon after she had put Jamie and the girls to bed. Netty, studying her closely, shook her head as she watched her leave the kitchen. "Poor sweet maid, some'at is up." She spoke aloud, but there was only Tom to hear her.

"Ye're imaginin' things." He said, looking up from the fire he was tending in the stove.

Netty shook her head. "No, mark my words. Some'at 'as 'appened. She d'look as though she've seen the ghost of the Grey Lady 'erself. Or worse."

Tom lent back on his heals. "She were some quiet, I'll give 'e that. Maybe she'm sickenin' fer some'at Maybe there be another baby in the offin'."

Netty turned her gaze away from the closed door. "No, I don' think so. I 'ope not anyways."

"Tis only natural like. They'm married after all." Tom made the simple statement.

"Yes, they be." Netty put a kettle on the stove. "For better or worse they d'say. But this'n be fer the worse, I d' reckon."

In the bathroom Ginifur drained what was left of the hot water into the bath tub, undressed herself and stood in the few inches of water. Scooping it up in the large tin jug she slowly poured the water over her hair and, as it trickled down her face it mingled with the salty tears that had finally found release. She felt unclean, and defiled. This puzzled her, for she had not felt this way after the night in Richard's arms. Then she had felt wondrous warmth fill every corner of her body and mind. Then, whilst his gentle hands caressed and explored her young and innocent body, whilst his soft lips kissed her eyes, face, lips and neck, all the while whispering sweet words of love in her ear, Ginifur had given more than her body that night, she had given her heart and soul to the only man she would ever love. Was that remembered night how love should be? She wondered. Or was it just a stolen night of exquisite pleasure, rarely experienced by either man or woman? Ginifur didn't know. What she was quite certain of though, was that what she had just experienced was more akin to abuse of both her body and mind. She would never know if it could have been different, for Adam was her husband now, and the law decreed that she must submit to his advances however distasteful she may find them. She washed her body all over, scrubbing at it hard in an effort to rid herself of the feelings bubbling up inside her. Stepping out of the bath, Ginifur continued rubbing herself so hard with the towel that she was in danger of damaging her fragile skin. Wrapping herself tightly in a warm robe she went and checked on the children before curling up in the chair by the fire in the nursery, and staring into the flames as the logs crackled and spat in the hearth. Ginifur shivered and drew the chair nearer to the fire, she was so cold, it was as though there was no heat in the fire. Then she physically jumped as she heard a soft tapping on the door. Surely Adam wouldn't follow her into the children's private quarters? Warily she called out. "Who is it?"

"Tis only me, m'bird." Netty opened the nursery door. "I've brought 'e some nice hot milk and a warm split 'n honey. Ye didn' hardly touch a bite of yer supper. The milk will 'elp 'e t'sleep, 'n the honey helps cure all ills. Ye're not sickenin' fer some'at are 'e?"

"No Netty. Just a wee bit tired that's all. I wish the Master was home. The girls miss him so."

Netty nodded briefly, thinking that they weren't the only ones to be missing him. "The Cap'n will be 'ome soon." She declared. "If not fer Christmas, at least e'll be with us fer the summer."

"Oh, I do hope so. He's been gone so long Netty" She stared into the fire.

Netty crossed the room and placed the tray holding the cup of milk and honey, and the soft and sweet yeast bread roll spread liberally with butter and honey, on a small table beside Ginifur, then standing up straight she crossed her hands across her ample middle. "Yes 'e 'as. So much 'as 'appened since 'e went away, 'n some of it not fer the better."

Ginny looked up sharply. " Netty! What on earth do you mean?"

Netty shook her head sadly. "Just me bein' maudlin'. But I reckon as there would be some things he'd 'ave put a stop to.

Drink up yer milk 'n get a good nights sleep. Ye'll feel better in the mornin'." She laid a large plump hand upon Ginny's head "Sleep well cheeld. Nothin's so bad, after a good night's sleep."

Ginny forced a smile. "Thank you Netty."

"Don' 'e worry about the doors. Tom locked up, there'll be no bogey men to disturb ye t'night, real or otherwise." The big hearted woman closed the door quietly, and with a worried frown she made her way back to the kitchen.

It was some time before Ginifur finally lay down on her bed, but even then sleep evaded her. Where had Adam got all those gold sovereigns? She searched her mind to see if she could find some logical explanation, knowing in her heart that there would be none. Now that she thought of it, Adam had been spending precious little time in the stables these last months. She recalled that Sam had said as much, and his wages reflected that. Not that this affected her life style, for they all ate in the kitchen and her keep was an extra to her wages. But Adam was never short of money, and visited the tap house in the village more frequently than he ever did before. She had also seen him coming home in the early hours of the morning, having been out all night. Where had he been on these occasions? She had never questioned it before. To be honest, she acknowledged to herself, it had caused her no great concern until this moment; at least he had been occupied elsewhere. Well, one thing was sure; she was going to find out. With this conclusion she finally turned over once more then, at last, she closed her weary eyes and was soon sleeping. Tossing restlessly, with a whimper escaping her lips once in a while, Ginifur did find sleep, but not a restful sleep of someone with no concerns on their mind.

When Adam woke next morning he sat on the edge of the bed and stared briefly at the pile of Ginifur's torn clothing on the floor before pulling on his shirt and trousers and leaving the cottage. He had not been so drunk that he didn't know what he had done. He knew, oh yes. But he felt no sorrow for his actions. Rather he was angry. But even then, not with himself. No. His anger was turned on Ginifur. Adam believed, after all, that it was Ginny's fault that he had behaved as he had. If she had acted towards him in the way a loving wife should have behaved, then he wouldn't have had to take her forcibly. She would have given herself to him in the way that Milly did when he visited her in the cottage above Kylyn Cove. Milly knew how to make a man feel wanted, wanted and

245

needed. Ginifur made it quite apparent that she didn't need him. She had Jamie. And Jamie was all she needed. At the thought of Jamie he slammed the door behind him and headed for the gates and the village beyond. Adam had a rendezvous to keep. He fully believed that if he could get Ginifur away from Tremanyon then they would be happy. Yes, even with the bastard Jamie. There would be more babies. Lots of babies, his babies. But it would take money and Adam now knew how to get that money. Lots of money.

With another Christmas to arrange for Rachel and Rebecca without their father or mother, Ginifur was too busy attempting to divert their attention to spare the time to bear any grievance towards Adam. Besides, it wasn't in her nature. Adam did not return for a couple of days and was surprised when she made no mention of the events of that night, and he briefly wondered if perhaps she liked it that way. He had known enough women to realise that some like to feel power in a man. Bur Ginny! Well there was no knowing what a woman liked, he decided. However, he had brought her something very special for Christmas and he believed that this would make it all right again. He decided not to press his attentions on her for a while; he had shown her he was master. That was enough for now.

Christmas Day passed in celebrations a little more than the last one after the shipwreck, but it wasn't until Boxing Day that Adam gave Ginifur her present. He came upon her when she was sitting at the Captain's desk in the Library. The door was open and he watched her quietly as she wrote in the large ledger that was open before her.

Ginny felt his presence and glanced up from the book. "Hello Adam. Did you want me for something?"

"No, yes."

Ginifur couldn't help but laugh. "Well! Which is it?"

Adam bristled, but fought his angry feelings back. "No, I wasn't lookin' for 'e, but yes, now that ye'r alone I do 'ave somethin' for'e. Ye'r never alone Ginny. I can't never get t'speak to 'e alone, let alone anything else." He shied away from the eyes that suddenly flashed at him accusingly, and he clamped his teeth together. No. He wasn't going to let her make him loose his temper, he wanted to give her his Christmas present. "I got this for 'e." Ginny eyed the small parcel. "It's a Christmas present, from me." Her eyes softened as she looked up from the offered gift. "Didn' really give 'e much when us was married, did I? 'appened so quick like. Still, I reckon this'll make it up to 'e." He grinned expectantly as she unwrapped the tiny box from its paper covering until it lay open in her hand. "Well, do 'e like it?" Ginifur lifted the gold pin from the box. Surrounded by engraved flowers the pin also was engraved with her name 'Ginny' in the centre. "There's a space at the back for 'e t'keep a snippet of hair. I'll cut 'e off one of m' curls for ye. Do 'e like it, Ginny?

Ginifur at last found her voice. "It's beautiful Adam. But you can't afford to buy something like this. Where on earth did you get the money? You aren't putting in the hours at the stables. I know, for your father has had to tell me, and Joe has had to help when you are not there."

Adam's face reddened with anger. "Always spoil things don' 'e, Ginny? That was me own money that bought that pin. Bought and paid fer in cash, every damn penny. Why can't 'e say 'Thank you' like any normal maid would do? Why do 'e 'ave t'spoil everythin'?" He snatched the pin from her hands. "Well I bought it for 'e, so ye'd best put it on yer dress I s'pose."

"I'll put it on my best dress, Adam. Thank you." She added. "It was a very kind thought indeed."

"No ye'll not. Ye'll put it on the dress ye're wearin' now. Let other folks know I can buy 'e gifts too." He angrily flicked the watch upon the chain.

"But this is my working dress, Adam. It's not right."

"Oh! 'n who's here t'say ye can't, eh? Who's here t'stop 'e wearin' the broach Ginny? I can't see nobody but ye 'n me, so which of us is it?" His anger was rising like a tide in his stomach. "It in't me, so it must be ye Ginny." He accused. "Tis ye, 'n ye knows it be true, don 'e? Who are 'e waitin' fer Ginny? I'm all 'e 'ave now. When are 'e goin' t'realise that. Who ever 'e was, he left 'e, remember? 'n it was me that was dumb enough t'pick up the pieces. When are 'e goin' t'give me a little in return?" Adam turned on his heels and strode out of the room.

Ginifur truly regretted her words. She had loved Adam once, not in the way that he wanted her to, but she had loved him. She thought she still did, but she didn't know this Adam, and she also knew that there was no honest way that he could have earned enough money to buy that broach. She was filled with doubts and misgivings. Should she have accepted it gracefully and not asked questions? But Ginifur knew what her answer was, and she had to find out what Adam was up to.

Between Christmas and New Year, Edward and Fanny Boscawen visited Tremanyon, bearing gifts for the children and Ginifur, but with no word from Richard. Reports from him had been received by the authorities in Boston but there was no personal letter for his family. Edward passed on the news that they had left Quebec for Louisburg and perhaps there would be more news in the spring. Edward would set sail for the New World in the summer.

As a special treat, Rachel and Rebecca were allowed to stay up on New Year's Eve, and they all saw the old year out by sending white haired Tom out of the back door, and seeing in the New Year by letting dark haired Adam, carrying the essential lump of coal for luck and salt for life, in by the front door.

Chapter Seven
1755 – *The Attack*

THE LATE BLIZZARD blew across the mountain, covering every rugged crag, wooded escarpment or river valley in a thick and virtually impenetrable white blanket of snow. Of Richard Liam and Jean-Paul there had been no word since news had reached Quebec of the safe arrival of the ship carrying them to Louisburg and Nova Scotia. At the end of November, General Montreaux had sent out a patrol, westwards, but they had returned as soon as the weather closed in. Now they were three weeks into the New Year, and still no word. It was the worst winter anyone in Quebec had been forced to endure. In addition to the usual snow and ice, the bitter north wind blew incessantly turning even the water in the jugs to a solid ice block unless it was near the warmth of a fire. It was the General's first experience of a Canadian winter and, as he stood beside the brazier in the timber building that served as his office, he glanced out at the snow laden sky. "No one can survive out there in this atrocious weather, surely?"

The orderly placed a jug of coffee on the brazier and handed a steaming mug to his commanding officer. "The trappers do. Don't ask me how, but they do."

"Experienced mountain men, perhaps! But not a Frenchman without any experience of these inhospitable conditions!"

"You are referring to the Comte to Varron and the two Irish trappers, Sir?"

General Montreaux sipped the sweet, dark liquid. "Yes, yes, I am."

"Rumour has it that the Irishmen were well instructed in the art of winter survival by a native Indian, Sir. It is only hearsay, but apparently they learned to find food where it would appear that there is none to be found and even endure extended periods of freezing weather. They say that they live like the Indian; they hunt like the Indian and even think like the Indian. If there is even a modicum of truth in these stories then there is a better than even chance that they could survive, and le Comte could not be in better hands."

General Montreaux watched as fresh falls of snow blocked out all visibility, and shook his head. "A better than even chance eh! What odds are you offering?" Of course the General had no way of knowing of Jean-Paul's previous experience as a trapper himself, or that he was well acquainted with the Canadian winters.

The trio could indeed have made the return a little earlier. Luck was with them all the way and they manage to find a boat to take them back to the mainland with no trouble at all. The overland return journey had been hard, for they had to keep up a good pace, but the autumn weather held out fine for them and they had covered the best part of the journey before the weather finally turned to snow. Richard was determined that not only would they return to Quebec with furs to sell, he was equally resolute that he would take home specimens of the delicate, milky white fur of the arctic fox and ermine for his daughters and Ginifur. It was this that had held them up and made their return a little more difficult.

Richard was surprised to find that he was being seduced by the breathtaking magnificence of the mountains which dominated the dramatic landscape, and the contrasting verdant pastures where, in summer, the moose, elk and deer grazed contentedly. In spite of himself, he found that he was falling in love with the country, the people with their determination to build a new life, and the exhilarating experience of his new occupation as a trapper. Indeed, if it wasn't for the children, he could possibly consider embarking on a new life here for himself. It was in the quiet hours, at night, when he was alone with his thoughts, that the call from home was the strongest. Then the longing to see his daughters' faces was so intense that he could almost conjure them out of the air. Then the yearning to see the coast of Cornwall, and Tremanyon, and his children, was almost overwhelming.

Even these extreme conditions didn't manage to alter his perception of this country. It only served to increase the knowledge that he had learned from Running Bear. Liam too, after his experiences of the last winter, had adapted to this harsh climate, and Jean-Paul actually found himself wondering why he had left. If it had not been for their extraordinary adaptability and fitness, they possibly would not have survived. But each obstacle became a challenge and only increased their determination to conquer it.

And so it was that, at the very moment the blizzard blocked out the view from the General's window, three figures, warmly wrapped in furs and wearing snow shoes, were battling their way towards the very gates of Quebec. The three figures and the struggling pack horses pulled behind them sledges laden with quality furs.

At the first sighting the cry went up from the stockade. "Mon Dieu. It is the trappers!! Open the gates; it is le Comte and his friends. They are alive!"

Word passed quickly from one ear to another and, by the time that Richard, Liam and Jean-Paul led the horses up to the livery stables, many people had turned out into the streets to welcome the intrepid travellers with resounding cheers and the news quickly reached the General's door. "Send a message to their rooms. Welcome then back and issue an invitation to dine with me tomorrow night." He poured himself a warming brandy. "It appears that your confidence in them was well placed. Henri." He added to his orderly.

At dinner the following night, the General listened with great interest to the doctored accounts of their travels, and requested that he might be the first to see the furs that they wished to sell. He ventured the suggestion that Richard might like to offer his services to France. Of course, they had been expecting it, and therefore Richard agreed to discuss this before he left Quebec.

Seven days later the blizzard passed over Quebec, and they woke to a crystal clear sky of azure blue above a landscape covered in a white blanket. The sun, reflecting off the snow, made the day time temperature warm in contrast to the temperatures of the last week or so. Three days later they decided that they would delay their departure no longer. Richard and Liam would leave to spend the rest of the winter at Elly's cabin, and they would meet up with Jean-Paul later in the spring. Whilst Richard went to discuss his proposed co-operation with the General, Liam left on a supposed day's hunting to meet up with Running Bear.

Running Bear made his way to the pre-arranged meeting point. His instinct told him that this would be the day. As they sat companionably on a sheltered bolder Running Bear told Liam of his concern that attacks had been stepped up on the settlements and, unlike last winter, there were still many French troops out on manoeuvres along the frontier. Liam agreed that they would meet up with him en-route to Twin Forks in a few days time, and then returned to the town.

From his meeting with the general, Richard learned that he wished him to collect any information from London that related to England's intentions for the future of Canada, and if they were to be sending yet more settlers. Any information he could glean was to be conveyed to the general when he returned to France later in the year. Richard agreed to do this for a handsome fee, although, of course, he had no intention of carrying it out. However, over the next few days he took note of the changes within Quebec itself. There was a build up of military personnel, both infantry and munitions. The walls had been reinforced and the new cannon had been installed on the battlements overlooking the St Lawrence river. On the landward side greater attention to reinforcements had also been made, and a stockade had been added as a first line of defence. It would appear that this was where the French expected any assault would be made, viewing an approach up the steep escarpment an impossibility. War with the Americas had been declared earlier in the year, when an attack had been averted and the militia scattered. It was Richard's considered opinion that if an attempt was to be made to recapture Quebec, it would have to be done from all sides. A frontal attack from the landward side as a diversionary tactic, whilst he considered the best chance of success would come from an assault from the river, up the rocky escarpment.

The day for the departure arrived. Jean-Paul would stay in Quebec until better weather set in, as previously arranged. In spite of the snow, they made good time. But everywhere there were signs of hostile activity. Burnt out homesteads, the settlers either dead and buried beneath the blanket of snow, or scattered far and wide. What ever the answer, there was no sign of them to be found on their journey.

They found Elly and her family were nervous, but resolute. They refused to move into Twin Forks, even though news of reported attacks on settlers had reached them. Running Bear had visited them not many weeks before, asking them to move into the community for he was concerned for their safety. But Elly firmly refused. Richard added his weight to these pleas, to no avail, and so it was finally decided that they would do their best to improve the defences of the homestead.

The remainder of the winter passed quickly and, although reports of raids on settlements had reached Twin Forks these had mostly occurred prior to Christmas. Initial fears soon diminished, and along with them came the belief that the perpetrators had long since departed from the area. However, in spite of the general improvement to moral, Richard and Running Bear decided to make improvements to the fortifications of the small settlement. Tuck had grown not only in height, and was now almost a man.

Richard could hardly believe that he was the same young lad of only twelve months before, and Liam teased him about the emergence of his first, down like, facial hair. He was now similar, in height and build, to Liam. His strength almost equalled Richard's, and he cut and carried long poles to be used in the stockade keeping up with Liam all the while. Running Bear suggested that when the thaw set in they should dig a ditch round the inside of the perimeter fence, this would be lined with short, vicious looking sharply pointed stakes, and then the ditch would be covered with lightweight twigs and branches, moss, and finally a dusting of fine dirt and leaves. He said it was hardly likely to fool a true native Indian, but then he didn't really believe that it was the natives that instigated these raids even if they were in attendance. The trap door in the floor of the cabin opened on to a hidden pit that was just large enough to hide Elly and the girls; although Elly insisted that she would die protecting the cabin and her children. But Running Bear had a better suggestion. When the ground had thawed enough, they would construct an escape route. This would involve loosening further floorboards beneath Elly's bed and not only digging a pit but constructing a tunnel to run from the cabin to the nearest timber line, where it would emerge in amongst the bushes. If the family should be so unfortunate as to need to use it, then he suggested that Elly seriously consider using this at the first sign of trouble. In their hearts they knew that Elly would rather die protecting her children, but it was the best that they could do in the circumstances. Running Bear stayed with them and so, when the weather changed into an early summer, they were ready to head west to Fort Deerfield and then on to Boston and home.

* * *

On the morning of their proposed departure Richard opened his eyes in the still dark of the cabin, wondering what it was that had woken him for dawn was still some while away. Sitting up on the mattress of hay that he had spread on the floor, he reached for his breaches and shirt and rose quietly to pull them on. Silently, on bare feet, he crossed the cabin floor and easing back the bar he opened the door and stepped out onto the porch.

Daylight still lingered below the horizon, the sky above the trees was tinted with the first wash of blue and purple. There was a curious stillness in the valley. Where normally the first strain of bird song would begin to break the silence of the coming dawn, in the trees and bushes beside the slow running river, now there was none. Richard glanced at the sky. Perhaps it was still a little too early, but he was filled with a sense of unease. Moving silently to the end of the porch he studied the stables and the coral beyond. The horses were restless, constantly on the move. Richard's eyes were drawn to the end of the valley, and the tree line. There was barely a breath of air to stir the trees, and there was no sign of the deer that usually came before dawn to graze before the sun arose.

Richard's ears had been finely tuned to the sounds of the mountains, but he sensed, rather than heard, Running Bear's silent approach. He was quite sure that it was Running Bear but, nevertheless, instinctively he raised the rifle to waist height and stepped back into the shadows at the back of the porch.

"You too are awake, my brother." Running Bear stepped up onto the porch. "We must stable the horses and feed them to settle them. But first we must wake Elly and the family."

"What is wrong? I don't like this silence." Once again Richard's eyes searched the valley. "Is someone out there?"

Running Bear glanced at the distant tree line. "Yes. But if we are quick we can be ready for them."

"A raiding party?"

The Indians face looked grim. "I fear it must be so. They are heading this way, but possibly this is not their target, maybe they will pass us by."

"You have been out there? You have seen them?" Richard asked incredulously.

"Yes. They are still some way off."

"Can we get the family out before they arrive?" Richard asked, yet fearing he knew the answer.

"It would be too dangerous. We cannot know which way they will turn. Come, let us go inside."

Liam had already risen and about to open the door. "Tis some quiet." He said. "I think that it was the silence that woke me." Tuck was half dressed and putting the coffee pot on the stove.

Richard knocked quietly on Elly's door and lifted the latch. "Elly! It's me, Dickon. Can I come in?"

When Elly answered he stepped just inside the room, where she sat up in bed with a shawl around her shoulders, and her dark eyes were large in her pale face. She spoke only one word. "Trouble?"

When Richard nodded she dismissed any vanity and threw back the covers. "I will wake and dress the girls. Is Tuck awake?"

"Yes he's making coffee. Get the girls dressed and then get Tuck to secure all the windows. You know the routine; we've rehearsed it enough times. Running Bear and I are going to see to the horses, I will leave Liam on the porch. When everything is secured, make the girls and Tuck eat something, yourself too. It may be a while before they can eat again." With this he turned and left the room, quite sure that Elly would live up to his expectations of her.

Keeping to the shadows, Richard and Running Bear crossed the yard to the coral where, moving easily amongst the horses Running Bear spoke to them quietly as he ushered them quickly towards the opened doors of the stables. Once they were all safely inside Richard secured the doors and then moved up and down the stables with a bucket of rolled oats and some hay. Then having checked the cattle and the pigs, the sheep were grazing at the far end of the valley and would have to take their chances, Richard released the dog from his chain and took her back to the cabin with him. Bess, the sheep dog was instantly aware of the unease, and whined at the closed door until Running Bear rejoined them, then she settled down in a corner with Kiery and Kathleen.

Liam and Tuck arranged the furniture around the perimeter of the room, and placed the ammunition on cupboards or tables beside each look out point. All the fire arms were laid out ready for use, buckets filled with water and blankets soaked in readiness to smother any fire. On the stove a pot of coffee bubbled, soda bread had just been taken out of the range, and a pan of bacon and beans sat in front of the fire. They had practised this routine many times, but Richard marvelled at Elly's outwardly calm appearance. The familiarity of the routine meant that the girls were not flustered or unduly concerned, and Tuck had been kept too busy to think of the very real possibility of an attack.

No one was hungry, but Richard insisted that they all ate something, and the coffee pot was soon empty. They took it in turns to eat and keep watch then, as Elly cleared the platters and pots away, made a fresh pot of coffee and settled the girls in the prepared area between the two bedrooms, each of the men took up their allotted position at the shuttered windows.

The shutters were thick and secure, but made with openings in the form of a narrow cross, just wide enough for the barrel of a gun or to view the area around the cabin.

Without taking his eyes from the surrounding valley, Richard kept up a conversation with Tuck, who was showing the first signs of strain. Liam joined in occasionally as Richard went into detail about their visit to Nova Scotia and some of their hair raising escapades whilst trapping. When Elly had finished her chores, she sat down with the girls and read them a story. Only Running Bear kept his silence.

Each minute that passed was an eternity. But, slowly, daylight filled the valley and the sun rose above the mountains to the east.

Richard's first inclination that something was happening was when he noticed the tell tale sign of a tightening muscle in Running Bear's neck, as he glanced across at him by the window on the other side of the door. At the same moment Running Bear glanced at him and briefly nodded.

"Elly!" Richard's voice was low and steady. "It is time."

Unhurriedly Elly ushered the girls towards the bedroom, and handed them down to the under floor chamber. "Don't move into the tunnel until Running Bear tells us to replace the floor boards. But don't come out. You will be safe down there and the men won't have to worry about knocking you over."

Kiery's lower lip trembled. "Ye're coming too, aren't ye Ma?"

Elly passed a rag doll down to her. "Now Kiery. We've practised this many times, you know that I must be up here to re-load the guns and we must do it just as Running Bear says. When it is time for ye to move into the tunnel, I shall come down with ye." Kiery and Kathleen managed to summon up a brave smile before Elly left the room, leaving the door open. The window to this room had been securely shuttered both from within and without. Liam stood guard at the western window, in the girl's room, Tuck was watching the north from the newly added box room where he slept, and Richard and Running Bear could cover the south and south east from the living area.

Running Bear's keen eyes had noticed movement in the scrub only seconds before Richard and Liam. Tuck saw nothing, but kept his eyes on the yard as he had been instructed.

Running Bear had warned them of the swiftness of an attack but, even prepared as they were, none of them expected the sudden onslaught. A bird call broke the silence of the air, followed by answering calls from various areas of bushy cover. Richard realised that none of them came from the area around the river bank and hoped that it would remain so. Briefly he thought about

Tremanyon and his daughters, and Ginny, and wondered whether he would ever see them again, and then he quickly thrust such thoughts to the back of his mind. He would need every ounce of concentration in the next few minutes.

Suddenly the attackers broke cover, sprinting across the area beyond the stockade. "Tuck!" Richard called out.

"Yes."

"Don't fire until they are within reach of the stables. Don't let them get to the horses. Liam! They are moving."

"I've got em."

Elly crouched on the floor, ready to reload the guns as they were needed.

The air, only a moment ago so quiet and still, was filled with a blood curdling war cry which was taken up as the attackers ran towards the first barricade. It would appear that they were indeed native Indians, but some of them did not move with the same agility as the others, and it was these that fell in to the first trap before warning was called. Those who made it to the second barricade paused momentarily, but a shout of command forced them on into the coral and, in the blink of an eye, the first real fighting started. Arrows flew, and gun shot filled the air with the acrid smell of burned gunpowder. The first wave of the attack only lasted minutes, but it seemed much longer. Then, by the time they had reloaded all the fire arms, the second attack started. This time they were fully aware of the traps, and the next wave of attackers scrambled over the stockade and nearly made it to the stables. However the area around had been completely cleared, and they would have to come out in the open to cross it. Elly picked up a gun and went to help Tuck to keep them pinned down.

Richard thought that they could only have a matter of minutes. There was no way they could continue to keep that number at bay. But the attackers fell back again, giving them a much needed break. "Elly! Get into the chamber. We've got to do it now."

Elly shook her head.

"Ma . . . you must. Who will look after the girls if you don't?" Tuck spoke bravely. "We agreed that you would, if it came to it."

Elly pushed back her stubbornness and, picking up a loaded gun, she hugged Tuck to her briefly before lowering herself into the chamber. Telling the girls to go further into the tunnel, she replaced the boards that hid it and settled herself against the side, the loaded gun across her knees.

"Tuck!" Richard's voice was gentle. "Get in with your mother." He instructed.

Tuck hesitated briefly, as he looked at the floorboards held by Liam and Running Bear. "No, Ma can look after the girls. Father would have fought to the last, that's what I intend to do."

Elly's eyes filled with tears as she reached up for his hand. They all turned their heads away as mother and son made their farewells, then quickly replaced the floor boards, put the bed and dresser back, and returned to their posts.

Running Bear knew that the next attack would be the last, and in hushed tones he agreed with Richard that they would each save two shots. One each for Tuck and Liam, and one for themselves, for they would be shown no mercy if captured. Silently they prayed that if Elly and the girls were found that they would be spared.

This time the lapse between attacks was longer. Each of the men had plenty of time to assemble powder and shot, and check and recheck the guns. Finally, when it came, it was almost with relief that they watched the natives attack once more. It wasn't that the numbers were so great, although they were, it was just that as one fell there was yet another to take his place, climbing over the dead or injured where they lay, until they were almost at the foot of the porch itself. The fighting was so intense that, in spite of their vow, Richard and Running Bear kept firing until the door suddenly burst open.

Richard turned and fired from his hip, the young Indian brave fell like a stone and the following war painted warrior was knocked off balance by his fall. Running Bear lunged at him with his knife, whilst Richard faced the warrior's companion who followed, falling upon him with his long bladed knife in his hands. Both Running Bear and Richard were immediately entangled in mortal combat, and Liam's instinct was to attempt to take aim on Richard's assailant but, in the confined space he soon realised that he would be in danger of killing Richard or Running Bear, or even both. By some miracle Tuck had the presence of mind to kick the door shut and push a broom handle under the latch. It wouldn't hold for long, but it might bring them valuable minutes. Liam glanced out of the window. For one moment it looked as though the attackers were uncertain of their next move, drifting back until, quite clearly, in French, the order came for them to regroup.

Running Bear's knife found its mark and the Indian fell away. Richard judged his move perfectly, and found the strength to thrust his knife deep into the Indian's side. The Indian's eyes opened wide in surprise, before Richard pulled away leaving his knife imbedded in the mortal wound. Briefly, before the dark enveloped him, the Indian noticed Running Bear step forward to speak to Richard, then he sank to his knees and died, unceremoniously, at Running Bear's feet. Running Bear stripped the feathered head-piece from the dead man's head. Renewed gunfire quickly brought them to their senses and as Richard picked up the dropped lance decorated with the gruesome reminders of previous raids, Liam raised his voice excitedly.

"There's shooting, coming from the river. They're fleeing. Be Jesus, the Indians, they're running away." They could all hear the sound of rapid gunfire and had mistaken it for their attackers. "It's Jean-Paul." Shouted a jubilant Liam. "It's Jean-Paul and Andy MacDonald."

"Tis the men from Twin Forks Ma!" Called out Tuck. "Do ye hear me Ma?" He ran to the bedroom, tugging at the furniture in order to remove the floorboards.

"Wait Tuck!" Richard brought him to a halt. "Wait until we know it is really clear." He opened the door and stepped out onto the porch, still with the lance in his hand and watching Jean-Paul and their rescuers scattering the attackers into the woodland at the end of the valley.

Behind him, Running Bear glanced around at the fallen bodies. It grieved him to see them lying dead or dying, motionless. Too late he saw the movement out of the corner of his eye. Hidden behind the woodpile, an Indian had recognised the lance and head-dress of his chief, and with a blood curdling yell let loose an arrow from his bow. Running Bear pushed Richard with one hand, and with perfect accuracy threw the knife with his other.

Clutching his belly the Indian fell across the logs, but Running Bear had turned away, quite certain his aim was true. Richard had slumped against the rail of the porch. The arrow, having gone clean through him, was protruding from his back.

"My brother!" Running Bear supported Richard as he sat beside him on the step. "I must break the arrow." Quickly he snapped the arrow head off and lowered his friend to the floor. Then he carefully examined the position of the shaft. "His aim was true, but I think you had moved enough for it to have missed your heart.

Does my brother trust me enough to remove the shaft? Pain prevented a reply, but Richard closed his eyes briefly before looking trustingly into Running Bear's eyes. "This will hurt." Running Bear warned needlessly. Richard acknowledged him again in the same manner and Running Bear positioned himself carefully over his prostrate body. With one hand flat on his chest, the arrow protruding between his second and third fingers, he took a firm grip on the feather trimmed shaft, and with one swift movement he removed it completely. Richard opened his mouth in agony, but no sound passed his lips for he slipped into unconsciousness. Using these precious moments Running Bear tore open Richard's shirt, exposing the wound and staunching the flow of blood with one hand, he felt for the pouch on his belt with the other. "Whisky!" He shouted at Liam and Tuck, both riveted to the spot, shock written all over their faces. "Whisky, do you want my brother to die?"

Liam found his feet and went quickly back to the cabin, returning with a half full bottle of poteen. "Tis all there is."

Running Bear removed the stopper with his teeth and sniffed at the liquor. "It will do." He said as he poured it into the wound and removed any traces of shirt threads. "Get Elly."

Tuck removed the floor boards, and Elly hurried to the porch where she took one look at Richard and immediately ran back into the cabin for her medicine chest, and a clean sheet which she immediately proceeded to rip into strips. Running Bear felt into his pouch and pulled out a small twist of animal skin which contained some powdered substance and this he sprinkled on the wound. Then he removed some dried moss which he packed into the hole where the arrow had entered Richard's body. Elly did not argue, or offer one of her own remedies, she was quite happy to leave it to Running Bear. She had seen his medicine work before. She glanced at Richard's face. But this time? Was there any medicine at all that would heal a wound such as this, for who could tell what damage had been caused inside? Elly bent down to press a folded wad of clean cotton onto the moss covered wound and then they carefully turned him over to dress the wound in his back in the same manner. This completed, linen straps were bound tightly around his chest.

"Will he live?" Elly looked from Richard to Running Bear.

"If the Gods will it." Running Bear glanced at Richard's face, drained of all colour. "He is strong. If the arrow has missed his heart then there is a chance. There was no poison on the arrow, he was lucky in that. He has a better chance than most." Kneeling beside his friend he carefully worked his arms beneath his body and, with one smooth movement, lifted him from the floor. Carrying him into the cabin, he laid Richard carefully on the bed in Tucks room. With great care, he and Elly removed Richard's clothing and when Elly had covered him with a clean sheet of linen and a home made quilt Running Bear gave her his instructions. Mix these herbs in boiling water, this much." He indicated a tin jug. "When he wakes let him sip it if he asks for water. The herbs will keep the heat from rising in his body and will help him to sleep. Sleep is the best cure for now." He turned to look about the room. Tuck and Liam had removed the dead bodies of the native Indians and attempted to make some order of the chaos. "I shall go to collect fresh herbs to help the healing. Do not move him. I shall be back." With these parting words he picked up his rifle and bow, strung his quiver of arrows on his back and went to retrieve his knife from the body on the woodpile.

Jean-Paul was just in time to see Running Bear's back, as he entered the copse by the stream, and a puzzled frown creased his brow.

For two days and nights, Richard slipped in and out of consciousness. Night or day, there was always someone at his side to help him sip the herbal water. On the third day, Running Bear returned with fresh herbs which he mixed to a paste. With Elly's help he removed the old dressing from the wound and cleaned it with fresh spirit brought over from Twin Forks. He spread the paste in the wounds, packed them tightly with fresh moss and bound them with fresh strips of Elly's linen. Richard showed no sign of fever, and fresh herbs were added to more boiled water to make a fresh potion for him to sip. Elly placed the soiled linen strips in a pan and put them on the stove to boil. This process was repeated every other day, without Richard ever opening an eye or showing signs of consciousness.

On the eighth day, when Richard finally opened his eyes and asked for a drink he was comparatively lucid. His eyes registered acknowledgement of his surroundings, and he recognised Elly who was sitting by the bed and managed a brief smile.

"Hello my fine fellow." Elly smiled back at him. He licked his lips. "Will ye be takin' another of Running Bear's drinks then?" There was a slight movement of his head to suggest that he would and Elly lifted the mug to his lips, gently tipping it so that the liquid poured out slowly.

Running Bear had been conversing with Jean-Paul, who was eager to set off for Fort Deerfield. He glanced across at the door to Tuck's room and pushed himself off the chair. "Is there improvement?"

"I think so." Elly replied. "Look, his eyes are quite bright, and I think he has recognised where he is."

Running Bear crossed the room in long strides. He smiled as he knelt beside the crude bed. "I see you my brother."

Richard's mouth opened. "I . . . see . . . you . . . also . . . my . . . brother." He whispered.

Running Bear smiled. "The worst is passed, I feel. Do not try to talk, save your strength. I think that you would like something to eat now." Richard inclined his head in answer. "Elly! Bring a little of that broth over here." Elly took a ladle of broth from the pot on the stove and, pouring it into a bowl, she passed it to Running Bear. With Elly supporting his body, Running Bear painstakingly assisted Richard to take a few spoonfuls of the broth. The effort tired him, but as he indicated that he had eaten enough he smiled. Indian men did not feed the injured, this was women's work. It was a mark of the strength of affection between the two men that allowed Running Bear to do this.

Richards's eyes wandered about the room. "Liam?" He asked.

"Liam is out with Tuck, they are mending the fences." Jean-Paul stood at the foot of the bed. "It is good to see you back in the world." He added. "As soon as you are fit enough we will set off for Fort Deerfield. Running Bear's medicine has been good, but we must get a doctor to look at your wound and, if we are not careful we will miss the White Rose."

At his words Richard looked agitated. "White Rose!" He repeated. "Must meet the White Rose. Must get back to Tremanyon." Vainly he tried to rise, but Running Bear gently pushed him back.

"Time enough to travel." He threw an angry look at Jean-Paul. "A few more days and you will be feeling stronger."

It was more than a few more days, it was the end of June before Elly and Running Bear agreed that he should attempt the journey to Fort Deerfield and, when they finally took their leave it was a sad family that was left behind.

Richard rode on horseback, with Running Bear either running or walking by his side all the way. Each night he would attend to the healing wound, redressing it with fresh herbs that he collected on the way and binding it with the supply of Elly's torn linen. But they soon had to construct a travois and line it with furs to lay Richard in for the last leg of the journey. By the time they had reached Fort Deerfield, Richard was showing signs of the strain of the journey, and he was running a fever. Running Bear could hardly contain his anger that Richard had not been allowed to recuperate properly before taking such an arduous journey and Richard was admitted to the infirmary at the fort. Running Bear refused to leave his side, even whilst the doctor examined the wound.

"I don't know how you treated this, Running Bear, but I think that it is fair to say that you have probably saved your friends life. There is no real sign of infection in the wound, but God alone knows what injuries may have been sustained inside him." He passed a hand over his face, and rubbed his chin thoughtfully. "This fever puzzles me. It could be the effects of the journey. It could be something more, I just don't know."

He cleaned the wound, examined the healthy healed tissue that surrounded it and looked deep into Richard's eyes as he listened to his uneven breathing. "I don't know what to suggest. His friends want to take him home, and the ship leaves in a few days time."

Richard slipped in and out of consciousness for the next two days but, on the third day, when briefly his mind was clear, he insisted that they returned to England. Running Bear gave a supply of herbs to Liam with instructions for their use, in contrast to those given by the doctor, but Liam promised faithfully to carry them out. When it came for them to leave, Richard and Running Bear were left alone to make their farewells. No one witnessed the pain that this separation caused to the two friends. The friendship that had sprung up between them was truly that of blood brothers. Richard assured him that it was not a true farewell, and Running Bear affirmed that he would always be by his side in spirit.

The homeward journey was arduous, and Richard's health deteriorated. His fever increased and his moments of lucidity were few.

Jean-Paul had been sitting by his bunk whilst Liam took some fresh air on deck. When he returned, Jean-Paul asked who Becky was.

"Why? Tis his daughter, of course."

Jean-Paul shook his head. "It cannot be his daughter. He has been asking for Becky's baby."

"Becky's Baby! Becky's Baby!" Liam puzzled. "Becky's Baby." The answer dawned on him, and he turned to the sea chest and retrieved the rag doll, complete with ribbon. "His daughter smuggled it into his chest, Dickon believes it to be a talisman." He snapped at Jean-Paul's surprised expression. Then he placed it next to Richard's hand. Richard briefly opened his eyes, saw the doll and took the ribbon between his fingers.

Somewhere during the journey the ribbon and the doll became parted. But the ribbon never left Richard's hands. He held it tightly in his grip, as though he feared that if he let go of it he would also let go of life itself.

Old Betsy

ADAM'S TEMPER HAD vanished as quickly as it rose, and he and Ginifur returned to a fragile truce only held together by equally fragile threads of what had, or might have been. However, the broach was not mentioned again, nor did Ginifur know what became of it.

Not wishing to face, or endure, a repeat of that awful night in the cottage, Ginifur smothered her own feelings of near revulsion by creating an invisible shield behind which she could disassociate her mind from her body, whilst submitting to Adam's harsh and inconsiderate approach to love making. Taking advice from Dr. Thomas, Ginifur confined these, what was for her undesirable and distasteful unions, to the first or last days of the month. But Adam was getting wise to this, and she feared a repetition of his previous act.

However, purely by chance, or so it seemed at the time, Ginifur met Old Betsy whilst she was walking home from Well Cottage one evening with young Jamie perched upon her hip.

Betsy had shown a keen interest in the child of her prophesies. And Betsy had read the signs, she knew that Jamie was not from Adam's loins. "Ye'll be 'avin a string o' babies about 'e one o' these days." She teased.

"I hope you are wrong there Betsy. I don't want another." Ginifur told her firmly.

Betsy nodded wisely. "Maybe not jest yet awhile." She rubbed her chin "Till then, there be no need to 'ave an unwanted cheeld." Betsy placed a bunch of gathered herbs in her basket and winked knowingly. "But I've read the signs. Ye won' 'ave no cheeld by that young 'usband of your'n, anyways."

"I've got Jamie!" Ginifur retorted indignantly.

"Ah, 'es. Ye've got young Jamie." She peered closely at the child on Ginny's hip, and Jamie smiled happily back at her. "Like 'is father i'nt 'e?" Ginifur turned white. "There be no secrets from Ol' Betsy, Miss Ginny, but yer secrets safe wi' me, never fear. 'Ere." From the Hessian sack, by her feet, she produced a small stone jar and a muslin bag filled with dried herbs. "Ye'll not get with another cheeld yet awhile. As I said, it's in the signs. But if ye are still afeared o' bearin' another babe, choose your own moment. Mix a teaspoon o' these 'erbs in boilin' water and drink

265

it every night for seven days after the bleedin' stops. Then, afore ye gives yerself to un, smear this much o' the cream inside of 'e." She illustrated how much she meant. "Tis only 'erbs, and can do no lastin' 'arm." Dubiously Ginifur took the proffered potions, disturbed by Betsy's apparent gift of sight. How could she possibly know that Adam was not Jamie's father, let alone know who he was. Betsy pushed another bunch of herbs into her basket and hoisting the sack over her shoulder she took another peek at Jamie. "Tis fer certin, there be no doubt about it. Tell me, did 'e know 'is middle name was James, or was it coincidence?"

"What do you mean?" How could Betsy possibly know what had occurred, she couldn't know that Richard Tremayne was Jamie's father. She just couldn't, could she? Ginifur had no idea if Richard even had a middle name. It hadn't occurred to her, for she had only been given one name, and so had Adam.

Betsy let out an amused cackle. "So, twas coincidence, or divine providence. Ye take good care o' yersel, Miss Ginny. You'm goin' t'be needed afore long." And leaving Ginifur staring at her retreating back she waddled off down the lane in search of more herbs.

Warily Ginifur placed the potions on her dressing table, where they stayed untouched for three weeks. It was only when her flux had been a whole week late that she was drawn to examine them. Placing a dab of the cream on the back of her hand she rubbed it gently into the skin. It didn't sting, it smelt slightly of herbs. Ginifur then examined the muslin bag of herbs. Just harmless herbs, she could not smell the scent of any of the known harmful ones. Ginifur pondered the problem. The only thing for certain was that she did not want another child, and the only quandary was what harm she might do herself. But Betsy's potions had not been known to kill anyone yet, so the only harm she could foresee was that she might never bear a child again. It didn't take long for her to make her decision, and from that night forward she faithfully carried out Betsy's instructions.

Ginifur's monthly courses arrived with a regularity that was uncanny. Needless to say this delighted Ginifur, but it was not what Adam had in mind. Once a month Ginifur would come upon Old Betsy, quite by accident it would seem, as she was picking herbs along the lanes. Betsy would hand her a fresh jar of ointment and a fresh muslin bag of herbs, and they would chat a while before parting. Ginifur even became a little fond of the sometimes feared woman. She was always referred to as Old Betsy, but in truth on closer inspection it appeared that she was probably only in her mid thirties. At a quick glance, her stoop possibly made her look older, but this was caused by a deformity of her spine. The cloak she always wore, with the large hood covering her head, of course did not help. Jamie saw none of these things, and smiled happily when she reached out to touch him.

Winter turned into spring, and spring into summer, and Jamie blossomed. He progressed quickly with all the encouragement he received from Rachel and Rebecca. Netty was horrified. She still held the belief that babies should not sit up until much later let alone be left rolling around on the floor and encouraged to crawl. So, on the occasion that Jamie took his first steps, when he was only ten months old, she nearly had an apoplexy.

Flouting all attempts to encourage her to dress him in skirts, as was quite normal to the time, Ginifur made Jamie trousers, with a bib and brace, so that he wouldn't hurt his knees when he fell. Ginifur's refusal to conform only served to anger Adam further, but both Simon and Samuel loved the child and thought that Ginifur was an excellent Mother, even if she did have singularly exceptional ideas on bringing up a child..

At the age of one year Jamie showed a keen interest in outdoor activities. He loved the horses and was often to be seen seated in front of Ginifur as she took a ride out on Damson, and he loved water and boats in equal measure, having already experienced the feeling of being afloat when he was taken out in Skylark with Simon and Ginny.

"He'll make a fine sailor, just wait and see." Said Simon. "Look at the way he is watching the sail t'see how the wind is catchin' it."

"'e'll be a fine 'orseman." Samuel suggested. "See the way 'e sits on Spangles."

All this could be easily explained as grandfatherly pride of course, but the truth was that they were each only stating the facts, and Jamie would soon be learning to sail the tiny boat that Simon was building for him. He would also shortly be joining Ginny on her gentler rides, mounted upon Spangles by Damson's side.

However, at this time, each of Jamie's achievements only provided further fuel for Adam's growing obsession to have a son of his own, and to increase his hostility towards Jamie.

267

The child had no obvious features which would give rise for anyone to think that Jamie was not indeed the child of Adam and Ginifur. He was slight of build, but well proportioned with straight limbs. His hair was dark, almost black, like Ginny, his skin was dark, his features striking and his eyes evenly spaced, like Ginny. He was a happy child, with Ginifur's disposition. It was only his eyes that were different. Bright, sparkling eyes, in an incredible shade of blue. Not cold and hard, as some blue eyes can be, but gentle and kind, and radiating an inner strength. It was the eyes that caused Adam's greatest rejection of the child, without him ever knowing the reason why.

Jamie gave Adam no real reason for this rejection. Jamie was an uncommonly well behaved child, instinctively knowing what was, or was not, expected of him. As if unaware of Adam's feelings, or in spite of them, Jamie would totter to meet him with a smile on his face. Hold out a hand to him, if he feared he might fall, and even offer him his last piece of fruit when one day Adam arrived after they had finished their meal. Jamie did not, in all honesty, deserve this hostility but fortunately he was seemingly unaffected by it.

May was a beautiful month, and Ginifur took the children on long walks across the headland. The bluebells lay thickly upon the floor of the woodlands, the tiny pink flowers of the wild campion, the early foxgloves, wild garlic and cow parsley filled the hedgerows, and the young leaves burst forth on the coastal Cornish elms and those planted along Tremanyon Avenue. Ginny's happiest moments were those that she shared with the children. On these occasions she could almost believe that she was completely happy. But these moments were short lived, and in the long hours of the night she admitted, only to herself, that she feared that true happiness would never be hers. But even in these darkest hours Ginifur's suppressed optimism could find a spark of comfort. For hadn't Fanny Boscawen informed her that although Richard and Liam had not returned on the last ship to return from Boston, the Admiral would be returning from Boston at the end of the summer in the White Rose. The fleet would sail with replacements and ammunition for Fort William Henry, and British troops were being built up along the borders with the increase of French attacks to border posts in the region.

Ginifur celebrated her 23rd birthday in May. It passed almost unnoticed. Adam forgot it completely.

Ginifur was increasingly worried by Adam's unexplained night time activities. Even though she did not spend all her nights with him she was still fully aware of his nocturnal habits, and sometimes unexplained long absences. But in spite of the fact that Adam's hours of employment had been cut back in the stables, he was never short of money. Ginifur was not happy with the company he was keeping either. For if Adam was not off on his mysterious activities, he was to be found in one of the Inns, drinking until the small hours. She feared the only explanation for Adam's change in behaviour and financial circumstances.

There were few in these isolated areas who did not have connections, or benefited from, the Free Traders. They were not in fact even thought of as outlaws, but as men plying a legitimate trade against the unfair imposition of taxes on a number of goods besides brandy. It had, of course, been common knowledge that the supply had been cut when the Militia caught the gang leaving Pentire Cove, but rumours had reached her that a new group had been formed and were working from near home. Veiled hints at the bravery of the boys who brought the goods ashore brought Ginny to the conclusion that they could be using Kylyn Cove and, if so, distributing them via the caves and tunnels was not to be ruled out. But if that was so, and they used the exit at the well, it would be difficult to hide it from her grandfather, and he had hinted at nothing untoward going on.

Using the information that she had gleaned from John Retallick, Ginifur had inspected the hidden area beneath the bridge and found the entrance of the tunnel to Tremanyon. It was covered with long, damp strands of Ivy, undisturbed for many years. She had even found the exit at the back of the cellars, this had been more difficult for the rings were fixed almost solid by long disuse, and it had taken many hours to free them. But she knew that it was there, and her determination was rewarded when, finally, the wall moved enough to enable her to enter the hidden tunnel. This find convinced her that the tunnel to the house had not been used for many a year. If the exit at the well was being used, then that was as far as it went. Further visits to Well Cottage convinced her that this was not the route if, of course, the cave and tunnel were being used at all. This only left the route out of Rosvarron and, of course, Monsieur de Varron was absent from home, as was Richard Tremayne. But at Rosvarron there was no one living in the house but the servants. Lady Catherine and her son were staying with her family in London. However John Retallick had said that the roofs to the exit at Rosvarron had caved in.

On more than one occasion throughout the summer, Ginifur considered the possibility of visiting the cave and exploring the tunnel beyond for herself, but it was probably the fear that she would find proof of the existence of local smugglers and Adam's involvement that made her hesitate. Whatever it was, Ginny never went near Kylyn Cave, and if it wasn't for the fact that it was the safest beach to take the children to she wouldn't have visited Kylyn Cove either.

June was the month for birthdays. Starting with Rachel at the beginning, Jamie in the middle and Rebecca bringing up the rear.

The hay harvest was good. Everyone at Tremanyon joined in, even the children. Netty would pack baskets full of food to take to the fields for the men and women, and to wash it all down there was home made cider, fresh lemonade, or hot tea poured from earthenware jugs. Men, women and children worked hard from the moment the dew had dried upon the meadow grasses until it began to fall again in the evening. They worked the field in staggered formation, down the swaths of grass, tossing it in the air to dry. If the day was really warm, and the air dry with little or no humidity, then it could be dried and stooked in a day. On the rare occasions that this happened, the quality of the hay was much better, and in truth it didn't happen often. But this summer, every field that was cut and dried for hay was dried and stooked in a day.

In August, the wheat and dredge corn gave forth a better than usual yield, and the prospect for going into a winter with full grain stores was good. On the farms there was plenty of grain, hay, potatoes and meat, and in the sea there was an abundance of fish. Such a different year from last year.

As each day passed, the hour of Richard's homecoming drew nearer and Ginifur's excitement was mixed with apprehension. Fanny Boscawen had told Ginifur that Lord Falmouth had sailed and they all hoped that Richard, Liam and Jean Paul would be there to meet them.

Pathways That Divide

THE FINE WEATHER continued long after the end of August with a hot Indian summer. In the middle of October Adam vanished for two whole weeks, without a word to anyone. Ginifur was beside herself with worry. No matter what had happened between them, she was married to him and Adam had been her friend since childhood.

When he finally retuned he was the worse for drink once more, and it would have been better if Ginifur had left him to sober up. But she had risen early and was in Garden Cottage when Adam opened the door and staggered through.

Startled, Ginifur turned. "Adam! Where on earth have you been? Your father and mother have been worried sick."

Adam sneered. "Me father 'n mother 'e say? I didn' 'ear 'e say that ye was worried."

Ginifur shook her head in disbelief. "Of course I was worried Adam! We all were, Netty and Tom included. We have got used to your short absences, but you have been gone for two whole weeks. Where have you been? What are you up to Adam?"

"Tid'n none o' yer business woman. Quit yer moanin'. What I'm doin is gettin' enough money to'get me wife 'n family outa 'ere." His lascivious eyes roved over her figure, and Ginifur managed to dodge his clumsy attempt to grab at her. This only served to anger him further, and his next attempt was more successful as he grasped her wrist and pulled her roughly towards him. "Me wife 'n family, Ginny. Do 'e 'ear me? Me wife 'n family. Me 'n ye,'n yer son. The bastard can come too o' course, but I want me own cheeld. So what news do 'e 'ave fer me this month? Eh?" Ginifur lowered her eyes to the floor and struggled to break free. "What news Ginny? Are 'e pregnant at last?" He raised his hopes as she still averted her eyes. "If 'e are, tis not afore time. God knows what took 'e so long, 'ow many times did yer fancy man 'ave t' try to get that brat into yer belly?"

Ginny's eyes flashed in anger. "It took once to conceive Jamie. And I didn't try." Adam's eyes were taunting her. "And I am not with child, Adam. Do you hear that? I am not carrying your child in my belly."

Adam's anger and resentment suddenly exploded as he put his full strength behind his hand and sent Ginifur flying across the room. "'ow can ye possibly 'ave one cheeld, 'n then take s'long t'ave another? What black magic are 'e practicin'? It in't natural I tell 'e. Look at all the others, year after year 'em 'ave babies, why not ye, Ginny? Why not? Tell me."

Ginifur felt a trickle of blood on her cheek, wiping it with the back of her hand and looking at the smear that it left in bewilderment. Shakily she grasped a chair in an attempt to pull herself to her feet. But before she could raise herself, another blow to the other side of her head sent her reeling again and then, before she could catch her breath, she was roughly lifted up until she could smell the alcohol on Adam's breath as he shook her, all the while shouting unintelligibly at her. Ginny heard rather than felt the ripping of her clothes, as the noise and pain in her head increased, caused by the beating she had received and the blows that he continued to rain down upon her, until she finally and fortunately, passed into unconsciousness.

When Adam finally ceased his tirade of abuse and realised what he had done, he glanced at the inert body of Ginifur lying at his feet. For one frightened moment he thought that he had killed her. However, a feint groan escaped her swollen lips and her body trembled as he bit his lip and wondered what to do. Adam glanced out of the window. There was no one about, it was still very early. What on earth was she doing in the cottage at this unearthly hour anyway? Could it have been that she was really worried about him? No, Ginifur didn't worry about anybody but Ginny and her brat Jamie. Adam grabbed his jacket and, opening the door, he left her lying there.

It was still early when Ginifur finally came round. As the last time, she returned to her room and bathed the wounds. But this time, when she had finished, she put Jamie on her hip and walked round to Kate's tiny cottage.

Kate answered the door immediately, and her mouth dropped open at the sight of her bruises. "Ginny!" She reached out and took Jamie from her "Adam?" She shook her head in disbelief. "Did Adam do this to ye?"

Ginifur's skin, that was either not bruised or scratched in some way, was white. Whether white with shock or anger Kate couldn't tell. "Come in Ginny, let me make 'e a cup o' sweet tea."

"No Kate. I'll be alright. But will you take Jamie for me and go to the Big House and look after him and the girls. I've go to get out for a while. I need some space, I need to be alone."

Kate looked unhappy. "Do 'e think ye should Ginny? It would be for the better, pr'aps, if ye went off t'bed with a drop o' brandy and milk."

"No Kate. Please, do this for me. And don't send anyone after me Kate, promise me. I may be out all day, but I'll come back. Never fear." She gazed at the bewildered child in Kate's arms.

"I knows that. Go on, away with 'e. Jamie 'n the girls will be just fine. You mind yerself Ginny."

Ginifur nodded and bent to kiss Jamie. "Be good for Kate, Jamie. I'll be back before bedtime." And she turned and left the cottage before Jamie saw the tears in her eyes.

Ginifur couldn't walk away without saying anything to Netty so, regardless of her appearance, she had to take the girls to the kitchen for their breakfast.

Netty's initial reaction was to close her eyes as she witnessed the result of Adam's latest abuse. "Fallen again, I see." She commented, in view of the presence of the children.

"Ginny was out riding early this morning, Netty, before we were awake. Damson threw a shoe and Ginny fell off." Rachel explained. "Do you think that Dr. Thomas ought to see her?"

"Dare say 'e should, but needless t'say 'e won't. But tis 'igh time someone knows what's agoin' on." Netty shook her head in amazement at Ginny's spirit and determination to cover the cracks in her marriage. She was only glad that Tom wasn't here to see her.

"I have asked Kate to come over and help with the children, she already has Jamie." Ginifur explained.

"Are 'e goin' t'see your Da?"

"No." Ginifur snapped, and then added more gently. "No Netty, and don't you tell him, please. I'm going for a walk. I will be alright, believe me."

"I 'ope so, my luvver, I do 'ope so." Netty bustled about the kitchen so as to hide her true feelings as Ginny left the room.

The autumn day was warm, and on any other occasion Ginifur would have been filled with happiness at the prospect of a few hours on her own. But this time there was no pleasure in her solitude. This time she needed the seclusion to regain her strength, revive her spirit and attempt to discover if there was any way to salvage something from her marriage. Ordinarily Ginifur would have ridden on Damson if she wanted to go out to the headland, where she could look out over Falmouth Bay, but there were two very good reasons why, on this day, even when it wasn't easy, she was walking out to the headland. Firstly, Ginifur didn't want Sam to see her this way, and secondly, she didn't think she would have the strength to mount Damson, let alone ride her. For the same reason Ginifur made her way quietly along Well Lane and past the cottage. Taking the footpath beyond the mill, she crossed the stream by the stepping stones before following the creak as it flowed into the main body of the river.

When Ginifur set out, each step she took seemed to cause her pain in one part of her body or another but, as she persevered, the exercise actually appeared to ease some of her physical pain. However it would take far more than exercise to relieve her mental anguish. Slowly but surely, Ginifur made her way along the riverside path until, after the long hard climb to Rhosinnis, the headland was finally in view.

Carefully Ginifur selected a sheltered and secluded spot, where she had a commanding view of the bay and the Lizard beyond. There were a few fishing boats in the bay, and a Clipper had dropped anchor in the Carrick Roads. Nearer to the rocks, at the base of the cliff, small boats were sailing along the lines of crab pots strung out along the coast.

Ginifur spread her shawl out over a soft bed of heather, and lay her weary body down to rest. She struggled with the problem on her mind. Was this how the future would be? Had her marriage to Adam sunk so low that there was nothing to retrieve? What would be the long term effect on Jamie, who didn't deserve to be brought up in an environment full of recriminations and hate? Hate! Hate? Ginifur realised for the first time that Adam really did hate Jamie. He hated him for what he was, there was no forgiveness in his heart for her or Jamie, even though Jamie was the innocent party. But what could she do? She was bound to Tremanyon, and to Richard Tremayne's daughters, as surely as she was bound to the headland itself. Ginny sat up and stared at the sea. She had told Kate that she needed to think, so she had better get on with it. Certainly crying wasn't going to do her any good at all. Ginifur took a long hard look at herself. It was true that she had a child to think of, but women sometimes had to bring up their children on their own. Look at Maggie Dowrick whose husband was lost when his boat floundered off the Black Rock. She brought up three children on her own, and a right credit they were to her too. She

274

worked at the pilchard cellars at Porthcarrow and Tremanyon. She worked her vegetable plot and made chutneys and jams, pickled and salted vegetables, and sold those that were surplus to her needs to pay for essentials. In haymaking time she helped in the fields, with the children helping or resting under the hedge, she picked potatoes and she helped with the threshing of the corn. Yes, she worked hard, Ginifur realised that this was inevitable, but she was fit and healthy and she loved her children.

Ginifur gave a deep sigh. If she was to even contemplate leaving Adam she would have to leave Porthcarrow and everything and everyone she loved and held most dear. If she was to leave Adam! If she was to leave Adam? At last Ginifur accepted that this thought had been lurking at the back of her mind. She was young, and strong. She had a good head on her shoulders, and she had received a good education from her grandmother. Besides this, she had worked in the cellars at Quay Cottage along with the women since she was seven, she could mend nets and she could work in the fields. She had saved all her money since she had been working for the Tremayne's for her father had refused to take a penny from her and she had little reason to spend any. Except for the few personal items that she needed to purchase, everything was provided for her in her employment at Tremanyon. All her food, all her clothes that she used for work, and even some that she didn't, for Annabelle had been very generous when she was alive and had passed on clothes that she no longer wore for Ginifur to cut up and alter. Perhaps she could pass herself off as a widow! Now that Ginifur had started her train of thoughts there was no stopping them. For a while she pondered on the possibilities and finally came to the conclusion that this was the only course open to her. She couldn't continue in this marriage of convenience to Adam. She should never have agreed to it in the first place. She would have to leave, even though it meant leaving everything she loved behind her. Of course she would have to wait until Richard returned to look after his children, but then. Then she would leave.

The decision, when finally made, was a relief. It was as though a load had been lifted from her shoulders, and she lay down once again, with her hands behind her head as she stared up at the few puffy white clouds above her. Whether it was the long walk that had tired her, or reaction to the early morning events, or even the fact that she had come to a decision about her future, whatever it was, within a few short minutes she was fast asleep.

Ginifur slept the sleep of the innocent. No memories of Adam's brutal treatment invaded her exhausted respite, and as she slept the sun moved slowly across the autumn sky. When her eyelids finally flickered, she shivered slightly. For as the sun sank towards the west, the warmth had been drawn out of the day. Ginifur stretched and opened her eyes. Although she still felt a little stiff, she sat up and stared hard at the horizon beyond the Lizard. The sea was empty now. No sails on the horizon. No fishing boats in the bay. Not even a crab fisherman was to be seen around the rocks. Ginifur's eyes were fixed firmly upon the horizon, willing the White Rose to appear, until she finally raised her eyes towards the sky. "Please Lord, send him home" She pleaded. "Send him home soon, for I don't think I can continue doing everything that is expected of me. I need to leave. Jamie and I have to get away and I can't leave Rachel and Rebecca until he comes home." Then once more lowering her eyes to the sea, barely audibly she whispered. "Oh, Captain! Come home soon, please. Rachel and Rebecca need you. We all need you."

Hauling herself to her feet she retrieved the shawl from the ground and wrapped it around her shoulders; she had been absent long enough. Tearing her eyes from the horizon she turned to make her weary way home. Her eyes were fixed firmly on the path in front of her, her mind going over the decision to leave Adam and Tremanyon.

If only she had lingered a moment longer, or even glanced back over her shoulder before the bend in the path. For if she had, she would have seen a set of white sails appear beyond the Manacles. And the ship, The White Rose, the south west wind filling her sails as she headed into Falmouth Bay.

The Homecoming

GINIFUR HADN'T SLEPT a wink of sleep. By three o'clock she gave up even trying, coming to the conclusion that making the decision to alter her life had made her too restless for sleep. The last time she had felt so restless was the night before Jamie was born. Then she hadn't slept either. She had turned out the linen cupboard and made an inventory of items that needed replacing.

Pulling back the curtains in the nursery, she gazed down at the gardens. They were barely visible for it was still quite dark. Ginifur ran her fingers through her hair, and gave a rueful smile as she paused on the thought that the darkest hour was just before dawn. Returning to her bedroom she dressed and made her normal tour of the house, but two hours early.

Ginifur normally rose at five thirty and spent an hour, before the children awoke, making a daily inspection. Taking note of the tasks that she would set Lizzie, Pearl and Peggy for the day. Always the perfectionist, today Ginifur found herself unusually critical and the list, by the time it was finished, was a long one. Glancing out of the drawing room window she watched the dawn and, as the sun rose above Dingerien Head, the early morning mist cleared and rays of pale sunlight spilled over the fields.

Ginifur pressed both hands against the flat of her stomach as an unfamiliar sensation took a hold of her insides, and she gave a puzzled frown. She felt . . . uneasy. A little queasy perhaps, not quite nauseous but! She put a hand to her chest. There was no pain, but a tightness. Perhaps it was just a reaction to yesterday. Whatever it was, she decided to go to the kitchen and find a bite to eat. Maybe that would settle her stomach.

Netty had taken out the first batch of bread from the oven. Ginny took a small split from the tray and broke it open to cool. "Is there any buttermilk Netty?"

Netty indicated the jugs on the table. "Big'n is milk, fresh from the cow. Little'n is the buttermilk." Then she screwed up her face as she asked. "'n how are 'e feelin' this mornin'? Ye' don' look as though'e 'ad a wink o' sleep."

Ginifur grimaced. "I didn't."

"No wonder. If'n ye asks me, which 'e won't, I'd say tis time that ye did some thinkin'.."

"Netty!"

"Don' 'e Netty me. Tis 'igh time the Cap'n were 'ome 'n all. Gallivantin' off round the world 'n leavin' too much on yer shoulders. Sure nuff, tis time 'e were 'ome." Ginny took a pat of butter from the cold shelf, spread a little on the warm split and ate it in silence. She had just finished the glass of buttermilk when Pearl arrived and, before leaving to see the children, she gave her a list of tasks to complete.

When the children had broken their fast and Rachel and Rebecca had settled to some school work with Peggy watching them whilst she did some mending, Ginny went to pick some flowers. Even though the master had been away for nearly two years it never occurred to her to leave the flower vases empty, and Tom had continued to grow a variety of flowers for cutting in the walled garden.

On her early morning round Ginifur had taken special note as to which flowers needed replacing. In particular, today, she was determined to cut some late blooms for the drawing room. She also planned to replace the displays in the hall, one on the side table, another at the foot of the stairs with a third one on the half landing.

"What do 'e want t'waste yer time doin' that fer? There be no one 'ere t'see it." Said Netty as she watched her set off with the trug in her hand.

"It's not a waste of time Netty. You never know when Captain Tremayne will be home, he may be on his way this very minute. He must return and find it just as he left it. It wouldn't do to let him think that we have let the standards slip in his absence."

"Well, if ye've set yer mind to it, ask Tom to bring in some tatties will ye?"

Ginifur took great care to select only the perfect blooms, laying them gently in the trug, with each flower head carefully separated from the next. Satisfied with her selection of flowers she then cut an armful of greenery, delicate asparagus fern, pittisporum and ivy leaves, and then she went to find Tom to give him the message from Netty.

Tom was in one of the glass houses. "'ello there, young Ginny. 'ow are 'e feelin' this mornin'? Feelin' a bit better are 'e?"

Ginny wondered what Netty had told him and said that she was feeling better then, in order to end the subject and change it for another said. "Netty said that she would like some potatoes, if you have dug some."

"'es, I 'ave. I'll bring em up shall I? When I come, will that do?."

"Mmmm, please.

"See ye've picked the last of the Cap'ns fav'rit flowers."

"Yes." Ginifur sniffed the small posy in her hand. "I thought I would put them in his bedroom. They will be the last till next year."

"'ardly worth it, is it? They won' last much more'n a day or so."

Ginifur shrugged her shoulders. "Oh I don't know. It makes the room smell nice, and it's been shut up for too long."

Tom grinned. "'n ye always 'as the last word, maid, don' e?"

Ginny smiled, she knew he was only teasing. "Don't forget the potatoes, will you?" She reminded him as she picked up the trug with her free hand.

Tom turned away. "No . . . I won' fergit the tatties."

As Ginifur wandered slowly back towards the house she became aware of the sound of a carriage approaching Tremanyon. What breeze there was blew from the east, and carried the sound with it. She could hear the horses as they came on at a steady pace up the avenue.

Hurrying herself, she arrived at the front steps as the first carriage rounded the bend in the drive. For there wasn't one carriage but two and they both bore the crest of Lord Falmouth. Ginifur ran up the steps and opened the door, laying the flowers down by the side table, then hastened back outside just as Lord Falmouth bounded up the steps.

"Ginifur!" His face was grim as he took hold of her arm and guided her back into the house. "I need a private word with you."

Ginifur's stomach lurched violently, and her heart suddenly began to pound in her chest. As Edward Boscawen opened the door to the drawing room she turned a fearful face upwards to him. "Captain Tremayne! Have you just come back from the New World? Has he . . ? Is he . . ? What . . ?"

Firmly but gently Lord Falmouth made her take a seat whilst he took up a position where he could look at her. He gave a deep sigh. "Now Ginny." He glanced out of the window as Liam and Jean-Paul alighted from the second carriage and paused at the bottom of the steps to converse with Lady Boscawen. "You know that we had hoped to bring them home on this trip." Ginifur could only nod, she dreaded to think what she was about to hear. "We all knew, at the outset, that the mission was fraught with danger. That there was always the chance that one, or other of them may get hurt, or even, perhaps, fail to return."

"Oh no . . !" Ginifur's heart sank.

"Richard was aware of the danger, as were Liam and Jean-Paul. But it seems to me to be totally unreasonable that such a misfortune should occur when their mission was, to all intents and purposes, over." He ran a hand over his face. "Richard received a near fatal injury whilst helping to protect the widow of a settler and her family, who were being attacked on their homestead."

Ginifur peered through tear filled eyes, clutching at those words. "Near fatal injury? You mean . . ?"

Edward's glance was tinged with surprise. "Injury? Why yes, you didn't think . . ? Oh I am sorry. I didn't mean to mislead you. But even so, I am afraid that the news is not good. Richard's wound was treated by a native Indian, his tracker and guide, and he probably owes his life to him. But he travelled too soon. The wound re-opened and, in spite of Liam's and the ships Doctor's ministrations, infection and fever have set in. He is a sick man Ginny, and will need a great deal of care and attention if he is to return to health. We have picked up Dr. Thomas on route, and we must get Richard comfortable as soon as possible. Is his room ready? Is his bed aired?"

Ginifur's relief was short lived, but at least Captain Tremayne had been returned to his children. And if God had seen fit to answer her prayer and send him home, then she meant to make sure that she did everything in her power to make him well again. Yes, even if it did mean that she would have to delay her own departure. "Oh yes. I have kept his room ready for him to arrive home at any day. The sheets are changed weekly and the bed-clothes are all aired." Ginifur just caught a glance of Kate as she ran, helter skelter, passed the window "Liam?" She asked.

"Liam is well, but tired. He has spent night and day by Richard's side, sleeping in a chair or on the floor. Refusing to let anyone take a spell, taking total responsibility for his care."

"Monsieur de Varron?"

"He too has returned safely. If you are ready, we will instruct them to carry Richard to his room?"

Ginifur nodded and rose unsteadily to her feet. Edward placed a hand beneath her elbow to aid her, and they returned to the hall.

At the bottom of the steps Liam broke away from Kate's embrace. Ginifur was stunned at his appearance. It could, of course, have been the strain, the tiredness. But he had aged much more than the two years he had been absent.

"Ginny!" Liam grabbed at her hands. "I did everythin' I could, believe me. Everythin' Running Bear told me to do, I did. But it wasn't enough."

Ginifur summoned up a reassuring smile. "I know you would have done all you could do, and if it wasn't for that maybe he wouldn't have come home at all. But he's home Liam, and we'll make him better. Believe me, we will. Hello Doctor Thomas." She acknowledged the Doctor at the steps of the first carriage with Jean-Paul. "You do know the way to Captain Tremayne's room, don't you?"

"Yes Ginifur. Is everything ready?"

"It is. Kate, go to the kitchen and get Netty to fill two warming pans and put them in the bed whilst we get the Captain ready. "Where is he Lady Falmouth?" She asked Fanny Boscawen who had taken her place beside her husband.

Edward opened the door of the carriage and held Ginny's hand as she put her foot on the bottom step to take a brief look at her master. Richard, like Liam, also had a beard, but beneath it his face was gaunt and his pallor unhealthy, tinged with yellow and grey. "Dear God!" She whispered before stepping down. "How will you carry him?"

"Liam and Jean-Paul have it worked out quite well." Said Edward from behind her. "Why don't you lead the way?"

The Fever

WHEN RICHARD WAS finally settled in his bed, Doctor Thomas gave him a thorough examination whilst Ginifur entertained Lord and Lady Falmouth, Jean-Paul and Liam in the drawing room. Having first asked Netty if she could prepare some food at such short notice she then took decanters of Brandy and Port to the visitors, together with a tray of assorted savouries quickly prepared by herself and Netty.

Although Edward knew the complete story of Richard and Liam's adventures, it was equally as interesting for Fanny Boscawen as it was for Ginifur. Liam and Jean-Paul shared the telling and they were both so explicit in their descriptions of the landscape that Ginifur felt that she would recognise everything if she was ever to see it for herself. They were both fascinated and concerned for Elly and her family. "Why didn't you send for them, Edward?" Fanny Boscawen puzzled.

"They would not leave. Elly was determined to stay, although she conceded to the request to move in to Twin Forks whilst the unrest continues." Jean-Paul told her.

"And Running Bear?" Ginifur wondered what had become of the native Indian.

"He has returned to his village, with the deep gratitude of our people. It was he who carried the reports back to Fort Deerfield and, if Richard survives this ordeal, he will owe him a debt of gratitude for having saved his life. If Running Bear had not been there I dread to think what might have been." Edward gave a deep sigh.

"If Richard survives!" Doctor Thomas had entered the room without them realising. "Of course Captain Tremayne will survive. However, I agree, that native should be congratulated for his administrations. The arrow, I am sure, has missed all his vital organs. But if it hadn't been for his prompt action he could easily have bled to death."

"So. What is your opinion of his state of health now?" Lord Falmouth pressed him for an answer.

"He is still running a fever. The wound appears to be clean, but has broken open again, and it is going to take time to heal. He has lost a lot of weight. If we can improve his body condition with some of Netty's cooking he will grow stronger. But most of all it is up to Captain Tremayne. He must want to live. Ginifur!" Doctor Thomas had voiced his opinions and turned to Richard's employee. "I would like you to accompany me to Captain Tremayne's room, in order for me to instruct you on his care. Liam! You too. In the absence of the Captain's manservant, Robert, it will be necessary for you to attend to his needs."

The doctor led the way back to Richard's bedroom. The room was dark and airless, even though it was the middle of the day, for the doctor had ordered the windows closed and the curtains drawn to keep the light out.

Richard Tremayne lay motionless upon the large bed. Propped against the stark whiteness of the freshly laundered linen, his face was gaunt and devoid of any natural colour, his skin like wax with an unhealthy sheen to it.

"It is so hot in here." Ginifur remarked.

"He must be kept warm, to encourage the fever to break. Give him nothing to eat, even if he asks for it, and only a little to drink." He ordered them. "Starve a fever, feed a cold." He added. "I have dressed the wound. Don't touch it. Bathe his head with cold water if you think he is too hot. But keep him warm, and don't let any cold draughts into the room. Dab his mouth with a wet cloth if he wants a drink, but don't let him drink too much. Now, let me see! Today is Thursday. By Sunday the fever should have broken, if it is going to. I shall call to see him on Monday morning and I will change the dressing then. Meanwhile there is not much that can be done. Call me if there is a change for the worse, but I must warn you, if there is a change for the worse there will be little that we can do about it but pray."

* * *

Richard was restless. His physical body was lying safely between freshly laundered sheets, fighting the fever that Ginifur and Liam were struggling to bring under control, but in his mind he was trapped inside Elly's cabin, with the flames licking at the roof. Richard and Liam had seen the end results of the homestead fires all along the border, and it wouldn't leave his memory. So now, as he tossed and turned with Ginifur bathing the sweat from his brow, and dabbing his lips with fresh spring water, to Richard he was still with Running Bear and Liam as they tried in vain to save the cabin and Elly's family. They had soaked everything that they could with the water that they had brought into the cabin and had covered the loose floorboards with wet bedding to try to stop the smoke from choking Elly and the girls, but it seemed that all their attempts were doomed to failure as the heat grew in intensity and Richard felt that he was almost on fire with the heat. He could no longer see Running Bear, Liam or Tuck. The smoke had filled the room. He tried to call out, but the words wouldn't come, and finally it seemed easier to stop fighting and let the flames do the work. Slowly the smoky scene faded into blackness, and now there was nothing. Only an empty void, full of dark silence. He could no longer hear the war cries beyond the cabin, nor feel the flames as they licked and crackled on the roof. So this was what death was like, nothingness. Richard was beyond caring and he let himself drift in the peaceful breeze that had suddenly appeared in the bright light that surrounded him.

Ginifur had sat beside Richard's bed for twenty-four hours without a break. In spite of the doctor's orders she had bathed his face and body, dabbed his dry lips with fresh, cool water as he had directed, and Liam had helped her to change his night shirt and sheets as soon as they became damp with sweat. Richard tossed and turned, calling out as he struggled with some inner turmoil that Ginifur couldn't ease.

Liam silently entered the room, bringing fresh water in a jug. "Will ye no take a rest, Ginny?"

Ginifur either didn't hear or chose to ignore the question. "He is worse Liam. If the fever doesn't break soon . . ." She wrung out a fresh piece of linen in the bowl and bathed the perspiration from his face. "What did Running Bear tell you to do when he had the fever?"

Liam glanced uncomfortably at the windows. "He said that he should have fresh air. Not to shut him up in a feted airless room, and there was a herbal mixture which we had to get him to sip, but that's all gone now."

"Did it work?"

"Yes, I think so. Anyways, 'e seemed to get better. Till we moved 'im."

Ginifur pushed herself up and striding towards the windows she threw the curtains aside and snapping open the lock she lowered the top sash window. "Don't you have any of the herbs left?"

Liam forlornly shook his head. "No."

"Do you know what they were?"

"No, I wish I did."

Ginifur took a long look at Richard who appeared for the time being to have given up fighting his inner battle. She struggled, for a few brief moments, with what her next step should be. Finally she came to a decision and turned to Liam. "I'm going to see Betsy."

Liam frowned. "D'ye think ye should, Ginny? Doctor left strict instructions, 'n ye've already broke two." He said glancing at the window with a slight smile.

"Betsy is no different to your Running Bear. You trusted him didn't you? You used the herbs he gave you, and they made him better. You said so. Betsy uses herbs too, she's no different." Ginifur stated stubbornly.

Liam looked uneasy. "T'be sure, I don't know Ginny. T'was different out there, there was no doctor. What will Doctor Thomas say if . . ?"

Ginifur watched as Richard suddenly thrashed at the sheet. "If we don't do something Liam, Captain Tremayne is going to die anyway." She finally voiced the word they had been refusing to use. "Look Liam"! If we don't break this fever he will die! Surely you can see that he is worse now than when he arrived home, and I'm not calling Dr Thomas, you heard what he said. If we cannot break the fever we can only pray. I've tried praying Liam, it's not working."

Liam knew that she was right; he had seen death staring at him before. "I'll stay with him."

Ginifur removed her apron. "I'll be as quick as I can." Liam was bathing Richard's face as she turned to leave the room.

Ginifur hurried to the stable where she told Sam that she wanted to get a breath of fresh air, and saddled Damson. Sam studied her as she yanked the girth strap tight. "Could'n find nothin' wrong with 'er." He commented.

"I'm sorry?" Ginifur looked up.

"Damson! Tom said as 'ow she threw a shoe, 'n ye took a fall. 'er shoes are all good fer she was only shod this week." He studied the bruise on her eye, now turning yellow. "Messed yer face up good'n proper too."

Ginifur looked uncomfortable. "I didn't look. I was a bit shaken, just didn't look. I just assumed she threw a shoe."

Sam didn't look convinced. "Not like Damson, t' take a wrong foot. You be a'right t'day?"

"Yes Sam. I won't be long." Ginifur put her foot in the stirrup and pulled herself into the saddle. Sam watched her ride out of the back gate and head off down the avenue towards the village.

Once through the village, Ginifur skirted the farmhouse at the bottom of the hill and took the narrow lane to the lonely cottage on the edge of the village. Betsy had been born in the cottage where her mother had died when Betsy was just twelve years old. Betsy had been an adept pupil and had learned the craft of herbal remedies from her mother. Now she cured animals and humans alike. She even mended broken limbs if you couldn't afford the services of the doctor.

Ginifur slowed Damson's pace as the cottage came into view. wondering whether she had acted too hastily. The track forked left, to Polskenna. The land to the right now narrowed to little more than a footpath. There was a time when you could drive a horse and cart over the hill to join the lane to St. Mary's. But few ventured along the narrow lane which passed within hailing distance of Betsy's cottage. Brave enough to call on her for a remedy when all else failed or they couldn't afford the doctor, but under normal circumstances folks were too superstitious, afraid to pass the time of day with a witch, even a white one.

As horse and rider entered the narrow, overgrown path Ginifur reined Damson to a halt and allowed her to drop her head to nibble at a tuft of young juicy grass. From the saddle Ginifur could see the cottage clearly over the hedge. The door was open wide, the windows too, and a spiral of smoke curled into the air from the lone chimney. The tiny garden was crammed with all manner of herbs and flowers, and in the sunlight it certainly didn't look fearsome. In fact it looked no worse that any cottage in the village, and it had been freshly lime washed too. Nevertheless, Ginifur hesitated. It really wasn't her place to doubt Doctor Thomas remedy. But even Gran was a big believer in the healing properties of herbs and often discussed their use with Betsy. She hesitated a moment longer then, picking up the reins that she had laid on Damson's neck, she was about to turn her head for home when a voice addressed her from the other side of the hedge.

"Well, Miss Ginny. Are 'e goin' t' turn that horse fer 'ome, or are 'e goin' t' come up t' the cottage fer what ye really came fer?"

Ginifur raised herself in the saddle to peer over the hedge, and realised that she wasn't surprised to find Betsy there. It seemed to be the most natural thing to happen.

Betsy lent on the hazel stick that she carried with her, to pull berries and herbs out of reach of her short arms. "I bin expectin' 'e. So, let me guess! The Cap'n i'nt no better? Be that what it is?" Ginny nodded. "I knawed it. Well if we'm not t' be too late, we'm better 'urry." She turned and waddled off across the field, leaving Ginny to make her own way up the path to the cottage door.

Tying Damson to the gate post Ginifur took a few steps towards the door. "Come in cheeld. There be nothin' t' be afeared of in 'ere. I don' bite, as ye well know, 'n I don' ride on a broomstick at the witchin' hour. But I do 'ave a cat, 'n the only bird is the one in the cage with a broke wing bein' mended."

Ginifur put a foot inside the door. Her eyes widened. The cottage consisted of one room, like Quay Cottage, and it was spotlessly clean. On the fire was a cauldron of boiling water. Dried herbs and flowers hung in bundles from the rafters in the open roof, filling the air with their sweet scent, and the long shelf at the back of the cottage housed an array of stone jars and bottles. At the table Betsy worked away selecting herbs and measuring them in her knowing way.

"Captain Tremayne was injured badly when he was away. He has come home sick with fever." Ginny informed her.

"Tell me some'at I don' know." Was Betsy's only comment.

"It was an arrow. It went straight through his chest. Doctor Thomas says that he thinks it has missed his organs, but he travelled too soon. The wound has opened up and he is running a terrible fever. I'm afraid he is going to die."

Betsy raised her eyes from the pine table. "So, why did 'e search out ol' Betsy?" She cackled.

"He was treated by a native Indian with a herbal poultice and drink. Liam said it made him better. He should never have travelled so soon."

"The wound? Tis open now?"

"It was when the doctor dressed it, and weeping."

"Mmm. Puss? Is there a discharge?" Ginifur nodded. "Any blood?"

"No, yes. It's sort of yellow, creamy."

"Do it smell?" Betsy screwed up her face until her eyes were just narrow slits.

"A bit, but I've smelt worse."

"In that case, I'll need t'see un." Betsy stated firmly.

"Can't you just give me something?" Pleaded Ginifur.

"I'll give 'e some'at fer the fever, but the wound! No, I need t'see it. Can't risk givin' 'e the wrong thing." She peered at Ginifur. "What do 'e think 'ould 'appen t' me if Cap'n died, 'n it was knawed I'd gived un some'at. No, I'll give 'e some'at fer the wound, but only if I sees 'im."

Ginifur turned to look out across the fields to Dingerien Bay. What was she to do? She was sure that Betsy could help Richard, but what would everyone say if she was to return with Betsy?

Betsy answered the unasked question herself. "Take these 'erbs. Mix a large spoonful in a bowl with boilin' water, add the juice of a lemon 'n a spoonful of 'oney. Let it simmer over a pan of boilin' water fer an hour. Then leave it t'cool, strain it 'n get the Cap'n t'sip it. Just a little at a time mind. Then do the same with the leaves, add boilin' water and simmer, but don' add no lemon or 'oney. When it's cool dip a compress in it 'n place it on 'is for'ead, 'n change it regular. Now when shall I come up t'see the Cap'n? Midnight? Will that suit 'e?"

Ginifur made a quick decision. Netty and Tom would be in bed and the house quiet. No one but she and Betsy, and Liam of course, would ever know. She held out her hand for the herbs, taking note of the size of the bowl that Betsy had showed her. "Midnight. I'll meet you outside the gate. By the hollow tree."

"Ye've got a wise 'ead on yer shoulders young Ginny. I tol' 'e ye'd be needed, didn' I? Tis all writ in the stars, cheeld. I've told 'e afore now. We can't escape what is ordered fer us. I'll see 'e at midnight." Betsy picked up the cat, who was rubbing against her skirts. "Say goodbye t' the nice lady, Blacky." But the cat just purred and looked at Ginifur from bright green eyes.

Ginifur's next problem, on returning home, was to prepare the herbs without anyone questioning her. But luck was with her. Netty decided that she wanted some apples and, totally out of character she wanted to go down to the apple store and choose them herself. "'aven't been t' the gardens all summer." She announced. "Time I saw what my Tom gets up to." And she set off with the basket. Pearl was polishing the silver in the dining room, Peggy was mending sheets in the laundry room and Ginifur had the kitchen to herself.

Carefully Ginifur followed Betsy's directions and then stood the bowls of steaming liquid into earthenware basins filled with ice cold water from the ice house. The ice was nearly all gone now, and it would be some months before it was refilled. Having stirred the liquids till they cooled, Ginifur strained them into a fresh bowl and a jug, so that she would know which was which, before carrying them up to Richard's room. "Is he any better?" Were her first words as she entered the room.

Liam shook his head. "T'be sure, tis in some state he is to ramble on as he has been."

"Could you make any sense of his words?"

"The only word I recognised was fire, s'pose it's cos e's so hot. I've been bathin' his 'ead, but it eases 'im not at all." Liam saw the jug and the bowl. "Is that the herbs?"

Ginifur nodded and held out the jug. "What do you think?"

Liam took the jug and sniffed at the liquid. "Can't say as I really remember truly, but I think it do smell a bit like Running Bear's herbs. What's the other?"

"To cool his head. It's got mint in it, I think." She sniffed the bowl and handed that to Liam.

"Mm, mint. So, are ye goin' t'use'em?"

Now that the potions were prepared Ginifur suffered pangs of uncertainty. "It seemed the right thing to do. But now, I just don't know."

Liam sniffed at the jug again, and then stared into the clear golden liquid. "I have t' admit, I was afraid when I first used Running Bear's medicine. If I was there now I'd still do it. What we're doin' now in't helpin' any Ginny. Ye said so yerself. I'll hold him steady, if ye can get him t' sip some of it."

Ginifur poured a little of the liquid into a small glass and, as Liam sat on the bed and raised Richard from the pillow, she put the glass to his mouth. As the smooth and fragrant liquid touched Richard's mouth his lips parted to allow a little to pass, and he swallowed it without a problem. "A little at a time, Betsy said. Not all at once." Ginifur repeated aloud to herself.

"Same as Running Bear." Added Liam as he lowered Richard to the pillow. "How long will it take t' lower his fever? Did she say?"

"No." Ginifur covered the jug and glass with a cloth. "I'll ask her when she comes tonight."

"Comin' here!" Liam exclaimed. "Ye can't be right in the head Ginny! What'll they say when word gets out?"

"Word won't get out unless you, or me, or Betsy lets it out. She will come at midnight, so that no one will see her come in or go out." Ginifur defended herself. "Netty, Tom, and Peggy and

Lizzie will all be in bed. Pearl will have gone home long ago. I shall meet Betsy outside and bring her through the front gate so we won't pass the stables or go near the Coach Cottage."

"Ye've been out in the sun too long. Ye'll be tellin' me next that ye've seen Kiara sunin' herself on Black Rock, and swimmin' with 'er in the sea." Liam shook his head in disbelief.

Ginifur pulled back the covers. "Smell that Liam!! Go On. Tell me the wound is healing! Tell me that's not rotting flesh I can smell. Go on. Tell me. Tell me he's getting better. Tell me I'm imagining it." She flung the angry words at him.

Liam's face was white with fear. "I can't tell ye that. Ye know I can not."

"Then help me Liam. Betsy is our only chance. I'll ride for Doctor Thomas if you say so, but I know he will only let him die. You heard him Liam. You heard him."

Liam stared at Richard. "Go and get some rest. I'll wait with him. You have to get some rest."

"I'll not go Liam, I just can't. If he's going to die then I am staying right here."

"I'll call ye when it's time to meet Betsy, I promise, or if 'e gets worse. Just get some rest. Look at 'e, ye'll fall down if 'e don't get some rest, then what good'll 'e be t' the Captain then."

"Oh, Liam, thank you. Thank you." Ginny brushed a tear aside. "You will call me, you promise?"

Liam nodded and turned away to bathe Richard's face with the herbal mixture. "I'll call ye, never fear."

Betsy Visits Tremanyon

GINIFUR PULLED THE hood of her cape up over her hair, and tugged it well down to hide her face. She let herself out of the front door and stopped to listen for a moment. It was quite light, for it was just before a full moon. But all was quiet. Somewhere in the distance an owl hooted. The breeze rustled in the few remaining leaves on the trees along the drive but, other than that, nothing. Ginifur ran lightly down the steps and at the side of the house, glanced up at the attic bedrooms. There was no sign of a candle light there, or in the bedrooms of the Coach Cottage that she could see above the Garden Cottage roof. Everyone was fast asleep; there would be no one to see her bring Betsy into Tremanyon.

Keeping to the grass along the side of the drive, avoiding the shingle, she made her way silently towards the gates. Once outside she slipped across the lane that led to the Home Farm and sheltered within the hollow of the ash tree to wait.

Ginifur had allowed plenty of time, and there were some moments to fill, so it was inevitable that she began to wonder about the wisdom of letting Betsy see Richard Tremayne. In fact, she was about to hurry back to the house when she became aware of a scratching noise on the outside of the tree.

"Are 'e in there, Miss Ginny?" Betsy's cracked voice came out of the dark. "Changed yer mind 'av 'e?"

"Oh no!" Ginifur said as she crept out of the hollow tree.

"Well, ye would'n be the first, 'n no doubt ye would'n be the last if ye did. So iffen ye've still a mind to, ye'd better lead me t' the Cap'n. Fer 'is time is runnin' short, I fear." She hitched a sack higher onto her shoulder.

"What do you mean?" Ginifur asked fearfully.

"Ye don' 'ave t'ask, ye knaws. Now come on cheeld, let's not be wastin' any more precious time."

As Ginifur led the way towards the front gates Betsy let out a low cackle. "Well, bless me boots! Never thought the day 'ould come when ol' Betsy 'ould enter Tremanyon through these gates. See this, yer Choughs!" She gave a mocking bow to the stone birds sitting atop the wall and Ginifur, glancing back, could have sworn the birds bowed their heads in obeisance. Shivering, and pulling her cloak tighter, she quickened her step, with Betsy trailing behind her trying to keep up.

Glancing anxiously at the house, before leading Betsy up the steps, Ginifur felt again the doubts nag in her head.

"Don' 'e be afeared cheeld. I'll do the Cap'n no 'arm, believe me. Iffen I don' see un, then thas a different matter. So. are 'e goin' t' take me in or no?" Betsy shifted her bag to the other shoulder and peered up at the lighted window above their heads as she waited. "'e aven't long."

Ginifur took the last three steps quickly, before she could change her mind. Taking the large iron key from her pocket she opened the door.

Betsy looked neither to left nor right, she didn't see the polished furniture, beautiful flower displays or expensive ornaments. Betsy wasn't in the least interested in any of the material objects that others set so much store by. If she was to pause and look she would only wonder why anyone would wish to clutter up their lives, and cause themselves the hassle of employing others to look after it. Betsy's cottage had a bed to sleep in, a chair to sit in, plus another should she ever have a visitor, which she never did. She had a Cornish range to cook on, a table to eat off and a cat for company. Betsy believed that she had everything that she needed to make her life comfortable.

In silence they climbed the stairs, as Ginifur led the way towards Richard Tremayne's bedroom.

Quietly opening the door, Ginifur let Betsy into the room. Richard's laboured breathing filled the room and Liam's anxious face turned towards the door. "He's much worse Ginny. The fever's risen again, and listen to him! He be strugglin' t' breath."

Betsy dropped her sack on the floor. "Go 'n fetch me a kettle of boilin' water, a bottle of spirit. Whisky, brandy or gin, please yer own mind to, but be quick about it." Ginifur signalled for Liam to do as she bid, and Liam left the room.

Betsy lifted one of Richard's eyelids with a bony finger. "Get they blankets off un, let me see the wound." Ginifur folded back the blankets and sheets, leaving Richard covered from waist down. His night shirt was soaked through. "Fergit yer modesty cheeld, get they clothes of un, 'n find un a clean night shirt." Betsy snapped as she fumbled with the buttons. "Do 'e want un t'catch a chill 'n add t' 'is problems?" Ginifur quickly undid the remainder of the buttons then, with Betsy to give a hand, lifted Richard up to pull the nightshirt from under him. As Betsy removed the dressing from the wound even she almost took a step back as the stench assaulted them. Betsy didn't flinch. "Get me some clean rags 'n hot water." She ordered as she pulled the last of the lint away from the foul discharge. "Iffen ye're a believer cheeld, ye'd best pray we'm not too late." She added. Ginifur filled a bowl with clean water from the jug and brought it to the side of the bed with the basket of clean rags put aside to bathe Richard's face and neck. Silently she prayed all the while she handed Betsy clean rags, one after the other, and took the stained ones away as she gently cleaned away all trace of the offending puss. Betsy straightened her crooked back as best she could. "Bathe 'is face 'n the rest of 'is body, 'n then get that clean night shirt."

Liam chose that moment to return with another kettle of boiling water and the spirit. He wrinkled his nose in distaste, and glanced at Richard's naked body, lying restless upon the bed. "It's the Cap'ns best brandy." He said as he put the bottle down.

"Then I'm sure the Cap'n 'll think it well used." Betsy cackled as she picked it up and considered taking a swig. "I'm gonna pour this over the wound cheeld, mop up the excess but don' 'e touch the wound mind." She proceeded to dribble the spirit in and around the wound until she was satisfied that every bit had been washed clean with the brandy. Then she opened the neck of her sack and drew out a handful of moss, a few packets, a jar and a drawstring cloth bag. "Put the moss in a bowl 'n just cover it with the boilin' water." She handed Liam the dried moss and turned back to the bed taking with her a packet and a jar of precious ointment. She sprinkled herbs into the liniment and then, all the while watching Richard's face, she carefully mixed them together. "Hold the jar cheeld." Betsy handed the jar to Ginny. Bony her fingers may have been, but they were also nimble and gentle as they quickly smothered the infected area with the sweet smelling ointment. Then she sprinkled it with a powdered substance from the other packet, reached out for the bowl and wrung out the excess water from the moss before packing it into the wound. "Make a pad o' that there linen." She ordered. "'n some fresh strips to strap un with." Ginifur quickly carried out the task and they strapped him tightly, pulled a fresh night shirt over his head, changed the sheets and lay him back on a clean pillow. "Cover un up, 'n put a hot water bottle at 'is feet. Now I've brought 'e some more 'erbs t' make more of 'is drink, 'n others t' bathe un with. Do 'e remember what t' do?"

Liam poured a little of the pre mixed solution into a glass ready to give to Richard when he next stirred, for the moment he lay a little more peacefully.

"Meet with yer approval do it?" Betsy asked him.

Liam looked her straight in the eye. "Running Bear used herbs, 'n they worked for him. Dressed the wound in much the same way too. What the doctor told us to do's not been much good."

"Try t' get un t' take a little 'n often. It'll bring the fever down." She stared long and hard at her patient. "e'll do. Reckon we caught it just in time cheeld. e'll 'ave ye t' thank fer that." Then Betsy turned and looked into Ginifur's eyes. "Ye can't run out on un now, can ye? You'm needed 'ere cheeld. Tis as I said, you'm needed 'ere, fer ye're a part of Tremanyon cheeld, 'n Tremanyon's a part of ye. Neither one can be separated from t'other." She ignored Ginifur's astonished look. "When do the good doctor intend t' return t' see t' 'is patient?"

Ginifur recovered her senses. "Monday morning. He said we were to call him if there was a change for the worse."

Betsy let out a cackle. " 'n ye did'n, did ye? Lucky fer the Cap'n ye did'n. Fer sure as the night comes afore the day, if ye'd called the doctor the Cap'n 'ould never 'ave seen another dawn. Well!" Once more she lifted an eyelid with a bony finger and peered into it as though she could see right into his mind. "Ye'll live Cap'n, I reckon. Yes, ye'll live t' see yer son, 'n that's a promise from ol' Betsy." She stood up and glanced about the room. "Keep the air movin', not too much night air when it be cold, but plenty durin' the day, 'n I'll see un again t'morrow night. Same time, same place eh Miss Ginny? Then on Sunday us'll put it all back just as the good doctor left un, 'n no one'll be any the wiser, eh?" Cackling to herself she bent down to retrieve her sack. "I'll see meself out, shall I?"

"No, I'll see you to the door." Ginifur found her voice and turned to lead the way out of the room. "Thank you for what you have done for Captain Tremayne. I don't know how I would have told the children, his daughters." Betsy smiled, her head nodding up and down as if it were attached to her body by a spring. When Ginifur opened the door for her to leave she hesitated, standing in the open doorway, her face cast in shadow. "What made you think I was leaving Tremanyon, Betsy?"

The wizened woman peered up at her through narrow eyes. "Well ye was thinkin' to, wasn't ye? But ye can't now, can 'e?

296

'Cos the Cap'n needs 'e, 'n that's a fact." And with this she tucked the now empty bag under her arm and, with her stick to steady her in the other, made to leave. "I'll see 'e t'morrow night cheeld. Same time, same place."

As Ginifur watched her make her way into the night, dark shadows reached out to envelope her as though they were ghostly capes. Slowly she made her way back to the bedroom where Liam was bathing Richard's face and hands. Her mind occupied on other things she began to tidy the room, clearing it of anything that might suggest that there had been another night time visitor. As she approached the bed Liam looked up.

"I don' know if I'm imaginin' it Ginny, but I could almost swear 'e do look more peaceful."

Ginifur glanced at Richard's face. "He is certainly not so restless." She picked up the discarded strips of linen from the tray on the side of the table, and then noticed a length of shabby ribbon. "Where on earth has this come from?" She asked as she picked it up and made to place it in the bag with the dirty linen.

"No. Don't throw that away!" Liam reached out to retrieve the frayed and dirty length of ribbon.

Ginifur glanced at the ragged strip in his hand. "What on earth could you possibly want that for?"

In his own mind, Liam was quite certain of the origin of the ribbon, even if he had no knowledge of the circumstances that led to it being found in Richard's possession. He studied the ribbon for some seconds. It was no wonder that Ginifur hadn't recognised it, for it was grubby and frayed. The once pretty length of bright emerald green ribbon was now drained of it's colour by Richard's constant handling. "Twas tied round the neck of Becky's doll. Cap'n, he thought of it is a talisman. He've been holdin' on to it as though it were the only thing that connected 'im t' life itself. He only let go of it a few minutes ago, don't 'e take it away yet, Ginny."

Ginifur stared down at the remains of the ribbon. "So that is what was clutched in his fist. But I don't remember a ribbon around the dolls neck when Becky and I packed it in his trunk." She peered more closely.

"No, it wasn't." Liam wondered how much he dared say. "He had it in his pocket. Tied it round the doll his self." Ginifur reached out for the ribbon. "Tis your ribbon, I'nt it Ginny?" When Ginifur's eyes met his they were misted with tears. "And Jamie? I know e's not Adam's child." Ginifur reached back to steady herself, and then slumped into the nearest chair. "He's Dickon's, i'nt he? He's the Cap'ns son."

"Dickon's?" Ginifur's face was filled with puzzlement and fear.

"The Cap'n insisted I called 'im by that name when we was away. But ye 'ave'nt answered me Ginny."

No quick denial sprang to her lips and, surprisingly, no fingers of fear clutched at her heart. In fact Ginifur felt a sense of relief wash over her. Relief that, finally, there was someone to share her secret. "What makes you think that?" She glanced anxiously at the sleeping form of Richard Tremayne.

Liam thought carefully about his answer. "T' be sure, Jamie is very like ye Ginny. I don' deny it. And if I 'adn't spent the last two years in 'is company, I probably wouldn't 'ave noticed the resemblance. But today, when I brought Jamie over from the cottage, the likeness was uncanny and I began t' wonder. Then, a few minutes ago when Betsy said 'Ye'll live t' see yer son.' Well, I knew that she knew too."

"Have you told Kate of your suspicions?" Ginifur wondered who else suspected that Richard was Jamie's father.

"No. Kate has no idea who Jamie's real father is. She knows that Adam is not, of course. fer ye tol' her that yerself." Liam assured her. "I won't be tellin' anyone, Ginny. Ye've nothin' ter fear from me. But what about him?" Liam nodded towards the bed. "Don' he have the right t' know?"

"No. It would only cause more heart ache. You won't tell anyone what you know, will you?" She pleaded.

"Do I take it that Adam don' not know who Jamie's real father is?" Ginifur shook her head. "Yer secret's safe with me, Ginny. Even if'n I don' believe ye should be keepin' it from him." He glanced back at Richard's sleeping form and, taking the ribbon from her fingers he placed it beside the bed.

Ginifur folded up the bag of dirty linen. "I shall dispose of these and then look in on the children, Liam. You must go back to Kate and your own children. I shall sleep in the chair here tonight."

"What about Adam? Will he mind ye stayin' here all night?"

Ginifur shrugged her shoulders. "Adam! I have no idea where Adam is, or when he will be back. He has become so secretive. He no longer helps Sam in the stables, that's why Joe is there now. Neither Sam nor his mother can get through to him. He goes off, without a word to anyone, for days, and sometimes weeks. We've been worried sick."

"Not only secretive, I hear." Liam eyed the bruises on her face, and those on her arms which were revealed when she rolled up her sleeves to attend to Captain Tremayne. "It don' sound like the Adam I knew!"

Ginifur gave a deep sigh. "It's not like the Adam I knew either. I should not have agreed to marry him. It all stems from that."

"Ye can't blame yerself, Ginny. Kate says as how he was determined t' wed thee. But if e's not working with Sam, what is 'e doin'?" Liam puzzled the question.

Ginifur shook her head. "I wish I knew. I do truly. But he has more money than can be honestly earned, I do know that."

"But ye can't be sure. Can ye?"

Ginifur shook her head. "No. I can't be sure, Liam. But I do suspect that he's involved in Free Trading. But it is only a suspicion, I have no proof." She looked up into his face. "Oh, Liam! What am I to do?"

Liam was moved by the sign of a chink in Ginifur's usual composure. She had always appeared to be so confident and assured. He knelt down and took her tiny hand in his large one. Gazing down at it, tenderly. "Tis only a suspicion, ye said it yerself. There be no proof that Adam is involved with the Free Traders." Ginifur shook her head. "Maybe, tis he wants t' surprise ye with good news."

"Oh, Liam!" Ginifur shook her head. "I've given up looking for the good reasons, there are none." She took a deep breath. "Now, go home to Kate. I'll be back here in a few moments and I shall be quite comfortable in that big chair by the window. It's bigger than some beds!" She added by way of a joke, to show Liam that she hadn't lost all her spirit.

"If'n ye're sure!" Liam rose from his knees. "I'll be back at first light." He assured her.

Ginifur pushed herself out of the chair and with a quick glance at Richard, to reassure herself that she could leave; she followed Liam from the room. She disposed of the dirty linen in the fire in the kitchen, made herself a nice cup of tea, and took it back to the bedroom.

Sitting in the deep, winged chair by the window, Ginifur stared out at the moonlit garden as she sipped the warm sweet liquid. Her mind leapt from one subject to another. Adam, and her belief that he was somehow involved in Free Trading. Jamie, her son. Richard's son. Did she have the right to hide his true beginnings?

Richard lying there in his bed, so ill that he might not recover, might never explain why he was carrying her hair ribbon so tightly in his hand. Herself, the new life that she had promised herself, now gone for she had to remain here. She couldn't leave Tremanyon now. Not now that Richard needed her to nurse him back to health, for she could never trust this task to anyone else. Slowly she turned away from the window, placed the cup and saucer on the table at her side and glanced around the room.

Ginifur entered the room frequently during the course of a week. Checking that Pearl had not missed the dust in the corners of the room, opening a window to let in fresh air or placing a posy of flowers on the dresser to dispel the feeling of emptiness. She would examine the room thoroughly, missing nothing, yet possibly seeing nothing of its contents. But now that there was nothing to attend to, there was time to gaze about her and study the carefully chosen furnishings and ornaments. Ginifur's eyes wandered across the room to the large canopied bed where her gaze lingered on its occupant. Beneath the unnaturally heightened colour of fever, his thin, pale face was now cleanly shaven, the skin transparent and tinged blue around the eyes, skin tightly stretched across high cheekbones, and his nose straight and narrow beneath hollowed eyes. In the figure lying before her she could hardly recognise the fit and handsome man who left this house just two years ago. At least no one would immediately recognise the similarities he shared with his son.

Ginifur's eyes moved towards the table beside the bed, and the crumpled, faded ribbon. Any doubts that this was her ribbon were swiftly fading, but why would he have kept it? Why should he have held on to it so tightly? What meaning there was in it, if any? Only time would tell. But there was still Adam! Adam, whom Jamie believed was his father. Adam! Who all but himself, her father and Sam, and those nearest to them, believed him to be Jamie's father. Adam! Whom she had loved as a brother, and could never love as a wife should love her husband. A tear slid slowly down her cheek. As her eyes slowly moved round the room she studied the canopy of the bed, the drapes gently moving in the light breeze from the gap at the top of the window, and she remembered the gentle rustle that they had made as she had lain there in Richard's warm embrace. Quickly she looked away. For the very first time she realised that Annabelle's dressing set had been removed from the dressing table. Only Richard's silver backed brushes and mirror lay there, with the silver tray in which he placed his watch and coins. Where were Annabelle's treasured pieces? When had they been removed? Why couldn't she remember? She had always checked things so thoroughly, so why hadn't she noticed before? For some reason she turned her head to look at the pictures on the wall. The miniatures of Richard, Annabelle, Rachel and Rebecca still hung from their ribbons beside the fireplace, but Annabelle's portrait above it had been replaced by one of Richard, resplendent in his uniform of the Cornish Regiment. When had that happened? Had they all been there that night? Had Richard removed them before his departure? She certainly hadn't, and there couldn't possibly be anyone else who would dare to do so or have any reason to. Her heart gave a leap of hope that he had tried to leave her a sign, only to be dashed by the memory of her marriage to Adam. Why hadn't she seen these things before? And what difference would it have made any way. Ginifur pushed her imaginings to one side, for imaginings they surely had to be. If Richard himself had indeed removed the pictures and Annabelle's personal items, it was only because their presence caused him too much grief. She was a naïve child to think that in her wildest dreams that it was anything remotely to do with her. The ribbon? It was no more than a piece of ribbon, attached to a favourite doll of his beloved daughter. Nothing more.

Richard stirred, and Ginifur brushed away her tears with the back of her hand. She pushed herself out of the chair and rested her hand across his forehead. His face was not so hot, his colour not so high, the perspiration appeared to be less. Could the fever be breaking? Could the worst be passed?

Ginifur gently bathed Richards face and hands, put the glass to his lips for him to take a few more sips, straightened the sheets and spent the next few minutes gazing down at his face. Then she turned away, settled herself back in the chair and it was but only a few moments before tiredness crept up on her, her eyes closed, and she fell into a dreamless sleep.

True to her promise Betsy returned on Saturday night, when she pronounced that the worst was indeed over. She redressed the wound with her prepared herbs, it looked far less angry, and Ginifur was able to tell her that Richard had managed to take the prepared drink at regular intervals.

Rachel and Rebecca were miserable. Desperately waiting to see their father. And Jamie, for the first time, was tearful due to

Ginifur's preoccupation with the invalid. Adam still hadn't returned, and Kate, Netty, Peggy and Lizzie tried their best to keep all the children occupied.

The following day, when Ginifur entered the room to relieve Liam, Richard had been washed and shaved and was wearing a clean night shirt. Liam had placed another pillow beneath his head and Richard's eyes were open. Neither of them had heard her enter the room and she paused for a moment at the door. The once bright blue eyes were pale and dimmed to a lifeless grey as Richard concentrated on Liam's moving lips. A lump rose in Ginifur's throat as the thought crossed her mind that, perhaps, the damage went far deeper than the visible wounds.

Ginifur stepped slowly into the room, her soft tread making no sound on the thick carpet, but her shadow fell across Richard's face and his eyelids fluttered. With great difficulty he turned his head towards her.

Ginifur managed a bright smile. "Good morning Captain Tremayne." She hardly recognised her own forced voice and glanced at Liam, silently pleading for help.

"Captain Tremayne 'as said that 'e would like something t' eat Ginny. I was goin' t' see if Netty could make up some broth. T'was what we gave Dickon back at Elly's cabin. Not too much, Running Bear said, just a little at first." Liam pushed his chair away from the bed and Richard's eyes returned to his face.

"I'll go." Ginny said.

"No." Liam told her firmly. "Ye must stay here and tell the Cap'n about 'is family. Maybe the girls could come and see 'im later. Just fer a moment or two." He smiled reassuringly at Richard. "I won't be long Cap'n. Tis Ginny 'erself who's been nursin' ye back t' health. Ginny 'n old Betsy, between 'em. T' be sure, I don' think ye'd 'ave made it without them." Richard attempted to raise his hand, but he was too weak. "Ye're safe now Dickon, we're both safe, and at 'ome at Tremanyon." His assurance was tinged with genuine affection and Ginifur found herself wondering about the relationship that had developed during their long absence. How would they manage to return to Master and manservant?

Painfully, Richard managed to speak the first word since his return to English soil. "Tremanyon." His voice was barely a whisper, and his eyes filled with tears so that Ginifur was forced to turn away and gather up his discarded night shirt to hide her own.

302

When she had recovered her composure Ginifur turned to find Richard's eyes upon her. The corners of his mouth moved upwards in a semblance of a smile. Even this miniscule movement was obviously a great effort for him and it tugged at Ginifur's heart strings. She settled herself in the vacated chair, where her face was almost on a level with Richard's. "You will hardly recognise Rachel, Captain Tremayne, she's grown so tall in the past two years. She's quite a young lady now, and Rebecca . . ." Ginifur chatted on in an attempt to fill him in on the happenings at Tremanyon during his absence.

That evening Betsy returned for the last time. Ginifur feared that Richard would object to her visit and treatment, and send her packing. But she needn't have worried. Richard found Betsy both interesting and amusing. When the dressings and bandages were removed she was well satisfied with the results of all their efforts. Clean dressings were applied to the wounds and they were bandaged once more in a similar fashion to those done by Dr. Thomas.

"Don' reckon as 'ow we oughta tell the good Doctor about me visits, eh Cap'n? We'll jest let un go on an' think tis 'is fancy treatment that cured 'e. T'will be our secret, the four of us." And the old crone cackled happily when Richard thanked her for saving his life and asked what payment he owed her.

"Get on with 'e." She objected. "Jest let young Ginny bring me some 'oney from they 'ives that old Tom Teague tends. Tis payment enough t' see 'e back on the road t' recovery. T'wouldn' do at all if ye wasn't t' make it, like. No, 'n that's a fact. Jest send me along some 'oney, that'll suit me fine." Betsy retrieved her black cape from the chair by the door, slung her bag over her shoulder, and waited for Ginifur to see her downstairs.

When Dr Thomas arrived the following morning he was extremely surprised to see Richard propped up against soft pillows with his daughters sitting on the bed chatting away. He accepted without question, Ginifur's explanation for the clean dressing and was quite taken aback by the clean wound with fresh skin starting to appear to the outer areas.

"To tell the truth, Richard, I doubted that you would see the following dawn." He admitted. "Your recovery is truly amazing." He missed the smile that passed between the conspirators. "I must commend your nursing skills, young Ginny. You never fail to amaze me." He began to rebind the wound, adding. "I think that your recovery has been greatly aided by Ginifur's ministrations."

303

Richard's voice was weak. "I know so." He agreed. "She, or Liam, have been by my bedside night and day, I will never be able to show them enough gratitude." A smile spread over his face as Ginifur felt the blood flush her face and neck, and hastily she looked down at the floor.

Adam arrived home that night. To Ginifur's surprise he was pleased to hear the news that Captain Tremayne had returned, and appeared genuinely sorry to hear of his wounds and subsequent illness. She was even more surprised, safe to say she was astonished, by his suggestion that Captain Tremayne would soon be better with Ginny to look after him. She waited for the expected display of anger and unreasonable jealousy. But none came.

If Adam had any memory of the incident of that awful morning, he showed no sign of it, or gave any indication of remorse. And Ginifur, who was never one to bear a grudge, was happy to put it behind them

Jamie waited to see what Adam's reaction was going to be, before taking his first step towards him. Both Mother and son were quite taken aback when Adam greeted him with apparent affection and then produced a beautiful carved rocking horse for him. "It came from France." Was his only comment, and the thought crossed Ginifur's mind that maybe she had been too hasty in her decision to leave him. Perhaps there was still a chance to salvage something from their ill-fated union. Watching Jamie's delighted face as he rocked back and forth on the wooden horse; Adam placed an arm about Ginifur's shoulders. "You get the Cap'n better, Ginny. Don' 'e go 'n worry' 'bout me. I'll be busy fer the next few days an' I'll grab a bite t' eat in the kitchen, or get Mother t' make me a pasty. But I could do with some clean clothes, if ye've got a moment or two t' spare." He indicated the bag, by the door, and for the first time Ginifur noticed that he wore new clothes. New leather boots, light brown even weave trousers, woollen jacket and a linen shirt. Adam acknowledged her surprise. "I'm comin' up in the world Ginny, an' I'm goin' ter take ye with me."

Ginifur bit back the questions that rose to her lips. "You look very handsome." She assured him, and was rewarded with one of Adam's smiles that had been lacking in recent months.

True to his word, Adam was, for most of the time, otherwise engaged, rarely at Tremanyon. And, when he was, he appeared to be a changed person. Nevertheless Ginifur always had one or more children with her in his company, believing that, if the occasion arose, he would keep his anger under control in their presence.

It was another two weeks before Ginifur was faced with the question she had feared most

For a few days Richard had been out of bed, sitting in the sunlight by the window of his room. But this was the first time he had ventured down stairs. With Liam and Simon on either side of him the three-some negotiated the stairs in high spirits. Richard's narrow brush with death had made him appreciate the little things in life once more, and found himself growing close to his loyal and devoted employees. James Thomas followed as they made slow, and for Richard, some-times painful progress to the drawing room. Awkwardly he was lowered into his favourite chair and Ginifur arranged a blanket about his knees. Dr. Thomas made a brief examination to satisfy himself that Richard had suffered no ill effects from his exhaustion, and then bade them farewell. Liam and Simon stayed for a while, answering Richard's questions about the goings on of the Estate, then they too took their leave and Richard was alone with Ginifur.

For a time they talked about the house, the Estate and the workers, and his children. But eventually, after a pause in the conversation, Richard turned a puzzled look at Ginifur and asked. "The children keep referring to a little boy named Jamie and I don't appear to have any recollection of him. Who is he Ginifur? He's not one of Kate's and Liam's is he?"

Ginifur's heart fell, and felt as if it continued to fall as she struggled to contain herself and her voice. She knew, of course, that this moment had to come, and that he would have to learn of her marriage to Adam. "He's mine, mine and Adams. We were married whilst you were away, Sir."

Richard concealed his surprise. "Of course! I did know that you were friends, but I hadn't realised that your relationship had developed so far."

Ginifur wanted to shout out. To say that it wasn't so. To tell him that she had only married Adam to give her son a name, and to save herself from revealing the true identity of his father. "Lord Falmouth insisted we made a temporary home in the Garden Cottage, but I have slept in the house with the children the whole of the time you were away, save for one or two nights when Peggy slept in the west wing. I gave you my word that I would watch over them, I knew my duty."

"I don't doubt you, Ginifur. I knew that they would be in safe hands." He was watching closely. "How old is the lad?"

Ginifur hesitated. "Nearly eighteen months, Sir." She wondered what he would make of that statement.

"Eighteen months?" He studied her face carefully, until she lowered her eyes and studied the carpet. What was the matter with her, Richard puzzled? She didn't show the signs of a young woman in love, only recently wed. "He appears to have won the hearts of my daughters." He added.

"He has, Sir." And almost added that this included everyone else but Adam.

"You must bring him to see me. Let him come with the girls, when you bring them down later."

Ginifur knew there was no point in delaying it, it would have to come sooner or later. "I will, Sir. Now, is there anything else that you need Captain Tremayne?"

"I don't think so Ginny." Richard continued to study her face.

"Then, if you will excuse me, Sir, I should return to my duties."

"Of course, of course. Don't let me detain you." Richard was puzzled at her brisk attitude. Something was worrying the girl, he was sure of it. "I shall see you later?"

Ginifur raised a smile. "I will bring the children down later, when you are rested, after your exertion." She told him and Richard nodded his head thoughtfully, his mind somewhere else. She bobbed a light curtsey and took her leave.

For a while Richard sat quietly, wondering about Ginifur's demeanour, and the child he had yet to see. He wondered if he would have Ginifur's colouring, her smile, and found that he was eager to meet her son. But tiredness soon got the better of him, his eyes closed and he fell asleep

When the time came for Rachel and Rebecca's afternoon visit to their father, Ginifur's heart was racing. Nervously she buttoned her son's little shirt and breeches, and then brushed his dark wavy hair. Jamie's blue eyes searched hers questioningly. She was not usually this nervous.

Rebecca, always the sensitive one, slipped a hand in hers. "Aren't you feeling well, Ginny?"

Ginifur put on a brave smile. "I'm just a little tired, Becky, that's all."

Rebecca's biggest fear raised its ugly head. "You're not going to be ill are you?" In Rebecca's mind, when people became ill they so often died. Mamma had died and then, so nearly, her Papa too. Rebecca couldn't imagine life without Ginifur. She was haunted by dreams that one day Ginny would die also, and leave her alone. Sometimes those dreams manifested themselves into dreadful nightmares, and she would awake to find herself sobbing, safely within Ginifur's comforting arms until sleep overtook her once more.

Ginifur re-assured her that she was not going to be taken ill and satisfied with the children's appearance, with Jamie safely in her arms, she led the way into the drawing room.

Richard looked up, a smile on his face, to greet the children. "There you are!" Rachel was the first to his side. "I still can't get over how tall you have grown." He told her. "You really are quite a young lady now. Turn around. Let me see you. Is that a new dress?" Rachel was extremely flattered, and showed of her new dress proudly. Rebecca stood quietly beside his chair until Rachel had ceased her parading. "And you!" Richard played affectionately with one of her long curls. "You are so like your mother. She will never die whilst you live." Rebecca's china blue eyes gazed back at him. Ginifur's patience had finally been rewarded, and Rebecca's hair was securely fastened behind her ears with a pale blue ribbon, allowing golden ringlets to fall down her back and over her shoulders. Rebecca's dress was the same pretty shade as her hair ribbon, with an over mantle of a deeper blue. As her mother before her she loved pretty, delicate colours where Rachel preferred more vibrant shades which suited her nature.

Jamie, when placed on the floor, for once was showing signs of shyness. Whereas normally he would go forward to great visitors with a smile upon his face, now he hung back. With one hand firmly holding on to Ginifur's he seemed to study the man sitting in the chair by the fireplace. Jamie's little face puckered thoughtfully. He was sure that he hadn't seen this man before, but there was something familiar about him. Rachel and Rebecca were happy in his presence so, he supposed, was his mother. Nevertheless, he didn't venture further into the room until the dark haired man turned his attention on him.

Faded blue eyes looked into Jamie's bright ones. Eyes that Jamie was sure that he'd seen before. "So, you must be Jamie!" Richard held out his hand. "I have heard so much about you from Rachel and Rebecca. Would you like to come here and talk to me?"

Jamie took a hesitant step forward, encouraged by the feel of his mother's hand on his shoulder, urging him on.

"Say hello, Jamie." Rebecca encouraged, and Jamie obliged her when he had reached the man's chair.

307

Richard smiled at the small boy, and briefly thought about his young son who had died at birth. He would not have been a lot older than Jamie now. "Hello Jamie, here." He patted the rug that covered his knees. "Come up here and we'll become better acquainted." Jamie did as he was bid and clambered up onto the gentleman's lap, where he found a picture book of Rebecca's. He had seen it before, but it was one that he liked to look at and he was soon pointing to pictures and saying the odd word in his delightful baby manner. "You must leave them all here for a while, Ginny, if you have something to attend to." Richard said as he settled the child more comfortably on his lap.

Ginifur hesitated. "If it pleases you, Captain Tremayne. But be sure to send one of the girls to find me if you tire of them." Richard assured her that he would, and with grave doubts and worries she conceded to his request.

* * *

Richard's health improved rapidly from that day forward. He and young Jamie became almost inseparable. Whilst the girls were at their lessons Jamie would sneak away to find Richard in his chair or later, as he grew stronger, taking a few steps around the garden.

The autumn, that had been fine and warm, grew colder as the days shortened. Ginifur and the doctor were fearful that Richard would catch a chill and bring back the fever. But no, the air appeared to be doing him good. As his strength returned, the walks grew longer, and all the while he would be accompanied by young Jamie. When Jamie's legs grew tired he would ride on Richard's shoulders for a while to rest them, but was soon eager to return to his feet and his place by this man's side.

Ginifur feared the day when someone else, besides Liam, recognised the likeness of Richard to her son and start to put two and two together. Somehow the colour and brightness took longer to return to Richard's eyes, and the other similarities were still hidden by his slowness in returning to good health, and in any case the similarities also applied to Ginifur. With the exception of those startlingly blue eyes. Thankfully the question did not appear to rise, or if anyone had there suspicions they certainly were keeping it to themselves.

After Adam's brief appearance he once more took his leave, saying that he would be away until after Christmas. He had remained cheerful throughout the last eight weeks, and been understanding of Richard's needs and Ginifur's nursing of her master. He had played with Jamie, taken him out riding with Sam, and on occasions, walked him down to Well Cottage to see Jamie's great grandparents. John and Anne were pleased to see them. They, like everyone else, adored the little lad. Adam would stay for a while encouraging John Retallick to reminisce of his youth, and John never suspected that he was actually being quizzed.

John and Anne had heard rumours that their grand daughter's marriage was not a happy one, but found themselves being convinced that this was not so. Adam seemed unchanged from the boy they once knew and, outwardly, appeared to be a devoted father to Jamie.

In all the weeks that Adam had been home, he had not once forced his attentions on Ginifur. When he bade her farewell he placed an affectionate arm about her shoulders and placed a light kiss on her cheek. He picked up Jamie, and threw him, screaming with delight, high into the air before catching him up and giving him a hug. "Look after yer Ma, boy." He said, then turning to Ginifur. "I shall have a real surprise for 'e when I return." Ginifur found herself wondering whether it was a surprise that she would like, or one she would not. With a final wave to his parents, Adam mounted the horse that he had arrived on and left.

As Christmas approached there was a flurry of activity. The house was filled with excitement and Richard surprised them all by extending an invitation to Christmas Dinner to Simon, Kate and Liam and the children and, of course, Ginny and Jamie.

The friendship that had been formed in the New World continued. Liam, after a brief spell of calling Richard 'Captain' was instructed to return to using Dickon when they were without visitors present. Liam now acted as Richard's manservant and friend and, after Adam took his leave, Richard insisted that Liam and his family move into the much better accommodation in the Garden Cottage. There were only two bedrooms but Joe, who had taken Adam's place in the stables, and had never had a room of his own, now had a room in the loft, over the stables. In the summer it was quite cool with the door left open, where they hauled up the hay, and in the winter the warmth from the stables below kept it quite snug. Joe was delighted to have his own space, he got on well with Sam, and was an able and willing worker.

Richard was almost his old self once more. He took to riding the estate, with Liam at his side, visiting the tenants and workers at Rhosinnis and Kylyn Farms and, occasionally he called at Rosvarron.

It was at Rosvarron that he heard the rumour that the Free Traders were once again using Kylyn Cove.

"It was a few nights after we had returned." Jean-Paul looked thoughtfully out of the window. "I couldn't sleep. I still felt that I was rocking about on board ship. I was looking out of the window and saw a light flash out at sea, beyond that spit of land." He hesitated. "You know the place I mean."

"The Point?" Richard suggested.

"Yes, that's it, The Point. The spit of land enclosing Kylyn Cove. The flashes were in sequence. Three long, one short and then one extra long one, repeated again after a pause. The sky was dark but, as I watched, the clouds parted just long enough for me to catch sight of a boat. Two masts, but not from these shores. Like those that they sail out of St Malo, most certainly French. I thought for a moment that she was in trouble, then realised that she was hove to, drifting slightly. Then I remembered the rumours that the Free Traders that were caught off Pentire had been replaced by another group. But surely there are none left living of those who plied their trade out of Kylyn all those years ago?"

"Only one." Richard laughed. "John Retallick, and it has been many a year since he sailed out of Kylyn Cove, I would think." This information had come to him from Edward Franks, spoken in the greatest confidence, and he had been told by the previous owner of Tremanyon, Squire Durance. Jean-Paul bit his lower lip thoughtfully. "What about that son of his? He can sail a boat."

Richard pulled a face and shook his head vehemently. "No. Not Simon. I'm quite sure of it. No, not Simon."

"Well, no doubt about it, the Free Traders are about." Richard didn't doubt him. "Have you heard anything? Or been offered any cheap Brandy?"

Richard shook his head. "No, Jean-Paul. None, not even from you." They shared a conspiratorial grin

"Never fear, I shall deliver a supply to you before Christmas, mon ami." Jean Paul told him. "Brandy, coffee, and tea for yourself, and fine silk and lace for your daughters." He laughed as Richard smiled. Have you had those furs made up yet?"

"They will be ready for Christmas." Richard informed him with another smile.

Jean-Paul's wife, Catherine, entered the room with her young son Jean-Louis by her side, and the maid with refreshments. Conversation did not return to the Free Traders, but it remained in the back of Richard's mind.

Chapter Eight
1756 – Recriminations

ADAM RETURNED, AS promised, after Christmas. It was, in fact, the second week of January that he arrived on a blustery evening, to find that he and Ginny had new quarters within the Big House.

The two rooms, that had previously been Ginifur's and the girls, had been turned into a bedroom and small sitting room. They could be entered from either the staff staircase to the attic rooms or from the main landing, which made it easy for Ginifur to get to and from the new nursery wing.

There was now no excuse for Ginifur not sharing Adam's bed. Richard said that until alternative arrangements could be made Jamie could continue to sleep in the nursery. After all there were four bedrooms and Peggy would sleep in Ginifur's room, calling for Ginifur if needed.

That night Ginifur was more nervous than a virgin bride on her first night of marriage. But she assured herself that if Adam was to hit her, or knock her about as he had done the last time, someone was sure to hear and come to her assistance.

Whether or not it was the latter fact or not, she had no need to fear. Adam was as thoughtful as he had been when they were first married. "Ye poor maid." He said, when she finally came to bed. "Ye're all tuckered out aren't 'e? Well, come 'ere 'n rest yerself." He pulled back the covers to let her in, then placed an arm around her waist. "Ye're cold 'n all. Look at the way ye're shiverin'!" She was shivering, it was true, but it wasn't from cold. "I'll rub yer arms 'n legs. That'll soon warm 'e up."

Ginifur tried hard not to recoil, for she was sure of what would follow and she had none of Old Betsy's herbs or ointment. She made a mental note to pay her a visit on the morrow. Adam rubbed her arms, and then her legs, and then to her utter amazement, placed his arm once more around her waist and wished her a good night. Having acknowledged him, and wished him the same, she then lay motionless, not daring to move a limb. But after only a few short moments Adam's breathing became deeper and regular. Her fears had been for nought. Neither did he attempt to do more

311

than to cuddle up to her on subsequent nights, and Ginifur's fears began to fade. She was in grave danger of letting her guard down.

No mention was made of Adam's promised surprise. He had brought her a gold chain and locket, set with an amethyst type stone, which he said was Sark Stone from the Island of Guernsey, and for Jamie he had a model boat. Although he spent most nights at Tremanyon he was away for the best part of the day, about his business he told her when she asked. Ginifur didn't question him too closely as to the nature of his business, and he didn't tell her.

Adam had been home for six weeks before there was any sign of his previous behaviour. He had returned from Tregony earlier than expected, agitatedly tapping his riding boots with his short whip. His wardrobe of clothes was quite large now, and far exceeded Ginifur's few dresses.

"Where's the boy?" He snapped, and Ginifur's smile of welcome faded.

"He's gone to Rhosinnis with Captain Tremayne and Liam." Ginifur informed him, puzzled at what had happened to bring about his change in temper, for he had left Tremanyon earlier in the day in good spirits.

"'e spends too much time with the Cap'n, and 'is daughters, soon e'll be gettin' ideas above 'isself. Think e's some'at special, speakin' just like ye 'n them. That's what ye want I s'pose, t' make a gent of un. Better ye left un with me; I'd make a man of un. Well if e's not 'ere I'll take the 'orse 'n go on down to Kylyn Cove. See if Will is about, maybe we could go fishin'." He laughed as though he had made a joke, and then spun on his heals and left the house. He had just arrived at the step beside the private little chapel when he remembered something and turned to catch her watching him from the back steps. "Oh! I fergot to tell 'e. Better make the most o' the next few weeks, fer they'll be the last ye'll spend 'ere on Tremanyon." He grinned in pleasure at the shock on her face. "I've bought a cottage on the cliffs, over Treloe way. We'll move in as soon as I've finished another little job I've lined up." He didn't wait for her reaction to this news, leaving Ginifur shaking in her shoes.

In a state of shock Ginifur somehow found her way to the kitchen where she slumped down into the chair normally reserved for Tom when he came in from the garden.

Netty was busy making bread and only glanced up, briefly, thinking that Ginifur was just taking a short rest. It was a few minutes more before she realised that Ginifur hadn't spoken, that her face was as white as a sheet, and that she was shaking from head to foot. She dropped the dough with a heavy thud, and hurried round the table. "Ginifur! Cheeld!! Whatever be the matter? Ye look as though ye've had the fright of yer life." A sudden thought crossed her mind. "My life! It's not the boy? It's not Jamie, is it?" Ginifur shook her head. "The Cap'n then! Have 'e taken a fall off that flighty 'orse of 'is?" Ginifur shook her head again, and Netty's fears abated. "Well then! What on earth is worryin' 'e cheeld?" Then she huffed dismissively. "It's that no good 'usband of your'n, i'nt it?" She glanced at Ginifur's bowed head, face in her hands. "Yes, it 'as t' be young Adam. Smarmy Jackanapes. 'e 'ave been up t' some'at I know. I tol' my Tom 'Wait 'n see' I said, I think e's up t' some'at, ye just wait 'n see." She dusted the flour off her plump hands, and then lifted Ginifur's young slender ones comfortingly in hers. "Are 'e goin' t' tell me about it then?" Ginifur nodded. "Then I'll mash a pot o' tea, then us'll make ourselves comfy like, 'n ye c'n tell me all about it."

By the time Richard arrived home with Liam and Jamie, Ginifur had related her story to Netty and was feeling a little calmer.

"Maybe tid'n true." Said Netty. "Maybe e's tryin' t' frighten 'e."

"I had thought of that." Ginifur admitted. "But I don't think so. He's always threatened to take me away from here. I don't know how, but I think that somehow he has finally found a way. I dread to think of how he came about the money."

Netty shook her head knowingly. "No good'll come of it, that's fer certin. No good, at all. Are 'e goin' t' tell the Cap'n?"

Ginifur thought hard before answering. It had crossed her mind to ask for his help, but she quickly dismissed it. "No, not yet anyway. Not until I really know what Adam is up to."

She glanced at the window as she heard a horse approach around the side of the house, and was just in time to catch a glimpse of Jamie perched in front of Richard on his favourite horse. The sight of them together brought on a pain as if a knife had been twisted in her heart. Maybe it would be for the best, she thought. To start a new life, away from Tremanyon, away from Richard and all she loved.

Adam didn't return that night, or the next. Ginifur lay awake until the small hours, expecting to hear his feet on the stairs, and finally she fell asleep just before the dawn.

It was on the third day, when Ginifur and Jamie were returning from Well Cottage, that her suspicions about Adam and the Free

Traders were aroused once more. She had just shut the gate when she saw Will Davies making his way towards Kylyn Cove with another fisherman from Porthcarrow.

"'ave 'e seen Adam, Ginny?" Will asked as they came abreast of her.

"Not since Tuesday." She admitted. "When he said he was going to find you and go fishing."

Will looked askance at Fred Wilmot. "We'm not goin' fishin' till Friday. 'e was s'posed to 'ave met a man in Treg'ny, then come back to meet us in the Inn. 'e never turned up."

"I'm sorry. I don't know where he is." Ginifur apologised.

"Well I 'ope e's back by t'morrow. When ye see un tell un t'get 'n see me dreckly. e'll know what tis all about, jest remind 'im that we'm goin' fishin'." Will and Fred burst out laughing and continued their way down the lane.

Ginifur promised that she would, then taking Jamie by the hand she led him home.

Adam arrived home that evening. This time was like the other times. All signs of the amiable Adam had vanished, and in his place an angry, unreasonable and belligerent young man stood his ground.

The children were all asleep in the nursery, and Richard had gone to the stables where Star was having a difficult time foaling. Netty and Tom were at the far end of the house, in the kitchen. There was no one to come to Ginifur's aid.

Bravely she asked him what he had meant by his parting remark to her, a few days ago..

Adam pushed her roughly to one side and taking a jar of cider he had brought with him into their sitting room, he sat down heavily almost knocking over the chair and table.

"Adam! Don't have another drink, please. You've had too much already." She pleaded.

"Quit nagging, woman. When I've had enough it'll be me what says so, not thee. I'll 'ave no woman tellin' me what I can or can't do." He tipped the jar up onto his shoulder, sending a shower of golden liquid down his throat and over the floor halting Ginifur's attempts to mop it up with a jeer, and pushing her so hard against the door that she hurt her back on its sharp edge. Ignoring the look of pain that flashed into her eyes he answered her initial question. "I meant 'zactly what I said. I've bought a cottage over Treloe way, 'n ye, me 'n the brat are goin' t' live there. We'm leavin'

314

this place 'n never comin' back. I mean it Ginny, never comin' back. D'ye 'ear me." He goaded her.

"No! This is my home." Ginifur couldn't believe that he meant what he said. "It's yours too. We were born on Tremanyon."

"Your 'ome is with me Ginny. Where I go, ye go. That's the law."

Ginifur protested. "I won't go. I won't leave my family."

"I'm yer family now, remember? Me, 'n the bastard. But we'm goin' t' put that right, aren't we? Ye'll 'ave my cheeld or I'll be knowin' why."

"I won't have any more children." She blurted out, in response.

"Who said so? I don' believe 'e." For a moment Adam seemed uncertain.

"Well, I haven't had another since Jamie, have I? That's not normal is it?" She suggested. "Maybe I can't have any more, or perhaps . . ." She left the question hanging in the air

"Well it i'nt me, if that's what ye're thinkin'. Ye're bewitched. Been usin' Black Magic, 'ave 'e? Would'n mind betting ye've been seein' ol' Betsy." Adam accused her.

"I'll not leave Tremanyon, Adam. Rachel and Rebecca need me. And how am I to see Da, or help Gran and Gramps as they get older?" She reasoned.

"I need ye. Ye've put your'n and the Tremayne family afore me fer too long."

"I won't go."

Adam lifted his hand and, with a violent backward swipe, sent Ginifur flying across the room catching her head on the table as she fell and leaving her stunned.

"No!" A little voice shouted from the doorway, and Jamie flew across the room to his mother's side. Neither Ginifur nor Adam had realised that the door to the landing was ajar, and their voices had carried to the nursery wing. Adam had barely reached the child's side, his darkened eyes focused angrily on the frightened figure clinging to his dazed mother. He was about to reach out to grab him when Jamie was whisked into the air and over his shoulder.

Adam lifted his eyes to where Jamie was held safely in Richard's arms. Richard glanced at the stunned Ginifur who, apart from a bump to her head and the already signs of bruising, appeared to be unhurt, and then turned his cold fury onto Adam. "What on earth do you think you are doing, man?"

Adam raised himself to his full height. "Tis between me 'n me wife. Tis nought to do with ye."

Richard realised that Adam was now indeed a man, and as tall as him. The two angry men faced each other eye to eye. Adam's deep brown eyes stared into Richards's bright blue ones. For the colour was now returning to Richard's eyes.

"What happens in my house is very much to do with me." Richard informed him as he glanced from one to the other. "How long has this been going on? Has he treated you like this before?" Ginifur didn't answer, she looked at the floor. "I see. Well, get out Adam. I'll not see Ginifur, or any woman treated like this."

"She's comin' with me I tell 'e, I'm takin' 'er away from 'ere. Away from Tremanyon and the likes of ye. I've bought a cottage. Ginny and the boy are comin' with me. She don' need your job no more, I've enough money t' look after 'er, 'n the b . . . boy."

"The boy!!" Richard exclaimed. "The boy! Doesn't your son have a name?"

Adam laughed. A hysterical, deranged laugh that curdled Ginifur's blood in her veins. "Oh yes, the Boy 'as a name alright. But my son? My son I'nt born yet."

Ginifur caught her breath as Adam halted in his tirade, catching sight of Jamie clinging to Richard's shoulder. However frightened the lad was he hadn't cried, but his bright blue eyes had darkened with anger and his face was set in a steely expression. That very same look was on Richard's face. The same deep blue eyes, bearing the very same expression. Suddenly the answer was there, staring him in the face, and Adam went cold. Ginifur, watching the expressions on his face change from anger to puzzlement and then understanding, knew that her secret was discovered. She very nearly called out to him to stop. But Adam turned to look at her, halting her words even as they formed in her throat.

"Now I knows. Ye're nought but a whore, Ginifur Retallick. Nought but a bloody whore, 'n a kept one at that. But ye're my wife, fer good or bad. Get up. We'm leavin', bring that bastard ye call yer son, we'm leavin', now."

Richard held back. It wasn't his place to come between a man and his wife, but he looked down at Ginifur, still dazed and leaning against the wall. "Is that what you want to do Ginifur? Do you wish to go with your husband and son?"

Ginifur was silently crying, her head buried in her hands.

"Is that your wish, Ginifur?" Richard pressed her. "You must answer me"

"Get up Ginny." Adam ordered as he reached to pull on her arm

Richard rounded on him. "Get back, man. She will make up her own mind, and in her own good time. Neither you nor any one is ordering her out of this house after all she has done for me and my family."

A sneer rose on Adam's face. "'n only ye would know just 'ow much, Ye 'n Ginny both."

Richard appeared to not hear this remark and continued to Address Ginifur. "Ginny! You must answer me. If it is your wish to leave this house tonight, then so be it, but if it is not your wish, then I'll not force you. No woman should have to endure a beating." He turned his eyes on Adam, who flinched as if he had been physically hit. "If I ever find you are raising a hand to her or Jamie again, I'll not be responsible for the consequences."

"Get up, Ginny. We'm goin'." Adam shouted at the huddled figure on the floor.

Ginifur made no sign of moving. "I think you have your answer, Adam." Richard scowled. "When Ginifur has recovered from this assault, she can take the time to make up her own mind. If she wants to, then she can follow you when she is in a fit state to do so. At the moment she can't stand unaided, let alone follow you. Now, get out of my house, and don't you ever step through the door again."

Adam's face was white with fury, and he was almost speechless with anger. With one final glance at Ginifur's bowed head he pushed past Richard and Jamie to find Netty with the girls on the landing. "Ye're all in this t'gether. But ye jest wait. I'll get me own back. Jest ye wait 'n see." He shouted over his shoulder as he ran down the main staircase in a final act of defiance, and out of the front door.

Miserably Ginifur waited, not knowing what would happen next as Richard handed Jamie over to Netty. Then bending down he pulled her hands away from her face, and gently brushed a strand of hair back from her eyes. "I won't pretend to understand what all this was about Ginifur, but I do know that I will not stand by and see you either beaten or unhappy." Placing a hand beneath her arm he carefully eased her up from the floor, supporting her while she regained her balance. "Now, you must get some sleep. You have had a nasty shock." He noticed her glance uncomfortably at her bedroom door. The one that she had shared with Adam. "The guest room is made ready. Why not sleep there." He suggested.

"Oh no!"

"But I insist. Then tomorrow, or when you are ready, we will discuss this problem, if you wish, and try to resolve the situation." Richard led her across the landing, opening the door to the guest room. "I don't need to tell you where the lamp is." He joked. "Try to sleep, you'll feel better for it. Nothing more can be done tonight." He brushed her hair with his hand, wishing he could take her in his arms and comfort her. But she was another man's wife. And Jamie? If Adam wasn't his father, then who was? Goodnight Ginifur." He said as he turned to leave the room.

"Goodnight, Sir, and thank you."

"Think nothing of it." He said, pulling the door closed behind him.

Richard turned to find Netty still on the landing with Jamie in her arms and Rachel and Rebecca at her side. Taking Jamie from her Richard led the children back to their bedrooms, where he settled them down and then sat in Ginifur's nursing chair in Jamie's room till long after the child had fallen back to sleep pondering on Adams angry words.

* * *

Adam slammed the door behind him with an almighty crash, leaped down the granite steps and landed uncomfortably on the pebble drive, where he spun round to kick the carved base that held aloft one of the pair of Choughs on guard at the bottom. He stared up at the closed door, resisting the urge to run back and apologise for what he had said and done. Why should he? He wasn't to blame. He had married Ginny, given her bastard son his name, and now he had bought a cottage, away from Tremanyon. Away from Tremanyon! He gave a mirthless laugh. Even if he did succeed in getting Ginny and her son away from Tremanyon, he would never be away from the Tremayne family. For Adam had seen Jamie in Richard's arms. He had seen the resemblance for the first time, he knew that Jamie was Richard Tremayne's son, and he thought that Richard knew this too. Angrily he spun on his heals and strode towards the front gate and the Inn at the top of Porthcarrow Hill, where he would meet up with Will Davies and Fred.

On Friday night, Jean-Paul once again saw lights flashing off Kylyn Cove, and heard muffled hoofs along the lane behind the house. When the boat sailed, Adam sailed with it, as he had many times before, and leaving no word of his whereabouts.

* * *

If Richard harboured any suspicions that he was Jamie's rightful father, he gave no sign of it. If he thought over the events of the night before Adam's departure, he kept it to himself, and Ginifur never noticed the times that he watched her when she wasn't looking. He was kind and considerate and, now that his health had returned, made no extra demands on her time.

Jamie had grown used to Adam's long absences, and his bouts of bad temper were not unknown to him. It had upset him to see his mother lying on the floor, but the Captain had been there, and he had soon forgotten the incident. Life, as Jamie knew it, soon returned to normal.

Ginifur's days were fully occupied. She had no time to dwell on Adam or what would happen when he returned. But at night, before sleep brought her much needed rest, there were doubts and self recrimination. Adam had gone away before, but this time it was different. This time Ginifur blamed herself, and each day she would wake, wondering where he had gone, when he would return.

So it was with a certain amount of relief that, at the end of March, they received a hand written note, delivered by Will Davies. Ginifur had taught Adam to read and write when they were children. The spelling was poor, but the writing was legible. Richard handed her the note in the Library. It was sealed. "I hope it is not bad news." He offered as she slit the seal and unfolded the single sheet of paper.

Relief was quite evident on her face, tinged with surprise, as she nodded. "He's in France!" She informed Richard. "Apparently that's where he has been when he's been away all the other times." Richard nodded as she read on. "Of course, he's Free Trading."

"You think so?" Was his only answer.

"I know so." She held out the letter. "If I had any doubts, this has dispelled them. He will return with the next consignment, and expects me to be ready to leave Tremanyon with him when he arrives."

Richard scanned the laboured writing. Adam gave no date for his impending return, but informed Ginifur that he expected her to be ready to leave immediately he arrived. "At least you know where he is. Will you tell Sam?"

"Yes. They have a right to know. If you will excuse me, I will go and tell Sam now. Adam's mother is worried sick."

Richard nodded his agreement. "Tell Sam to take the news to his wife right away." He watched Ginifur's retreating back, and was left wondering about her innermost feelings.

The Free Traders

THE WARM SPRING day brought a brief respite from the cold wet days that they had recently been forced to endure. The dark clouds rolled away, leaving a clear blue sky, washed clean by the prolonged rain, dotted with a few white fluffy clouds like freshly laundered pocket handkerchiefs hanging on the light southerly breeze to dry. Richard suggested that he and Ginifur took the children for a walk. They had been cooped up inside for days on end and were getting irritable with their enforced confinement. Even Rebecca, who was usually quite content to paint or draw, and was not a child with boundless energy, was fidgety and morose.

Ginifur suggested that they took the children to the beach to watch the seaweed gathering, and this they did, taking the narrow lane to the beach where the shipwreck had occurred. At the bottom of the avenue they took the sanding lane to the beach. The sanding lanes were the ones that the carts took when they went to the beach to collect shingle for the drives of the larger houses, or seaweed such as today.

When they reached the beach they joined the throng of cheerful villagers, all collecting the dark brown, shiny, slippery seaweed. Sam and Tom had already arrived at the beach and they were handing out the baskets. Ginifur had brought the children's over-alls, the ones that they used for painting or when they were out collecting nature samples. She slipped these over their dresses and, pulling on one herself, they eagerly joined the villagers filling the baskets whilst Richard looked on. When the baskets were full they were heavy. Men and women alike carried the baskets. When they were ready to be carried back to the wagons they bent down, pulled a leather strap over their forehead and pushed their arms through the shoulder straps, like bal maidens. Basket after basket was filled and carried this way, until the beach was almost completely clean. If the sand was firm enough the carts could be drawn further down the beach and the weed pitched up with forks. But more often it was too soft. Besides the wagon and cart from Tremanyon, there was a wagon from the home farm, a wagon from Rosvarron, another from Trelander House, one from Kylyn Farm and two from Pentonvrane, which was miles away and meant that the east winds had kept the nearest beaches to them clear of seaweed. In addition to these wagons, the villagers had brought buckets and baskets, hand carts and dillies. They too would make the fertiliser for their own vegetable plots, so essential for their families. When they had finished, Ginifur removed the overalls and placed them in the basket she carried, and wiped their hands with a damp cloth she had brought for that purpose then, reluctantly, she followed Rachel and Rebecca to the spot where the shipwreck had occurred.

It was the first time that Richard had seen the place where the events of that fateful night, when the ship was washed onto the rocks. He too was amazed at Ginifur's heroism, and Ginifur began to wish that she had suggested somewhere else for their walk. On their way home they took a detour through Lerryn Wood, to pick the last remaining daffodils, some primroses and the first of the bright bluebells. On her return Ginifur placed a large handful in a vase in her room.

The sweet perfume wafted on the breeze from her window as Ginifur picked up the lamp to take to her bedroom. As she placed her hand upon the door knob to close her door, she froze. She thought that she had heard the side door creak on its hinges as someone opened it. Ginifur thought that she had locked the door after Liam went home, hanging the key on the hook by the cloaks.

She cocked her head to one side as she listened for further movement. The door to the lower staff staircase had been secured with a bar and a bolt on Richard's instructions. Only the door to the landing was open. It wasn't locked. There was no key. There was someone coming up the stairs. Ginifur could hear the stealthy tread, and the blood ran from her face. Surely Adam wouldn't dare to set foot in the Big House again! Ginifur shrank back against the wall. The footsteps had stopped right outside her door. She wanted to call out, but no words came from her lips. Then there was a light tap on the door.

"Wh . . . who is it?" She managed to whisper.

"It's Liam, Ginny." Liam's voice was hushed, and she breathed a sigh of relief. "Can you open the door? I need to speak to you."

Ginifur's hand was shaking as she turned the handle and peeped on to the landing. "What on earth is the matter, Liam? Is it Kate? Or one of the children?" Was her immediate response.

"No." Liam assured her.

"Then what can bring you here at this time of night?" She opened the door further and let him into the tiny sitting room, replacing the lamp on the table. She glanced at her watch. "It's gone midnight, Liam!"

"I know, I know. But something's come up." He glanced around the room, uneasily.

"Liam!" Ginifur frowned as she watched Liam fidgeting uneasily.

"Would ye be knowin' where Adam is?" He finally asked.

Ginifur looked down at the table. "Why do you ask?"

"Would ye be knowin' where Adam is?" He repeated urgently.

Ginifur looked into his face. "I do. But why are you asking?"

"And are ye really believin' Adam is truly involved in Free Tradin'. Do ye, believe that, Ginifur?"

Ginifur's brows drew closer together. "You know I do. But why are you asking me now. At this time of night."

"Be Jesus, I wish I wasn't that I do. But if ye are right, 'n e's comin' back into Kylyn tonight, e'll be in fer a fright. That 'e will."

Ginifur stared at him. What could Liam know about Kylyn Cove? "Why?"

"Tis the Militia, Ginny. They've been tipped off, and are lyin' in ambush, along the lane to Rosvarron and on the cliffs.

It took some while for Ginifur to answer, her mind in upheaval. "How do you know?"

"Tiny Tindle was hidin' with the ponies in the moor, when 'e saw 'em comin' up the lane 'n e's got eyes like a cat, that one, sees better at night than in day. I found 'im cowerin' inside the gate, afraid t' go 'ome 'cos there're guards on the road by the blacksmith. Say's there's no way to warn 'em, and 'e thinks everyone will point the finger at 'im."

"Oh no!" Aghast, Ginifur turned towards the window and both their backs were to the door. Neither of them had heard further footsteps on the landing.

"What's going on?" Richard stood in the doorway, his white linen shirt unbuttoned, stuffed hastily into his breeches. He looked from Ginifur's frightened face to Liam's. "Well!" He addressed Liam in an unusually gruff manner. "Is this a social call Liam, or do you have a better reason for being in my house at this time of night?"

The blood that had previously drained from Ginifur's face immediately flooded back as she reeled around. "Of course it isn't a social call. How could you think such a thing?"

323

"Well?" Richard repeated, not taking his eyes from Liam's blank expression.

"It's the Militia." Ginifur blurted out. "The Free Traders are going to fall into a trap, and probably Adam with them." She grabbed her cloak, hanging beside the door, she had forgotten to take it off downstairs when she came home.

"And where do you think you are going?" Richard raised his eyebrows in surprise.

"I'm going to the cove, of course. What else do you think I'm going to do? Wait here until they are all captured!" She retorted.

"Ye can't do that, Ginny." Liam objected. "Ye'll be caught too. Sweet Mary, think of Jamie! Think of your son."

Ginifur had fastened the cape and was lifting the hood over her hair. "I won't be caught. I know how to get to the cove without being seen." She glanced at Liam's worried face. "Thank you for telling me Liam. Don't worry. I promise I will be all right." She looked briefly up at Richard. "But if not, look after Jamie for me." She attempted to step passed Richard.

"If ye insist on this madcap escapade, then I'm coming too." Liam responded, glancing angrily at Richard.

Richard's apology was evident by the expression on his face. How on earth could he possibly have thought that the two people who he respected, even loved more than any but his daughters, would even consider the immoral deed that had sprung to his mind? He cursed himself angrily and turned on his heals, his voice coming back to them loud and clear. "If you think you can both go gadding about the countryside at this time of the night, and leave me here worrying, you can think again. Short of locking you both up, and knowing your resourcefulness Ginifur Retallick, that wouldn't last long . . ." He grunted in exasperation. "And you had better get into something less cumbersome than that dress of yours Ginifur. We might have to move fast!"

Ginifur glanced down at the full skirt of her dress. He was quite right, of course, it would hinder her if she needed to run or climb. "What about Kate, and the children?" She asked.

"Is Peggy still sleepin' in the nursery?" Ginny nodded. "Then I'll go 'n tell Kate that I'm comin' with 'e. She'll want me t' go, Ginny." Liam turned to retrace his steps. "I'll se ye both down stairs. " He called back to her.

Ginifur opened a drawer in the chest and pulled out a pair of Adam's trousers. They were new, and Adam had left in such a hurry they had been forgotten. She wrinkled up her nose in amusement. Oh well! She was going to try to warn him, wasn't she? Hastily she pulled her dress over her head and thrust her slim legs, clad in flimsy pantaloons, into the trousers. When she pulled them up, they came almost up to her armpits. Rummaging in the draw she found a leather belt and a woollen shirt. Shrugging herself into the oversized shirt, she buckled the belt securing the trousers about her narrow waist.

"That's better. Here." Richard held out her cloak.

How long had he been there waiting for her? Ginifur searched his face for a clue. But there was none, and she let him slip the cloak over her shoulders. "You don't have to come." She protested.

With his hands still firmly on her shoulders Richard studied her from head to toe. She looked even more fragile in the set of oversized clothes, and his heart filled with wonder at the strength in her. All he wanted to do was to take her in his arms and hold her tight, to protect her. He pushed all these thoughts angrily to one side. "No, I don't. Do I?" She glanced up into his eyes, trying to gauge his thoughts. "What sort of man do you think I am, Ginifur? If you think I could watch you go out there on your own, you can't think much of me as a man. My instinct is to try to stop you. But I know that is impossible. You would probably try to climb out of the window if you had to." Ginifur picked up the lantern, and pulled the storm cover down. "So . . ." He shrugged his shoulders and indicated the door. Richard had chosen dark breeches and a long dark coat. He wore no hat.

Liam was at the bottom of the stairs, similarly dressed and carrying another lantern. "I don't s'pose we'll be needin' these." He said. "They'll only let everyone know we'm comin."

"Yes we will." Ginifur lifted the bar securing the door to the basement. Richard and Liam bit back the questions rising in their minds following her down the stairs and out of the basement and into the small courtyard where they turned to the left and not up the steps.

"Ginny?" Liam ventured.

She turned to face them both. "I know that it must sound rather far fetched, but there is a tunnel leading from the house down to the river." In the light of the lanterns she saw the surprise on their faces.

"I'm not saying I doubt you Ginifur, but . . ." Richard was cut off mid sentence.

"That's good. I wouldn't want you to doubt me." Whether she was aware of it or not, her statement had a double edge and Richard didn't further the subject as she opened the door to the cold room. "And whilst I think of it, nobody else knows about the tunnel except me and Gramps. The Free Traders have not been using it, Captain Tremayne." Richard winced. How he longed to hear her use his given name. He wanted her to drop all the formality, but she was married. For better or worse, Ginifur was married to Adam. Oh yes, indeed, he did remember the night before his departure. He remembered every single moment. He could smell the sweetness of her skin, feel its silken smoothness. He could feel his fingers as they ran through her hair, and the softness of her lips beneath his own. Richard knew that it wasn't lust that made him feel this way; he had loved her then as he loved her even now.

The lantern lit up the small room where cured meat hung, and butter was kept cold on the marble slabs. Without hesitating Ginifur had made for the far wall. Liam stared at her in disbelief. The wall abutted solid earth. They were below ground level. Against the wall there was a frame on which hung pots and pans, hooks and butter pats, cheese rings and muslin.

Ginifur gripped a ring embedded in the wall with both hands. With great difficulty she twisted the ring anti clockwise. There was a grating noise from behind the wall and, slowly, very slowly, a whole section of the wall behind the frame moved inwards until there was a space large enough for a man to step through. Without a word to either Richard or Liam, Ginifur picked up her lamp and stepped through the space. Liam was the first to recover, and was the next into the tunnel beyond, followed by a speechless Richard.

The air on the other side of the wall was stale and musty. The passage was dark, narrow, low and damp under foot. The last time that Ginifur had entered the tunnel it had been in the summer time, now water trickled down the uneven walls and the scurrying of rats could be heard, quite clearly, hurrying along the uneven floor.

"Have 'e been down 'ere afore?" Liam ventured.

"Yes, once." Her voice came back to them as she stepped towards the black hole to lead the way.

"How long have you known about it?" Richard wanted to know.

"Not long." Was her short reply.

"Who told you that it existed?" Richard pressed her further! "Your grandfather?"

Ginifur sighed. "Yes."

"Does Adam know of it?"

"I can't be sure, but I don't think so. I am fairly sure that Grandfather would not let the secret out to anyone but family. It was always the way with the channel, I am sure it would apply to the tunnels too, but I'm quite positive that it hasn't been used for a long time. Sh . . . We must be quiet now, and be careful, the passage slopes downwards from this point."

Obediently they did as she bid. The passage did indeed become quite steep. The floor beneath their feet was slippery with green algae which they could glimpse in the weak light of the lanterns, and the rope that had once been secured to the walls in iron rings to serve as a hand hold had long ago rotted completely away. It took all their concentration to keep on their feet until the ground levelled out and Ginifur drew to a halt.

"We must put the lamps out now." A thought struck her. "Did you bring a tinder box, Liam?" She whispered. He nodded, showing her the tinder box before he doused the lantern.

Suddenly, with both lamps extinguished, they were plunged into darkness. In the silence they could now hear running water, bubbling over the stones on the creek bed. Inch by inch they pressed forwards until a glimmer of light appeared behind a dark curtain. Ginifur pushed aside the long strands of ivy which disguised the entrance from the outside, and stepped out onto the wet and slippery stones beneath the low bridge just before the entrance to Well Lane. Richard and Liam could just see her face, and needed no instruction to keep silent. All three listened for any noise above the babbling water. Then, keeping to the dryer shale, they made their way up stream.

At the other side of the bridge, they came out to where the undergrowth tumbled down to the river bed, completely obscuring them from above. Their eyes had become accustomed to the dim light and they could see each other quite well. Ginifur indicated that they were going up, into the undergrowth, but it looked pretty impenetrable.

A few feet to the side, Ginifur bent under a low tree trunk that had fallen across the narrow stream. Within seconds her upper body had disappeared and only her legs and feet were visible as she scrambled up the incline. Once Ginifur's feet had vanished Liam followed, Richard once again brought up the rear.

They found themselves in a thicket, upon a narrow winding fox or badger run and in a few moments they were at the back door of Well Cottage.

The door was never locked, and Ginifur slipped inside. At her grandparents bedroom door she paused to listen to their steady breathing before creeping across the floor to the side of the bed where her grandfather slept. Putting her lips to his ear she whispered to him. John Retallick eyes flew wide open.

"Sh . . . Grandfather. It's only me. Ginifur." She reassured him as he raised himself up onto an elbow.

"What's amiss cheeld? Is it your Da? Or Jamie?"

Her grandmother stirred, and Ginifur quickly explained why she was there, and told them that Liam and Captain Tremayne were with her. Whilst she went to fetch them inside, John and Annie quickly dressed.

When they were all assembled Ginifur explained that they wanted to get into the tunnel that led to the caves, to warn Adam that the Militia were on the cliffs.

John shook his head. "Ye can't do that cheeld. No one's gone down there for years. There could 'ave been a rock fall, anythin'." He continued to shake his head. "No. No. Besides I may not even be able to open the entrance. It's been closed so many years now, probably won't budge."

"It's our only chance, Grandfather." Ginifur pleaded. "If Adam is out there, he is in great danger." She grabbed hold of his arm in desperation. "Please Grandfather. How do we get down into the well?"

"Down a well!!" Exclaimed Richard. "Wells are filled with water!"

"Not this one." Admitted John, and sighed. "Well, I s'pose ye'll try t' do it, with or without my help." Continuing to shake his head he sent a pleading glance to his wife for help or assistance.

Anne Retallick made her opinion quite clear by adding. "She'll not forgive you if you don't, John. You take them to the well, and I'll keep watch on the lane." Ginifur rewarded her with a grateful smile.

John Retallick reached for an old coat which hung beside the door, and shrugged it on. Opening the door he indicated for them to follow and they proceeded down the path to the track that led to the well.

At the well, John struggled over the granite water filled trough set into the ground, and struggled to release the locking mechanism which moved the railings to one side to let him through. Behind the water outlet was a large slab of granite. Another struggle with another locking mechanism, and Ginifur was about to give up hope when a rusty, grating noise growled from beneath. It seemed to hang on the air and they all looked nervously about them, listening for any sound that it had been heard father afield. Once the mechanism had been released it was not too difficult to push aside the slab from over an empty shaft. "There be a wooden ladder strapped to the wall. It 'aven't been checked in years, so be careful." He sat on the rim and put one leg over the edge.

"Grandfather! What are you doing, you are not coming too." Ginifur exclaimed.

"Just ye try t' stop me cheeld. Just ye try t' stop me." The second leg followed the first and his feet felt for the rung of the ladder as he lowered his body into the dark hole.

Ginifur reached out to touch him, but Richard stayed her hand. "You can't ask him to stay behind Ginny. If you want to go into the cave, it looks as though you will have to let him come with us."

Ginifur capitulated. In all honesty she had no option, for her grandfather had now vanished from sight below the rim. With Richard above her and Liam below, they followed John Retallick down into the abyss without mishap. The rungs were no longer good and strong, but they held, with only one or two missing.

At the bottom of the ladder they regrouped in the dark, until Liam had relit one of the lanterns, before making their uncertain progress along the narrow tunnel. Here again the floor of the passage was uneven, but not so damp. At intervals there had been small rock falls, but nothing to halt their passage and they were quickly cleared. After what seemed quite a while, certainly it seemed longer than the last tunnel, a pin prick of light ahead made John tell them to dim the lantern even further and to be as quiet as possible. As the light became brighter, and the pin prick of light much larger, muffled voices could be heard ahead of them until, quite clearly, they heard one voice call out above the rest.

"Quiet. Quiet I says." The party in the tunnel came to an unsteady halt. "Did 'e 'ear that? Where did it come from? Adam! Is that ye?" If Adam, was there he didn't answer, and Ginifur's fears were confirmed.

"Don 'e be s'jumpy, Ben. Get away with 'e. Let we get this up t' the 'orses." This time the voice was much nearer the light.

John Retallick put a hand out to still the rest of the group, and stepped nearer to the light. "Is that ye, Ben Tuckett?" There was a sudden hush, followed by a tremulous voice.

"Who be that? Where are 'e?"

"Tis me. John Retallick. And I'm 'ere." John stepped out of the tunnel into the light, to be surrounded by puzzled questions.

"What are 'e doin' down 'ere?"

"Where did 'e come from?"

"Ow did 'e know we was 'ere?"

John cut short the questions. "I'm not alone. Come out." He called, and Ginny, Richard and Liam stepped into the large cave.

"It's the Cap'n!"

"What's 'e doin' 'ere?"

"Christ! It's Ginny Retallick!"

"Quiet." Ordered John, and his seniority received the respect that he deserved. Anyway, hadn't he too once been a Free Trader? "Ye'd better listen to me grand daughter, here, 'n Liam."

Ben Tuckett stepped forward, taking the lead for the band of smugglers. "Well Maid! What 'ave ye got' say that involves the likes of we?" He jeered.

"The Militia are lying in ambush in Rosvarron Lane, and are on the cliffs above the entrance to the cave. Your ponies have been let loose, and Tiny Tindle is in hiding at Tremanyon." She looked from face to face. "Where is Adam?" She received no answer.

"Where is Adam Sawle?" Demanded Richard.

"So, 'e couldn' keep 'is trap shut." Mumbled one. " 'e 'ad t' tell 'er."

"Are 'e sure that it i'nt 'e, Adam, that tol' on we?" Asked another.

"Of course he hasn't told me. Do you think I would stand by and let him risk so much, just for money. And Adam wouldn't risk being captured by giving information to the preventative men. What I know is only what I have worked out for myself. Now, where is he?" Snapped the now angry Ginifur.

"Where is 'e Ben?" John Retallick voice was cold and demanded their attention.

Ben Tuckett wavered for only a moment more. "Adam's still out there, John. Come over with the Frenchie, e'll be on 'is way back in now. We unloaded the shipment a whiles back, they came in on the early tide, but Adam 'ad some things t' attend to afore they set sail again."

"Oh no!" Ginifur reached out and caught Richard's sleeve. "What if they've got as far as the cliff?"

"Where's the entrance to the beach?" Richard demanded to be told as he glanced around the cave to see more than one entrance to yet further tunnels.

"Tis that one there, Cap'n." John pointed to the low passage.

"Leave your contraband here." Instructed Richard. "You men follow John and Liam back to the cottage. We'll meet you there with Adam."

Liam didn't argue, as Richard grabbed Ginifur by the hand and made for the other tunnel.

In the outer cave Ginifur and Richard paused beside the boulder before pushing aside the branches of the bush and creeping out on their hands and knees onto the ledge above the beach. Their eyes, that had become accustomed to the dark of caverns, could see quite clearly even though there was good cloud cover. Neither of them spoke, listening to the night sounds. A stone was dislodged above them. It rattled down the cliff, to land on the rocks below with a crash, and was followed by a hushed voice. "Watch where ye're puttin' yer feet, ye daft bugger. Some one'll 'ear us."

Ginifur's eyes searched the cove, the channel and the sea beyond. Suddenly she gripped Richard's sleeve and pointed towards the rocks at the entrance. A tiny boat, and its occupants, was heading towards the cove, totally unaware of what lay in wait for them. There was nothing they could do to warn them and there was silence above, on the cliff. They knew that the boat must have been seen by the watchers there as well.

Each minute of the wait seemed an eternity for Ginifur, until the tiny boat cleared the channel and entered the cove. The boat held two occupants, one of whom Ginifur was certain had to be Adam. The other was someone who could steer his way through the treacherous rocks, probably Will, for Adam certainly did not know the way. She wanted to call out, to warn them. She couldn't even shine the lamp for they had left this back at the entrance to the caves. Richard laid a gentle hand on her shoulder, holding a finger to his mouth for her to keep silent. There was a chance, maybe, that they hadn't been seen yet.

The two men, and Ginifur was now quite sure in her own mind that they were Adam and Will, slipped over the side of the boat and dragged it up the beach. As they lent inside to retrieve something from within the hull a strong and sharp voice broke the silence of the night. "Halt, in the name of the King. Halt or we'll fire."

Ginifur's silence was finally broken. "Run, run for the cliff. It's your only chance." She called out.

The two figures sprang away from the boat and began to sprint across the beach. Ginifur and Richard waited for the gunfire, but Ginifur had unwittingly, earned them a few precious moments.

"Fire, ye idiots. I said fire!" An angry voice called out in the dark. "Do ye want 'em t' get away?"

"But one of 'em is a girl Sarg! You 'eard 'er. There's a girl down there." A voice faltered. "I ain't never shot a girl!"

"Fire, I said. Girl or no girl. Fire, or I'll 'ave ye all charged." The voice ordered. One tentative shot was followed by another, then another and another. One of the two men fell, and the other paused to check his accomplice while the soldiers re-loaded. But he was dead, there was nothing that could be done for him, and he made another run for the cliff.

Ginifur held her breath. Was it Adam? She couldn't tell. Another shot rang out. The runner stumbled at the bottom of the cliff, and began to drag himself upwards. He was just below the ledge.

"We've got 'em both Sarg'." A triumphant voice called out gleefully. "The second one's under the cliff. Ye can't see 'im from 'ere, but I got 'im alright."

Richard lay down on the ledge and leaned over. Adam was just below him, clinging to the rock face. "Quick man!" Richard attracted his attention. "Give me your hand."

Adam glared up at the man he hated with every breath in his body, and then Ginifur's face appeared beside him.

"Adam! Quick, we haven't much time. Let him help you, please." She pleaded with him.

The sound of running feet along the top of the cliff, heading towards the path to the beach, echoed in the night air and, with a final glance at his fallen friend on the beach below, Adam reached up to the helping hand. It took all Richard's strength to pull Adam the few remaining feet to the ledge, and they stumbled into the hidden cave with only seconds to spare.

As Ginifur tore the blood soaked clothing away from Adam's chest they could hear the puzzled voices on the beach.

"This one's dead. Where's the girl?"

"I thought ye said the other one was at the bottom of the cliff."

"Get a light someone."

A light glowed beyond the bush, as someone lit a flare on the beach.

"She must 'ave climbed the cliff Sarg. I was sure she was 'it. I saw 'er fall."

"Well ye was wrong. Get back up and search for 'er. She can't 'ave got far. Not if she've really been 'it as ye claims." The sergeant ordered.

"Ginny!" Richard shook her shoulder. "Come. We must move."

"He can't be moved, Sir. He's hurt real bad." Ginifur stared at the gaping hole in Adam's chest.

"We have no choice." Richard tore his shirt into strips. Pressing a wad of the linen into the wound he tied the rest of the strips tightly round Adams chest, then lifted him from the floor. Adam was no light weight, but could feel no pain from the awkward handling, for mercifully he had passed out. With no light to guide them, their progress was slow. But eventually the lamp left in the centre cavern guided them on to where John awaited them

"Who's hurt? I heard shootin'. Are 'e alright Ginny? Ye're sure? Ye're certin'?" Then having satisfied himself that she was indeed alright, he saw the limp body of Adam as Richard placed him on the floor. "Is 'e dead?" He asked.

"No. But he will be if we don't get him home soon." Richard stretched his back, rubbed his arms and then bent to pick Adam up once more. "Any way, I thought I told you to lead the others out."

John chuckled. "'n ye would know 'zactly which exit to take would 'e?" He asked.

Richard glanced around the cavern again, once more noticing at least ten other exits. "Point taken John, then lead us out of here."

Ginifur's grandfather shuffled towards the right exit to the well, wondering all the while how they were going to get Adam up the shaft. By the time he had solved the puzzle they had reached the ladder. Telling Richard to leave Adam at the bottom of the shaft with Ginifur, they hurried to the surface where John fetched a rope. All the time working in silence they threw the rope over the centre bar where it snaked down to Ginifur at the bottom. Quickly she secured it under Adam's arms then, as slowly as they dared, Richard and John hauled him to the surface. "I know it id'n the

333

best way." Whispered John. "But tis the only ways I c'n think of just now."

Richard had to agree. Adam had lost a lot of blood, and they had to get the wound clean as quickly as possible.

Liam had led the shaken smugglers to the bridge over the lane. There they dispersed singly into the night, some along the creak edge to the main river, some up through Primrose Bank and the fields beyond, some following the stream for a while before being enveloped by the silent night. Liam had then returned to the cottage to wait for Richard and now helped Richard to carry Adam and retrace their steps up the slippery slope of the tunnel and back to the house.

Once Adam was laid out on the bed, and Ginifur began to undress him, Richard turned to Liam. "Take Lamorna, and ride to Dr Thomas. If anyone stops you, say that I have had a relapse. The fever has returned, and you think I am going to die." Liam took one glance at Adam's grey face and spun on his heels.

Dr Thomas came immediately. He gave Liam a fresh mount, and ordered his stable hand to rub Richard's horse down and stable him for the rest of the night.

When they returned to Tremanyon, Ginifur and Richard had cleaned the wound, and removed the worst traces of dirt and sand. But the shot was still in Adam's chest.

"Take her out of here." James Thomas said as kindly as he could. "Give her a glass of brandy, Liam."

Ginifur tried to object, but Liam persuaded her to leave and took her downstairs.

"I can see young Ginny's been busy." James Thomas bent over Adam's motionless washed body. And removed the temporary dressing. "I don't know that I want to know how he came by this wound, got something to do with the Militia scouring the country-side, has it? No, don't answer me. They swallowed Liam's fairy tale anyway. In any case, it would appear that they are looking for a female, so it can't be Adam, can it?" He glanced up at Richard with a conspiratorial smile. "However, I think that you had better lay low for a few days, until your fever subsides that is." Methodically he inspected the wound, listened to Adams heart, pulled his eyelids up and inspected his eyes, and checked him for other wounds. Finally he redressed the wound and pulled the covers up to Adams neck.

"Well James! What are his chances? Will you be able to remove the bullet?"

James Thomas opened his valise and took out a bottle. "Laudanum." He pronounced. "It will ease the pain. His chances . . ." His words hung on the air whilst he stared at the inert body for a moment. "As to his chances?" He repeated. "Very small indeed. In fact I should tell you, none. He has lost a lot of blood and the shot is too deep for me to remove, even if I did have the necessary instruments with me. I believe it is close to his heart and any movement could, and most probably would, be fatal." He snapped the bag shut. "He may not even wake again, probably better if he doesn't. I'm sorry Richard. I can do no more for the boy than to make his end as comfortable as I can." Then picking up the bag he turned away from the bed. "Will you tell Ginifur, or shall I?"

"No. I'll do it." Richard told him. "I owe her that much."

James Thomas shook his head. "She hasn't had much luck, one way and another. Deserves better from life, she does."

"The child? Jamie. He's not Adam's." Richard spoke about Jamie's birth for the first time.

The good doctor, bit his bottom lip, and looked Richard in the eye. "There is such a thing as patient confidentiality you know that." Richard acknowledged this with a nod of his head. "But I assume you know something about Jamie's birth or you wouldn't have mentioned it. So, in answer to your question, yes. I do have reason to believe that he is not Adam's son."

"You attended her?" Richard asked.

"I did. And I count it an honour to have done so."

"Did she never say who he was? Jamie's father?" Richard pressed further.

James Thomas shook his head, remembering the days after he had first brought the subject up with Ginifur. "No. Never." He looked back at the bed. "She'd have gone to jail rather than disclose the name of the child's father. Who ever he was, she loved him a great deal, of that I have no doubt. Fine little lad, isn't he?" He looked deep into Richard's eyes. "Yet, who ever he was, he never came back to claim him."

Richard held the door open for him to pass. "So she married Adam to save her son from being born in jail. Dear God . . ." Richard whispered. "If only I had known."

"Eh! What did you say?" The good doctor was already half way down the stairs.

Richard walked down the few steps to catch him up. "I said thank you, for what you have done."

"Think nothing of it. Couldn't really do anything for him anyway, I'm afraid. When the time comes, I'll record his death as an accident. Broke his neck in the fall from that flighty horse of his, that's what I'll record." He picked up his cloak from the chair in the hall. "Let me know when the time comes, and tell Ginifur that I am truly sorry."

Richard showed him to the door. Dawn was flickering below the dark horizon as he watched the doctor ride away. Then, with a heavy heart, he made his way back into the house.

Ginifur took the news badly but, when she had recovered her composure, returned to sit beside Adam's bed. Once again Kate and Peggy stepped in to take charge of Jamie and the girls. Rachel and Rebecca were now of an age to amuse themselves when necessary.

For two whole days Adam remained unconscious, and all that time Ginifur stayed by his side.

The Last Goodbye

RICHARD ENTERED THE bedroom, taking in the sight of the dark rings beneath Ginifur's eyes, the lack of sparkle in their usual bright green and the worry etched on her face. "You are tired lass. Please go and get some sleep. If you don't, you'll be no use to Adam when he wakes, or to Jamie."

"No. Not until he wakes. I'll not leave here until he wakes." She rested her weary head against the back of the high backed chair and, as her glance returned to the figure lying in the bed; Adam's eyes flickered and opened. "Oh Adam! I'm so glad that you are awake at last." Ginifur took his hand in hers. "You have been unconscious for so long."

Adam's eyes searched hers and then travelled upwards to Richard standing behind her shoulder. "I reckon, as I owes ye my thanks, Cap'n Tremayne. I wouldn't want my family to go through my trial as a Free Trader."

"No thanks needed, Adam. I'm glad I was able to help." Richard assured him.

Adam's eyes closed once more. "Don't try to talk anymore, Adam." Ginifur pleaded.

Her words brought Adam struggling back to consciousness. "I must talk now, there's so much I 'ave t' say."

"Later . . . Later . . . when you are better. You can talk then." Ginifur entreated.

"There won't be no later, Ginny. You knows that 'n I knows it too. I aven't much time left 'n I've got t' put things right."

Ginifur was stopped from saying any more by Richard's hand pressed on her shoulder.

"I'm sorry about all they things I said and done, Ginny. I never meant any of 'em. Don' know where they came from even; I think it were some demon inside me." He struggled to breath. "Another thing, I never would 'ave took 'e away from Porthcarrow 'n yer Da. The cottage! It weren't at Treloe, but only a little ways from 'ere, on the other side of the village."

"It doesn't matter Adam, it's all behind us now." Ginny assured him.

"C'n ye ever fergive me fer hittin' ye like I did? I don' know what come over me, fer I'd never dream of hittin' a woman in me right mind." His eyes clung to hers.

"There is nothing to forgive, Adam. The blame was mostly mine." Ginifur tried to ease his mind.

"It wasn't" The angry outburst set off a fit of coughing, and specks of blood appeared at the corners of his mouth.

"Please, Adam! Don't try to talk anymore." Ginifur pleaded with him.

Adam struggled to catch hold of her hands and the exertion was almost too much. He struggled once more to continue. "I'm dyin' Ginny. Please fergive me, or I'll die in torment. Ginny, please. Please fergive me."

Ginifur would have agreed to anything to stop him speaking, but it was easy for her to say. "Of course I forgive you Adam, but there is really nothing to forgive."

Adam breathed a sigh of relief. "Twas all my fault. It was me that pressed ye into marriage. It was me that didn' keep t' my side of the bargain. I knew that ye loved Jamie's father. Ye tol' me so, ye never deceived me or led me to believe otherwise. If I'd given ye the space ye needed, then maybe, in time ye might 'ave learned t' love me too."

"I did love you, Adam. I always loved you." Ginifur tried to reassure him, and it was the truth. She did love him, and always had. It was, just different.

A semblance of a smile flitted across Adam's face. "Yes ye did. But as a brother, Ginny. Not as a lover. Not as ye loved 'im. Not as ye loved Jamie's father." He looked up at Richard Tremayne. "And, do ye know, I believe 'e loved thee too. I believe 'e still does, 'n I believe e'll do the right thing by ye when I'm gone."

"Adam, don't talk so." Tears streamed down Ginifur's face.

"Cap'n." Adam addressed Richard.

"Yes Adam." Richard smiled benevolently down on him.

"Ye'll look after me wife, won't 'e? Ye won' turn 'er away. 'n ye were right Cap'n, a man should be proud of a son like Jamie. Ye'll take care of my son, Cap'n, fer e's the only one I'll ever 'ave now. I don' 'ave no others either, by the way, what ever I made thee think Ginny. Guess it weren't you that couldn' get with child, but me as couldn' deliver." Adam was gasping for breath, forcing himself to continue, his eyes latching on to Richard's own. "Jamie?" He continued when his breathing eased. "Ye'll treat 'im like yer own, Captain Tremayne. Give 'im a chance t' make some'at of 'is life?"

A lump rose in Richard's throat. "I give you my word, Adam. I will give Ginifur and your son my care and protection for as long as they need it. And Jamie! Jamie will be given a chance to make something of his life, I promise." Richard assured him.

"Yes." Adam's eyes closed once more. "I believe ye will." He took a deep breath. " 'n I believe we both now know the truth of it too."

Ginifur let go of his hands. "I'll go and get your Ma and Pa." She insisted.

"No, please stay." Adam's eyes flashed open once more. "Don' go Ginny, I'm afeared of dyin' alone." Cradling his hand in hers she stroked it gently with her fingers. "Remember when we was just tackers, and used to go out to the Point." He reminisced. "Ye used to say ye could 'ear Kiara singin' on the rocks? Ye even said she swam with ye in the cove."

"Yes, but you never believed me. You said you didn't believe in mermaids."

"I did though, I could 'ear 'er meself. Saw 'er too, with me own eyes. Did'n dare own up t' it though. The boys would 'ave laughed me out of the village." He struggled to focus upon her face. "T'was a sweet sound, weren't it, Ginny? I'd swear I could 'ear 'er callin' t' me now." He smiled up at her. "Them was 'appy days, Ginny, weren't em?"

Tears almost stopped her from seeing his smile. "Oh yes, Adam. Very happy days indeed."

Adam smiled again, before adding. "Remember me that way, Ginny. Remember me as I was back then, when we was young, 'n 'appy. Not as I 'ave been these last months." Then slowly his eyelids closed for the final time, and Ginifur was left sobbing as her head fell upon his lifeless hand.

Richard left her to grieve for a few moments, tears running freely from her eyes and each sob tearing at Richard's heart. When the sobs began to ease he lifted her from the bed and, as she turned away from the silent Adam, she lent against his strong supporting body for comfort. Richard's arms slid about her tiny frame. His hands stroked her silken hair as he whispered words of comfort in her ear. This was not the time for questions and anyway, if he was honest, he knew most of the answers already. There was only one question that he didn't know the answer to, and that he couldn't ask her yet. No, not yet.

True to his word, James Thomas signed the death certificate as a riding accident, and Adam was buried in Porthcarrow Churchyard a few days after he died at Tremanyon. Behind his coffin walked his widow and son. Behind them, his parents and, behind them walked Richard and his daughters. The Church at the top of the hill was full. Everyone in the village had turned out to say farewell, among them Ben Tuckett and Adam's free trading friends. None of them had been caught that fatal night, and behind closed doors they laughed at the Militia's attempts to trace the gun shot girl they thought was on the beach that night.

The family and close mourners returned to Tremanyon, where Netty had laid out refreshments for them. The villagers had a spread, provided for them by Richard, in the Inn. It was immediately after the guests had gone that Richard left to answer a request to visit Lord Falmouth at Tregothnan, and a few days later he sent word that he had been summoned to London. He gave no indication as to when he would return, but assured Ginifur that he would, as soon as circumstances allowed.

Adam's death had come so suddenly, without warning, and Ginifur's feelings were in turmoil. She struggled with the feelings that she had been at fault, and Sam and his family assured her daily that she was in no way to blame. "Adam chose to become a Free Trader." Sam told her. "It was this that was 'is downfall, not you maid."

Ginifur turned a tired face towards him. "I didn't love him enough."

"Ye loved 'im as much as ye could. Adam shouldn' 'ave asked fer more than ye could give 'im." Sam grieved for his son, but he could not lay the blame on Ginifur's shoulders.

But Ginifur still had some grieving to do on her own. She had lost her dearest friend and so it was probably for the best that Richard had been forced to leave Tremanyon to give a final report to The House, thus allowing Ginifur time and space to try to come to terms with her husband's death.

A New Beginning

RICHARD WAS DETAINED in London for over six weeks, engaged in meetings with William Pitt, amongst others. English troops were suffering heavy losses in the America's, in their fight for Canada, and considerable confusion arose over the policy of the government. Popular demand for William Pitt was rising, and Pitt's attacks on the Duke of Newcastle were increasing. He declared. "I am sure I can save this country, and nobody else can." It was the belief of Edward, Lord Falmouth, and his friends that it would not be long before William Pitt was returned to office after his disgraceful dismissal in 1755.

Richard resented the lengthy stay in London. He would quite happily have turned right round and gone home, if it hadn't been for the fact that Edward and Fanny had accompanied him to the capital.

It was Fanny who arrived at the house in Hampstead, one evening when Edward had been detained at a cabinet war meeting. After a busy round of the dressmakers, milliners and wigmakers, she had taken a light lunch with friends, enjoyed a drive around the park in the summer sunshine and arrived in a happy state of mind. She sprang down from the open landau and skipped up the steps, handing her fashionable summer cape to Robert as she asked. "Where is Captain Tremayne?"

"He is in the garden, Ma'am." Robert informed her. "Shall I notify him of your ladyship's presence?"

"No, Robert." She waved a delicately gloved hand at him. "I'll tell him myself." And she brushed past him as she headed for the door which led out of the hall to the rear of the house. "Will you kindly arrange for Mary to bring tea into the garden room?"

Robert gave a brief bow to her retreating back. "Certainly, Lady Falmouth."

Fanny's skirts rustled as she swept through the garden room. The fragrance from the orange blossom, on the imported trees which Robert so carefully attended to, filled the warm conservatory and in the garden the early summer shrubs were blooming. "Richard!" She called out, as she spied him leaning against the trunk of an apple tree at the far end of the lawned area. "Richard!"

She repeated. But Richard didn't hear her voice until she was right beside him. Richard's eyes came into focus. "Where on earth were you?" She laughed. "You certainly weren't here. No, don't tell me. I expect you were back in Cornwall, on your beloved estate. I see the same look in Edwards's eyes on too many occasions for you to deny it." Richard smiled. "There, I knew it. Perhaps you would be kind enough to tear yourself away from your day dreaming for a minute and join me for tea. Robert has asked Mary to serve tea in the garden room." She informed him.

Richard took her hand in an elegant move, kissed her gloved finger tips, and placed her hand upon his arm, saying. "I cannot imagine a more enchanting lady to take tea with."

"La!" Fanny's laugh rang out like that of a young girl. "I don't know if you are an incorrigible liar, or a fool Richard." And she laughed again at the shocked look upon his face. "Either way, I think that it is high time that you took a hard look at yourself, and what you want out of life. I also think that it is high time that you and I have a good talk, Richard, don't you?" Richard looked sideways at her, an eyebrow raised in question. "And don't look at me like that Richard. I think you know only too well what I am talking about, and most importantly, who. " Placing her other hand upon his she took the lead and headed back along the lavender bordered path, towards the house.

In the glass covered garden room Fanny settled herself in the chair and dismissed Mary, who was hovering in waiting to pour the tea, by telling her that she would do it herself. When Mary hesitated, Lady Falmouth had never poured the tea before, Fanny told her that she was quite capable of pouring tea if she so wished to. Richard smothered a smile and waved Mary away.

"What's all this about, Fanny. Tea for two, I think that there is something on your mind. You haven't had too many hats made up have you? Or too many dresses? Are you trying to embroil me in some scheme of yours to deceive Edward?" Richard laughed as she first poured the milk into the two china cups, and then followed with the tea, handing a cup and saucer to Richard with a smile.

"Richard! What am I to do with you?" She took a sip from her cup and replaced it in the saucer before turning to him again. "You and I, and Edward if he would only let himself, know only too well that your heart is not here in London. All this intrigue, talk of war in the colonies, it isn't for you Richard. The city hems you in, even in the garden you search the sky as if you wish you could fly out of here." Richard only stared at her in silence. "Take a hard look at yourself, Richard. Focus on what you really want out of life. You won't find it here, my dear." She reached across to touch his knee. "The place you so constantly dream of, and of those that you love most in this life, none of them are here, Richard. They are all in Cornwall."

Richard sighed. "But Edward . . ."

"La . . !" She repeated with a shake of her hand. "Edward! Edward, if he was honest, would agree with me. His only loves are Cornwall, Tregothnan and that beloved ship of his. Myself and the family fit in somewhere, I am sure, but it what order I couldn't quite say."

Richard objected. "You will always be the first love in Edward's life, Fanny." He assured her.

"Very gallant of you indeed. Richard." She smiled. "But I am not a fool. I have always known that Edward's first love is his Cornwall and Tregothnan, and the second the White Rose." Then she lent back against the cushions to study his face more clearly. "But you, Richard? Who comes in what order do you think?"

"The girls are, of course, my greatest reason to live. And I miss them so much. I have been away from home so long that the days drag by. I do not really see that I am doing any good by being here."

"The girls! Yes, or course, the girls." Fanny bit her lip as she considered her next question. "But is there one particular girl who may be on your mind?" Richard's surprise at the question, made her smile. "I have lived a few years Richard, and seen many things. There is not much that will surprise or shock me."

Richard stood up and went to the door overlooking the garden. He hadn't thought that he had acted in any way which might have made his thoughts clear to anyone. Let alone Fanny and Edward. He turned to study her concerned face. "He is not Adam's child, you know." There it was out. What would she have to say to that?

Fanny pushed her chair back and came to stand beside him, taking his hand in hers she looked up into his face. "Edward and I . . . Well, you see, we never really believed that he was." She smiled at his surprised expression. "Oh yes. He is indeed Ginifur's son. There is a lot of her in him. And folks could easily be fooled into thinking that he was Adam's son, for why shouldn't he be. But for those who know you well, and love you too, Richard, they cannot be so easily fooled. Ginifur's mother may well indeed have had blue eyes, but Jamie did not inherit them from her, did he?"

"How long have you known?" Richard asked. "Is Ginifur aware that you do not believe that Jamie is Adam's son?"

"Firstly, no, Ginifur doesn't know what I think, or Edward. Secondly! I think I knew on the first day I saw the babe. Ginifur gave a very logical explanation for the child's blue eyes, but I am no fool, Richard, Ginifur didn't love Adam, but she did indeed love Jamie. Yes, many children are born by an act when love is not involved. But that would not happen with Ginifur." She drew him back to the chairs where she pulled hers a little closer to him. "As you know, I visited often whilst you were away. I promised I would, but I would have anyway. The more I saw Jamie grow, the more sure I became of the identity of his true father." She let his hand fall. "Did Ginifur tell you before Adam died, or after? Or had you suspected it anyway, and asked her yourself?"

"The answer is no, on all counts. At least, at first, I don't think I suspected." He took a deep breath, and stared out at the garden again. Fanny let him take his time. "And no, she hasn't told me. Not before, nor since. Well she is still grieving for Adam. But Adam, he knew. He . . . on the night that he died . . ."

"There is no need to say anymore." Fanny reassured him "Now, I am going to get to the crux of the matter." Fanny spoke sharply and Richard looked round. "Did you take advantage of a vulnerable young woman who in spite of herself, and took great pains to hide it, was very much in love with you?"

Richard frowned, and rubbed his chin in thought. "Perhaps I did. Of course I don't like to think so. Yes, I was sorely grieving after Annabelle died, and I blamed myself for her death too. It was Ginifur who bore the brunt of it all, cared for Rachel and Rebecca, cared for Tremanyon, cared for me without me really realising it. That night, I found her beside Rebecca's bed, comforting her." He paused. "Shall I go on?" Fanny nodded. "How can I explain? I looked into her face, as if seeing it for the first time. It was a woman's face, no longer a child. Yes, I wanted her, I needed her but it was more than that. Can you understand Fanny?" He pleaded.

"Yes Richard, I can. Do you want to go on?"

Richard took in the look of genuine concern on her face, and continued. "Yes. I picked her up. and took her to my bed." He shook his head in disbelief. "Why am I telling you this?" He asked in wonder.

"Because there is no one else, Richard." Fanny told him. "Who else is there? I am here and believe me, I do care."

"When I awoke, she had gone from my bed. I needed to see her. To tell her . . .To tell her that I would be back. Tell her . . ." His voice tailed off.

"That you loved her, maybe?" Fanny suggested.

"I think so. I'm not sure what I would have told her. But she had gone."

"Gone?" Fanny said in disbelief.

"No, not gone. But she had left the house and gone to Quay Cottage I discovered later. I left Tremanyon without speaking to her again."

"You left, without any explanation!" Fanny couldn't believe what she had heard. "Surely, you could have found her?"

"Liam looked, Kate said that she had gone to Quay Cottage, he went as far as the walled garden but couldn't see her returning . . . and Edward! Edward was waiting in Falmouth." He tried to explain.

"So. That was the last time you saw her. Before you left, that is." Fanny surmised.

"No, not exactly." Fanny raised a painted eyebrow. "We were sailing out of the Carrick Roads when Liam saw her. She had sailed out to the bay, to see us off. It was then that I knew. Knew that I had to return, to tell her that I needed her beside me, always."

"And you came home to find she had married Adam." Fanny finished for him

"Yes." He agreed. "I was surprised. For I had never seen anything that made me think that they were anything other than good friends. No one told me that Jamie was not Adam's son, but I . . ! I don't know. I think in my heart I have known from the moment he climbed onto my lap." He shrugged his shoulders. "I thought to myself this should be my son. So now, Fanny. What do I do now? What must you and Edward think of me?"

"Richard! What Edward or I might think is of no relevance. What I want is for you to do what is in your heart. Follow your heart Richard, forget what anyone else may think and do what is right for you, Ginifur and Jamie. Folks will forget in time, they always do and anyone who meets Ginifur could not fail to fall in love with her, believe me." Once more she took both hands. "Edward and I did. Go home Richard, go home."

* * *

345

The month of May passed by slowly, as Ginifur adjusted to her new life. The trees were clothed in fresh foliage, bluebells, and primroses, which had carpeted the woods, faded along with the may blossom, and the days lengthened as the June days came around and spring turned into early summer.

Each afternoon Ginifur would saddle Damson and ride out over Rhosinnis to the headland. Sometimes she would take Jamie, and Rachel and Rebecca, and sometimes she would ride alone. Today, for some reason, she felt like going further field. She left Jamie with Kate, and Rachel and Rebecca, who had begged to be allowed to go into the kitchen to try their hand at baking, with Netty, and Ginifur turned Damson's head towards the village and Dingerien Head beyond.

The day had been overcast but as she looked up to the headland, the clouds were suddenly torn apart to allow a patch of blue sky to peep through. By the time she had reached the headland, breathless and flushed with her heart pounding from the gallop, the sky had finally cleared and the light wind abated.

Letting go of Damson's reins, Ginifur allowed her to wander free amongst the young heather and gorse. She wouldn't go far away. Then she chose a smooth rock, with soft young heather at its base to sit upon, which afforded her a view of the whole of the bay and the coastal path from Porthcarrow.

Settling herself upon the cushion of heather, Ginifur lent back against the warm, smooth rock and stared out over the bay. From here she could look down onto Pentonvrane. A long house, nestling amongst the trees and its garden leading to the very edge of the cliff. Beyond Pentonvrane, on the other side of the bay, the village of Porthcarrow hugged the hill, cottages tumbling down towards the sea and tiny boats bobbing up and down on their moorings at their feet. Her eyes roved the cliff, settling briefly on a lone rider as he took the coastal path from the beach towards Pentonvrane until her attention was attracted to the cottage on the far side of the valley, its windows winking in the sunlight.

The day before, Mr. Franks had paid Ginifur a visit, bringing with him the deeds to Adam's cottage. It was fully paid for. Not only was there a cottage, it came with a group of buildings and the surrounding fifteen acres. It included a shippon for the three cows, and a pig sty for the two Cornish Lop sows and boar. Edward Franks had ridden over with Ginifur and Jamie to see the cottage and give her the keys. Ben Tucket was there. Ben had taken care of the animals when Adam was away on his trips, and he offered to continue to look after them until she decided on her future.

Ginifur had been quite taken aback. The tiny cottage was spotlessly clean and freshly lime washed, inside and out. Floral curtains hung at the windows and the furniture was more than adequate. It contained three rooms. A living room, complete with a Cornish Range, and two bedrooms. Not only had Adam left her and Jamie the cottage and the land, he had left a substantial amount of money in the bank, and a locked box for which there was no key. Edward Franks told her that he had the key in his office and, on Adam's instructions, the box was to be opened by Jamie when he reached the age of twenty-five. Ginifur was puzzled, but didn't question this, handing the box back to Edward Franks. Needless to say, Ginifur's circumstances had changed dramatically. There was no reason why Captain Tremayne should be held to his promise to a dying man. Ginifur was financially able to bring up her own son. Richard's letter to her and the children was received nearly two months ago, and she had firmly convinced herself that he was now regretting his promise to care for her and Jamie. Ginifur made the decision that, when he returned, she would tell him that he was discharged from all responsibility for them.

Ginifur had been so absorbed in her thoughts that she wasn't aware of the horse coming up from behind, until its shadow fell across her. "I'm sorry Damson." She said, pushing herself up off the heather. "I have been ignoring you, haven't I . . . Oh!" She exclaimed as she came face to face with Lanhoose. But, more than that, upon his back was Richard Tremayne, with Jamie happily seated in front of him. "Oh . . . Sir!" Ginifur flustered. "We didn't know . . .We hadn't heard . . . I'm sorry . . . If I had realised that you were returning today, I would never have left the house."

Richard laughed. "Don't worry Ginifur." He slid to the ground and then lifted Jamie down to run to his mother. "I wanted to surprise everyone. Jamie wanted his mother so, when Sam said you had ridden out here, we decided to come and look for you."

"I'm sorry, Sir. You shouldn't have troubled yourself." Ginifur reached down to retrieve her son, balancing him on her hip.

Richard turned his gaze across the bay. "It was no trouble. I have a good enough reason to take Lanhoose out, and avail myself of the opportunity to inhale some of this beautiful fresh air. Ginifur, you have no idea how insufferable the air is in London"

He breathed deeply, inhaling the fresh salty air scented with the wild flowers that grew in abundance on the headland.

Jamie wriggled in his mother's arms, so Ginny put him down where he happily sat himself on the ground watching Damson and Lanhoose grazing contentedly a few feet away. Ginifur was left staring at Richard's back. "Rachel and Rebecca will be pleased to see you home, Sir. They have missed you very much."

Richard slowly turned. He studied Ginifur's face, and she lowered her eyes, avoiding his searching ones. "They have?" He asked with a smile twitching at the corner of his mouth.

"Oh yes." She assured him, glancing up once more. Her heart racing at the sight of him standing so close to her. "Very much."

Richard took a step closer. "And you, Ginny? Have you missed me also?" He reached out to put his hand under her chin, forcing her to look back at him.

Ginifur felt the blood rush into her face. She wished that she could turn her head away, but he held her chin firmly between finger and thumb. "Of course, Sir. The house is never the same when you are away." She whispered.

Richard's smile reached his eyes and he laughed. "The house! I see, the house!" He stifled another laugh and withdrew his hand as he glanced at Jamie before looking back at her face. "And Jamie! Has Jamie missed his father?" Richard's eyes held hers for a long moment before she lowered them once more.

Ginifur's already racing heart beat even faster, the blood pounding in her head as she grasped for an answer whilst Richard waited patiently. "Adam was often away for long periods. I don't think Jamie realises that he won't be coming back."

Richard placed a finger under her chin once more, gently raising her face till she was looking up at him. "I didn't ask if he missed Adam, Ginny. I asked if he missed his father." Ginifur, searching his face for an indication of his feelings found none, but he continued before she could speak. "Adam knew who Jamie's father was?"

Ginifur blinked back the tears. "I think so, at the end."

"He said that you loved him very much, Jamie's father. Is that true?"

Ginifur didn't answer immediately, wondering what his purpose was, but finally she decided that only the truth would do. "I did, Sir." She told him, and added. "With all my heart."

Richard took a deep breath and looked briefly away. "And now, Ginifur? Do you love him still? Are you still in love with Jamie's father?" He turned and put his hands on her shoulders so that she could not move away.

The conversation had already gone too far. Ginifur knew that there was no going back now. What ever the outcome of this conversation, she had to continue, and there was always the cottage on the other side of the bay for her and Jamie to go to. She held her head high and looked Richard straight in the eyes. "I do, Sir. And I always will."

Richard smiled. "Do you love him enough to consent to marry him, Ginifur?" Ginifur's eyes opened wide, sparkling with unshed tears. But there wasn't enough time to answer, for Richard hurried on. He needed confirmation that his suspicions were correct. "Jamie is my son, isn't he Ginifur. Adam knew that when he died, didn't he? He suspected as much on the night he left for France."

Ginifur's legs grew week. "When did you know?" She asked.

"I think I knew on the very moment Jamie climbed onto my lap. I said to myself 'This should be my son'. Later, as my suspicions grew, I couldn't bring myself to ask you. You had a husband, Ginifur. I didn't know your true feelings, you kept them well hidden. You still are, Ginny, you still are."

Ginifur found the strength to pull away. "I'll not marry again to give Jamie a father. Adam, left me well provided for, I can bring Jamie up alone." She had raised her voice, bringing Jamie to his feet and anxiously looking from one to the other. Jamie had never heard an angry word pass between his mother and Richard, it disturbed him and he was alarmed.

"Ginifur." Richard reached out for her hand. "I am not asking you to marry me because of Jamie. I am asking you to marry me because I cannot imagine my life without you." He laid his heart bare for her to see.

"But, no. It's impossible." She tried to pull away again, but Richard forced her to look into his eyes.

"No buts, Ginifur. Nothing is impossible. In all those weeks, when my life hung in the balance between this world and the next, the only thing that kept bringing me back was the memory of your sweet, gentle face, and the sight of your tiny figure as you waved farewell to us when we sailed in the White Rose." Now it was time for Richard to search her face for assurance. "Was Adam right, Ginifur? Did you truly love me? Do you love me still?"

Ginifur's eyes swam with tears. "I do." The whisper passed her lips

"Then, will you marry me, Ginifur?" His husky voice made her tremble, and her answer was barely a whisper.

"If it is your wish, Sir."

Richard spoke roughly for the first time. "No, Ginifur. Not for my wish alone. Not unless you love me too. For believe me I do indeed love you Ginifur Retallick. Not unless you believe me, and it is what you truly desire." His fingers dug into her arms, pressing her for the answer he wanted to hear.

What she truly desired? Ginifur couldn't believe what she was hearing, and she gave him her answer. "It is all, and more than I could ever dream of, Sir."

Richard's laugh came out as a roar. "My name is Richard, my beloved. If we are to be married Ginifur, I think it would be better if you call me Richard." He cupped her face in his hands. "Say. I will, Richard. Go on Ginny. Say it. Tell me that it is what you truly wish." He teased her.

Ginifur's tears were now tears of joy. "I will Richard." She whispered at first. Then louder, and louder. "Oh yes. Yes I will marry you. I would love to marry you Richard Tremayne." And Richard took her in his arms briefly, before whisking her light frame into the air and whirling her round and round in sheer happiness.

Jamie looked up from his spot in the heather. He didn't know what was happening, but it didn't matter. The two people that Jamie loved most in the entire world were laughing and happy. And if they were happy . . . Jamie was happy too.

Authors Note

The characters in this book are purely fictional, who are not based on any person either living or dead, and any resemblance to real persons living or dead, is coincidental. Where names and occupations have been taken from reports of the times, this is for information purposes only, and no likeness is intended towards the real life characters.

The events portrayed are not based on any factual incident either, however, Lord Falmouth (Admiral Edward Boscawen) did actually live in this period of time as did William Pitt.

There is, of course no evidence that William Pitt and Admiral Boscawen ever met to discuss the Canadian/French war or ever met socially in Cornwall. However, I believe there would be little doubt that they were acquainted. William Pit the elder was the grandson of Thomas Pitt who purchased Boconnoc House with the proceeds of the Pitt Diamond which was sold to the Regent of France. William was the second son of Robert Pitt and Lady Harriet Villiers and he grew up at Boconnoc. In 1756 the seven year war broke out and Pitt was Secretary of State with sole charge of the direction of the war and foreign affairs and in 1758 the army began to make inroads into the French control of Canada including the capture of Fort Duquesne which was renamed Pittsburgh. Pitt did indeed play an important political role during the Colonial Wars, and Admiral Boscawen was successful in the recapture of Louisburg in 1758. Subsequently General Wolfe set out from Louisburg to capture Quebec in 1759 where he led the assault, scaling the steep cliffs, known as Heights of Abraham. The following day he was wounded three times and died at the peak of the battle at the age of 32. The French Commander died on the next day and the French fled Quebec. They finally surrendered on September 18th 1760.

Lord Falmouth joined the navy at the age of twelve. He was made a captain at twenty six and rear admiral at thirty six. Admiral Boscawen's career in the Royal Navy covered many sea battles, particularly against the French and was also credited with playing a major role in the improvement of health on board His Majesty's ships, by implementing an improvement to personal hygiene and the provision of a better diet. He was accused of promoting

'Cornishness' on his ships, whether this was true or not I have no idea, however, it was a fact that there was little need for 'The Press Men' in Cornwall and Admiral Boscawen's ships always had a full complement of crew. The White Rose is a fictional ship, however Admiral Boscawen's ship in 1744 was the 'Dreadnaught' from whence came his nickname.

Lord Falmouth, Admiral Edward Boscawen, died in 1761, after the capture of Laos, when he was only 50 years of age. At the time of writing I do not know what happened to his wife Fanny, she and her husband had five children and I believe that she lived to a great age.

After the fire in 1512 the House of Commons met in St Stephens Chapel in the palace precincts. The House of Commons was not rebuilt until 1834 following a further fire and this was when the Big Ben bell was added, weighing 13 tons. For the purposes of my story I use an imaginary location beside the Thames.

The inspiration for the stories around Tremanyon came from the house that was once my home, and the headland that I love so much, but the names and places have been altered to fit my fictional story. Although we find ourselves now living far across the country in Essex, it will be no surprise to anyone who knows me and my family that, although I am not born 'Cornish' (only married into a long established Cornish family) my heart remains in Cornwall. The house is now in others hands, but I delight in the fact that the Quay Cottage remains my own special place. It is here that my husband and I, children and grandchildren feel most at home.

My husband's family still farms the land that surrounds the cottage – and we return there as often as we possibly can.

Acknowledgements

The history of Tremanyon is based on information that was given to me by the only living survivor of the Johns family of Trewince, in 1962 and I regret that I cannot remember her name. She was in her latter years when she arrived at the house to ask if she could look over the estate, for she was writing a book about the Johns family who rebuilt Trewince in 1750 after a fire destroyed the earlier Queen Anne Manor. Whilst a member of staff showed her around the estate she allowed my mother and I to copy pages from her manuscript. Oh how I wish there were such things as scanners in those days, for there was much that we could not copy. From that day on I began to weave the stories that I would write . . . one day. I only wish that I could thank her for her help.

I also wish that I could thank my mother in law, Emily Elizabeth Symons, who both encouraged and helped me whilst I was writing this book and told me that I must give her the first copy. Born in 1905 in Gerrans, she was a true Cornish Gentlewoman and is remembered with great affection by her family and friends alike.

I must give a big thank you to all the local families who live on the Roseland Peninsular who accepted me and my family into the community all those years ago, and I hope that they will forgive me for using this beautiful part of Cornwall and changing the description of the area and names of the villages to fit my story.

My thanks to Les Merton for giving me the confidence to proceed with the publication of Tremanyon, and for all his guidance and help with this . . . my first book.

Last, but not least, I must mention my husband Michael who refused to let me put the manuscript for the Tremanyon books in a cupboard to be forgotten.

My research was mostly done through 'on line' facilities and the faithful Encyclopaedia Britannica. What would we do without readily available information today?

TREMANYON
– Time brings many changes / Jamie –

The opening chapter of the
second book in the Tremanyon series

Chapter One
1781 The Homecoming

THE BRITISH FRIGATE was a fine sight with its sails filled with wind as it made a slow approach past the headland, gliding gracefully into the Carrick Roads where it hove to in the sheltered waters. The noisy rattle of the chain disturbed the silence of the late afternoon and was quickly follwed by a resounding splash as the anchor hit the water, falling to the sea bed of the deep bay and take a firm hold in the sand and rock.

"Detail a landing party, Mr. Trenchard," Captain Maynard ordered before turning to the younger man in uniform standing beside him. "The cutter will take you ashore from here, and we will probably get a faster turn around as you suggested. Just tell Mr. Trenchard where you want to be dropped off."

Jamie Tremayne glanced hungrily at the bend in the river, hiding Quay Cottage and his first view of home for over five years. "I am truly grateful to you for bringing me home. I was not looking forward to the journey from London by coach."

"It was a pleasure to have your company. Captain Tremayne, tell me, have you truly decided to leave the sea? I understand that Admiral Kemp had high hopes for you."

Jamie smiled. "My promotion was gained purely by the untimely death of Captain Ferris, and my being the most senior officer available when we were so far from home."

"You underestimate yourself. You will be greatly missed by your crew." Captain Maynard shook his head and glanced at the cutter being lowered into the calm waters of the bay. "I was sorry to hear the news about your father's untimely death. Are you going home to take over the estate?"

Jamie's brow creased into an unfamiliar frown. "No . . . I believe that my brother will take over the major part of the estate. But I believe that my father has left me Rhosinnis, it covers a large part of that headland there in front of us." Jamie indicated the headland to the east of Falmouth Bay. "The land adjoins Tremanyon and I will be able to keep an eye on my mother."

"Surely your brother will do that! You have a promising career ahead of you in His Majesty's Navy. Admiral Boscawen was your Godfather I understand. He would have been proud of you. I beg you to reconsider, don't throw your life away buried in some backwater."

Jamie laughed. "It is no backwater, believe me. Admiral Kemp has given me a year to reconsider. But I have been away too long and I want to go home. I believe that my future is here . . . in Cornwall." He glanced out into the bay at a fishing boat approaching from the Lizard. "I'm sure that is one of our boats." Jamie narrowed his eyes against the lowering sun. "Yes . . . It's Guinevere." A thought crossed his mind "Captain, do you think that your cutter could intercept that fishing boat. I could transfer to her and you will be able to continue your voyage without more ado."

The older man put up his hand to shield his eyes, as he followed the progress of the oncoming fishing boat. "I'm sure it could. But there is no need I assure you."

"I would be grateful. I quite fancy arriving home in one of our own boats."

"As you wish." Captain Maynard glanced at the cutter, the eight men in place with their shipped oars. "The cutter awaits you. Give your orders to Mr. Trenchard and he will intercept the fishing boat Captain." He extended his hand. "May I wish you well in your new venture. However, I must add that I hope that I will see you again, in uniform and where you belong."

Jamie took a firm grip of the offered hand. "Thank you. I promise to think things over very carefully before giving my final answer to Admiral Kemp. I wish you a successful voyage and a safe return to England."

Captain Maynard's eyes followed Jamie as he clambered swiftly down the rope ladder slung from the deck to the cutter where he turned to give a final salute. Captain Maynard returned the salute and then made his way back to the poop deck.

The order given to release the boat hooks, the seamen dipped their oars into the water and with strong strokes sped the cutter through the water, towards the oncoming fishing boat. Jamie stood in the bow, drinking in his surroundings. Jamie had learned to sail in these waters with his mother and grandfather. He had walked and ridden over every inch of the headland in front of him with his father and mother, and much of the surrounding countryside too. He was home . . . and he should have been home sooner. If he had come home sooner then, maybe . . . No! Jamie pushed the thought aside and concentrated on the crew of the fishing boat.

IV

The cutter had not escaped the interest of the fishermen as they headed for home. "Where d'ye think they'm goin'?" Tommy Sawle asked of no one in particular.

"T' be sure, I don't know. Tiz a fine uniform that gentleman is wearing though. Our Jamie's a Captain now, and would be lookin' as grand as him I'm a thinin'." The helmsman's accent was a rare mixture of Irish and Cornish, both soft and musical. He too watched the approaching boat and the uniformed figure standing in the bow shielding his eyes from the sun. Where the devil would they be going, he thought, there was nothing but open water ahead of them. Unless . . . Aiden Fierney frowned. What interest would they have in a small fishing boat going about her honest business?

Suddenly the figure removed his splendid hat and hailed across the narrowing expanse of water that divided the two boats. "Ahoy there Guinevere!" He hailed them. "Have you room for a passenger to Tremanyon?"

Aiden handed the helm to Ben Rowse as he watched the cutter draw nearer. "Bring her about Ben." He instructed and as he took a closer look a smile spread across his face. "Jamie! Jamie! Is that really you?"

The crew of the cutter shipped their oars as the tide carried them the last few feet and Jamie pulled the boat hook to take a hold of the fishing vessel. Looking up with a grin on his face he answered. "It is that Aiden. Luck has been with me for sure. The Tribute saved me a long journey by coach and now I can travel home on one of our own boats." He threw his canvas sack over into the well of the boat and clambered swiftly aboard where he gripped Aiden firmly with his strong hand before putting an arm of friendship about his shoulders. "How are you my friend?" He asked before turning to call to the cutter. "Thank you, a safe journey to you and the crew." With a swift salute of the crew the cutter drew away and began its return to the Tribute.

As Guinevere's sails filled and resumed her course Jamie stood beside Aiden as they passed below St. Maries.

"Are they expecting ye at the Big House?" Aiden asked.

"Yes and No. I did write to mother saying that I would be coming home, but I gave her no specific date. How is she?"

"She is well. Coming to terms with a life without your father." Aiden took a quick glance at Jamie's' face, which was turned towards the small cove ahead.

"My brother and sister?"

Jamie didn't notice the slight hesitation before Aiden answered. "They are all well."

There was a moments silence as Jamie listened to the slip slap as the boat hit the waves that then ran splashing along the hull. "Could you drop me off at Rhosinnis beach, Aiden? I have been too long at sea and have the sudden yearning to feel good firm Cornish soil beneath my feet. I will walk around the river to the creek and hail Gramps at the cottage to row across and fetch me."

Aiden frowned briefly. "Do ye fancy company? I could come with ye . . . the boys can take Guinevere in."

Jamie smiled his agreement. "That would be good. I've so much to catch up on."

Jamie's concentration on the approaching beach and the jetty running into the water from the protected wall was such that he didn't see Aidan's expression darken, or hear him say quietly to himself. "Yes . . . there is. More than ye would wish, an' not much of it will be to your likin', I be thinkin'."

As the boat pulled away Jamie turned to Aiden. "You have no idea how good it is to feel this earth beneath my feet." He unbuttoned the gold braided jacket and loosened the neck of his shirt. "Come on, let's go home."

Side by side, the two friends jumped the tiny stream that ran through the wall and pushed open the gate. There was still some warmth in the fading sun and Jamie removed his jacket and slung it carelessly over his shoulder. "Where was my father going when he took that fall?"

The suddenness of the question surprised Aiden but he quickly recovered and offered the only one he had. "T' be sure I'm not knowing the answer to that one. Your mother believed that he was going over to Killow Barton and that was why there was such a delay in finding him. We were all searching in the wrong place. It wasn't till mornin' we found him in the valley behind the Mill.

Jamie glanced back at Aiden as they followed the winding river path, too narrow to walk abreast, but Aiden was looking down, watching the uneven path. "He was going to see Robert Fry?"

Aidan gave a reluctant. "I suppose so." Whilst hoping that Jamie would not continue the subject. "Surely Mrs. Tremayne wrote and told you the details!"

Jamie drew to an abrupt halt. "I only had a brief letter from Lady Falmouth, forwarded by the Admiralty. I have had no letters from home for the last three years, just before father died. It isn't

VI

unusual for letters to follow us from port to port and not arrive until we get home." He explained unconvincingly. "However, I'm glad that Father and Mother have been keeping an eye on Clara. I haven't received any letters from her either. I expect she was miffed when I was so suddenly shipped off again when she was expecting me home on leave. I only hope that they received my letters to them." When Aidan said nothing he continued. "Of course they did. Letters to home always arrive safely. But I did so miss receiving all the news about Tremanyon. You have no idea how much one looks forward to news from home."

Aiden did finally manage to find something to say. "I can imagine."

The tiny path along the river now rose through a plantation of trees. Jamie studied the undergrowth. "Why haven't the orders been given to keep this wood properly managed? What on earth is Jack playing at? I would have expected better from him." Aiden didn't answer. "Have you lost your tongue Aiden? You've usually got a lot to say for yourself."

"Jack Newton is no longer the bailiff at Rhosinnis." Aiden informed him in a rather terse manner.

"Jack! Not bailiff at Rhosinnis!" Jamie repeated parrot fashion. "He wasn't old enough to give up, and where would he go? Jack was born on Rhosinnis, Aidan. he was happy there. What reason would he have to leave?" Jamie couldn't believe the news.

"Ye'd best ask your mother." Aiden answered flatly.

"Ask Mother! What on earth would she have to do with it? Come on Aiden, just what are you trying to hide from me?" Aiden didn't answer nor look at Jamie. His gaze firmly fixed on the village on the opposite shore. "What happened to friendship Aidan? I thought that we had no secrets from each other."

Aiden looked sheepishly at his feet and kicked a stone off the path. "That was before . . ." He offered by way of an explanation.

Jamie looked baffled. "Before what? Before I went into the Navy, that didn't bother you . . . before . . . as you put it. Before I became a Captain? That shouldn't mean anything! All I want is home here in Cornwall, on this peninsular." He sighed as he looked about him. "Why did Jack leave, Aiden?"

Aiden finally looked up taking stock of the set of Jamie's head and body language, and relented. "He didn't leave, he was pushed."

"Pushed!" Jamie shook his head in disbelief.

VII

"The Squire, as your brother wishes to be known. He gave him notice to quit. Said that he no longer required Jacks services, he could manage on his own." They had halted by a stile, and the path that would lead over the hill and back down to the river. "That was nearly three years ago now, after your father died. He got rid of four men too, and told the others that remained that they would have to work harder to make up for it or they would be out on their ears. He halved the workers at Kylyn too."

Jamie stared at Aiden in disbelief, before letting his eyes wander over the nearby fields. The hedges were overgrown, and in less than three years the brambles had taken hold and were encroaching on the fields. Docks, thistles and other obnoxious weeds were to be seen in pastures that had once been as clean as Tremanyons lawns. "Why! Why would Beau do that?" Jamie studied Aidan's closed expression and wondered exactly what had happened since his Father's untimely death to bring this about. Aiden had always been so open, so easy to read, a close companion with whom he shared many secrets. It appeared that this was not the case now.

"I'd rather not comment till ye've spoken to your mother and brother, Jamie." He added at last.

Jamie sighed unhappily. "I was so looking forward to coming home, Aidan. With all the fighting I've seen, I thought that the one place that would always remain the same, it would be Tremanyon." He placed a hand on Aidan's shoulder. "But I tell you this, Aiden; whatever else has changed, our friendship will always remain."

Aiden gave him a brief smile. "I hope it is so, Jamie . . . that I do n' all. But time brings many changes, I fear. With a heavy heart Jamie took the next step towards the head of the creek, where Quay Cottage stood on the other side.

Once only a single floor, the dwelling above the pilchard cellar had been extended and another floor added in 1757, when Jamie's maternal grandfather had re-married. This gave them two bedrooms and a box room with a living room and kitchen below. Simon Retallick and his new wife were thrilled with their new home and to everyone's surprise Eva gave birth to a son, Joshua, in 1759. The result of this was that Jamie had an uncle who was younger than himself and Ginifur had a half brother younger than her son. Over the intervening years Joshua and Jamie's relationship had been that of brothers, but this relationship did not develop between Josh and Beau who was born in 1758

Guinevere's crew had alerted Josh of the news of Jamie's impending arrival and he had sighted the two men as they came around the riverside path. By the time that Jamie and Aiden had clambered down to the rocks Josh had rowed the boat over and was waiting for them. "Welcome home, Jamie." He tended his greeting. "Tis been a long time."

"Too long, I gather." Jamie added ruefully. "But thanks "Uncle" for those kind words." He quipped and Aidan's and Josh's laughter at this joke lightened their spirits for a moment or two until they reached the other side of the creek. "Where's Gramps? I thought that he would have come down to meet me when he knew I was back. Haven't you told him?" As a thought crossed his mind he added fearfully. "He's alright isn't he?" And Jamie glanced anxiously up at the cottage.

Josh hastily assured him. "Yes . . . yes. Da and Ma are both well. I thought Ginny would have written and told ye, I married two years back now. Tess and I live in the cottage. Da and Ma have moved into Well Cottage to look after Gran, Gramps died last spring. Da still keeps the books for the quay boats, but he has more time for himself. He and Ginny go fishin' out of Kylyn Cove. It has helped her, I think, since your Pa died."

Jamie shook his head. "Is anything the same? The sooner I see Ma the better. Are you coming Aiden?"

Aiden shook his head. "No . . . I'll see ye later never fear. Don't worry about your bag and fancy hat, I'll bring them up when I've finished here." He watched Jamie's retreating back. "Be Jesus . . . What a welcome home there is in store for him." Josh looked bewildered. "He's had no news from home since his father died, and then only recently from Lady Falmouth telling him of his father's death." Aiden explained.

"Nothin! Not from Ginny? Nor 'er over Killow Barton?" Aiden shook his head. "Dear God. What a welcome he has t'be sure." Josh whispered.

Aidan turned his eyes away from the receding figure. "Ginny kept that quiet." He said. "Never said a word about him coming home."

Joshua pondered these words. "If tis true about him not receivin' no letters from home, tis a fact that she've not heard from him in these last three years. Not even after his father died."

"So Da said."

"Never did believe he could behave so . . . he'd always written so regular. I always thought there had t'be a reason. Though for the life of me I can't think what could have happened." Joshua contemplated the question.

"Be Jesus . . !" Aiden exclaimed. "If she's not expecting him, she's going to have one devil of a shock. I'd best catch up with him." He made to leave but Josh caught hold of his sleeve

"Wait, Aiden, as soon as I heard the news of Jamie's arrival I sent young Timmy up with a note for Ginny. She will know by now." Joshua assured him. "And Liam and Kate and the girls will be near by, never fear."

Aiden shook his head. "May the blessed Mary help them all." He said as he sadly turned away to see to the unloading of his boat.

ABOUT THE AUTHOR

CAROL WAS BORN in Moreton-in-the-Marsh, Gloucestershire, during World War Two and she and her mother spent the remaining war years following her father round the United Kingdom whilst he served as a Squadron Leader in the Royal Air Force until the end of the war. During the duration of the war they lived in a caravan, made by her father and grandfather, which was transported by rail and road to farm land near to the air base that he was stationed on at the time. After the war they continued to move from home to home in both Essex and Norfolk as her father developed his new career in civil aviation, and by the time that she was fifteen she had attended eight schools, including a brief spell at boarding school in Berkshire. Leaving college at sixteen, after secretarial training, she was fortunate to find a job as a typist for seven retail sales reps. at Samuel Courtauld's Ltd in London, and at seventeen was a private secretary to the manager of Retail Promotions Department.

At the age of eighteen she came to live in Cornwall to assist her mother with the running of a Holiday Complex on the Roseland Peninsular and it was there that she finally felt that she could begin to develop roots in a part of the country that she came to love. It was in this house that she began to weave the stories that she would write, one day. With Irish and Welsh ancestors she has always thought of herself as more Celt than English and she found herself feeling that she had finally come home. In Cornwall she met her husband to be, Michael, a son of the neighbouring farmer, and they married in 1962. Two of their sons were born in Cornwall before the family left to take up the offer of work abroad, across the Tamar, where the family was completed with a girl and another boy.

However their links with Cornwall and family were so strong that they returned frequently where they stayed in the house she continued to think of as 'home' until it was sold.

When the house and business were eventually sold they were fortunate to be able to keep the cottage by the river, and it is to here they return as often as they can to be surrounded by the farmland of the family farm and their family.

Although, at present, they live on their own farm beside the River Crouch on the far side of the country in Essex, the long term aim is to return home to Cornwall to spend their latter years in the county they love and which is so much a part of them.

COMING SOON

TREMANYON
– Time brings many changes / Jamie –

ALSO AVAILABLE FROM PALORES

KOKOPELLI'S DREAM – by Juliana Geer

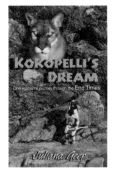

Following a powerful dream, Ana Clair embarks on a search for her destiny. On her journey she encounters books and people that take her beyond her horizon. There is her psychic friend in Cornwall, the Aztec flute player in Canada and the Very Old Man of the Mesa in Arizona. Then there are the children. Together they fulfil the prophesy of the Hopi people and realise Kokopelli's dream – the collective dream of mankind.

ISBN 978-906845-12-4

WHERE SHADOWS LIE – by Katie-Louise Merritt

The rebellious member of a loving family, Kitty feels she is somehow different and apart. As a child, she courts danger and excitement, protected always by a presence only she can sense and hear. When two men vie for her love as a young women, she takes a path that strangely follows a haunting figure from her childhood, leading to a devastating revelation.

ISBN 978-906845-04-9

EDGE OF A LONG SHADOW – by Nigel Milliner

The silence screamed out to be broken.

'Have you ever studied the shags and cormorants from the lookout . . . how they just sit there on the rocks doing damn all for most of the time? They dive around for a while looking for fish and then, when they've got what they need, they go back to the rocks and hang their wings out to dry.'

'What about it? That's the role nature designed for 'em.' Alf did not look up.

'Well, don't you think we're rather like that in Pengarth . . . We old bits of flotsam in the lee of Shag Rock? Just doing what we have to do, then sitting around drying our wings for the rest of the time until the next meal'.

ISBN 978-906845-00-1